Love's
SWEET
Beginning

Books by Ann Shorey

AT HOME IN BELDON GROVE SERIES
The Edge of Light
The Promise of Morning
The Dawn of a Dream

SISTERS AT HEART SERIES
Where Wildflowers Bloom
When the Heart Heals
Love's Sweet Beginning

Love's SWEET Beginning

A NOVEL

Ann Shorey

Revell

a division of Baker Publishing Group
Grand Rapids, Michigan

© 2014 by Ann Shorey

Published by Revell
a division of Baker Publishing Group
P.O. Box 6287, Grand Rapids, MI 49516-6287
www.revellbooks.com

Printed in the United States of America

Library of Congress Cataloging-in-Publication Data
Shorey, Ann Kirk, 1941–
    Love's sweet beginning : a novel / Ann Shorey.
       pages cm. — (Sisters at Heart ; book 3)
    ISBN 978-0-8007-2072-8 (pbk.)
    1. Nurses—Fiction. 2. United States—History—1865–1898—Fiction.
I. Title.
PS3619.H666L69 2014
813′.6—dc23   2013034504

Scripture used in this book, whether quoted or paraphrased by the characters, is taken from the King James Version of the Bible.

14 15 16 17 18 19 20   7 6 5 4 3 2 1

For Ann Kathryn Roberts, with love.
You're my joy and my inspiration.

St. Louis, Missouri
April 1868

Cassie Haddon jammed a pillow over her ears, hoping to block the sound of raised voices. In the hallway outside her room, her mother and uncle shouted at each other in tones no pillow could smother.

"You've imposed on my hospitality far too long," her uncle's deep voice growled. "It's time you and that useless daughter of yours moved on."

Cassie cringed. Heaven knows she tried to be helpful. It wasn't her fault that she'd reached the age of twenty-five without possessing any useful skills. Until the war, she'd always had servants to wait on her.

"If my Phillip were alive, he'd be appalled at your behavior. You're his brother. You have an obligation to take care of us." The thin walls did nothing to diminish her mother's shrill pitch.

"Don't put on airs with me, Eliza. After eleven months, I've more than fulfilled any obligation I may have had toward you. You have a brother of your own drifting around somewhere. Go find him."

At the thought of being forced to leave, Cassie dropped the pillow and ran to open the door. "Please don't send us away. We have nowhere else to go. I promise I'll help more—I just need someone to show me what to do. Your wife shoos me off when I try to do anything."

Eliza Bingham lifted her chin, her hennaed curls bobbing. "Don't beg, Cassie. It's unbecoming to a lady." She shifted her gaze to her brother-in-law. "We'll be on our way first thing tomorrow. And may our fate be on your head."

She grabbed Cassie's arm and tugged her into their shared bedroom, slamming the door behind them.

Once inside, Cassie sank onto the edge of the bed and stared at her mother. "How can we leave? Where on earth will we go?"

"Noble Springs. The last word I had about my brother, he's working for the railroad there, laying track for a spur line."

In spite of her apprehension, Cassie couldn't prevent a tickle of excitement at the prospect of returning to the town where they'd spent a brief sojourn the previous year. Since the end of the war, Mother had ricocheted from place to place seeking someone to care for them. If she were to locate Uncle Rand and settle in his home, Cassie would finally be free to make a life of her own. She'd learn skills to take care of herself. Find work. Put down roots. She didn't want to end up like her mother—helpless.

"I'd love to go back to Noble Springs. What a perfect idea."

"We'll see how perfect things are when we get there. Rand's accommodations may be even less comfortable than this house." She removed a paisley shawl that covered a trunk in one corner of the tiny room, then snapped open the clasps and lifted the lid. "We'll pack tonight, and have Rudy take us to the rail station in the morning. I'll show him he can't bully me."

From the set of her mother's jaw, Cassie knew she'd follow through with the plan. What she didn't know was how Mother proposed to find her brother once they reached Noble Springs. Cassie hadn't seen him since she was a child and remembered little of his appearance—other than the coppery hair that her mother claimed crowned her side of the family.

She opened a bureau drawer and removed a stack of underlinens. When she was halfway to the open trunk with her arms full, her mother stopped her.

"Not now. Wait until I pack our quilts and pillows. My goodness, how many times do I have to show you the correct way to fill a trunk?"

"But how will we sleep without our bedding?"

"We'll roll up in our dressing gowns. They'll be the last thing we pack in the morning. I want to be ready to leave here at daylight. I don't care if the train doesn't depart until noon or later. We're not spending one more minute than necessary in this house."

Sighing, Cassie dropped her chemises and drawers back in the bureau and lifted a quilt from the bed. Together they folded the red and green thistle pattern into a rectangle, placing the covering in the bottom of the trunk.

Cassie sat next to her mother in the swaying passenger car. If she didn't get some air, she believed she'd faint to the floor. Rain had been falling since they left St. Louis, so opening a window was out of the question. She leaned forward and put her head between her knees.

Her mother elbowed her. "What on earth are you doing? Sit up."

"I . . . I think I'm ill. Everything's spinning."

"You'll feel better once we have something to eat. We should arrive in Noble Springs within the hour." She slipped her arm around Cassie's shoulders and helped her into a sitting position. "Rest your head against me and take deep breaths."

Cassie leaned into the embrace. The rocking of the train reminded her of happier times, when as a child she snuggled next to her mother for comfort. There'd been few of those moments since her father's death.

She relaxed to the sound of rhythmic clacking as the iron wheels rolled over the tracks. The next thing she knew, the engine's long whistle signaled their approach to the station in Noble Springs.

The train came to a stop with a billow of steam and the clash of cars rolling together. She rubbed her eyes and peered at the station house through a fogged-over window. The small wooden building looked forlorn in the rain.

"What do we do now? How will you find Uncle Rand?"

For a moment, uncertainty crossed her mother's face. Then she straightened her shoulders and pulled her umbrella and carpetbag from the overhead rack. "We'll leave our baggage with the stationmaster, and go inquire at West & Riley's. The grocer knows everybody. He'll know where my brother is living."

When they descended onto the platform, Cassie's dizziness returned. She grasped her mother's arm to keep from falling.

"I don't know if I can walk that far."

"You'll be fine. It's only a few blocks. Once we're there, we'll have a light meal in the restaurant before we hire a buggy to take us to Rand's house."

The thought of food did little to restore Cassie's equilibrium. With deliberate steps, she moved to the shelter of the station and rested on a bench beneath the overhang while her mother arranged for storage of their baggage. The falling mist blurred the signs on the buildings across the street. Drips of moisture splashed from the roof of the station to the boardwalk at her feet.

Four blocks in this weather sounded like four miles.

⸎

Cassie and her mother shared the umbrella as they pressed through the drizzle toward the combination grocery and restaurant that served as Noble Springs' unofficial information center. If Jacob West, the owner, didn't know who was doing what, his cook, Mrs. Fielder, usually did.

As they picked their way around puddles dotting King's Highway, she felt a twinge of nostalgia at the sight of Rosemary Saxon's cottage, surrounded by its white picket fence. Her stay with Rosemary had been a blessing during the months of her mother's ill-fated marriage to Mr. Bingham.

She gave herself a mental shake. Rosemary's last name was Stewart now. She'd married the doctor, Elijah Stewart, last August, and now lived in his two-story brick home in the next block. Cassie decided she'd pay a call on her friend as soon as she and Mother were settled with Uncle Rand. Then she'd visit Rosemary's sister-in-law, Faith Saxon, at Lindberg's Mercantile. The thought tickled her insides. Imagine how surprised the two women would be to see her back in Noble Springs.

When they entered West & Riley's, the savory aroma of roast turkey wafted toward them from the entrance to the restaurant portion of the building. In the grocery, shelves were stocked to the ceiling with boxes, bags, and cans filled with food. Her stomach rumbled. Maybe Mother was right—she needed something to eat and she'd be fine.

Mr. West hurried toward them, wiping his hands on his apron. His face creased in a smile. "Miss Haddon. Mrs. Bingham. Good to see you again. Are you in town to visit friends?"

Cassie's mother shook her head. "We've returned permanently. I'm hoping you'll be able tell us where Rand Carter lives."

"Happens I know." Mr. West combed his fingers through his dark hair. "He's not far from here. A block up Third Street. Cottage across from Cadwell's boardinghouse." He raised a questioning eyebrow. "He's only been in town six months or so. If you don't mind my asking, how is it you know him?"

"He's my brother."

"I'd never have guessed." He flicked a glance in Cassie's direction.

Her skin prickled. Judging by Mr. West's tone, Rand Carter might not be the refuge they sought. But from the determined expression on her mother's face, Cassie knew she intended to march straight to Uncle Rand's door, no matter what reception awaited them.

Mother gave the grocer a dismissive nod. "Thank you, Mr. West. Since he's so close, we'll be on our way."

Cassie gazed with longing at the empty tables in the restaurant before turning to follow. She tried to ignore her growling stomach.

"We'll eat at Rand's house," Mother whispered after they stepped out of the building. "We don't have money to waste." She strode to the corner and turned north on Third Street. Cassie hurried to keep pace.

She felt a sense of relief when she noticed a modest brown cottage trimmed with red shutters across from the boardinghouse. A brick pathway, surrounded by patchy grass, led to the porch. The dwelling didn't look as bad as Mr. West's reaction led her to believe.

Her mother paused and drew a long breath. "Well, here we are." Her grip on Cassie's arm tightened. "Thankfully, my own brother can't turn us away."

She marched up the porch steps and rapped on the door frame. After a moment, a middle-aged man answered the summons. His graying hair was combed straight back from his forehead and he held a pair of spectacles in one hand. His workman's trousers were clean, but patched. He inclined his head in their direction.

"Yes, ladies? If you're here to collect for war relief, I don't have—"

"I'm sorry to disturb you." Mother's voice squeaked. She cleared her throat. "I was told my brother lived here. His name's Rand Carter."

"That's me."

"But . . . you're not my brother."

"Never said I was."

Cassie swayed and grabbed a porch railing for support. She'd used all of her strength to walk this far. Now where would they go?

2

When Cassie looked up, Rand Carter was scowling at her, his spectacles perched on the bridge of his nose.

"Won't do you no good to pretend to be sick, if that's what the two of you are playing at. I barely got enough money to scrape by—I can't be giving to beggars."

Her mother pushed between them. "I assure you, we're not beggars. I was told my brother lived here."

"Well, he don't."

"But you have his name."

"There's probably a dozen Ransom Carters in Missouri. I'm just one of 'em."

"Ransom," Mother said, with a catch in her voice. "My brother's name is Randall."

Cassie closed her eyes and wished her mother would stop talking so they could leave. First knocking on a stranger's door, then being mistaken for a beggar. She didn't think the day could get any worse.

Rand Carter stepped inside the threshold of his cottage, his hand on the edge of the door. "Good luck finding him." The latch clicked.

Reeling, Cassie grabbed her mother's arm as they descended the steps. "Who told you your brother lived in Noble Springs?"

For once, Mother's dignified manner fled. Her cheeks reddened. "Mrs. Otis, from back home in Mississippi, mentioned his name in a letter. She didn't exactly say he was here."

"What did she say?" If she hadn't been so light-headed, Cassie would have stamped her foot.

"She was just passing local news, and mentioned that she'd heard Rand got a railroad job after the war, and was working near Noble Springs. She figured I'd want to know where he was." In her agitation, Mother allowed the umbrella to drift to the left, and a trickle of cold water found its way down Cassie's neck.

She tugged her cloak higher and stopped across the street from West & Riley's.

"What are we going to do now?" Her voice trembled.

Mother closed her eyes for a moment. When she opened them, she'd regained her regal bearing. "We'll ask Mr. West if he knows of a Rand Carter who works for the railroad, of course. I'm afraid I didn't make myself clear earlier. Then, if worse comes to worst, we'll go to your friend Miss Saxon."

Cassie gasped. Heat flooded over her, despite the chilly afternoon. "She has a husband now. We can't just appear at her door with no warning. Whatever will she think?"

"She's always favored you. I'm sure she'll be delighted."

"Mother, please—"

Her mother stepped off the boardwalk, lifting her skirts above the toes of her boots. "Stop fretting." Her tone left no room for argument.

Cassie followed her across High Street and allowed herself to be led into West & Riley's. The first words of the fifth commandment repeated themselves in her head. *Honor thy father and thy mother . . . honor thy father and thy mother . . .*

The war had taken her father, so she owed double honor to her mother.

Mr. West's eyebrows shot upward when he noticed they'd returned. "Your brother wasn't home, Mrs. Bingham?"

"He's not my brother." From her tone, she blamed Mr. West for the mistake. She leaned the damp umbrella against a wall. "The Rand Carter I'm looking for works for the railroad. He's in his middle forties. Red hair. Taller than you."

Mr. West shook his head. "Doesn't sound familiar. I'll ask around next time the road crew comes in."

Cassie's shoulders sagged. The last thing she wanted to do was to knock on Rosemary's door and ask to stay with her and Dr. Stewart. How could her mother—

"Miss Haddon, are you unwell?" Mr. West took her arm. "Come. Sit down for a moment."

"I'm sorry," she said as he led her to a chair inside the near-empty restaurant. "I don't know what's wrong with me. I haven't had anything to eat today, but—"

"We'll fix that now. You rest. Mrs. Fielder will bring your supper."

Mother lifted her hand to stop him, her cheeks crimson. "I'm afraid our funds are limited. Perhaps a bowl of soup rather than a full meal?"

Cassie stared. Mother brought them here with little in her purse but train tickets? Dizziness assailed her again, and she closed her eyes against the sight of her mother's discomfiture.

"Two plates of food." Mr. West made a *pfft* sound. "It's nothing. You'd be doing me a favor. Mrs. Fielder cooked far too much today, and as you can see, the supper hour is over."

"Well, if you're sure . . ." Mother settled onto a chair next to Cassie.

"I'm sure." He strode into the kitchen.

As soon as he was out of earshot, Cassie turned to her mother. "We have no money?" Her insides churned.

"I was so certain Rand would be here . . ." Worry lines furrowed her brow. "I have a few dollars, but not enough to last more than a day or two." She lifted a knife and fork from the table and inspected them for cleanliness, then removed her gloves. "Let's eat every bite of this meal. Then we'll decide what to do next."

Mr. West approached and placed steaming plates of food in front of them. At the sight of turkey slices and sweet potatoes swimming in gravy, Cassie's stomach rebelled. Gulping, she pushed the meal away. All she wanted to do was find someplace to lie down until her dizziness passed.

"Eat your supper." Her mother forked up a mound of sweet potatoes. "Mr. West was kind enough to provide this food for us. The least you can do is show some appreciation."

"Is something wrong with the meal, Miss Haddon?" Concern shone in his dark eyes.

"No." She waved her hand in front of her face. "I just feel so dizzy. I thought I was hungry, but now . . . now I'm afraid I may be ill."

"I'll send someone for the doctor."

"No, please. I . . . we can't pay. This will pass, I'm sure."

He cocked his head, an amused expression on his handsome face. "You remember Doc Stewart?"

"Certainly. He and my friend Rosemary were married last summer."

A shadow passed over his features. "Yes. They were." He drew a breath. "Since you're Mrs. Stewart's friend, I don't believe you need to worry about payment. But if there's a charge, I'll be responsible."

Her mother rested her fork on the edge of her plate. "Cassie, please allow him to summon Dr. Stewart." She gave Mr. West a bright smile. "We were just talking about the doctor before we entered your store. Possibly his wife will have a tincture that would help."

Cassie covered her face with her hands, wishing she could sink through the floor. Ransom Carter had called them beggars.

Perhaps they were.

$\mathcal{J}$acob's shoulders tensed when Dr. Elijah Stewart strode through the door of the restaurant. The sight of his rival for Rosemary's affections continued to have that effect on him, despite the months that had passed since Rosemary and the doctor were married.

He forced his lips into a welcoming smile.

"Miss Haddon's been taken ill." Jacob gestured toward a table at the back of the room, where she sat with her head cradled in her arms. "I'll be happy to pay your fee for this visit."

"Not necessary. She's my wife's friend, as you know." The doctor crossed to Miss Haddon's side and placed his medical bag on the table. Jacob followed a few paces behind.

Miss Haddon raised her head. "You really didn't need to come, Dr. Stewart. Mr. West was kind enough to bring me some broth and allow me to rest here until I felt better."

From the flush that suffused her features, Jacob felt sure she must be feverish. And who could blame her? Mrs. Bingham would wear anyone down to a nub. From what Miss Haddon had revealed while they waited for the doctor, her mother had dragged her onto the train from St. Louis without breakfast, and until they reached his restaurant, they'd had nothing to eat. Of course, Miss Haddon hadn't said one unkind word about her mother in the telling. He shook his head and watched as Doc Stewart counted her pulse.

After a minute or two, and several questions, the doctor lowered his burly frame onto a chair next to his patient. "I don't find anything medically wrong. You're overwrought. I prescribe rest—at our house." He leaned back in the chair and grinned at her. "Rosemary will be beside herself with joy to see you—and your mother too, of course. My buggy's waiting."

"I hate to impose . . ." Miss Haddon's face flamed brighter.

Mrs. Bingham hurried toward them. "Thank you so much, Doctor. You're too kind. I know Cassie's eager for a visit with dear Rosemary." She slipped her hand under her daughter's arm and helped her to her feet.

While they crossed the room, Jacob ducked around them and held the door open. Miss Haddon's gaze locked with his. Her green eyes shone. "Thank you for everything. I'm grateful for your concern." She held out her hand, and he took it.

"If you need anything while you're here, I'd be pleased to do all I can to help."

"Just don't forget to ask about my brother," Mrs. Bingham said.

Her domineering attitude raised his ire. "No, ma'am, I won't." He hoped he sounded courteous.

He stood in the doorway for a moment after Doc Stewart's carriage turned the corner and traveled south. Aside from her current state, Miss Haddon had blossomed during her time in St. Louis. If it weren't for that mother of hers, she'd be a lovely wife for some lucky man.

Blowing out a breath, he closed the door. The last time he'd considered a wife, she married someone else. He wouldn't risk his heart again.

꧁꧂

Cassie leaned back against the seat during the brief carriage ride, her pleasure at the prospect of seeing Rosemary tainted by the circumstances. She would have given anything to visit her friend as an equal. Instead, she and Mother would come at the door as—

She bit the inside of her lip.

Beggars.

The doctor stopped the carriage in front of his house and tied the horse to the hitching post. "I'll stable him later. Right now I want to watch Rosemary's face when she sees you."

Grinning, he escorted Cassie and her mother up the porch steps and knocked. Behind the closed door, a dog barked.

In a moment, Rosemary answered the summons. Her eyes widened.

"Cassie! Mrs. Bingham. What a wonderful surprise." She reached down and grabbed the sable and white dog by the collar. "Bodie, be still."

He wagged his tail and pushed his head against Cassie's leg.

Rosemary smiled. "He remembers you." She stepped away from the entrance. "Please come in."

Her figure had filled out since Cassie saw her last. She wore a peach-colored dress covered by a white, full-length apron, which couldn't quite conceal her plumpness. Her eyes sparkled when she gazed up at her husband. "What a treat. How did you manage this?"

"I thought you'd be pleased. I'll explain later—right now I need to stable the horse." He bent to kiss the top of her head. "I won't be long."

Cassie gazed around the spacious entry, surprised at the elegance of her surroundings. In her letters, Rosemary had mentioned leaving her cottage when she married, but she hadn't described her new home with any detail.

To one side, a flight of polished oak stairs led to a carpeted landing. On her right, a hall table held a fluted silver tray containing a number of calling cards.

After hanging their cloaks on a hall tree, Rosemary gestured through an archway toward a comfortably furnished room. A lamp glowed on a table placed within the curve of a bay window, illuminating upholstered armchairs and a high-backed sofa. Flames crackled over logs in the fireplace.

"Please, be seated. I'm anxious to hear what brings you back to Noble Springs."

Cassie settled onto one of the chairs near the fire and waited to hear how her mother would respond to Rosemary's question.

Mother took a moment to fiddle with the lace collar at her neck, then cleared her throat. "We came here planning to live with my brother. I was told—erroneously, it turns out—that he was working for the railroad in this area."

"You're saying he's not here?" Concern wrinkled Rosemary's forehead.

"No, he isn't. I plan to write to the railroad company first thing tomorrow. They'll be able to tell me where he is."

Rosemary leaned forward. "In the meantime, please consider yourselves our guests." She rested a fond gaze on Cassie. "It will be like old times to have your company."

"You're very kind. We appreciate it." Mother shot an "I told you so" glance in Cassie's direction.

She squirmed on her chair. When her uncle Rudy told Mother they'd be his guests, the visit had stretched to nearly a year. Cassie promised herself they wouldn't abuse the Stewarts' hospitality in the same fashion.

Late that evening, Cassie and Rosemary sat alone in the kitchen sharing a pot of mint tea. A plate of lemon-thyme bread rested between them on the table.

Grateful her stomach had settled, Cassie lifted a slice and nibbled one corner, then rested the treat on a dessert plate beside her teacup. "You and the doctor—"

"Please, call him Elijah."

"I'll try. It's hard to break old habits." She moistened her lips and began again. "You and Elijah are so gracious to take us in like this. Mother . . . I don't understand how she could have left my uncle's home without—"

Rosemary squeezed Cassie's hand. "Having you here is a blessing. I've missed you dreadfully." She hitched her chair closer until their knees touched.

"But still, to arrive without warning . . ."

"I'd have been devastated to learn you were in Noble Springs and staying at the hotel."

"No chance of that." She inhaled the fragrance of mint as she sipped her tea. "Mother was so sure she'd find her brother that she didn't think about the cost if he wasn't here." She lowered her voice, although her mother had retired to the guest room for the night over an hour ago. "We never should have left St. Louis, no matter how poorly my uncle treated us."

"Will you please stop apologizing?" Rosemary smiled and pushed the plate of sweetbread closer to her. "Try another bite or two. You're looking better by the minute."

Cassie surveyed her friend. Her skin bloomed with health, and her glossy hair shone in the lamplight.

"You're the one who looks wonderful. I know it's rude to ask, but are you . . . ?"

Rosemary blushed. "Yes. In June sometime, we think."

She rested her hands over her abdomen. "We're planning to turn our guest room into a nursery soon."

A bite caught in Cassie's throat. Her friend couldn't have her nursery until the guest room was vacant.

Apparently reading her expression, Rosemary said, "Not that soon! You and Eliza are welcome to stay as long as necessary."

How long would that be? If they couldn't find her uncle, she and Mother had nowhere else to go.

Cassie stood in West & Riley's with her arms folded across her chest, listening to her mother berate Mr. West.

"We all know a railroad crew spent the past two weeks in Noble Springs. The *Observer* had a long story about how much money their presence brought to the community. What I don't understand is why no one told you one thing about my brother. Are you sure you asked?"

Mr. West's face grew thunderous. "I wouldn't lie to you, ma'am. I've told you before, the railroad has workers all over this part of the state. You can't expect them to know each other."

Cassie stepped forward. "We appreciate your help. You've been very kind."

"Wish I could do more, Miss Haddon." His expression relaxed. "One of these days your uncle will turn up. Just be patient."

Time was running out for patience. As each day passed, she felt more self-conscious about their presence in Rosemary's home.

"I'm trying, Mr. West." She took her mother's arm. "It's a lovely day. Let's enjoy the sunshine while it lasts."

With an irritated huff, Mother tugged her arm free. "I'm quite capable of walking without assistance." She stalked out the door. Once they were on the boardwalk, her steps slowed. "I just don't know why I haven't heard from the railroad. They must keep a list of their workmen."

"It could take weeks for a response."

"No matter. I'll wait."

Cassie's heart plummeted. The thought of imposing on Rosemary's kindness for an indefinite period made her cringe. She tightened her jaw as they approached the Stewarts' two-story brick home. In St. Louis, her uncle called her useless. She'd show him. She'd show everyone.

Rosemary's dog, Bodie, left the porch and scampered down the walk when he saw them. Cassie bent and scratched him behind the ears. To her surprise, her mother stroked the fur on his back.

"I thought you were afraid of Bodie."

"I've grown used to him. If we have to live here, I might as well accept the dog."

Cassie straightened. "We don't have to live here."

"We certainly do. We can't even buy tickets to St. Louis, not that Rudy would take us in if we got there." The look she gave Cassie was tinged with fear. "I'm afraid I've brought us to a dead end." Her lip trembled. "I don't know what to do next," she whispered.

Taken aback by her decisive mother's vulnerability, Cassie gave her a hug. "We'll be fine." She sounded braver than she felt. First thing tomorrow, she'd make a plan.

Tonight, she'd pray for guidance.

4

The next day, while Cassie helped Rosemary wash the dishes after the noon meal, a portion of a Scripture verse that had come to her in the night circled through her mind. *If any would not work, neither should he eat.* She was more than willing to work. If she could escape her mother's scrutiny for an hour or so, she'd put her plans into action.

After drying the final plate, she draped the towel over a peg and turned to Rosemary. "I need your help. You mentioned that this afternoon you intend to call on one of Elijah's patients who has a new baby."

Rosemary smiled. "Yes, Mrs. Wright. I'm eager to see her little one. I'd be pleased to have you accompany me."

"Thank you, but I have something else I need to do. Would you mind taking my mother instead?"

Her friend's cheerful expression faded. "Do you think she'd be willing? She's done little since you've been here other than sit in your room reading books and writing letters." A flush colored her cheeks. "I'm sorry. That sounded harsher than I intended."

"It's the truth." Cassie bowed her head. "While my father

was alive, he made certain we were both waited on hand and foot. Mother hasn't accepted that those days are gone forever." She met Rosemary's compassionate gaze. "That's why I hoped you could keep her busy this afternoon. I'm going to go out and find a job."

"Doing what?" Rosemary blurted, then clapped a hand over her mouth. Her expression softened. "I mean, you've never really worked either. I don't think—"

"I'm not useless. You found a job and took care of yourself. Why can't I?" She turned toward the entrance to the dining room. "If you don't want Mother's company this afternoon, I'll find another way."

"Why don't you just tell her what you plan to do?"

Cassie pivoted to meet her friend's puzzled gaze. "She'd never let me go. To her way of thinking, ladies don't soil their hands with work. But if I present her with the *fait accompli*, she'll have to agree."

At least, she hoped that's how things would turn out. Last night the solution to their dilemma seemed so clear. Now the doubt in Rosemary's eyes brought out her own uncertainty.

Then a glance at the dress her friend wore—gathered under the bust to conceal her condition—reminded Cassie that she and her mother must find a home of their own, and soon. For that to happen, she needed a job.

"Where do you plan to seek employment?" Rosemary's soft voice cut into her thoughts.

Hope shot through her. "Does that mean you'll take Mother with you this afternoon?"

"Yes, I'll be happy to."

She threw her arms around Rosemary. "Thank you. You're a blessing. I'll go help her get ready."

"Now, tell me where you're going."

"I'll tell you when I return." She left the kitchen and sped up the stairs.

⮑⮐

As soon as Mother departed with Rosemary, Cassie drew her green plaid taffeta walking dress from the wardrobe in their bedroom. Once the frock had been her best choice for paying calls. But after more than a year, signs of wear showed around the hem and sleeves.

By folding the cuffs to the inside, she hid their frayed edges. If she had time, she'd also stitch the hem up an inch, but at best she had an hour or so before Rosemary returned from her call on Mrs. Wright.

Cassie slipped out of the simple blue cotton garment she wore and stood in her petticoat, nerves fluttering. She didn't know which worried her the most—the reception she might receive when she asked for work, or her mother's reaction if she were fortunate enough to be employed. After a moment, she took a deep breath and dropped the green taffeta over her head. The time had come to step out in faith.

Standing in front of a framed wall mirror, she settled her straw bonnet over her auburn braids, then tied the emerald green ribbons beneath her chin. A closer scrutiny in the glass revealed pale skin. She pinched color into her cheeks, then hurried down the stairs.

Bodie met her at the door, tail wagging.

She rubbed his ears. "Not now. I'll walk you when I get back." She slipped outside and closed the door in his hopeful face.

Moving briskly, she crossed King's Highway and strode north. At the corner of High Street, she straightened her shoulders, drew a breath, then marched through the door leading to West & Riley's restaurant.

Since the noon hour had passed, no patrons sat at the tables, although stacked dishes here and there testified to their presence earlier. The room smelled faintly of ham and scorched cornbread. She heard voices and the clinking of cutlery coming from the kitchen, so she turned in that direction. The door swung open before she reached the entrance.

Mr. West blinked at her as if he'd seen a vision.

"Miss Haddon? Are you in need of groceries? My helper should be somewhere about."

"I came to see you." She squelched the tremor in her voice. "About a job."

He raised an eyebrow. After a glance at her attire, he shook his head. "I'm sorry. I don't need any more help."

"I beg to differ. From the looks of the tables, you are lacking a waitress to fetch and carry plates in and out of the kitchen. I noticed the other evening that you were doing the serving." Perspiration moistened the palms of her gloved hands as she continued with her rehearsed speech. "As the owner of the business, that's hardly the best use of your time. There may be customers in the grocery right now, and no one there to assist them."

One corner of his moustache twitched as he appeared to fight a smile. "Well said. But you're a lady—a real lady. This is no place for you."

She peeled off her gloves, draping them over the back of a chair, then moved to one of the tables. After stacking soiled dishes together, she swept up knives and forks and dropped them onto the top plate.

"I assume you want these in the kitchen?"

He nodded. No doubt about it, he was smiling. Grinning,

in fact. If it weren't for the skeptical expression on his face, she'd have thought he was pleased.

She grabbed the stack, wishing she hadn't put so many heavy dishes into a single pile. The crockery plates weighed far more than Rosemary's china. Tightening her grip, she pushed through the door with her shoulder and deposited her burden next to the washbasin.

An older woman pulled her hands from soapy water and stared. "What in heaven's name are you doing? Did Mr. West say you could come in here?" She pushed a strand of gray hair away from her forehead with the back of one reddened hand.

"More or less." Mr. West spoke from the doorway. "Miss Haddon, would you please come with me?"

"Certainly. As soon as I clear the rest of the tables."

"Now. Mrs. Fielder will finish in the dining room."

Mrs. Fielder huffed out a breath. "In due time, sir. I've only got two hands."

He rolled his eyes heavenward, then turned and marched through the door, motioning for Cassie to follow him.

Before leaving, she glanced around the kitchen for someplace to clean congealed gravy from her fingers. Mrs. Fielder frowned at her. "What is it you're wanting now?"

"My hands. They're sticky. Have you a towel I could use?"

"Mercy sakes. You carry half a dozen plates and you think your hands are sticky?" She gestured at a roasting pan and baking sheets waiting to be washed. "An hour up to your elbows in the dishpan will fix that." Then her expression softened. "There's towels on that shelf behind you. Help yourself."

"Thank you." Heat stung Cassie's cheeks as she made quick work of wiping her fingers. She hurried after Mr. West, praying her efficiency at clearing the dishes had made a good impression.

He sat at one of the tables farthest from the kitchen. When he saw her, he pointed to an empty chair facing him. "Please have a seat." He rubbed his moustache with his thumb. "I don't understand why a lady like you would want to work here. My trade is mostly workmen from the boardinghouse. Some of them can be rough around the edges—not like the gentlemen you're no doubt used to."

She bit her lower lip. "I need a job, Mr. West. I want to be able to support my mother and myself."

"Why not set up as a seamstress or milliner?"

"I can barely stitch a straight hem. I've never made a dress in my life." She leaned across the table, her hands clasped together as if in prayer. "The only work I've ever done is help with dishes after a meal."

He leaned back in his chair, arms folded across his apron. "I take it your mother hasn't tracked her brother down."

"No, and we can't continue to impose on Rosemary and her husband. If I had a way to earn some money, I could find us a little cottage to rent."

She wondered at herself, giving so much personal information to the grocer. Except for seeing him away from the store a few times when he called on Rosemary last spring, he was a stranger. Why should he care what happened to her and her mother? She gave his face a brief survey. At least he didn't appear hostile.

She lifted her chin. "I can start tomorrow. Tell me what time to be here."

"Six o'clock. We're busiest at breakfast."

She jumped from her chair. "Thank you, Mr. West!"

"Wear something less . . . noticeable. And Miss Haddon—"

"Yes?"

"I'm willing to try this for one week. Then we'll see."

With purposeful steps, Cassie strode out the door and hurried toward Rosemary's house. Once she was beyond sight of the restaurant, she paused, her heart galloping.

Six o'clock in the morning. She'd never been anywhere that early in her life. She prayed she'd awaken in time.

After Miss Haddon left, Jacob plodded into the grocery and leaned against a counter. What had he done? He raked his fingers through his hair. Mrs. Fielder wouldn't be happy. Miss Haddon likely wouldn't last the first day. Then he'd have to dismiss her, and she wouldn't be happy either.

He paced to the rear of the store, straightening stock on the shelves as he walked. He could work with other men without a problem. But for some reason, ladies baffled him. He needed a cook, so he'd hired Mrs. Fielder. So why did he hire Miss Haddon?

The last serving girl he employed had left to get married, and he hadn't replaced her. Up to now, he hadn't seen any need. Still didn't, for that matter. He closed his eyes and pictured Miss Haddon in her rustling taffeta dress, marching to the kitchen with her bonnet ribbons streaming behind her. No one looked less like kitchen help than she did.

He poked at a case of canned beans with the toe of his boot. Even if she lasted only one day, he'd have to make sure none of his customers got the wrong idea about her presence in the restaurant. Instead of freeing him to spend more time in the grocery, she'd be taking him from his other duties. He should have said no and sent her on her way.

Growling in his throat, he bent and stacked the cans on a shelf. He'd allow her to fail. When she recognized the work was too much for her, she'd leave on her own. Then he wouldn't have to deal with the tears he feared would come if he'd denied her the job today.

⁂

"Cassiopeia Rosetta Haddon! I'm thankful your father isn't alive to see how far you've sunk."

Cassie flinched at her mother's rebuke. "I don't see where I had any choice. We can't continue to live on Rosemary's charity." She kept her voice down so they wouldn't be overheard.

Mother rose and paced the length of their shared bedroom. "But to lower yourself to a servant's level. How could you? I've tried so hard to teach you to be a lady." She dabbed a tear from the corner of her eye. "Didn't you pay any attention to me at all?"

"You taught me how to make lace, appreciate classic literature, play a piano, and write a fine hand. I'm grateful, but none of those things will help me earn our keep."

"A lady marries well. Her husband earns their livelihood." The bed creaked as Mother sank onto the edge and covered her face with her hands. "Your reputation will be ruined. I'd hoped once we found Rand that he would introduce you to a suitable bachelor. But now . . ."

Cassie settled beside her. "We don't know how long it will take to find your brother." She softened her voice. "In the meantime, I must do something to provide for us. I pray you'll try to understand."

She kissed her mother's cheek, then crossed the room to the wardrobe and drew out the blue print dress she'd worn before leaving for West & Riley's that afternoon. If she borrowed one of Rosemary's aprons, the garment should fill Mr. West's definition of "not noticeable."

Mother sniffled. "That's your oldest dress."

"Exactly. I plan to wear this to the restaurant in the morning. Mr. West advised me to wear something inconspicuous."

"My heavens. Now the man is telling you how to dress." She fanned herself with her hand.

Cassie drew a deep breath and held it for a moment. "He's my employer now. He has the right." She stumbled over the words. He also had the right to send her packing if she couldn't do the work.

5

*L*eaves on a butternut tree across the street from West & Riley's trapped the early morning sunlight, sending filtered shadow over the alley behind the restaurant. Cassie shivered, more from nerves than cold. She hurried through the kitchen entrance.

"I'm not late, am I?"

Mrs. Fielder paused in the act of kneading dough and rested her hands on the worktable. "Mr. West said you'd be here. Didn't say what time, so guess you're not late." She gave Cassie's garments a quick glance. "At least you wore an apron today and changed from that fancy outfit."

Cassie ran her fingers along the sleeve of her blue dress. "This one's easier to care for." She smiled, hoping to make a friend of the cook. "Please tell me what you want me to do."

"The men will be here for breakfast in a few minutes—most of 'em, anyway." With a floury hand, Mrs. Fielder pointed to shelving piled with brown crockery. "The plates are over there, knives and forks in that tray against the wall. Best get everything on the tables right away. Put a setting in front of each chair—but you already know that, eh?" She raised a skeptical eyebrow.

Heart thudding, Cassie nodded and took three plates from the shelf. Before she reached the door, Mrs. Fielder snorted.

"Three at a time? You'll be ten minutes just carrying plates. There's twenty-four chairs out there."

Cassie backtracked, adding three more pieces of the thick crockery to her load. As soon as she entered the dining room, she thumped the stack onto the nearest table. A quick survey of the room showed four rectangular tables, each surrounded by six chairs. Some part of her mind must have noticed the furnishings when she visited yesterday. But yesterday she hadn't paid attention.

Sighing, she walked around the table, centering a plate in front of each chair. Then she stepped back and studied the arrangement. One of the plates sat off-center. She made a quick adjustment. As she did so, she sensed she was being observed.

When she looked up, she noticed Mr. West standing in the doorway that joined the grocery to the restaurant. He watched her without saying a word. Unnerved, she hastened back to the kitchen.

Mrs. Fielder slid a pan of biscuits into one of the two ovens and banged the door closed. "You'll need to move faster—this isn't a ladies' tea. When you finish with the plates, the cups are on that tray under the window."

"Yes, ma'am." The words stirred echoes in her memory. She'd grown up listening to servants respond in the same fashion to her mother, never imagining one day she'd walk in their shoes.

Under Mr. West's silent, but intent, gaze, she set the remainder of the plates in front of the chairs, then turned to gather tableware from the kitchen. Before she reached the door, he cleared his throat.

She stopped.

"Miss Haddon. If I may make a suggestion."

Her heart thrummed. "Yes, sir. What is it?"

"You could save yourself several trips if you put the knives and forks on top of the plates when you bring them out."

Heat climbed up her throat and burned her cheeks. How obvious. A few minutes on the job and she'd already earned a black mark.

"You're right. Thank you." She kept her gaze on the floor until she reached the kitchen, then grabbed two handfuls of tableware and dashed back to the dining room. Heedless of alignment, she dropped a setting at each place. As she finished with the last table, the outside door opened and two men entered.

"Well, if you don't brighten the morning," the first one said, removing his hat. He wore a red flannel shirt tucked into dusty black trousers. Stubby whiskers prickled from his cheeks. "Mrs. Fielder sick?"

Cassie inched toward the kitchen. "No. She's . . . making breakfast."

The second man laughed. "We figured as much. That's why we're here." He stepped to one of the tables and scraped a chair across the floorboards. "I smell coffee. Don't see no cups, though."

Oh mercy. She'd forgotten the cups. A second black mark. "I'll bring them right now."

She whirled and pushed through the door, nearly colliding with Mrs. Fielder.

"Heard voices. Time to start serving." She carried the largest coffeepot Cassie had ever seen.

"Just a moment. I forgot the cups."

"Humph. In that case, you take care of the coffee. I've got to tend to the eggs." The cook thunked the pot at the rear of the range and picked up a spoon.

Cassie's knees wobbled. She doubted she could lift the pot, much less pour without spilling on customers. Cool air slid over the floor as more men entered, their voices loud above the clinking of Mrs. Fielder's spoon against the skillet.

This was the moment she'd dreaded. Mr. West had cautioned her that the men he served weren't all gentlemen. No matter. She needed this job. She jutted her chin in the air and marched into the dining room carrying a tray full of cups.

Close to a dozen heads turned in her direction. Some were hatless, others wore slouch hats even though they sat at the table. Cassie marked them as the ones who weren't gentlemen. With quick movements, she circled the room, plunking a crockery mug next to each plate.

"You going to fill these?" The boy who spoke couldn't have been more than sixteen or seventeen.

"'Course she will. That's her job." Middle-aged, with coarse features, the speaker reached out, placing his hand on Cassie's waist. "Ain't that right, missy?"

Revulsion shuddered over her. She twisted away. "Yes. If you'll excuse me, I'll return in just a moment with the coffee."

Mr. West strode across the room and caught up with her next to the kitchen door. "It would be best if Mrs. Fielder handled the coffeepot," he said in an undertone. "You fill the platters. She can serve the tables."

"Yes, sir." Equal portions of gratitude and embarrassment swept through her. She scurried to Mrs. Fielder's side to relay his message.

The cook huffed out an exasperated breath. "Wish he'd make up his mind. First he wants you to serve, now me." She shoved the spoon into Cassie's hand. "The bowls are next to the stove. Fill 'em with eggs. Put the biscuits and bacon on the platters. One for each table. Bring 'em right in. Those gents don't have all morning."

Mr. West didn't think her capable of pouring coffee. If she couldn't do the simple task of dividing the food, she knew he wouldn't let her stay.

Hands shaking, she scooped spoonfuls of scrambled eggs into four bowls, doing her best to ensure each bowl contained an equal amount. When she reached to the warming shelf for the bacon, her fingers slipped on the greasy edge of the tray. The contents spilled over the top of the range like so many twigs. Grease splatters smoked. Bacon strips shriveled.

At that moment, the door swung open and Mr. West stepped across the threshold. "Customers are waiting. Where's the—" His voice choked off. He grabbed a serving dish from the table next to the stove. Using a long-handled fork, he raked the darkening strips off the stovetop and onto the platter.

Cassie watched, horrified at what she'd done. "I'm so sorry." The words emerged in a faint whisper. The pan slipped from her nerveless fingers and clattered to the floor.

He set his jaw in a tight line. "Take one of those towels over there and clean the grease off the range before a fire starts. Then clean the floor. I'll send Mrs. Fielder in for the biscuits." He turned his back and stalked into the dining room.

The smell of smoldering fat spurred her from her paralysis. She snatched a towel from the shelf, wadding the thick cotton fabric around her right hand. Perspiration beaded her forehead and sizzled on the broad iron surface as she leaned over to reach splatters in the back corners.

Mrs. Fielder banged into the room, dumped the biscuits into bowls, and stamped out again without saying a word. She didn't have to. Disapproval radiated from her body like quills on a porcupine.

Cassie dropped the soiled towel into a basin and slumped against the worktable. *Lord, help me. Keep me from more accidents.*

If she finished well, she hoped Mr. West would be pleased enough to overlook the bacon incident.

Jacob stepped into the kitchen after the final supper patron departed. Reflected sunset sent a saffron glow through the window, tinting Miss Haddon's auburn hair gold. Bent over the dishpan, she paid no attention to his presence until he spoke her name.

She turned then, wiping water from her hands with one corner of her food-spotted apron. Her green eyes were shadowed with fatigue.

"Yes, sir?"

He pulled a chair away from the worktable. "Sit a moment."

After a glance at Mrs. Fielder, who stood with her back to them using a brush to scrub the stovetop, Cassie crossed the room and sat. Anxiety marked her features.

"I know I'm slow, but I'll have everything washed before I leave."

"I'm not worried about the dishes." He hoped the sympathy he felt showed on his face. "You look worn-out. This is more work than you've ever done in your life, am I right?"

Her features tightened, as if she were bracing herself for a blow. She straightened her sagging shoulders.

"I can do this, Mr. West. Please give me a chance."

The scrubbing sounds stopped. He knew the cook was listening to their conversation. He'd hoped to speak to Miss Haddon alone, but if he waited much longer she'd probably collapse. The surge of protectiveness he felt surprised him. He had to send her home. Now.

"Be reasonable. Today was nothing. When there's a full railroad crew in town, we have men standing in line to be served."

"All the more reason you need help." Her eyes sparked. "You said you'd give me a week. This is just my first day."

He rubbed the back of his neck. "From what I've seen, a full week would probably kill you. Wouldn't do me any good, either." Shaking his head, he reached into his pocket and pushed three silver quarters toward her. "Here's a day's pay. I hope you find something you're more suited for."

She glared at him. "I'm tired of being told I'm useless."

"I never said—"

"You can keep your money." She rose and swept her cloak and carryall from pegs near the door. "Good night, Mr. West."

The screen door banged behind her.

He blinked at the intensity of her reaction. She had to recognize that the restaurant was no place for an innocent girl like herself. A fresh flare of anger burned through his gut at the memory of the customer grabbing her waist at breakfast. He'd had to use all of his willpower to stop himself from taking the man by the collar and throwing him out. To have her continue working here would only invite similar incidents.

The *scritch*, *scritch* of brush on iron told him Mrs. Fielder had returned to her task. For a brief moment, he wondered whether he should ask her opinion about Miss Haddon.

Then he slapped his hand on the table. No. He'd done the right thing.

6

assie's fists clenched and unclenched as she marched along the block between the restaurant and Rosemary's house. A week would probably kill her, he'd said. Such presumption. True, she'd never felt this tired, and her feet throbbed from standing most of the day. But nothing a night's rest wouldn't cure.

There had to be some way to persuade him to let her come back to work.

When she reached the Stewarts' porch, she realized she still wore her soiled apron. Her face burned. As if the day hadn't ended badly enough, here she'd walked past the businesses lining Third Street wearing servant's garb. She jerked the apron off and crammed it into her carryall before climbing the porch steps.

Once inside, she paused in the entryway to remove her shoes from her aching feet. She'd taken a few steps toward the sitting room when she heard voices.

"When I invited them to stay, I had no idea they'd settle here! I don't mind Cassie—at least she helps you around the house—but her mother—" Elijah let the remark hang unfinished.

"How can we turn them away? They have nowhere to go."
Rosemary's angry tone matched her husband's.

"Neither does our baby. It's time I started on the nursery."

"Nonsense. You have more than a month."

Cassie pictured her friend standing toe to toe with Elijah, unwilling to give ground. Heat swept over her at being the cause of the argument.

She needed to find a home for herself and her mother. Soon.

She tiptoed to the entrance, opened the door again, then slammed it. The voices stopped. The back door banged. In moments, a flush-faced Rosemary hurried from the kitchen and clasped Cassie's shoulders.

"I never dreamed you'd be so late! Have you had supper?"

Cassie eyed her friend. She wanted to assure her that she and Mother would be gone soon, but how could she do that without revealing she'd been eavesdropping? Indeed, how could she offer any assurance when she'd just lost the first job she ever held?

The starch left Cassie's bones. She tottered over to the sofa and slumped against the back, dropping her carryall on the floor.

"Yes, I've had supper. When the men left after meals, Mrs. Fielder and I had time to eat." She massaged her temples. "I didn't know I'd be this late, either. Mr. West didn't tell me ahead of time that I was to stay through supper."

"Well, tomorrow you'll know."

"Um, yes. I will." Here was the perfect opportunity. She needed to tell Rosemary that she'd been dismissed. Cassie opened her mouth, but the words stuck in her throat.

Apparently mistaking her silence for fatigue, Rosemary took her hand. "You look like you need a cup of mint tea. Let's go to the kitchen."

Rosemary stopped in front of the stove and pushed a kettle

over one of the round eyes on top. "While we wait for the water to boil, tell me about your job. What did you have to do today?"

Thankful for a question she could answer without dodging the truth, Cassie said, "Set tables and wash dishes. Over and over."

"But . . . weren't you going to help serve?"

"Mr. West didn't trust me with serving. First thing this morning, he sent Mrs. Fielder out with the coffee and I spent all day in the kitchen. Unless it was time to prepare tables for the next meal—then he allowed me into the dining room." She couldn't help the trace of sarcasm that tinged her last sentence.

Rosemary patted Cassie's shoulder. "Jacob's a practical man. Maybe he thinks you need another day or two to learn how he wants things done."

Another day or two. She'd only been allowed twelve hours. She bit her lip at the memory, a knot of anger forming in her chest. Slow or not, anybody could wash dishes. He had no reason to send her away.

Rosemary moved from the stove and gazed out the window into the fenced backyard. One hand stole to the corner of her eye and brushed away what might have been a tear.

Cassie followed her gaze. Elijah stood in one corner and tossed a stick for Bodie. The dog raced after the prize, then dropped it at Elijah's feet to be thrown again.

Watching them, Cassie squirmed inside. If she and Mother weren't here, Rosemary and her husband wouldn't be quarreling. They'd be enjoying a quiet evening together—maybe drinking mint tea. She drew a deep breath and released it in a long sigh.

"Where's my mother? Did she go to bed this early?"

Rosemary's expression flattened. "She went to your room

following supper. Apparently she's none too happy about you working for Jacob West."

Another opportunity to give Rosemary her news. Cassie let it pass. Instead, she cleared her throat. "No. She isn't. But I'm praying she'll come around."

At that moment, the kettle came to a boil, splattering hissing drops of water over the stovetop. Rosemary hurried to grab the handle and pour hot water over the leaves in the teapot.

Cassie glanced between Elijah, out on the lawn, and her friend, who watched him through the window. She took a step toward the doorway.

"If you'll excuse me, I can't keep postponing what's sure to be a confrontation with Mother. Why don't you call Elijah in and enjoy this tea together?"

She left the kitchen without giving Rosemary the opportunity to reply.

Cassie's mother lay on their bed atop the coverlet, a folded cloth resting on her forehead. "Well, I hope you've learned a good lesson. When you take a servant's job, you work servant's hours." She spoke without turning her head.

"The work was hard, but I did it." Cassie couldn't keep the pride from her voice. "I felt useful for the first time in my life. If that was the lesson, it was a good one." She wouldn't give her mother the satisfaction of telling her that Mr. West had dismissed her. After overhearing Rosemary and Elijah, a determination to earn a living stiffened her spine. She would not impose on her friend a day longer than necessary.

Her mother whipped the cloth aside and swung her stocking

feet over the edge of the bed. Sitting upright, she beckoned with her index finger. "Let me see your hands."

Cassie stepped closer, extending her reddened palms.

"My heavens! What did he have you doing?" She squeezed Cassie's fingers. "My poor girl. I hope you told him you didn't want his scullery job."

"I said no such thing."

Mother looked horrified. "Surely you don't plan to continue."

"I do and I will. I'm truly sorry to upset you." Cassie bent and kissed her mother's forehead, then withdrew from her grasp.

One way or another, she'd fight for a second chance.

***

The hinges on the screen door gave a rusty squeak when Cassie stepped into the restaurant kitchen the following morning. She didn't see Mrs. Fielder, but the range ticked as the iron surface heated. Apprehension prickled along her arms. Mr. West must have built up the fire. She'd hoped she could avoid him, at least for now, by being early.

She drew a fortifying breath. No matter. She'd start by setting the tables and worry about him when he appeared. After removing half a dozen plates from the shelf, she counted out an equal number of knives and forks and carried them into the next room.

When she stepped into the dining room, Mrs. Fielder stopped sweeping the floor and stared at her.

"What are you doing? Mr. West told you not to come back."

"So he did. You might say I paid no attention." She walked around a table, placing a setting in front of each chair.

Mrs. Fielder's mouth lifted in a half smile. "Wouldn't have

guessed you had this much spirit." Chuckling, she carried the broom toward the kitchen. "Go ahead and finish those tables. We'll see what he says when he gets here," she called over her shoulder.

Relieved the cook hadn't sent her home, Cassie blew out the breath she'd been holding and returned to the kitchen for another stack of plates.

She'd nearly completed the last table when Mr. West stomped into the dining room. "Miss Haddon! Why are you here?" His deep voice sounded like a growl.

"You had no cause to dismiss me. So I decided not to leave." With deliberate motions, she laid a knife and fork next to a plate, then straightened, planting her hands on her hips. "Anyone can set tables and wash dishes. Did you find me incompetent at those tasks?"

"No." He narrowed his eyes. "But by the end of the day, you were near collapse. This isn't a proper job for you. I can't be responsible—"

"You're not responsible for me. Kindly allow me to decide what's proper." She swallowed the pounding in her throat. For the first time in her life, she was standing up for what she wanted. She enjoyed the sensation.

A moment of silence passed between them. Mr. West's gaze traveled over her blue print dress, her clean apron, and stopped at the toes of the worn boots she'd borrowed from Rosemary. A smile hovered under his moustache. "I see you came better prepared today."

"Yes, sir, I did."

She waited, feeling the bump of her racing heart.

"You're to work in the kitchen." He gave her a hard look. "No waiting tables. Understood?"

"But I—" She clamped her lips over the remainder of her retort. "Understood."

Shaking his head, he turned and stalked to the grocery entrance.

Cassie suppressed a whoop of joy. Speeding to the kitchen, she hurtled into the room and seized a tray of cups. She'd not lose this chance.

*J*acob sat at a table in his small office space in one corner of the storeroom. A pen, ink, and an open ledger rested beneath a glowing oil lamp. He'd postponed his monthly report to Colin Riley, his partner in Boston, until he could think of a way to explain his hiring of Miss Haddon. Colin had warned him more than once about being overly charitable.

Jacob massaged the back of his neck. He didn't believe his partner would be persuaded by a description of Miss Haddon's sweet face and shining green eyes as the reason behind his decision to add her to the expense side of the ledger, although if he were honest that's what he'd have to say.

The middle of May was fast approaching. Two weeks had passed since her employment. If he didn't post a letter soon, Colin would no doubt send someone to check on him.

Jacob wanted to avoid such a visit at all costs.

He groaned and lifted a sheet of paper, then copied the income and expense figures for April at the top of the page. Thankfully, income exceeded expense even with the addition of another employee. After writing a draft for Colin's share of the profits, he scribbled a brief message beneath the figures:

You'll note I've added another person to the kitchen. She's been a great help to Mrs. Fielder. With summer coming on, the cooperage and wagon shop will be hiring more men. I hear a brickyard will set up here soon, as well. New customers should easily cover the additional salary.

He stopped and tapped the pen holder against the table-top. Should he say more about Miss Haddon? No, he'd stop now. Too many explanations opened the door to too many questions.

After dipping the nib in the ink again, he signed his name. In the morning, he'd take the letter to the post office and send it on its way.

"Mr. West?" Miss Haddon's voice spoke behind him. He started, dropping the pen. She'd appeared as if his thoughts of her had brought her to the doorway.

"What is it?" His voice sounded harsher than he intended.

She took a step back. "Please excuse the interruption. I know it's time to go home, but a man came to the kitchen door to talk to you. Mrs. Fielder made him stay outside, but she told me to come get you." Her eyes opened wide. "I hope you don't mind."

"Not at all. I'll come with you right now." He gentled his voice, berating himself for causing the apprehensive expression he saw on her face. Frightening her was the last thing he wanted to do.

He followed her from the grocery through the dining room, then to the kitchen. Mrs. Fielder stood near the door wearing her cloak.

"The fellow's in the alley. He wouldn't say what he wants."

"Thank you both. Before I talk to him, I'll see you out the front entrance." When he caught a surprised look pass between Miss Haddon and Mrs. Fielder, he hastened to explain. "No telling who's out there. Best if he doesn't know you're out walking unescorted."

By including the two of them in his comment, he hoped he'd hidden his concern for Miss Haddon. The drab clothing she wore to work couldn't disguise her beauty. He wished he could offer to see her home, not merely tonight, but each night. He shook his head at his folly. At thirty-eight, he was practically middle-aged. She couldn't be more than twenty-two. She'd never be interested in him.

When they reached the street entrance, he turned the key in the lock and swung the door wide. "See you tomorrow."

Miss Haddon gave him the full benefit of her deep green eyes. "Yes, sir. I'll be here."

He paused a moment after closing the door to gather his straying thoughts. With an unknown visitor waiting in the alley, he needed to be alert. As far as he knew, Colin was the only person in Boston who knew where he was, but he couldn't be overconfident. Life had a way of sneaking up on a man.

Bending over, he patted one of his boots. The outline of his Pepper-box pistol reassured him of the weapon's presence. Thus prepared, he strode to the back door and inched open the screen door. He heard the visitor before he saw him.

"Mr. West?" A tall dark-skinned man stepped from the shadows, his hat tucked against his chest. Tight curls covered his scalp.

"I'm Jacob West."

"My name's Wash Bennett. I was wonderin' if you need your kitchen swamped out nights after the ladies are to home." Wash moved closer to the entrance.

Nothing about his slow drawl indicated Boston roots. Likely he was a freed slave, searching for work. Jacob relaxed a bit and pushed the door wide. "Come on in. You hungry?" He stepped aside and allowed the man to enter.

"No sir." Wash's skinny frame belied his words. "Not lookin' for a handout. I work for my food."

Jacob gazed around the kitchen, taking in spills in front of the worktables and stove. Most nights he stayed behind to scrub the floors after he balanced the day's ledger entries. If he hired Wash Bennett, he'd be free to leave that much sooner.

A moment of silence passed between them. Pity swept over him at the sight of Wash's hopeful face. So many former slaves needed work. He couldn't help them all—but he could help one. Jacob rubbed his moustache with his thumb, then pointed to a mop and bucket in the far corner. "I could use someone. How soon can you start?"

"Right now. I'll shine the place up real good." Wash rolled up the sleeves of his faded chambray shirt. Ropy muscles stood out on his forearms.

"One thing first." Jacob walked to the box where he stored bread and removed the wooden cover. He placed a loaf on the table and cut four slices, then spread them with butter. "Eat this now, then go to work. Tomorrow I'll have the cook set aside some supper for you."

Tears brimmed in the man's eyes. "You're a blessin', sir. Thank you."

Embarrassed, Jacob nodded. He thought of the unsent letter to Colin on the table in his office. He'd wait until next month to tell him about Wash Bennett. For now, he'd sit in the dining room and watch to see how his new employee carried out his duties.

It wouldn't do to be too trusting.

As Cassie walked toward the Stewarts' house, she pondered the change she'd seen in Mr. West. She wouldn't have thought him afraid of anything. Yet his reaction to the news that someone waited for him behind the restaurant left her puzzled. Perhaps the lateness of the hour was the explanation. When she reached King's Highway, she paused and forced her employer from her thoughts.

More immediate concerns awaited her in the brick home across the street. Her friend's baby would be born in a few more weeks. Despite sending repeated letters to the railroad company, Mother hadn't received any news about her brother. Tension vibrated in the air whenever she and Elijah were in the same room.

Cassie waited until a group of riders passed, then stepped off the boardwalk to cross the wide street. Her mind jumped from one solution to another, always returning to the same thought. She'd have to take what little she'd earned so far and try to find a place to live.

The atmosphere when she entered the house reinforced her decision. Rosemary sat alone, a half-knitted baby sacque resting on what was left of her lap. Woofs from the back garden told her that Elijah had probably taken Bodie and gone outside. As usual, Mother would be in their shared room, either reading or penning demands to the railroad. The contrast with the happy scene at her arrival last month brought tears to her eyes. How could her mother be oblivious to the disruption caused by their presence?

Rosemary pushed her knitting aside and smiled at Cassie. "Come sit with me. It's lonely in here. Elijah seems more interested in throwing sticks for the dog than chatting with me in the evenings."

"I suspect he'd like to be upstairs creating a nursery for your little one, but Mother and I are in the way." Cassie took her friend's hand. "We'll be gone by the end of the week. I promise."

Rosemary's smile wobbled. "Please don't do anything rash. I don't want you to feel unwelcome. If it were up to me . . ."

"You've done everything you could to make us welcome. So did Elijah. We've overstayed."

"Then tell me about your plans." A frown crossed her friend's face. "I hope you're not leaving Noble Springs."

Cassie shook her head. "I'm happy here. I like working for Mr. West, in spite of being confined to the kitchen."

"You said that with a certain smile. Is it the work you like, or Jacob West?"

"Well . . ." She thought of his deep, resonant voice, and the kindness he tried to hide under a gruff manner. Knowing she'd see him every day spurred her toward the restaurant in the early mornings. "I must admit, I like both him and the work." A flush heated her cheeks.

"He's an honest man with a good reputation in town." Rosemary's eyes twinkled. "He's a bachelor too."

"Mother doesn't like him."

"Things change."

"Mother doesn't."

Her friend blew out a breath and shifted on the sofa. "She can't control your life forever." She lowered her voice. "I'm concerned for her state of mind. More and more she shows signs of melancholia."

Cassie had to agree. After her first few days at West & Riley's, Mother had stopped complaining about her absences. As far as Cassie knew, she ventured from their room only for meals and to walk to the post office for more stamps and paper. The money she'd brought with her must be nearly depleted by now, with no results to show for her efforts.

Surely if they lived under their own roof, Mother would

come around and take an interest in making a home for the two of them. Eventually she'd have to accept the fact that she'd never find her brother.

Nerves skittered in her throat. She'd given herself five days to find a place for them to live. Now that the words were out of her mouth, she prayed she could keep her promise.

he next morning, Cassie hurried with her kitchen
duties in order to have a free moment to speak to
Mr. West when he arrived. After throwing several handfuls
of ground coffee into the coffeepot, she pushed the brew to
the back of the range to steep. She'd positioned a large bowl
on the worktable and opened the flour bin when Mr. West
entered the kitchen.

Her heart gave a little hop. If he said no to her request,
she had no idea what she'd do. She dusted her hands on her
apron and crossed the room to where he stood.

"I have a favor to ask, sir."

"You don't need to 'sir' me all the time, Miss Haddon."
His expression softened when he looked at her. "What is it
you need?"

"We aren't too busy between noon and supper time. I have
some business to attend to. By the time I leave at the end of
the day everything's closed." She knew she was talking too
fast and slowed herself down. "If I could have a free hour
this afternoon, I'd appreciate it."

"Of course." He cleared his throat. "I've been meaning to
tell you how pleased—"

Mrs. Fielder bustled in from the dining room, broom in hand. "Never seen the floors look so good." She stopped beside Mr. West. "You must've worked extra hard last night."

He glanced between her and Cassie, appearing annoyed at the interruption. "I hired that fellow who was here. Name's Wash Bennett. He'll come in and mop the floors after you leave."

Mrs. Fielder sniffed. "How d'you know he won't rob you blind?"

"I don't. But in the meantime, I'd like you to set a plate of food out for him before you go home."

Cassie watched him, enjoying the way his gravelly voice vibrated in the room. He wasn't one for long conversations. She wished he'd talk more so she'd have the pleasure of listening to him speak.

"Humph." The cook's response could have been a yes or a no. She swished away and thumped the broom against the wall. "Don't think I won't be checking the pantry every morning."

"Fine. You do that." The skin around his eyes crinkled when he smiled. "Now, Miss Haddon, as I was saying, you may take an hour off."

"Thank you, sir."

He raised an eyebrow.

"I mean, thank you."

One hour. She knew where her first stop would be. Where she went after that depended on the answers she received.

That afternoon, Cassie walked the three blocks to Lindberg's Mercantile, hoping to see her friend Faith. She often brought her baby son to the store for a while each afternoon, although Thaddeus Cooper, Noble Springs' former sheriff, now managed the business.

She passed the lawn surrounding Courthouse Square and turned left on King's Highway. The mercantile sat across the street in the center of the block. Cassie prayed she wouldn't have to deal with Sheriff Cooper. Somehow she hadn't lost the awe of him she felt when he'd served as sheriff. She'd much rather ask Faith her questions.

Familiar scents of oiled floors and leather surrounded her when she entered the building. For once, the bolts of colorful fabric displayed near the left of the door didn't tempt her to linger. She had enough time for a conversation with Faith, but not for daydreams over items she could no longer afford.

Cassie glanced toward the rear of the store, noticing Faith's "woodstove regulars," Mr. Grisbee and Mr. Slocum, were in their usual places with a checkerboard between them. They'd stopped their game, apparently waiting to hear why she'd come.

When Sheriff Cooper ambled over, she bit back disappointment. After offering a polite greeting, she said, "Faith isn't here today?"

"Nope. Baby's sick. Expect you'll see her Sunday at church, though." He sounded dismissive.

She straightened, trying to make herself taller in response to his six-foot stature. "Perhaps you can answer a question for me."

"Ask away." He tucked his thumbs in the pockets of his vest.

"I'm in need of a place to rent, Sheriff." She licked her dry lips. "Have you heard of anything nearby? Not too dear?"

There. The words were out of her mouth. She held her breath, waiting for his response.

He gave his head a slow shake. "You fixing to stay in town this time? Not going to run off to St. Louis again, are you?"

"If I were, I wouldn't be seeking a place to live." She pasted what she hoped was a charming smile on her lips to soften her sharp retort.

"Well, afraid I can't help you. Have you tried the boarding-house?"

"My goodness, no. Share lodgings with a houseful of men? There must be something else available."

A chair scraped on the wooden floor. She turned to see Mr. Slocum striding toward them.

"Miss Haddon. Happens I might know of something." He stroked his tidy gray goatee. "Probably nothing a lady like you would want, though."

"Please, Mr. Slocum. Tell me about the house and let me decide."

"Well, it's not exactly a house. More like a cabin, or maybe you'd call it a shed."

She put her hand to her throat. "A shed? Is it habitable?"

"Probably. When I first came here twenty-some years back, I built this little place to keep the weather out while me and the wife put enough by to build a proper house. Now I use it to store firewood and such. Wouldn't take much to move everything out—if you're interested."

Somehow she'd pictured a sweet cottage like Rosemary had before she married Elijah. By no stretch of the imagination could Rosemary's home have been called a shed. But if Mr. Slocum and his wife had lived in this place, how bad could it be? A glance at the wall clock behind the cash drawer told her that her hour was speeding past. She didn't have time to waste.

"I am interested. If it's not too far away, may I see it now?"

"Not too far at all, just over on Third Street, near the boardinghouse. Mind you, the cabin hasn't been lived in for years. You sure?"

"I'm sure." She felt like part of her had detached and watched from a distance. Timid Cassie Haddon, finding somewhere to live for herself and her mother. A month ago she'd never have dreamed she could do such a thing. But then a month ago she never dreamed she'd be earning seventy-five cents a day working in a restaurant kitchen.

Her uncle couldn't call her useless now.

⁓

Cassie followed Mr. Slocum along a gravel path that led behind his white clapboard home. Flowers budded on a lilac bush growing next to the house. A small cabin—indeed that's what it was—sheltered in a back corner behind a plowed garden plot. An oak tree spread dappled shade over the entrance. She noted that the door hung straight on its hinges, and the two windows she could see were protected by shutters. A stone chimney rose at the rear of the building.

The door creaked when Mr. Slocum tugged on the latch. Inside, cobwebs draped over what appeared to be a full cord of wood resting in the center of the main room. Broken chairs, a legless tabletop, and an iron bedstead leaning against the wall filled what was left of the space. To the left, a doorway led to what must be a second room. She noticed a stovepipe penetrating the back wall, and prayed it might be connected to a small stove. With the firewood blocking her view, she couldn't be sure.

For a long moment, Cassie stared, trying to imagine how she'd convince her mother to live in such surroundings.

"Told you it wasn't much," Mr. Slocum said. "But you can have the place for four dollars and fifty cents a month."

"Four dollars. No more."

His gray eyes crinkled at the corners. "Reckon I can live

with that. You've got grit, Miss Haddon. Never would have guessed."

"It comes over me at odd times." She returned his smile and then waved her hand at the woodpile. "Now, please tell me how long before all this is cleared out. I'll need to clean before Mother and I bring our things over."

"Let's see. Today's Thursday." He pushed his hat back from his forehead and took a hard look at the contents of the room. "I'll get Grisbee to help me. The place will be all yours Saturday for sure."

She thanked him and then walked the short distance to West & Riley's with her heart thumping. Four dollars was almost a full week's pay.

Another thought sprang to mind. She'd talked to Mr. Slocum as if she and Mother were poised to settle in the cabin. But they lacked one tiny thing. Furniture.

They lacked two things if she considered her mother's reaction. What if she refused to leave the Stewarts' house?

When she was a child, her father used to chide her about jumping before looking to see where she'd land.

She'd really done it this time.

Cassie paused inside the kitchen door to don her apron while trying to control her whirling thoughts. She and Mother could get by with a bed, a table, and two chairs. Assuming she could afford the furniture. She wiped sweaty palms on her apron. She had only a few dollars left after giving Mr. Slocum a month's rent.

"Are you going to stand there all afternoon?" Mrs. Fielder's sharp voice slashed through Cassie's worries. "Mr. West told me to take the leftover beef from the noon roast and make meat pies for supper." She gestured toward a bowl filled with chopped potatoes and onions. "Those need to be fried up, then mixed with beef and gravy and dumped into those pans."

A row of brown stoneware pie pans waited on one of the two worktables. Cassie hesitated. "I don't know how to fry potatoes." A memory from childhood stirred. "I can make piecrust, though. Cook used to let me help her."

Mrs. Fielder planted one hand on her round hip. "Well, why didn't she teach you to fry potatoes, then?"

"Mother wouldn't let her. She was afraid I might burn myself."

Shaking her head, the woman blew out a long-suffering breath. "Fine. I'll take care of the potatoes. You make the crust. We'll see if you can manage that."

Within a short while, the kitchen filled with the aroma of frying onion and potato. Cassie stood at the worktable cutting lard into flour. Thankfully, for a few minutes she could think about something other than the dilemma that awaited her. For those few minutes she'd revisit the happy times she'd spent helping their cook. Before everything changed.

The two knives she used made a scratching sound, like fingernails on a slate, against the oversized crockery bowl. When she sprinkled water over the crumbled mixture, Mrs. Fielder stepped away from the range to watch.

Cassie kept her eyes focused on her task.

"You need more water." Mrs. Fielder lifted a half-filled cup, her hand poised to pour.

"No." Cassie pushed the woman's hand away. "Cook said to use a light hand when adding liquid. Too much makes a tough crust."

They stared at each other for a moment. Then the tight lines around Mrs. Fielder's mouth relaxed. "Go ahead then. Soon as I fill those pie plates, you top 'em and we'll put 'em in the oven. 'Proof of the pudding,' and all that. Just remember, I'll make sure Mr. West knows who made the crust."

Cassie checked the contents of the bowl. She'd done everything the way she remembered, although she'd never had to prepare pastry in such a large quantity before. Her nerves jumped. What if her distraction over renting the cabin caused her to forget a key ingredient? She poked the mixture with her finger. The consistency felt right—a little bit damp and yielding, but not sticky.

The beef filling sent a savory fragrance over the room as Mrs. Fielder scooped spoonfuls into each pie pan. After sprinkling flour over a cloth, Cassie patted a handful of dough into a ball and rolled the first crust flat. If her efforts turned out like cardboard, she hoped the meat and potatoes would be enough to give the patrons a satisfying meal.

Her stomach fluttered. She should have offered to wash the dirty pots, sweep the floor, chop vegetables, anything, instead of yielding to impulse and claiming she could make piecrust.

Before she'd left earlier, Mr. West started to say something about being pleased. She hoped he meant with her work. What would he say now, once he saw the results of her pastry making?

After the step she'd taken today, she couldn't afford to lose this job.

$\mathcal{O}$nce the supper patrons left, Cassie entered the dining room and began clearing tables. To her relief, a quick glance showed her that the pie pans were empty, and no one had folded the crust to one side in order to eat the filling alone. Then she shrugged. Over the past weeks, she'd learned that hungry men would eat anything put before them. The platters always came back to the kitchen empty.

Tableware clinked on crockery plates as she gathered soiled dishes. Soon she and Mrs. Fielder would take time to eat their own supper. Then she could judge for herself the success or failure of the piecrust.

"Miss Haddon. A word, please." Mr. West's peremptory tone stopped her midway to the kitchen. He crossed the dining room from the grocery entrance.

She lifted her chin, the better to meet his criticism head-on. "I'm sorry. I've been distracted all afternoon. After this, I'll leave the cooking to Mrs. Fielder, I promise."

He reached for her arm and then dropped his hand before touching her. "What are you talking about?"

"The meat pies. The crust was dreadful, wasn't it?"

"That was the best piecrust I ever ate. Light. Flaky. Almost floated onto the fork." His dusky skin flushed darker. "I sound like a woman."

You could never sound like a woman, she felt like saying. *Not with that gravelly voice.*

He cleared his throat. "Thing is, I'd like you to start baking pies for desserts. Mrs. Fielder is a good cook, but she has limits. Pie is one of them."

"I . . . I've never really made a whole pie. Just the crust. Our cook did everything else."

"Well, how hard could it be? Crust, apples or something, and bake."

Cassie felt light-headed. She'd been afraid she'd lose her job, and instead he'd added a complication.

She still had to face Mother when she went to Rosemary's tonight. Then worry about making the cabin livable. And now Mr. West wanted her to leap into something she'd never done.

She gazed into his eyes, warm and brown as molasses, and heard herself say, "All right. When do you want me to start?"

"Saturday. I'll get in a supply of dried apples tomorrow, and see to it they're waiting for you when you arrive Saturday morning. Mrs. Fielder can help you find whatever else you need." His face wore the delighted expression of a man who'd discovered treasure in his backyard.

She groped for a chair and sat. "Not Saturday. Please. I was going to—"

"Going to what?"

"Ask for the afternoon off." Her words tumbled together. She drew a deep breath and held it, feeling a pulse throb in her neck.

"First today, now you want Saturday. I was afraid of this." He fingered his moustache as he stared at her. "If you're going to work here, you need to be committed. This isn't an off-and-on pastime."

"I assure you, I'm not a dilettante. I need this job—never more so than now."

His eyebrows rose. "And why is that?"

To her surprise, his voice sounded gentle, almost like he cared about her answer. The worry she'd bottled up all afternoon spilled over.

"I found a cabin to rent. Mr. Slocum said we could have it on Saturday."

"'We' is you and your mother?"

She nodded.

"So you'd like to take the afternoon to settle there?"

"Yes. Please." She studied his face, trying to read the thoughts behind his noncommittal expression. If he refused, she and Mother couldn't possibly be settled in the short time between the end of her workday and full dark on Saturday. Spending the Lord's Day laboring was out of the question.

He straddled a chair facing her. "All right. Take the afternoon. Just remember, I'll be expecting pies on Monday."

"Thank you. I . . . I appreciate everything you've done for me." She jumped to her feet and grabbed a stack of plates to go to the kitchen.

"Miss Haddon."

She paused.

"I'd be happy to lend a hand. Let me know if you'd like some help."

"Oh! Thank you. I will."

Her heart gave a happy bump at the thought of spending time with him away from the restaurant. Then she chided herself. If he helped, the move would be completed sooner. Then he'd be assured she'd be back at work on time Monday to bake his promised pies. It wasn't as if he were personally interested in her.

⊰≫≪⊱

"I won't even consider such a thing." Cassie's mother sat in a slipper chair under the window in their bedroom, her hands folded on her lap desk. "Leave this comfortable house to live in two rooms?" Her red hair cascaded down her back in a thick braid. She wore her wrapper, although the sun hadn't set.

Cassie arched an eyebrow. "You're living in one room now. Except for meals, Rosemary tells me you spend no time downstairs."

"Well, that's different. I could if I wanted to."

"We can't wait any longer to hear from Uncle Rand." She knelt beside the chair and took her mother's hands. "Rosemary and Elijah need this room for their baby. They've been more than gracious to us, but the time has come for us to have our own place to live."

Mother jerked her hands free. "If you call a rotting cabin a place to live. I certainly don't."

"Would you rather stay in a boardinghouse full of workmen? Right now, that's our only other option."

"How dare you speak to me in that tone of voice? What happened to my respectful daughter?" She narrowed her eyes. "You've changed since you started working for that Mr. West. He's put these notions into your head, hasn't he?"

"I make my own decisions."

"You don't make mine."

"This time I have. The rent is paid for the first month. We'll move in Saturday after I finish cleaning the rooms. That way we'll be all settled and ready for church on Sunday morning."

"You don't know the first thing about cleaning a house." She sniffled. "My own daughter, scrubbing floors. How did we ever sink so low?"

Cassie bit back a sharp retort at the sight of her mother's tears, and used a soothing voice instead. "Lots of families are suffering as a result of the war. Things are bound to be better soon. Who knows? Uncle Rand may pop up any day."

Mother stood and stared out the window. Gripping the sill, she asked, "What about furniture?"

Cassie felt a surge of triumph. Asking about furnishings meant her mother was thinking ahead to living in the cabin.

"We won't need much. I'll see what I can do." She infused her voice with confidence she didn't feel, then put her arm around her mother's shoulders. "I need to go tell Rosemary our plans."

"Your plans, not mine."

Instead of responding with further argument, she kissed her mother's cheek. "I'll be back in a few minutes."

As she descended the stairs, Cassie wondered at the strangeness of life. She'd always believed she would live under her own roof after she married. But Garrett Fitzhugh, her fiancé, had died two years ago in Jefferson City. Then a train derailment left her and Mother in Noble Springs following Garrett's funeral.

Now here she was, preparing to make a home for the two of them by herself. So many changes in such a short time. She prayed the Lord would help her mother accept more changes to come, beginning with Saturday's move.

She found Elijah reading in front of the bay window in the sitting room. Bodie lay at his feet. The dog gave his tail a lazy thump, but didn't rise.

Elijah lowered his magazine. "You look like you need a cup of Rosemary's mint tea." He smiled. "She's in the kitchen at the moment."

Tiredness weighted her shoulders at the memory of everything that had happened since she left the house that morning. "It has been an eventful day. I'll let her tell you my news later."

He nodded and returned to his reading.

"I heard you say you'd had an eventful day." Rosemary stood in the kitchen entrance.

"Indeed I did. I rented a cabin for Mother and me from Mr. Slocum. We'll move in on Saturday."

"No. That soon?" She sank onto a chair.

"I promised you we'd be out by the end of the week."

"You know I'd never hold you to such a promise." Rosemary rested her fingers against her cheek. "You have no . . . possessions. Is he renting furniture to you as well?"

Cassie huffed out a breath and sat facing her friend. "That wasn't part of the bargain. We only need a bed and a couple of other things."

"Like a table and chairs, curtains, rugs, dishes . . ."

A headache stirred in her temples. She hadn't thought about curtains, rugs, and dishes. Or pots and pans, knives and forks, or a scrub bucket and mop, for that matter.

She straightened her shoulders. She'd do what their house-keeper had always done. Make a list. Then buy what she could.

On Saturday morning, Jacob stood with Jesse Slocum surveying the empty cabin.

"Didn't know this place was back here until Miss Haddon said she'd rented it." He shifted on one foot and looked the older man in the eye. "You think they'll be safe?"

"Don't see why not. Any trouble, they can come get me. I'm usually here."

"Unless you're in the mercantile."

"Yup. But daytime's not what you're worried about, is it?"

Jacob flushed. He hadn't realized his worry showed. Sooner or later, Miss Haddon's innocent beauty was bound to attract attention from the men in the boardinghouse across the street. He doubted her mother had the grit to stand up to a threat to their safety.

"I feel responsible for her. Somebody's got to care." He stepped inside the entrance, his boots crunching on wood chips and bark scattered over the floor. Flames flickered behind the open damper in the small stove at the back of the room.

Jesse pointed to a glowing red area around the stovepipe. "Thought I'd better make sure this thing wasn't rusted through anywhere. Works fine." He took a stick from a box of firewood on the hearth and pushed the damper closed. "We'll let it burn itself out. Don't need heat today anyhow."

Ducking his head beneath the lintel, Jacob moved into the second room. A few fingers of light spread from gaps in the shutters. Pegs lined two of the walls about four feet from the floor. An iron bedstead was pushed against a corner. New rope crisscrossed the side rails, forming a platform for a mattress tick. He turned to Jesse.

"When did Miss Haddon have this brought over? Thought they weren't moving until this afternoon."

Jesse scuffed a few dead leaves to one side with the toe of his boot. "Well, this old thing was left out here when we built the big house. Wife wanted everything new." He shrugged. "Figured the ladies could use it."

Jacob hid a smile. Perhaps he wouldn't have to concern himself with their safety after all.

Back in the main room, he took a piece of paper from his pocket and scratched "bed" from his list. The challenge now would be to see how many necessities he could provide without the Haddon ladies knowing he'd done so.

On Saturday afternoon, Cassie lifted her shawl from a peg next to the kitchen door. Her hands shook. She had so much to do. One afternoon in which to shop for supplies, clean, and arrange their possessions in the small cabin. She'd stopped by there on her way to work. Wood chips littered the floor, left from the firewood Mr. Slocum had moved to a lean-to beside the alley. Cobwebs netted the grimy windows. Mother was right about one thing. She didn't know the first thing about cleaning a house.

Today, she'd learn.

Mrs. Fielder spoke behind her. "You got everything you need to live in that old place? I heard you came here with nothing more than a trunk full of pretty clothes." She cleared her throat. "Between me and my daughters, we might be able to scare up a skillet for you, and maybe a kettle or two."

Grateful tears welled in Cassie's eyes. She turned, laying her hand on the older woman's arm. "Bless you. You heard correctly. Anything you can spare would be very welcome."

"Now, no need to take on so. Can't hardly find my way around my own kitchen for all the clutter. Glad for a reason to make some room on the shelves."

After thanking her again, Cassie pushed open the screen door and set off for Lindberg's Mercantile. Mrs. Fielder's unexpected kindness lightened her steps as she strode past the businesses along the boardwalk. A smile hovered on her lips. The woman's brusque exterior hid a warm heart.

Still smiling, she pushed open the mercantile door. At the sound of the tinkling bell, Faith Saxon glanced up from the counter where she stood, then hurried toward her. "Mr. Slocum told me you're moving into his old cabin today." She hugged Cassie.

"I am." Cassie returned the hug, then stepped back. "I

was hoping you'd be here this afternoon." She took a quick glance around. "Where's little Alexander?"

"He's asleep behind the counter in the buggy Curt made for him."

"Your husband is a man of many talents." She tiptoed over to the buggy and gazed down at the sleeping baby. His blond hair lay in wisps over his forehead. "He looks more like you all the time," she whispered.

"Today's his two-month birthday. I baked a Dolly Varden cake for him this morning." Faith's blue eyes sparkled. "He won't get to eat it, of course, but Grandpa will certainly enjoy a slice or two. It's his favorite."

Cassie liked Faith's grandfather. In spite of his age and memory troubles, he accompanied Faith and Curt to church each Sunday, and never failed to greet her and Mother in a courtly manner. She'd never known either of her own grandfathers. Her father's father died before she was born, and her mother evaded questions about her own parents.

Wishing she could settle in for a visit instead of having to hurry to the cabin, she stepped away from the baby and drew her list from her handbag. "I came to buy a few things before I can start cleaning. There isn't much money, so my list is small. To begin, a bucket and scrub brush and some towels. Oh, soap and a broom."

"I think you're very brave. I can't imagine scrubbing out a dirty old cabin. Spiders, mice, and who knows what running around inside." She shuddered.

Cassie shook her head. "I can't either, but it needs doing before we can live there. I'm praying I can have everything spotless before Elijah brings Mother over with our trunk this evening." Her mind flashed to the interior of the cabin as it looked that morning when she peeked inside. Maybe spotless was too tall an order. As clean as possible might be more realistic. She drew a deep breath. With the Lord's help, she'd do her best.

Faith took the list from Cassie's fingers and scanned the contents. "You're right, this is a small list. Dishes, four yards of blue gingham, a lamp, tableware. Are you sure you've thought of everything?"

"It's all I can afford. I'm hoping to get Mother interested enough to sew curtains with the fabric."

"You don't have to do this." Worried wrinkles creased Faith's forehead. "Curt and I can make room for you."

"Thank you, but no. We were in the way at Rosemary's, and it would be no different in your house. Now that I have employment, I can take care of my mother by myself."

After paying Faith for the purchases and securing her promise to have Curt deliver the items she didn't need right away, Cassie stuffed everything else but the broom into the bucket. With her hands full, she walked to the corner of King's Highway and then turned north toward High Street. After a couple of minutes, someone fell into step behind her. The back of her neck prickled.

She increased her pace.

So did the person following.

assie wanted to run, but with both hands full she couldn't lift her skirts out of the way. The best she could do was a modified trot. She cast a frantic look over her shoulder when she reached High Street.

A dark-skinned man wearing a battered slouch hat was closing the distance between them. Heart racing, she pivoted to face him.

"Come any nearer and I'll scream for help." She brandished the broom like a club.

He stopped a safe distance away and pulled off his hat. "Sorry to scare you, missy. Mr. West told me to go to that store and fetch your parcels for you."

Her heart slowed its wild pounding. Without his hat, she recognized Wash Bennett, the man who came in at the end of each day to scrub the restaurant kitchen.

She held out the broom and bucket. "I'm sorry, Wash, I didn't expect you. I welcome the help. Thank you. But how did Mr. West know where I was going?"

"Don't know, missy. He never said." Wash looped one arm through the handle on the heavy wooden bucket and grabbed the broom with his free hand. "Where you takin' this?"

"Just a couple of blocks down the street. Cattycorner from the restaurant." She started in that direction, then paused when he didn't join her. Surely he didn't plan to take her purchases and run away. "Wash? Are you coming?"

"Just waitin' for you to get ahead. Wouldn't do for me to be next to you."

"Those days are gone. You don't have to walk behind me."

"'Fraid not all folks think like you. If'n you don't mind, I'll keep my distance."

She gave a reluctant nod and set off toward the cabin. After a moment, she heard Wash's footsteps behind her.

Cassie stopped in front of the two wooden steps set against the rock foundation. She noticed that someone, probably Mr. Slocum, had opened the shutters so afternoon light could fill the interior. She'd have to sweep the wood scraps out before she could scrub the floor. Or should she wash the windows first? She wished she'd watched when their housekeeper cleaned her parents' home.

When Wash caught up with her, he placed the bucket on the ground and leaned the broom against a wall. "I'd best not tarry." His gaze darted toward the alley. "If anyone sees me with you . . ."

"I wouldn't want to bring trouble down on you. Thank you for helping me." She dug in her handbag and held out one of her remaining coins.

Shaking his head, he took a step away. "No need, missy. Mr. West done paid me already." He turned and strode along the path to the street.

Her gaze followed him until he was out of sight. The thought that Mr. West had paid Wash to help her left her dumbfounded. Why would he do such a thing? Shaking her head, she stepped inside the cabin.

The bedstead in the other room was the first thing she noticed. A clean straw tick rested between the rails. Then she saw a square table and two chairs pushed against the wall. Moving closer, she bent her head to get a better look at the chairs. An exact match to those in the restaurant. First sending Wash, and now this. She'd seen enough of her employer to know he had a soft heart when it came to other's needs, but she hadn't asked for help.

Her thoughts jumped to the task before her when something scuttled across the floor and disappeared under the bed. She ran back outside and grabbed the broom. After dragging the bed away from the wall, she chased the rodent around the cabin until it scurried out the open door.

Heart pounding, she leaned against the frame and marveled at herself. Ladylike Cassie Haddon, chasing mice. None of her childhood friends would believe the tale. They'd never believe what she planned to do next, either.

After unbuttoning the cuffs on her blue work dress, she rolled up the sleeves, then carried the bucket over to the lean-to and filled it from the pump. The weight of the water dragged at her arm as she staggered back to the cabin. A few drops sloshed over the edge when she plunked the wooden container next to the waiting broom.

Dust flew as she swept. The afternoon sun inched lower in the western sky, prodding her onward. *Just keep going. If you stop, you'll never finish in time.* She shuddered at crackling cobwebs and scattering spiders when she brushed the broom over the window glass. She wished she knew how their housekeeper had accomplished all these tasks in a home far larger than this tiny cabin.

Cassie wiped perspiration from her forehead and dropped

to her knees next to the bucket. After plunging the brush into a lye soap and water solution, she began scrubbing the floors in a back corner of the bedroom. Dip the brush. Drag the bucket. Each dip brought her closer to the front door.

When Elijah arrived with her mother at dusk, the damp floors gleamed in fading light that pooled beneath clean windows. A resin-fresh aroma rose from the scoured pine boards. Cassie had moved the table and chairs near the stove in the main room. A shelf nearby held the skillet and pots Mrs. Fielder had promised, along with the dishes Curt delivered from the mercantile.

Cassie had never been so tired, not even after her first day at the restaurant. Her back ached. Her fingertips were raw from scrubbing. Yet she couldn't stop smiling at what she'd accomplished. Just let her uncle—or anyone else—try to call her useless now. She'd made a home for herself and her mother.

Elijah was first up the steps. He set their trunk inside the door and whistled as he stared around the room. "I'd never have believed you could do all this in such a short time. I stopped by yesterday while Jesse was repairing that table. Figured then you'd need a week to clean out the years of neglect. And you did it in an afternoon."

She basked in his look of admiration, at the same time making a mental note to thank Mr. Slocum for providing the table.

Her mother appeared in the doorway, dressed in her best traveling suit. She'd done her hair in an elaborate twist at the back of her head.

Cassie held her breath, hoping for praise.

Mother sniffed. "At least the place feels sturdy enough. I was afraid it would fall down around our ears."

Elijah sent Cassie a sympathetic glance.

She blew out a breath and then slipped her arm around her mother's waist.

"Welcome to your new home."

~

The lamp Cassie purchased sent a warm glow over the cabin's interior. Once she unpacked the trunk and spread their red and green thistle pattern quilt over the bed, she settled onto one of the two chairs, unable to keep a smile from her face. The small dwelling looked almost . . . homey.

She turned to her mother, who sat across the table. "We'll be comfortable. I know you'll get used to being here."

The lamplight caught the glitter of tears in her mother's eyes. Her lower lip quivered.

Mother seldom cried.

Cassie's heart plummeted. She jumped to her feet. "You must be tired. Rosemary sent over some of her teas. Would you like a cup?"

"No . . . no, thank you." She covered her face with her hands and sobbed.

"I know this isn't what you're used to, but it's all I can do for now." Cassie wrapped her arm around her mother's shoulders and hugged her close. "Please, try to make the best of things."

"It's not you. I can see how hard you've worked." She drew a trembling breath. "I feel like I've failed. This isn't what I wanted. I dreamed of you with a fine husband, children, a home like your father and I had. I did everything I could to prepare you for such a life. And now look." She waved her hand at their surroundings, tears running unchecked down her cheeks. "You . . . you're kitchen help. Spending your meager wages to put a roof over our heads."

"Mother—Mama—you know this isn't your fault. I'm glad I have my job. We're blessed to have a place of our own, however small."

"My dreams are ashes." She rose and turned toward the bedroom. "You may feel blessed. I don't."

Cassie crumpled onto a chair, her mother's pain tearing at her heart. Nothing she could do would return their lives to what they were before the war. *Lord, I'm powerless to help my mother. The apostle Paul says in your Word that he has learned, in whatsoever state, to be content. Please, let this be true for her as well.*

Cassie rose early on Monday and dressed for work as quietly as possible to avoid waking her mother. Tiptoeing around the main room, she set a plate and knife next to a covered pan of cornbread. A jar of honey and a bowl of butter waited on the shelf. She would have breakfast at the restaurant, but Mother would need to prepare her own meal. Thanks to both Faith and Rosemary, they were supplied for the next few days.

She took one last glance at her mother's sleeping form, then slipped out the door. Her shoes crunched on the gravel path that led around Mr. Slocum's house and out to Third Street. The morning she'd been dreading had arrived. Mr. West expected her to make pies, and beyond preparing crust she had no idea how. Thankfully, Mrs. Fielder would be there to offer direction. Even more pressing, she needed to determine whether the chairs in her cabin had come from the restaurant. Mr. Slocum said they weren't his. Neither Faith nor Rosemary claimed ownership. That left Mr. West as the likely donor.

She clasped her hands together and rested her fingers against her lips. He'd granted her a favor by giving her time off, sent Wash to carry her purchases, then provided furniture. The poor man would soon realize helping her decreased his profits. A headache pecked at her temples. What if he decided she'd become a liability and discharged her?

Drawing a deep breath, she crossed the empty street and entered the kitchen. Her headache burrowed deeper when she saw a row of pie pans spread out on one of the worktables. Jars of dried apples sat to one side.

She swallowed. First she'd set the tables in the dining room, then speak to Mr. West about her chairs. The pies could wait a bit.

Mrs. Fielder pushed open the door, eyes bright with curiosity. "Did your mother like the cabin?"

"She's . . . adjusting. I don't believe she's ever lived so humbly."

"Humbly? There's folks would be glad to have a snug roof over their heads."

Cassie held up her hand. "I know. I'm thankful to Mr. Slocum. Mother seems to be having a difficult time right now, and I don't know how to help her."

"Humph. She doesn't realize how lucky she is to have a daughter like you."

The balm of Mrs. Fielder's kind words spread over Cassie, smoothing the edges of her worries. She moved close to the older woman and squeezed her hand. "Thank you, Mrs. Fielder. You're very kind."

"Call me Jenny."

"Thank you—Jenny." She walked to a shelf, taking down a stack of plates. "I'll have the tables ready in a few minutes."

"Good. I'll make the biscuits and be out of your way so you can start on the pies."

"About the pies—"

"Don't worry. You'll have the kitchen to yourself after breakfast. I promised one of my daughters I'd watch her babies while she renders up some lard. She worries about them underfoot with the hot fat bubbling."

"But I need you to—"

"Now, don't worry. I'll be back in time to cook the noon meal. You won't have to do a thing but make a few pies while I'm gone."

Cassie'd never seen anyone render lard. When their cook needed fat for cooking, she'd taken a jar full from the root cellar—a jar like those waiting near the pie plates in West & Riley's kitchen. She drew in a long breath.

Piecrust, apples. As Mr. West had said, how hard could it be?

She dropped knives and forks on top of the plates she held and then hastened into the dining room. Mentally, she counted chairs as she arranged place settings. When she reached the table nearest the grocery entrance, she saw four chairs, not six.

Her stomach tightened. The chairs in her cabin came from the restaurant.

Mr. West stood behind the counter inside the grocery, talking with a customer. Nervous perspiration popped out on Cassie's forehead. She had to say something to him. It wasn't seemly for him to help her set up housekeeping. If her mother found out . . .

As soon as the customer left, she stepped through the entrance. "Mr. West."

He turned, his expression welcoming. "Good morning. I trust you and your mother are comfortable in your little cabin."

"Yes. But those two chairs—" She bit her lip. "They're missing from the dining room. You brought them over, didn't you?"

"You needed them." He studied her face. "Don't look so worried. I can easily buy more."

"How much do they cost?"

"Miss Haddon. They're a gift."

"Truly, I appreciate your intentions. Sending Wash to the mercantile was a generous act. But if anyone found out you helped furnish the cabin, talk would fly around town about my morals. I can't have that—neither can you." She hid her trembling hands beneath her apron. "Please, take the price from my salary."

"I never intended to cause harm." Pain settled over his features. "Forgive me."

He looked so distraught that she reached out and grasped his arm. His solid, muscled arm. She jerked her hand away as if she'd touched hot coals. "I know you didn't." She softened her voice. "If you'll let me pay for the chairs, I'd love to keep them. And I thank you."

His dark eyes burned into hers. "You're welcome. Since you insist, I'll deduct a small amount each week, so as not to cause hardship. And Miss Haddon . . ."

"Yes?"

"I'm looking forward to apple pie with my dinner."

Her heart drummed as she returned to the kitchen. She'd never met anyone as kind as Mr. West. She prayed he'd be pleased with her efforts.

Jenny Fielder paused at the door leading to the alley and tossed Cassie a wave. "I'll be back in a couple of hours. Don't worry about a thing."

The screen door banged behind her.

Cassie plunged her hands back into the greasy dishwater and scrubbed the last bits of egg from a cast-iron skillet. She wished there'd been time to ask Jenny more about baking an apple pie, but the woman had been so busy hurrying through her breakfast chores that she bit her responses off in abbreviated sentences. "Hot oven." "Don't crowd." "Mind the time."

After placing the skillet on the stovetop to dry, Cassie marched to the worktable and stared at the ingredients for her pies. At least she knew how to make the crust. She sifted, measured, and cut chunks of lard into flour. As she sprinkled water over the mixture, her confidence increased. She was worrying over nothing. Line the pans with crust, fill with apples, and bake. The customers would be pleased, and so would Mr. West.

In the next half hour, she lined six pie pans and covered the remaining crust with a damp towel to keep the dough

Love's Sweet Beginning

from drying while she added the apples. After opening the first jar of apples, she shook a quantity of the dried fruit into a crust and distributed the pieces evenly inside the pan. Moving down the row, she repeated the process with the five remaining pie plates.

Cinnamon. She remembered their cook always flavored apple pie with cinnamon, so she went to a narrow shelf near the range and found Jenny's supply of spices. A narrow jar labeled "Cinnamon" contained fragrant sticks of the sweet spice. She shook out one curled stick for each pie. They probably softened as they cooked, like carrots.

She held her hand at the open oven door to check the temperature as she'd seen Jenny do. Not hot enough. She arranged three pies on the oven shelf, careful not to crowd them together, then added more wood to the firebox.

The tension that clamped her shoulders receded. She poured a glass of sweet cider from a crock on the table and gathered the bowls she needed to wash. Now that her task was nearly complete, she felt foolish for her worries. How hard could pie-making be, indeed.

Jenny paused at the entrance to the dining room. "Please divide each one into six pieces while I take the coffee in."

Cassie nodded and scraped blackened crust from the edges of the pies. Except for the burned parts, her efforts looked perfect. Next time, she'd pay more attention to how long they stayed in the oven. She took a knife and cut through crust and filling. As soon as the pies were sliced, Jenny whisked the pans out to the waiting customers.

Wishing she could watch the men taste her baking, Cassie paced between the closed door and the worktable. The third

84

time she passed the table, Jenny patted a chair beside her. "You might as well sit down and rest for a moment."

"Is Mr. West eating with the other men?"

"Yes. He's sitting near the grocery, guess so he can get up if a customer comes in."

Cassie hoped he had one of the slices without a burned edge.

After a couple of minutes, the door swung open and Mr. West entered carrying a plate containing a wedge of pie with one bite missing. Behind him, men's voices rose and chairs scraped against the floor.

Prickles ran up Cassie's arms. Something was wrong.

He walked to the table and folded the top crust back over withered apple pieces. A cinnamon stick lay crosswise over the filling like a minus sign.

Her breath stopped. She cast a frantic glance between Mr. West and Jenny. "What did I do wrong?"

Mr. West cleared his throat. "Mrs. Fielder will have to answer that question. I'm not a cook. Near as I can tell, you've wasted a lot of expensive apples. From now on, go back to your other chores. Let Mrs. Fielder handle the baking." He set the plate on the table with a thunk, then turned and strode from the room.

She tried to stop the tears that rolled over her cheeks. She'd wasted food, disappointed Mr. West, and probably jeopardized her job. She dropped onto a chair and stared at the offending pie. Learn from your mistakes, her father had often told her. After a moment, she drew a deep breath and turned to Jenny.

"Why . . . what . . . do you know how this happened?"

Jenny poked a fork into one of the apple slices and bit off a corner. She chewed and chewed, then swallowed. "How long did you soak the apples in that cider Mr. West bought?"

"Soak the apples?"

"They need to sit in hot cider for an hour or so. Puffs them up." She lifted the cinnamon stick, a smile twitching at the corner of her mouth. "See that brown powder on the shelf over there?" She pointed to a stubby bottle sealed with a cork.

"Yes."

"That's ground cinnamon. Mix a spoonful into the sugar for each pie."

Cassie burned with embarrassment. She'd done none of those things. Lowering her gaze, she stared at her hands clenched together in her lap. "You must think I'm hopeless." Her voice trembled.

"No." Jenny squeezed Cassie's shoulder. "You should've seen the first pie I tried to make. At least you can do crust. Mine come out like hardtack. I'll write you a recipe so you know better next time."

"Mr. West said there won't be a next time. From the look on his face, he's not likely to change his mind."

She stood and dumped the pie into a slop bucket. Failure weighted her movements.

Jacob's steps dragged when he left the store on Monday evening. The expression on Miss Haddon's face when he showed her the ruined pie was etched in his memory. She couldn't have looked more shocked if he'd slapped her. Then what did he do? Complained about wasted food and slammed the plate down on the table. He'd tried so hard to show her kindness. Now she was afraid of him again.

He kicked at a pebble in the alley on his way to fetch Jackson, his stabled horse. A letter from Colin Riley crackled in his pocket. Perhaps if the message from his partner had contained better news, he wouldn't have been so short with Miss Haddon. He shook his head. The damage was done.

The horse nickered when Jacob approached. Water from the trough in front of him ran down the animal's lips and dripped on the ground.

"Ready to go home?" Jacob rubbed Jackson's neck, then brushed dirt and dust from his hide before dropping the saddle onto his back. Once they left the stable, he turned west along the darkened streets. After months of traveling this route, his mount knew the way as well as he did.

As they passed lighted windows at the edge of town, Jacob felt a pang of sorrow. Men returning after a day's work were welcomed into warm houses with lamps burning to dispel the gloom. When he reached his own home, he'd be groping in the dark for matches to light his lamps. No one would greet him at the door with a smile and a kiss.

For some reason, he thought of Miss Haddon's bright smile. Her eagerness to please. He'd shut down that eagerness as surely as if he'd slammed a door in her face.

He groaned. It wasn't as if she'd be interested in him anyway. Once the younger men in town learned of her presence, one of them would win her heart and she'd be gone.

He gripped the reins tighter as he continued on the road beyond Pioneer Lake and up the track toward his home. An occasional spark flew when Jackson's hooves struck a rock. A stream gurgled in the darkness. When they reached the top of the rise, his house's silhouette stood black among shadowed oaks and hickory trees. Two stories, with a veranda across the front. He'd had the home built the previous fall, its solid presence assuring him that he'd risen above his unfortunate beginnings.

Now the letter from Colin Riley threatened all he'd accomplished.

As soon as Jacob stabled his horse, he marched into the house, lighted a lamp, and flung himself into a chair in the parlor. Gritting his teeth, he removed Colin's letter from his pocket. Maybe the news wouldn't seem as bad this time.

Jacob,

Your report for the month of April has yet to arrive. Normally, I wouldn't worry. You've proved yourself reliable over the years you've been in Missouri. But things have changed with me.

My health is failing, and I've decided to sell the business to a younger man. Keegan Byrne has worked for me for the past year, and seems quite eager to carry on with Riley's Grocery as it was when you were here.

Which brings me to my point. Keegan will expect a draft from you within the first ten days of every month. I've explained our long history to him, but he's full of modern ideas and thinks I'm too lax in enforcing payment.

I wish I could give you this news in person. As far as I'm concerned, I have no doubt you will continue to prove as honest with Keegan as you have with me. It's done my heart good to see your success.

Sincerely,
Colin

Jacob heaved a long sigh. The news was no better with a second reading.

He wondered how much Colin had told Keegan Byrne about their initial meeting. One thing for certain—he wouldn't be so much as one day tardy sending his partner's share to Boston. Having Colin come to Noble Springs would be hazardous enough. He couldn't risk a visit from someone who knew him only as a name in a ledger.

Over the years, he'd done all he could to keep his Boston past secret. As Colin acknowledged, he'd proved himself honest. No good could come from his history reaching the ears of people in Noble Springs. Particularly Miss Haddon.

❧

The following morning, Cassie moved as silently as possible through her table-setting duties. After the way Mr. West spoke to her yesterday, she had no desire to call attention to herself. She planned to arrange tables, wash dishes, and stay away from him at all times. If he couldn't find anything to complain about, he couldn't dismiss her.

When he walked through the dining room to unlock the street door, she fled into the kitchen and busied herself slicing bacon.

Jenny stopped stirring pancake batter to watch. "Cut 'em a bit thinner. Get more out of a side of bacon that way."

Cassie nodded and made the next slices smaller.

"You're quiet today." Jenny's spoon scraped the side of the bowl, around and around.

"I keep thinking about those dreadful pies. What if none of the men come back for breakfast?"

Jenny snorted. "They'll be back. Can't keep a man away from food." She fished in her pocket. "Here's a recipe for dried apple pie. This afternoon, you make a crust and I'll show you how to plump the apples. We'll just do one little pie. Mr. West will never know." Her eyes sparkled with mischief.

"Bless you. I'm determined to learn how to do it right, even if I never have another chance in the restaurant." Jenny's kindness lifted her heart.

At the sound of footsteps coming toward the kitchen, they stopped talking and turned their full attention to their tasks. Mr. West paused in the doorway and cleared his throat.

Cassie kept her head down.

He took a couple of steps into the room. "Careful with that knife, Miss Haddon. Wouldn't want you to cut yourself."

She lifted her head far enough to gaze at him through her lashes. Did he think she was that incompetent? "Yes, sir."

Jenny raised her eyebrows. "She knows how to cut bacon."

"Good. Well, I'll leave you to it, then." Face flushed, he turned and strode out of the kitchen.

The two women exchanged a look.

"Do you think he heard us about the pie?" Cassie whispered.

"I doubt it. Can't think why he'd come in here now, though. We generally don't see much of him until the breakfast rush is over."

Cassie knew why. He was checking up on her. Another mistake and she'd surely lose her job.

Jacob sat at the table in his office reviewing ledger totals. In the background, subdued murmurs of conversation filtered through the dining room wall. He seldom came to the restaurant on Sundays, but today was the last day of May. His report and accompanying bank draft would be posted first thing tomorrow. Mr. Byrne could take his modern ideas and line a birdcage with them.

"Mr. West?" The cook's voice brought him back to the moment. "I brought you a bite to eat." Mrs. Fielder set a sandwich and a piece of pie on the table.

He swiveled in his chair. "You made pie? Ginger cake is what I wrote on the menu board." Then he recognized how ungrateful he sounded. "Sorry. I mean, thank you."

She responded with a grin. "Try the pie and tell me what you think."

Mrs. Fielder had a heavy hand with pastry. To please her, he cut off a bite and popped it in his mouth, not expecting much.

Juicy chunks of apple surrounded by sweet cinnamon-flavored sauce swept over his tongue. Flaky crust crumbled as he chewed. He stared at the cook. "This is the best pie you've ever made." He forked a larger bite.

"Miss Haddon baked this yesterday. She's been practicing. I didn't tell her I planned to give you some."

He dropped the fork to the plate. "She's been practicing?"

"The poor girl was heartsick at the way her pies turned out. She's afraid you'll dismiss her." Mrs. Fielder folded her arms over her chest. "So she's been making little pies, day after day, until she got the feel of it. I thought it was time you knew."

Afraid she'd be dismissed? No wonder Miss Haddon found a reason to leave the room whenever he visited the kitchen. "That happened a couple of weeks ago. You don't mean she's been worrying about her job ever since?"

"Well, why wouldn't she? She's right proud of renting that little cabin. Without what you pay her, where would they go?"

He leaned back in his chair and studied Mrs. Fielder's flushed face. "What do you think I should do?"

"That's up to you, isn't it?"

After she left, he stared at his half-eaten slice of pie. Admiration for Miss Haddon's persistence glowed within him. He'd never met anyone quite like her.

He rubbed the back of his neck, wondering whether he dared to get to know her better.

❧

Late Monday afternoon, Cassie stood at a worktable rolling out a small circle of piecrust to fit over the filling in a seven-inch pie plate. She glanced at Jenny.

"I'll slip this in the oven with the biscuits at suppertime. If it turns out well—"

"Of course it'll turn out well. For the past week every pie has been perfect. When are you going to tell Mr. West?" Her tone held a challenge.

"I don't think he cares. He said for you to do the baking."

Their employer appeared in the doorway between the kitchen and dining room. "You don't think I care about what?"

Cassie startled, then tossed a clean towel over the unbaked pie. "Um, whether we have biscuits or cornbread tonight?" She noticed that the round pan showed beneath the towel, and bunched a corner to disguise the shape.

A grin creased his face. He stepped over to the worktable. "So, what's under there? Biscuits or cornbread?"

She shot an alarmed glance at Jenny, who met her gaze with a smile and an encouraging nod. "Tell him," she mouthed.

Cassie hung her head. "No, sir, it's an apple pie." She flipped the towel aside. "If you're worried about the expense, please take it out of my pay."

"I won't do anything of the kind. I was much too hasty the other day, and I'm sorry. Mrs. Fielder brought me a sample last night. It was perfect. Would you consider making pies for our customers—please?"

"Oh, yes, I will!" She wanted to shout for joy, but instead cast him a shy smile. "Th . . . thank you for giving me another chance."

She looked into his dark brown eyes and saw more than an employer. The warmth in his gaze brought a flush to her cheeks.

❦

The sky glowed brilliant orange as Cassie left the restaurant that evening. When she reached the corner of High Street, she glanced west in time to see a halo of light reflected on the horizon following the descent of the sun behind the hills. How appropriate—the heavens were celebrating with her.

Assuming customers liked her pies as much as Mr. West did, she hoped her job at the restaurant would be secure. For the first time in her life, she'd be accepted as a competent, productive person. She hugged her arms around her middle. Best of all, she'd earned Mr. West's admiration. If she kept a journal, she'd put a star beside today.

Her steps light, she crossed the street and followed the gravel path that led to her cabin behind Mr. Slocum's house. Flowers hung like tassels on his lilac bush. Reaching up, she broke off a cluster and brought it to her nose, savoring the fruity-sweet fragrance. As soon as she entered the cabin, she'd put the sprig in water to celebrate this day.

Mother greeted her at the door. She wore her wrapper with a towel draped over her shoulders, her long hair hanging loose over her back. The earthy smell of henna filled the air.

Another good sign. Mother was taking an interest in her appearance again.

"I thought you'd never get here. I have the best news!" Mother clutched her hand and tugged her into the room. "A letter came from the railroad today. Rand is in Calusa. We can go there as soon as we get tickets."

The lilac bloom fell from her fingers. Jacob had apologized, given her another chance, and then promised so much more with his eyes. Her heart fluttered when she pictured the look he'd given her. *Now* her mother wanted to leave?

"Just think. You won't have to work for that grocer anymore. I don't like the way he looks at you." Mother clasped her hands. "Rand will take care of us. Our future will be secure."

Glancing inside the bedroom, Cassie noticed the open trunk, and a plain blue blanket covering their bed. Not the thistle quilt. "You've started packing already?" She stepped into the room. The quilt was folded inside the trunk, along with their extra linens.

"Of course I have. The train for Calusa departs around

nine in the morning. I checked." Mother followed her to the doorway. "You can pack everything but your traveling clothes tonight, then go to the restaurant tomorrow and tell that Mr. West we're leaving."

Cassie teetered on decision's ledge. Her thoughts spun. She'd vowed to honor her mother, but she was content here. More than content, happy.

Drawing a deep breath, she squeezed her hand over the cold metal clasp on the trunk's domed lid. Her mother hadn't been this animated since they left St. Louis.

Cassie released her grip on the clasp. Steps dragging, she crossed to the pegs where her two better dresses hung. Setting the plaid taffeta aside for the journey, she laid her rose chintz over the bed and folded the yards of fabric into a rectangle compact enough to fit inside the trunk's maw. The process brought an uncomfortable reminder of the night they'd packed to leave St. Louis.

Then, she'd had no skills. Now, leaving meant a return to living under an uncle's roof and abandoning all she'd accomplished. Blinking back tears, she mentally erased the star she'd planned to put next to today in her imaginary journal.

assie drew a steadying breath and surveyed the main room of her cabin. The cups and plates she'd purchased rested on a shelf next to several glass tumblers. Gingham curtains framed the windows with bright blue checks. A single lamp glowed in the center of the table, its light illuminating the lilac sprig lying on the floor next to one of the chairs.

She brushed past her mother and filled one of the tumblers, then seized the purple bloom and thrust it into the water.

"I can't do it. I'm not leaving."

Mother narrowed her eyes. "Of course you are."

"No."

"What's happened to you? I've spent more than a month looking for my brother, and now that I've found him you stand in my way." Her mother sank onto the edge of the bed.

The straw tick rustled when Cassie sat next to her. She laid a gentle hand over her mother's. "I didn't say you couldn't go. I said *I'm* not going."

"It's the same thing. You know I don't have money for a ticket."

"I'll buy your ticket." Her stomach lurched at the thought

of depleting her funds with the rent due soon, but she stiffened her resolve. "I'm glad you found Uncle Rand. Nevertheless, I'm content here in Noble Springs, and here's where I want to stay."

"Do you expect me to make that trip alone? I could be robbed, or worse."

Robbed of what? Cassie wanted to ask, but didn't. She blew out a lengthy sigh. "All right. I'll accompany you to Calusa. But as soon as you're settled with Uncle Rand, I'm coming back home."

Home. The word was a balm to her soul. For the first time since the war, she'd found a place that felt like home. Here's where she'd stay.

Then the thought of purchasing two train tickets—one for a round-trip—intruded. Plus she'd earn no salary for several days. And as if things weren't bad enough, tomorrow she'd have to go to Mr. West and tell him her plans.

On Tuesday morning, Cassie entered West & Riley's kitchen with hesitant steps. Her green plaid traveling dress swished when she crossed the floor to Jenny's side.

The cook's eyes rounded. She placed the bowl of eggs she held on a worktable and surveyed Cassie's attire. "You're fancy today. What if you spill something on that pretty dress?"

"I'm not staying." Tears stung her eyelids. "I'm so sorry to leave you with all the work. Mother found her brother, finally. We're taking the train to Calusa in a couple of hours."

"Oh no!" Jenny grabbed Cassie's hand and led her to a chair. "You can't just up and leave." She dabbed her eyes with a corner of her apron. "Never mind about the work. I'll miss you. You've made the days here a pleasure."

"Please don't cry. I plan to return as soon as Mother is settled."

"Good for you! I knew you had spirit." A frown etched her forehead. "You'll need it when you talk to Mr. West. He's not going to be pleased."

"I know. Is he here?"

"In the grocery."

Cassie gazed at the pie plates stacked in front of her and swallowed disappointment. Her dream would have to wait a few days.

"I'd better go see him before I lose my courage." She squeezed Jenny's hand, then rose and marched toward the grocery.

Mr. West's welcoming smile faded the moment he noticed her dress. "Miss Haddon? You look lov—very nice, but that's a strange choice for a workday."

"I'm sorry." She bit her lip. "I'm not dressed for work today. Mother found her brother—in Calusa—and we're taking the train there in a couple of hours. I promised I'd accompany her." She knew her words ran together. Pausing, she willed herself to slow down. "I know I shouldn't be asking for more favors, but she's my mother, and I owe her honor."

A perplexed expression crossed his face. "You owe *her*? How can you leave when I—when we need you here? Seems like you've already done more for your mother than could be expected. Now you're going to run off to Calusa."

As his voice lowered, her heartbeat increased. She wished she could say she'd changed her mind, just to see a smile reappear on his face.

"Only for a few days. As soon as she's settled I'll come right back."

He shook his head. "We'll see. With respect, you seem to be tied to her apron strings more than most."

"I hoped you'd understand. How could I say no?"

"You're the only one who can answer that. Have a safe journey, Miss Haddon." He turned away from her and began stacking tins of condensed milk on a shelf.

She glared at his back and then flounced out of the store, telling herself she'd enjoy every moment out of his unreasonable presence.

Cassie waited next to her mother at the ticket window inside the train depot. Through the open door, she watched Elijah heft their trunk onto a baggage cart. For Mother to ask for his help in the midst of office hours took more nerve than she'd ever have believed her mother possessed. There seemed to be no stopping her once she had Uncle Rand in her sights.

"Calusa's the end of the line, ladies." The ticket agent's voice drew her attention back inside the depot. "If you want to go farther west, you'll have to take the stage."

Mother smiled at him. "Calusa's the end of my search. We're not going any farther."

He grunted and handed them their tickets. "You ought to get there around four this afternoon, depending on how many folks get on and off at the stops. You can board any time now."

"Thank you." Cassie swept the tickets into her handbag and hurried out to Elijah.

"I can't thank you enough for fetching our trunk for us." She hoped he could see the apology in her eyes. "I had no idea Mother had imposed on you to such a degree."

"Took only a few minutes. I know you'll be happy to see

her settled." He glanced toward a passenger car where a conductor assisted her mother up the steps, then turned his attention back to Cassie. "Rosemary's sorry she couldn't come to see you off, but she's staying close to home these days." He grinned. "Doctor's orders."

Another reason to be glad she'd found the little cabin. As soon as she and Mother left Elijah and Rosemary's home, they'd converted their spare room to a nursery. Elijah's mother's rocking chair waited in one corner, and pink, blue, and yellow ruffles adorned the cradle. Any day now Rosemary would hold her infant in her arms.

The train whistle blew. Steam whooshed from beneath the engine. Cassie held out her hand and Elijah clasped it between his. "Hurry back."

"Indeed I will." She dashed for the passenger car.

When she stepped through the entrance, Mother stood and waved to her from a seat halfway down the length of the crowded car. Making her way along the center aisle, Cassie took note of their fellow travelers. Families with small children, older couples, and several cigar-smoking men who leered at her. Salesmen, she guessed. She quickened her pace.

Slipping onto the wooden seat next to her mother, she noticed a dignified-looking gentleman across the aisle. His black suit and black cravat suggested preacher. He nodded at her when he caught her gaze, then turned his attention back to a book he held in his lap as the train jerked into motion.

Coal smoke twisted through half-open windows, adding a sulfurous tinge to the effluvium from the salesmen's cigars. She coughed and held a handkerchief to her nose.

In contrast, her mother relaxed against the seat back, smiling. "Just think. In a few hours I'll see my brother. I was beginning to despair."

Cassie lowered the handkerchief. "Do you know where to meet him?"

"Not exactly. Mr. Dunkle—the man who wrote to me—said Rand was employed as a grader on the line. He did say the workmen's housing was close to the tracks. He also said Calusa is a new town, built because of the railroad. So it shouldn't be hard to locate my brother there."

Eyebrows raised, Cassie stared at her mother, wishing she'd asked her question earlier. She'd been so focused on what she'd say to Mr. West that she'd forgotten how vague Mother could be with details.

The train clickity-clacked around a bend and rolled west. A grove of oak trees blocked her view of the track ahead.

<hr />

Dust devils blew along deserted streets. Instead of a station house, the town's only identification was a square sign reading CALUSA next to a telegrapher's shack. From her vantage point on the train's platform, Cassie counted eight frame buildings and several shanties across the broad street. Telegraph wires overhead hummed in the wind.

A man jumped from the baggage car and dropped their trunk on the dusty boards, then glanced around, apparently seeking waiting passengers. Seeing none, he hopped back through the open doors. Steam shot from beneath the wheels as the engineer guided the train along the track to the wye junction, then backed the cars to the turning point. Once he had clearance, the engine rolled east along the turn, taking the train toward Noble Springs.

Cassie looked up and down the platform for someone

to assist them with their trunk. By the time they'd reached Calusa, all other passengers save the gentleman across the aisle had disembarked at various towns along the way.

Mother clapped her hand over her hat. "Let's get out of this wind before we're blown away." She pointed at a square building facing them across the street. A sign painted over the doorway read RESTAURANT, but no light shone through the dingy windows. "We'll ask inside where the workers are housed."

"We can't just leave our trunk here." Cassie cast a dubious glance at the weathered structure.

"Pardon me, ladies. Is someone coming to meet you?" The man in preacher's garb stopped next to them and dropped his valise at his feet.

"I'm here to join my brother. He isn't expecting me, but I imagine the proprietor of the restaurant will tell me where he is," Mother replied in a dismissive tone, then turned away and took Cassie's arm. "Excuse us, please."

Cassie glanced between their trunk and the stranger. With no depot and no stationmaster, she had to trust someone. He looked safe enough. Ignoring her mother's frown, she tugged her arm free.

"Do you know who might look after our trunk until we find my uncle? I hesitate to leave it sitting here."

"I'd be pleased to offer my services." He swept off his hat, revealing sparse white hair circling the crown of his head. "Reverend Alfred Greeley," he said in a voice that Cassie felt sure would carry to the rear of a crowded sanctuary. "And may I know your names?"

"I'm Miss Haddon, and this is my mother, Mrs. Bingham." Mother gave him a tight smile, her lips compressed.

He nodded acknowledgment. "You said you were crossing to the restaurant? If you wish, I'll accompany you and watch through the window while you inquire as to your uncle's whereabouts."

"Thank you, Reverend." Cassie marveled at her boldness in speaking to a stranger. She prayed the man was who he said he was.

Once inside, Cassie noted with a shudder that the restaurant looked nothing like Mr. West's tidy establishment. One long table ran down the center of the room. Flies zoomed between the open kitchen and the tabletop. Stale, greasy odors clogged the air.

A man wearing an apron crossed the room toward them. Rolls of fat jiggled around his waist. "Afternoon, Reverend. You're early for supper. Won't be ready for another hour." He eyed Cassie and her mother. "This your wife and daughter?"

Reverend Greeley's face reddened. "No, Gus. They won't arrive for another month. Mrs. Bingham here"—he inclined his head in her direction—"is seeking her brother."

Mother stepped forward. "His name's Randall Carter. He's one of the railroad workers here."

Cassie twisted her hands together and held her breath, waiting for Gus's answer. What if Mother had been misled again?

"Rand? Sure, I know him. Drives a grading team."

She shot Cassie a triumphant glance. "Could you tell me where he lives, please?"

"One of them railroad houses across from the tracks. Second one from the west end." He rubbed his palms over his prominent belly. "Not there today, though. Went out with a crew this morning. Won't be back 'til tomorrow sometime."

"You're sure?"

"'Course I'm sure. Cooked their rations, didn't I?"

"We'll take our trunk to his dwelling and wait for him there."

A knot of alarm filled Cassie's throat. They couldn't plant themselves in her uncle's home without his approval. She shook her head, but Mother didn't notice.

Gus held up his hand. "Probably not the best idea, but you do what you want. None of my business." His heavy footsteps thudded back to the kitchen.

Reverend Greely left his post at the window and approached them. "The Travelers' Rest Hotel is a short distance away. If you'll forgive my intrusion, I suggest you spend the night there. It's clean and secure. I'm going there myself. We can send someone back for your trunk."

Cassie studied him. He seemed trustworthy, but in Noble Springs the preacher lived in a parsonage, not a hotel. Reverend Greely's statement didn't make sense.

"Why are you staying at the Travelers' Rest if you're the preacher here?"

He held the door open for them. "I'll explain on the way."

She eyed him sideways as she stepped out into the blowing dust. To the east, beyond the workers' housing, she spotted a two-story building with a TRAVELERS' REST HOTEL sign beneath the roofline. If he guided them in any other direction, she'd grab Mother and run back to the restaurant. With a firm grip on her mother's arm, she followed the reverend.

By the time they reached the hotel, he'd given them a brief account of his stay in Calusa. Once his wife arrived, they'd buy land and build a house. In the meantime, he traveled back and forth between Calusa and their home in Coopers Glen, spending a week in each place.

He paused before opening the door to the hotel, and pointed to a whitewashed building on the next street.

"That's the Calusa school. On Sundays it's the church."

Relieved, Cassie nodded. Evidently he was as honest as he appeared.

When they entered the lobby, she made a quick assessment of the furnishings. Keys hung on a rack behind a simple desk at the back of the room. A parlor stove stood in one corner, with unoccupied rocking chairs and a worn-looking sofa filling the rest of the small space.

She gulped and stepped up to the clerk. "How much for one night?"

∾≫∾

The following afternoon, Cassie perched on the edge of the bed while Mother stood at the lace-curtained window in their room and looked out at the street.

"Rand's got to be here soon. The man in the restaurant said he was expected today." She pivoted from the window and paced across the bare wooden floor. "If he doesn't come, we'll just have our things moved to his house. That way you won't have to pay for one more night in this miserable hotel."

"We can't do that. We'd be trespassers." Cassie rubbed her fingers over the coarse weave of the bedcovering.

She didn't want to spend another night in Calusa, no matter where they slept. Mr. West's deep voice rumbled in her memory. *Have a safe journey, Miss Haddon.* His tone held a ring of finality. He didn't believe she'd come back.

In an hour or so, the train would arrive from the east and make its turnaround to Noble Springs. She fidgeted and checked through her packed carpetbag for the dozenth time, wondering what she'd do if her uncle didn't arrive. Whether she wanted to or not, she knew she'd stay.

Mother settled on the edge of the bed. "I do wish you'd change your mind and live here with me. I don't like the idea of you being unchaperoned around that Mr. West."

"We're never alone. Mrs. Fielder and Timothy Dawson, the boy who helps in the grocery, are always—"

At the sound of a knock on the door, they both jumped to their feet.

Before Cassie could stop her, Mother grabbed the knob and flung open the door without asking who waited in the hall.

"Rand! I knew you'd come!" She threw her arms around a red-bearded man in workman's clothing.

He took a step backward and disengaged her grip. "Settle down, Lizzie, and tell me what you're doing here. First thing when I got to town, Gus at the restaurant said my sister's looking for me." Yellow-stained teeth showed when he gave her a crooked grin. "You come all this way to forgive me for fighting in the Federal Army?"

Mother's face turned scarlet. "No need to bring up the past. Everything's different now. Our property's gone. Philip's dead." She held her hand out to Cassie. "You remember my daughter, Cassiopeia."

"Been a long time." He gave Cassie a brief nod, then raised an eyebrow at her mother. "What do you want from me?"

Cassie gaped at him. To hear Mother tell the story, she and Uncle Rand had a warm relationship, but this reception was decidedly frosty. She stepped closer, noticing the odor of sweat that clung to his clothing. "You'll be more comfortable if you come in and sit . . . Uncle Rand. There's a chair beneath the window."

"I'm fine right here, thanks." He shifted his feet. "I don't have all afternoon, Lizzie. My job keeps me going—the railroad's always sending me one place or the next. I'm home for a couple days, then off again. So, why are you here?"

Mother jutted her chin in the air. "I've come to live under your protection. We're family. Father taught us to look after each other, remember? You may be an important man with the railroad, but I'm still your sister."

Cassie cringed. This meeting wasn't unfolding the way she'd imagined. Her mother acted defiant, but her voice trembled. At her statement, Uncle Rand had taken a step backward, as if preparing to flee.

A train whistle shrieked in the distance.

As the sound died away, an anxious silence enveloped the room. Cassie held her breath, waiting for her uncle's response.

He fixed his gaze on her mother. "Don't know how much protection you'll get from me. Just told you I'm gone half the time. But our pa would be sore disappointed in me if I turned you away."

Mother reached for his hand. "I'd be grateful," she whispered.

He glanced at Cassie. "You needing protection too, missy?"

"No, sir. My home is in Noble Springs. I can take care of myself." She said the words with pride. For the first time in her life, they were true.

The train whistle sounded again.

Cassie slipped an arm around her mother and kissed her tearstained cheek. "Are you sure you'll be all right? I'll stay if you need me." Sudden pain drove deep in her heart at the reality of parting. Despite all her brave words, she felt tethered to her mother's side.

"She'll be fine." Uncle Rand spoke in a gruff voice. "Don't you worry about your ma."

"Being with my brother again is answered prayer. If only

you were staying . . ." Mother's lower lip trembled. "This is the first time we've ever been apart. I don't know how to say good-bye to you."

"I don't know how, either."

The floorboards vibrated as the train rumbled to a stop across the wide street. Cassie glanced out the window, then burrowed into her mother's embrace. "This isn't good-bye. We're only going to be separated by a few miles of track. I'll write to you every week."

"I promise to answer every one." Mother's lips curved in a wobbly smile. "After all, I've had lots of practice writing letters." She kissed Cassie. "Now you'd better go before the train leaves. I . . . I'll stay here."

Her chest aching with unshed tears, Cassie grabbed her carpetbag and dashed from the room. When she reached the platform, she waved her ticket at the conductor to prevent him from closing the entrance to the passenger car.

With one foot on the step, she heard boots pounding on the platform and a male voice calling, "Miss Haddon! Cassie! Wait!"

She whirled and stared into the face of Garrett Fitzhugh. Her dead fiancé.

assie clutched the train's handrail for support. This couldn't be happening. She'd watched Garrett's casket lowered into the ground. Thrown a handful of dirt over the polished surface. Felt her heart ripped from her chest as the preacher read words from Scripture over the grave.

And now Garrett stood next to the passenger car with Reverend Greely beaming beside him.

The reverend broke the charged silence. "Mr. Fitzhugh teaches in the school building that I pointed out. When I told him about meeting you, he was most anxious to pay his respects."

Garrett removed his hat and gave her an easy grin. His blond hair glinted in the sun's slanted rays. "From the look on your face, I'd guess you don't remember me."

"Garrett . . . how could I forget you?" Cassie leaned against the vestibule wall for support. Her heart battered against her ribs.

His handsome features clouded. "I'm Patrick. I had no idea you'd mistake me for my brother. I'd forgotten for the moment that we looked so much alike."

Grief she'd thought buried stung her eyelids. To see Garrett again—no, he wasn't Garrett. She reached toward him, grasping at air. "P . . . Patrick?"

She searched her memory for a recollection of Garrett's brother. He'd attended the funeral, along with numerous family members and friends. She remembered being told he taught school somewhere farther west, but beyond that he'd made no impression on her at the time. She offered him a weak smile. "Forgive me, please. You took me so by surprise. It's kind of you to come to greet me."

"I often wondered what became of you after—"

The conductor stepped into the vestibule, arms folded over his chest. "Best take your seat, miss. We'll be rolling soon."

She nodded, then extended her gloved hand. "Good-bye, Mr. Fitzhugh. It was a pleasure to see you again." Politeness required the remark, although seeing Garrett's brother had been anything but a pleasure. Stunning blow would better express her feelings.

He bowed over her hand. "The pleasure is mine. Godspeed, Miss Haddon."

Cassie collapsed onto a seat on the right-hand side of the deserted car. Her limbs trembled. Memories of Garrett tumbled through her mind. Like Patrick, he was tall and slender, with piercing blue eyes. They'd met at a dance in St. Louis and he'd been taken with her immediately—and she with him. When he proposed, Mother saw him as their best hope to restore their fortunes. Then, in a blink, he was gone. Struck by a runaway team when crossing a street.

Now, sitting alone in the passenger car, Cassie wondered what her life would have been like if they'd married. Her mother would be settled into the home Garrett was planning to buy for them, instead of living at the edge of nowhere with her brother. Cassie would be the lady of the house and not working in a restaurant to earn a living.

But she'd never have met Mr. West, with his arresting eyes and gravelly voice. The Lord had closed one door but another stood ajar. A tingle bubbled up inside when she imagined the surprised expression on her employer's face when she arrived at work tomorrow.

The train rocked into motion. Out of the corner of her eye, she saw Patrick Fitzhugh running alongside. He waved his hand at her.

She stood and struggled to open the window as the train gathered momentum. After several attempts, she succeeded.

He cupped his hands around his mouth. "Miss Haddon! I forgot to ask your destination! Where do you live?"

She leaned out the open window. "Noble Springs."

"I may—" The train's whistle blew the rest of his sentence away. He disappeared from her view, along with Calusa's bleak streets.

Closing her eyes, she leaned against the seat back. At the moment, the pain of leaving her mother overwhelmed any thoughts of Garrett or Patrick Fitzhugh. The image of Mother clutching Uncle Rand's arm burned in her mind.

She prayed he'd take the responsibility seriously.

❦

The following morning, Cassie awoke early despite having arrived in Noble Springs after ten the night before. The cabin felt empty without Mother's presence. Cassie's decision to stay in Noble Springs came at a price she hadn't anticipated.

She swung her feet to the floor. The sooner she left for the restaurant, the sooner she'd see Jenny—and Mr. West.

She padded to the main room and stirred the fire until coals winked among the ashes. After tossing a few small pieces of wood into the firebox, she placed a kettle on the stove to heat for tea. While she waited, she donned her blue print dress and arranged her hair in a neat coil at the back of her head.

Peeking into the oval mirror that hung over the bureau Faith had given her, she pulled a few tendrils loose in front of her ears. No sense in looking too severe when Mr. West arrived.

As soon as she finished her tea, she zipped out the door into the sultry morning. The butternut tree across the street from the restaurant cast an umbrella of welcome shade over the kitchen entrance. Excitement tickled her throat as she burst through the doorway.

"I told you I'd be back, Jenny."

The cook turned from the worktable where she'd been scooping scrambled eggs and potatoes into a shallow bowl. "Praise God you're here. I couldn't imagine how I'd get along without you today." Her grim expression telegraphed worry.

"Mr. West always helps—" Cassie bit off the rest of her comment when she noticed Wash Bennett standing between the two worktables. She'd never seen him at the restaurant early in the day.

She glanced between Jenny and Wash. A premonition twisted her stomach. "Something's wrong. Where's Mr. West?"

"He's home with a broken leg," Jenny said. "Wash here found him in the grocery last night when he came in to clean the floors."

Cassie swung around to face Wash. "What on earth happened?"

"His boot hung up on one of them crates in the back. Guess he didn't see it. He pitched facedown, snapped his bone like a matchstick."

She clapped her hands over her mouth. The image of Mr. West lying alone and injured brought quick tears to her eyes. "The poor man! What a blessing you were here."

"Yes, missy, it was the Lord's work for certain. After the

doctor left, I carried Mr. West home in his buggy, then come back here this morning to give you ladies the news."

"Who's looking after him?"

"Reckon I am."

Jenny tapped a spoon on the edge of the bowl. "I cooked this for his breakfast. There's plenty for you too," she said, leveling her gaze on Wash. "When you get back, just dump it in a skillet for a couple minutes to get the eggs good and hot."

"Yes, ma'am." He took the covered bowl in his large hands. "I'd best be going."

Cassie stepped closer to him. "Please tell Mr. West I'll have a surprise for him this afternoon. You are coming to get his supper, aren't you?"

"Yes, missy. I'll tell him. Might make him feel better."

After Wash left, Jenny wrapped Cassie in a hug. "I was afraid you wouldn't come back. I know how your mother is."

"I confess, leaving her was harder than I thought it would be. But she's with her brother, so I'm trusting him to watch over her well-being." She tried to imagine her mother in Uncle Rand's house, wishing she'd had time to see her settled before the train arrived. A lump rose in her throat and she swallowed. Hard. Yesterday couldn't be changed. Right now she needed to focus on their immediate dilemma.

"How will we keep the restaurant and grocery operating without Mr. West?"

"I don't know. I been studying on it since Wash told me what happened." Jenny grabbed a knife and attacked a mound of potatoes waiting to be diced.

Cassie stared at the floor as if the solution might be written on the spotless boards. Her mind roamed over the routine Mr. West had set for his business. Thinking out loud, she said, "Young Timothy comes into the grocery before Mr. West unlocks the restaurant door. We already know how to handle the meals. That leaves counting receipts and writing everything in those ledgers he keeps."

"You make writing in ledgers sound easy. I wouldn't know where to begin." Her knife whacked a potato into strips.

Memories of evenings spent with her father in his study filtered into Cassie's mind. Though several years had passed, she remembered his meticulous accounts of their crops and holdings. The process couldn't be too different than what Mr. West did with his business. It wouldn't hurt to try.

"Do you think he'd allow me to help?"

Jenny raised an eyebrow. "Don't take offense, but you couldn't find your way around the kitchen two months ago. Now you think you can manage the whole lot?"

Her conviction wavered for a brief moment, then she squared her shoulders. "I won't know unless I try. When Wash comes back at suppertime, I'll ask him to take me to Mr. West. We'll let him decide."

"He don't let too many people know where he lives. I doubt he'd welcome a visit."

"We'll see." She grabbed a stack of plates. "I'll get the dining room ready for breakfast, then start on pies."

After setting the tables, Cassie slipped into the grocery. Timothy paused in the midst of dusting the shelves when he saw her.

"You're the lady who works with Miz Fielder, ain't you? I never saw you up close before." His Adam's apple bobbed in his throat.

"That's right. I'm Miss Haddon."

He dropped the feather duster on a counter. "The swamper said the boss broke his leg. He ain't coming in today." He puffed out his chest. "I reckon I can handle things fine without him. Since you came to work, he's over in the restaurant lots more than he used to be. He leaves the store to me."

She swept her gaze over his patched trousers, worn shirt, and lanky blond hair hanging over his forehead. Likely he needed his job as much as she needed hers. "Mr. West has mentioned how much he depends on you."

Timothy flushed. "He has? I mean, good to know."

The aroma of frying bacon drifted through the doorway and reminded her she needed to be in the kitchen. She drew a quick breath. "Has he taught you how to enter receipts in the ledger?"

"No sirree—I mean, no, miss. Nobody touches them books but Mr. West."

She clasped her fingers behind her back so he couldn't see her hands tremble. "Since he's not here today, I'll take care of the ledger for him after you lock the grocery."

"I don't know . . . he never said . . ."

"He didn't plan to break a leg. We'll have to do all we can to help him until he can come back, won't we?" She gave him her brightest smile.

"Yes." He drew the word out to two syllables. "I reckon so."

"Good. Please come to the kitchen after you lock up, so I'll know it's time for me to tally the books." Perspiration prickled across her forehead. Her father had been protective of their finances. Mr. West might be angry, but after leaving for Calusa without his blessing, she needed to prove herself. Managing his accounts would be the perfect opportunity.

Cassie had a warm apple pie waiting on a worktable when Wash returned that evening. One of Mr. West's ledgers rested next to the dessert.

Wash glanced between her and Jenny. "This here pie must be the surprise you promised Mr. West. Looks mighty good." He hung his hat over a peg beside the screen door. "Soon's I mop this floor, I'll take him his supper."

Jenny nudged Cassie's side, then folded her arms and raised a skeptical eyebrow. "Go ahead, ask him."

Bucket in hand, Wash paused on his way to the pump. "Ask me what, missy?"

"Would you please take me with you when you deliver Mr. West's supper?" Her pulse thudded. Wash had to say yes.

She needed Mr. West's permission to continue with the ledger. And if she were honest with herself, that wasn't the only reason for her request. She wanted to see him.

The deep grooves on either side of Wash's mouth lifted when he smiled. "I reckon I could do that. He was right pleased to hear you was back. Seein' you might be a better surprise than a pie."

Jenny cleared her throat. "Now, Wash, you know Mr. West

doesn't like too many folks knowing where he lives. Maybe you shouldn't be driving Miss Haddon out there. I tried to talk her out of going, but—"

"He's been real good to me. I surely don't want to make him mad." He set the bucket on the floor, then faced Cassie. "Maybe I better ask him first. If he says yes, you can go tomorrow."

She shook her head. She'd tallied Mr. West's receipts, entered the amounts in his ledger, and placed the cash in a metal box she'd discovered in his office. She'd already stepped so far over the line of propriety that his anger at having her come to his house seemed minor. Either he'd be grateful for her help, or dismiss her on the spot.

"If he's upset, Wash, I'll take the blame." She moved the pie to one side and hefted the ledger, amazed at her daring. "Please. We'll leave as soon as you're finished with your chores."

Cassie sat in the back of the buggy while Wash drove them through town and on west in the direction of Pioneer Lake. Twilight bathed her surroundings in softness. When she was a child, she imagined at this quiet time that the earth was settling down to sleep.

She sighed at the memory as Wash slowed the buggy and turned onto a narrow road leading uphill. So much had happened since the war swept away her peaceful childhood. Sometimes she hardly recognized the person she'd become. The old Cassie would never have demanded to be taken to visit a single man in his home. Yet here she was, bouncing over a rocky track to confess to her employer that she'd taken the liberty to look into his business ledgers.

After cresting a rise, Wash stopped the buggy in front of a two-story frame house that rivaled many of the homes she'd seen in Noble Springs. A lattice-trimmed veranda spread across the front. Light spilling from tall windows brightened rocking chairs on both sides of the porch. Looking up, she noticed smoke curling from a chimney at the center of the roof. She couldn't understand why Jenny said Mr. West didn't like people knowing where he lived. Surely he was proud of his fine home.

"Here you are, missy. You wait right there. I'll help you with your things." The buggy rocked when Wash jumped to the ground. After he tied the horse to a hitching post, she handed him the pie and a bowl containing supper but kept the ledger tucked beneath her shawl.

He hesitated a moment before carrying the food toward the house. "Lordy, I hope he's not mad that I brought you."

"I pray he's not. But I promise I'll tell him it was all my idea."

"Yes, missy." Doubt weighted his words. He stepped in front of her to open the door.

A wide hallway lay before them, with a set of stairs on the left leading to the second floor. Halfway down the hall, a stream of light flowed from an open doorway to her right. Wash pointed. "There's the parlor."

Mr. West's gravelly voice called from within the room. "That you, Wash?" His tone sharpened. "Is someone with you?"

"Yes, sir." He moved aside so Cassie could precede him. "Missy Haddon came with me."

Jacob's face brightened when she entered the room. He pushed himself higher in his upholstered chair and reached for crutches lying on the floor within his reach. The motion shifted his right leg, which rested on a low stool in front of him.

He drew a sharp breath.

The sight of him reclining, leg splinted and bandaged, melted her heart. "I'm so sorry this happened to you. Please don't try to stand."

She wished she could reach out and smooth the tousled hair from his forehead. Instead, she extended her hand and he took it in his. Tingles skittered up her arm.

Still holding her hand, he enveloped her in his warm gaze. "Thank you." He glanced at Wash, who remained in the doorway holding the food. "Wash said you were sending a surprise. Looks like you made me a pie." A smile spread beneath his moustache. "Having you deliver it in person is a better surprise."

When Wash left, heading toward what she assumed to be the kitchen, she stepped away from Mr. West's side. "After you see what else I brought, you may not like the surprise quite so much."

He waved at a gilt-trimmed velvet sofa facing his chair. "I doubt that. Please, be seated and tell me the rest."

She sank onto the plush upholstery and took a quick glance around. Recessed bookcases framed both sides of the fireplace. All the furnishings complemented the elegance of the sofa. She wondered at the contrast between the simplicity of the restaurant dining room and the ornamentation in his home. Mr. West held a few surprises of his own.

"I need to tell you what I've—what we've all done to take care of the business while you're away." She pulled the ledger from beneath her shawl and laid it across her knees.

His eyes widened.

"After Timothy left today, I wrote the grocery and restaurant receipts in here. I copied the way you've done it."

"Let me see." He leaned toward her, his mouth set in a straight line.

Feeling the sting of his gaze, she passed the opened book to him.

Jacob tried to hide his misgivings when he accepted the ledger. He never allowed anyone to disturb the contents of his desk. But his careful planning hadn't taken into account Miss Haddon's desire to be useful. Running his finger down the row of numbers she'd entered, he mentally added the totals. To his amazement, her sums agreed with his.

He flipped the pages back to the beginning to see what he'd written in the book that might have revealed his life in Boston. As he feared, he'd noted names and addresses inside the front cover. Sweat dotted his hairline. Colin Riley and Keegan Byrne could be explained away. Not so the third name.

His breathing stilled. He stole a glance at Miss Haddon, trying to decipher her expression.

She cleared her throat. "I don't blame you for being angry. I know I intruded, but I wanted to help. You've been kind to me in spite of my failures. I hoped it would comfort you to know that West & Riley's would survive until you're able to return."

A few wisps of auburn hair had come loose and framed her face. She'd never looked prettier. He longed to cross the room to sit beside her and assure her he wasn't upset, although nothing could be further from the truth. Instead, he closed the book and gave her what he hoped was a genuine smile.

"I'm grateful that you—all of you—care about me." He gripped the ledger. "You did a fine job. Nevertheless, please leave the accounting to me."

If he'd struck her, she couldn't have looked more stunned.

She shrank back against the sofa. "Did . . . did you find errors? I checked everything twice."

Her visit had built on the intimacy he longed for between them. Now with one sentence he'd shattered the connection. "No errors." He tried another smile. "I've always kept my business dealings private. Guess I'm too old to change."

"I'll remember that in the future." Her voice sent a chill through him. She adjusted her shawl over her shoulders. "Perhaps I'd better be going."

He glanced at the darkness gathering beyond the windows and nodded. "Would you please go to the kitchen—it's the next door on the right off the hallway—to ask Wash to take you home? I'd go myself, but—" He gestured at his leg.

She stood, holding out her hand. "Would you like me to return the ledger to its *proper* place?"

His fingers tightened over the leather cover. "Thank you, but that won't be necessary."

"Very well. Good evening." She whipped through the doorway.

Within a few moments, Wash stepped into the room. "Missy Haddon says I'm to take her home now. Don't you want your supper?"

"It can wait. Please see her safely to her door."

"Yessir."

After they left, Jacob slumped against the chair back and closed his eyes. Memories from his life in Boston taunted him.

Miss Haddon must never find out who he'd been and what he'd done.

Cassie stepped away from the worktable and brushed a smudge of flour from her cheek. Six rhubarb pies cooled on racks near the door to the dining room. If Mr. West thought she couldn't do anything but bake pies, she'd make sure they were the best pies anyone ever tasted.

The muscles in her neck tightened when she heard his crutches tapping their way toward the kitchen. She slammed the lid on the flour bin and hastened to the sink, turning her back to the door.

Jenny shook soapy water from her hands and moved aside to make room for Cassie. "Sooner or later you'll have to talk to him. I don't know what happened last week, but I told you not to go out there."

"Nothing happened." She grabbed a dishrag and plunged her hands into the water. "He thinks my competence stops at the kitchen door, apparently. So we have nothing more to talk about." She scrubbed at burned-on gravy in a skillet.

Mr. West crutched his way over to the sink. "The word is out about your baking." He fished in his pocket and placed a sheet of paper in a dry spot next to the washbasin. "Here

123

are orders from two households in town. They each want a whole pie."

"I'm happy to hear that." She flexed her aching shoulders and read the names without meeting his eyes. "Thanks to Jenny's help, we're keeping up."

"I don't do that much." Jenny picked up a brush and stepped away to clean the cooled surface of the range.

He spoke close to Cassie's ear. "Look at me. Please."

She glanced at him sideways. The pleading in his eyes rattled her resolve to remain silent in his presence.

He moved his crutches in front of him, then shifted his weight and swung his good leg forward, bringing him closer to her side. His voice rumbled. "I know I've wounded you. Soon as we're finished for the night, I'd like to drive you home in my buggy so I can explain."

The scrub brush scratched over the range top. Jenny kept her back turned and appeared to be absorbed in scrubbing, but Cassie knew her ears were tuned to every word she and Mr. West said.

"That's kind of you, but you know I live just across the street. It's not a taxing walk."

"We can take the long way around. I'll have the buggy at the kitchen door a little before seven."

To be fair, she should listen to what he had to say. She dried her hands on her apron. "All right. I'll be ready."

⁓

Cassie sensed Jenny's gaze following her out the door as she threw her shawl over her shoulders and hurried to meet Mr. West. She couldn't imagine what he'd have to say that could explain his actions.

He waited next to his horse and buggy, a rueful smile on

his lips. "Forgive me for not helping you in. It's all I can do to hoist myself up." Supporting his weight on his crutches, he took her hand and held her steady while she put her foot on the step. After she settled on the leather seat, he made his way around the buggy and gathered the reins.

He placed his crutches at her feet and stepped up with his uninjured leg, then flung himself onto the seat. The buggy jounced when he landed. "Not polished, but effective," he said, grinning.

She dared a smile back. "I can see you've practiced."

"I wanted to be sure I could get in and out without falling."

"I'd help you if you fell."

"I believe you would." His gaze locked with hers for a breathless moment before he guided the horse out of the alley and rolled south. Instead of turning toward her cabin, they traveled down Third Street, past the church and Rosemary's home.

When they reached the street that paralleled the railroad, he stopped in front of a park across from the tracks. He pointed to the lattice-enclosed bandstand in the center of a grassy area. "If you like, we can walk over there and watch the sunset before I take you home."

After glancing at his right leg, which he had stretched as straight as possible on the buggy floor, she shook her head. "It would be a bit difficult for you to get out and in again, wouldn't it? I'm comfortable right here." Next to you, she wanted to add, but didn't.

"Miss Haddon . . ." He cleared his throat. "It's been a long time since anyone cared about my welfare. Takes some getting used to."

He'd given her the perfect opportunity. She drew a deep breath and turned to face him. "Your welfare was the reason I took it upon myself to make the entries in your ledger. I could understand your reaction if I'd made mistakes, but you said there were no errors."

His head jerked up. "You surprise me with your boldness."

"I surprise myself sometimes." She rubbed her sweating palms on her skirt. She'd gone too far to back down now. "You said you would explain. I'm listening."

Mr. West leaned against the seat back and fixed his eyes on the horizon. He spoke in a monotone, as if reciting from memory. "Before the war, a man named Colin Riley loaned me the money to open my business. He trusted me, so I trust him. Aside from that, I learned a long time ago to depend upon few people. So, I work alone." A corner of his mouth turned up in a half smile when he met her gaze. "Change comes hard, but if you'll bear with me, I'm willing to try."

She released a long breath. "You weren't angry with me?"

"No. But it would have been better if you'd asked first."

"How could I? You weren't at work."

His brows drew together, then his lips twitched. After a moment a husky chuckle erupted. "You've got me there. I'm not practiced with ladies—that must be obvious."

She straightened her skirt as a pretense to move an inch or so closer. "I like you just as you are." Her hand flew to her lips. Of all the bold things to say. Why couldn't she learn to think before she spoke? "I . . . I mean, you don't have to act in any special way." Oh, goodness, that was worse. She turned her head, certain that her face must match the color of the rosy sunset.

"So you wouldn't mind if we spent more time together?"

"Mind? Of course not." This was the moment she'd dreamed of—to sit beside Jacob and listen to his deep voice express his feelings for her.

"Good." He gave her hand a squeeze. "I have a question for you, but I want you to think before you answer."

Cassie thought she'd swoon from joy. Here's where he'd ask if he could court her. She drew in a breath. "What's the question?" Her heart trip-hammered while she waited for his response.

"If I hire a girl to help you, would you be interested in operating a bakery from the restaurant kitchen, just for your pies? Of course I'd increase your salary."

"What!?" Her voice rose to a squeak.

"I thought about this all last night. You've shown a good head for numbers, so you can keep your own records. We'd meet at the end of the day and I'd enter the totals in my ledger."

She felt like sinking through the floor of the buggy. Thank goodness he couldn't read her thoughts—her words had been bad enough. Speechless, she released his hand and scooted toward her side of the buggy seat.

He leaned toward her. "I know this is sudden. Take as long as you need to answer."

Moments ticked by while she struggled to form a response. Despite her dismay at the turn their conversation had taken, his proposition sounded appealing. She enjoyed the clockwork timing of baking pies between scheduled mealtimes. With a little rearranging, she and Jenny could make the kitchen a more efficient place to work. And with an extra helper she could handle more orders.

She dipped her head toward her lap. A few months ago, she hadn't known she possessed the ability to bake a single pie, much less take orders and sell them. The Lord had blessed her. She couldn't let embarrassed pride stand in her way.

Jacob shifted on the seat. "I thought you'd be pleased."

"I am. Thank you for the opportunity." She kept her head down, lest he see the disappointment in her eyes. How silly she'd been to think he wanted anything more than a business relationship.

18

On Friday evening, Jacob leaned against the doorway between the kitchen and dining room, watching while Miss Haddon bustled about the space, directing Wash as he rearranged the work area.

"That table under the window goes here by the door," she told him, leading the way across the room. "That way the shelves are opposite. Since the pie pans are stored there, they'll be easier to reach."

"Yes, missy." Wash maneuvered the thick wooden work-table around the stationary counter where the washbasin rested. The muscles in his arms stood out from bearing the weight.

She stopped next to Jacob and turned to him with a smile. "If I work on this side, Jenny will have the area around the range for meal preparation." Her eyes sparkled. "We've talked about this plan all week. I'm so glad you approve of the arrangement."

He shifted his weight on his crutches in order to stand taller. "You do whatever's necessary. This corner is your bakery. If there's anything else you need, just say so."

"Well, there is one thing. You mentioned hiring a girl to

help. Have you found someone?" She flushed. "I'm sorry. I shouldn't have asked. That's your business, not mine."

"Miss Haddon, I told you we'd work together on this enterprise. I've had an idea I'd like to—"

The table bumped against the wall. "This where you want it, missy?" Wash wiped his brow with his forearm.

"Yes. Thank you so much."

"Need anything else moved?"

"No. I'm sorry to have kept you from your other chores."

"Mr. West said I was to do anything you wanted. Just holler." He grabbed a bucket and headed for the pump in the alley. The screen door banged.

She lifted her warm gaze to meet his. "Anything I wanted? You're very kind."

Jacob fought down the jolt of pleasure that shot through him.

"Just doing what's good for business. After all, I asked you to take on a big job." He winced at the unintended gruffness in his voice.

"Oh. Yes, of course." Her expression flattened. "You mentioned an idea a moment ago. Please tell me more."

He pivoted so that he faced the grocery. "I need to get off this leg. Please come to my office for a minute. We can talk there."

She walked beside him through the dining room, matching her pace to his. Her skirts whispered over the wooden floor. "I forgot about your leg," she said, her tone regretful. "I'm sorry to keep you standing for so long."

"No need to apologize. I wanted to be there." He stepped to one side so she could enter his office, then used a crutch to point at one of the chairs. "Please, let's sit for a moment."

His senses jangled when she brushed past him, the crisp fragrance of lavender trailing in her wake.

She gazed around the storeroom for a moment, then perched on the edge of a chair. "You're going to tell me about your idea, Mr. West?"

He drew his chair close to hers. The lamp on the table enfolded them in an intimate circle of light.

"Wash told me about a woman he's met. Her name's Becca Rowan. Like him, she's a former slave. Since the war ended, she's been making her way north. She ended up in Noble Springs a few days ago." He rubbed his hands on his thighs. "Wash asked if I could give her a job. I'd like to hire her to help you, if you agree."

"Of course. What a perfect solution." She beamed at him.

"Not so fast. She was a field hand—I doubt she has any pie-making abilities. Maybe never worked in a modern kitchen." He pinned her with his gaze. "She'd be more work than help, I'm afraid—at least in the beginning."

Her smile broadened. "Sounds like me when I first came here. You gave me a chance—why shouldn't we do the same for Becca?"

"Are you sure?"

"Absolutely."

"Then I'll speak to Wash about her tonight. I'd like it if she could start tomorrow morning. I know Saturdays are busy, but she'd have a chance to learn her way around the kitchen at least."

She scooted back on her chair. "You're a kind man, Mr. West. Everyone in town respects you."

He'd worked hard to earn their respect. If anyone knew— no, that would never happen. He cleared his throat. Was she simply being polite? Did he dare—?

"I'm not as interested in what everyone thinks as I am in your opinion." He gave a half laugh to cover his embarrassment. Drawing a deep breath, he touched the back of her hand.

"When we're by ourselves, I'd like it if you'd call me Jacob." What if she refused, or worse yet, laughed at him?

A blush painted her cheeks. "I'd like nothing better . . . Jacob. My given name is Cassiopeia, but my friends call me Cassie."

Her name sounded sweet in his ears, yet did he dare allow her into his heart? His courtship of Rosemary Saxon had been prompted by practical considerations. He knew with Cassie he wasn't being a bit practical.

"Cassie. I don't suppose you'd want to go for a buggy ride with me on Sunday afternoon?"

She chuckled. "That's certainly a roundabout invitation. I would be pleased to go riding with you after church. In fact, would you care to join me for the services?"

"No, thank you. It's been a mighty long time since I've been inside a church. I don't plan to start now."

She raised an eyebrow, then rose and turned toward the entrance. "It's growing late. Please excuse me. I prefer to walk to my cabin while there's still some daylight."

He knew his response disturbed her. Nevertheless, his decisions were his own business. He struggled to his feet, grabbing his crutches as he stood. "I wish I could offer to see you home. I'll ask Wash to escort you."

"That's kind of you, but risky for him. Don't worry. I'll be there in five minutes or less." She paused in the doorway. "Please tell Wash I'm eager to meet Becca." She whisked through the opening and disappeared toward the kitchen.

Becca. For a few brief minutes he'd forgotten his intention to hire the woman. Cassie's presence had that effect on him. He laughed at himself. As a young man he'd seen others smitten by a pretty girl and wondered how they could be so calf-eyed. Then he'd been too busy surviving to think about girls.

Now he understood.

The next morning, Cassie stood in the restaurant kitchen admiring her new workspace. Sometime after she'd left last evening, Jacob had mounted a lamp on the wall over her table. She smiled at his thoughtfulness. Since her area had no windows, the light would help her to see well, no matter how cloudy the weather.

"What are we baking in this fine corner today?" Jenny asked. She leaned against the table, arms folded over her round stomach.

"Pecan, from the recipe you taught me last week—I hope. Mr. West planned to hire a helper for us last night. Her name's Becca Rowan—she's someone Wash recommended."

"She's colored?"

"Yes." She noticed Jenny's dubious expression. "Why?"

"I never did hold with slavery. He better pay her the same as us."

"I didn't think to inquire, but I expect he will. Wash wouldn't have asked him if he were an unfair man."

"We'll see. Once she gets started, I'll make it my business to find out."

Cassie smiled at her outspoken friend. A kind heart beat beneath the woman's peppery exterior. In certain ways, she reminded her of Mother.

At the thought of her mother, worry prickled at the back of her mind. Two weeks had passed, and she'd had no letter. Why hadn't she written?

She startled when Jenny squeezed her arm. "You're woolgathering. What does Becca have to do with pecan pies?"

"Oh! I'm sorry. I was thinking about my mother."

"Is she ill?"

"That's just it. I don't know. I've written to her twice, but

I haven't had a response." She bit her lower lip. "I pray I did the right thing by leaving her in Calusa."

"Bad news travels fast. You'd know if something was wrong." Jenny pulled her into a brief hug. "Now, let's talk about your first day in our bake shop."

Cassie forced her thoughts to the task at hand. "I plan to ask Becca to shell the pecans. Mr. West has a couple of sacks full in the storeroom. I noticed them last night."

Jenny raised an eyebrow.

"I . . . I was in his office. That's when he told me about Becca." Warmth crept up her neck.

She turned away when the screen door creaked, grateful for the interruption. A dark-skinned woman stood on the threshold, hands clasped together. From her unlined face and black hair, Cassie guessed her to be near her own age—middle twenties. The hemline on her faded turkey-red print dress stopped above the toes of her worn boots. When she stepped inside, she held her head at a proud angle, as if challenging them to look down on her.

"You must be Becca Rowan."

"Yes. And you're Missy Haddon. Mr. West told Wash you needed help." Her tone was respectful, but not subservient.

"That we do." She turned toward Jenny. "Mrs. Fielder and I are glad you're here. Goodness knows we can use another set of hands."

Becca took another step into the room. Her gaze swept the massive range with its side-by-side ovens, the worktables, the shelving along the walls. She held up her callused palms. "I never worked in a big kitchen. I been in the fields most of my life. Hope I don't burn nothing."

"When I came here, I didn't know the first thing about cooking—still don't, really. But Mrs. Fielder helped me, and I'll help you."

"Oh, I can cook all right—over a fire. Just never was allowed to work indoors with the kitchen help." She pointed to the rack of cookware next to the range. "Never saw so many fancy skillets and such."

"Well, first things first. Put on one of these." Cassie lifted a folded garment from a shelf.

Becca examined the square-cut white cotton apron. "You give this to me for free?"

"Mr. West supplies these for us. We wear a clean one each day. Before we leave in the evening, we drop the soiled one in that basket over there. The boy who works in the grocery—Timothy—his mother washes them."

"Lord have mercy. No one's washed clothes for me since I was a baby."

After Becca fastened her apron, Cassie showed her around the kitchen, then led her to the shelf where the dishes were stored. "Our first task is to set the breakfast tables, then I start making pies." She explained how to prepare the tables, and while Becca followed her directions, Cassie crossed to the grocery.

Jacob stood at one of the shelves, shuffling bags of coffee from back to front. He turned when she entered. "How's Becca getting along? Are you pleased with her?"

"She just got here, but I'm sure she'll do fine. In fact, I came to ask if you'd have Timothy carry over one of those sacks of pecans I noticed last night. I plan to put her to work shelling them."

"Consider it done." He leaned his weight on his crutches and moved around the counter. A grin tugged at his lips. "This is working out better than I thought. You're over here already—I don't have to wait until evening to have a moment with you."

Her insides tickled. "You're kind to say so, but I must—"

The outer door opened. A tall blond man stepped inside, then came to an abrupt stop when he saw her.

Garrett—no, Patrick—Fitzhugh removed his hat and bowed. "Miss Haddon. What wonderful luck. Your mother told me I'd find you at this establishment, but she said you'd be in the kitchen." He rubbed his forehead. "I must have misunderstood."

Without considering her actions, she backed up until she stood close to Jacob. His solid presence steadied her as she stammered out her question.

"My mother? What's happened to her?"

19

Cassie held her breath, waiting for Mr. Fitzhugh's reply. Jacob shifted on his crutches until his shoulder touched hers.

Mr. Fitzhugh's gaze bounced between them as though he'd just noticed Jacob. He stepped forward and held out his hand.

"You must be Mr. West. Miss Haddon's mother has mentioned you." From his tone, the mention hadn't been favorable.

Jacob grasped the extended hand. "Jacob West. And your name?"

"Patrick Fitzhugh. Miss Haddon and I are old friends."

Cassie gasped at the implication. They weren't friends at all. "I beg your pardon, Mr. Fitzhugh. We've only met briefly on two occasions. Why would you come in here and pretend a relationship that doesn't exist?"

"My apologies. I confess I was presuming upon your engagement to my older brother. Had he lived, we'd have known each other well." He sent her a winning smile. "Please forgive me for overstepping."

Jacob moved away from her side. Head lowered, he glared at Mr. Fitzhugh. "You've come at a busy time. Perhaps you and Miss Haddon could continue your conversation later." His growl sent a shiver through her. Few people would ignore the power in that voice.

Mr. Fitzhugh wasn't one of them. "I understand." He backed toward the entrance, then faced Cassie. "I'll be here until Monday. Perhaps you'd allow me to escort you to church tomorrow. Your mother told me where you're living and where you worship."

"My mother . . ." Cassie held out her hand. "Please tell me. Is she all right?"

"She's well." He shot a glance in Jacob's direction. "We'll talk more tomorrow, when you're free."

The door closed behind him with a sharp click.

Jacob leaned against a counter, a stunned expression on his face. "You were engaged? How long ago? Why didn't you tell me?"

"We're hardly that well acquainted, Mr. West." She deliberately reverted to using his formal name. "*If* such a time ever comes, rest assured you'll have all your questions answered." She tightened her jaw. "Now I really must get back to the kitchen. Please don't forget the pecans."

She strode through the dining room, her mind awash with new worries. Would Jacob lose interest in her because she'd once loved another? The prospect had caused her to answer his questions more sharply than she intended. Once again, her quick tongue had run away with her.

Then there was the issue of her mother's welfare. She wished she didn't have to wait until tomorrow morning to learn why Mother had sent Mr. Fitzhugh to Noble Springs.

The beginnings of a headache throbbed in her temples.

On Sunday morning, moments after tying the emerald-colored ribbons on her bonnet, Cassie heard a knock at her door. She checked her reflection in the mirror before answering. Worried green eyes stared back at her. Mr. Fitzhugh's news couldn't be too terrible, or he wouldn't have made her wait a day before delivering his message. Or would he? Perhaps Jacob's scowl intimidated him more than she believed.

Her jaw dropped when she opened the door.

"Jacob. Wh . . . what are you doing here?"

"I believe you invited me to accompany you today."

He wore an iron-gray suit with a bright white shirt that accented his dusky complexion. His dark hair was freshly trimmed. He'd never looked more handsome.

She glanced over his shoulder in time to see Mr. Fitzhugh approaching on the gravel walk. Sucking in a breath, she met Jacob's eyes. "Yes, I did invite you, but you declined."

"I changed my mind." He nodded toward the alley, where his black buggy waited, its bright red wheels gleaming in the sunlight. "Shall we go?"

"I already agreed to Mr. Fitzhugh as my escort." At that moment, the blond man arrived at her doorstep.

Church bells pealed through the morning air. Cassie turned her eyes toward heaven. *Lord, what do I do now?*

"Mr. West." Mr. Fitzhugh touched the brim of his hat. "I didn't expect to see you this morning. I trust you'll excuse us. Services are about to begin."

"I was going that way myself. No reason two of us can't escort Miss Haddon. Last I heard, God's not particular."

Cassie looked down to hide a smile. Jacob not only offered to go to church, he was arguing for the right. Wonder upon wonder. She rested her hand on his.

"Would you mind if we all rode together in your buggy, since it's close by?"

"Fine idea." He pointed toward the alley with one of his crutches. "This way, Fitzhugh."

Cassie followed him, Mr. Fitzhugh at her side. Strolling close to Garrett's brother gave her a sense of walking through the past. She couldn't remember how many Sundays she'd spent in her fiancé's family pew in St. Louis.

Mr. Fitzhugh bent his head down to whisper near her ear. "Perhaps we could have a few minutes alone after church?"

"I'm sorry. I've promised the afternoon to Mr. West. But I must talk with you before you leave tomorrow. Could you come to the restaurant in the morning?"

"There's nothing I'd like better."

They reached the buggy, and he helped her in before Jacob could make his way around to the passenger side.

Sandwiched on the front seat as they traveled toward the church, Cassie felt tension crackle between the two men. When she'd invited Jacob to attend services with her, this hadn't been what she intended.

Mr. Fitzhugh brought news of her mother. She welcomed him for that reason.

Aside from that, she wished he'd go back to Calusa.

<hr />

As they made their way down the center aisle of the church, Cassie sensed people stirring to gawk. When they passed Faith and her family, her friend's eyebrows shot to her hairline.

Cassie mouthed, "Talk to you later," before leading the way to an empty pew on the left side of the sanctuary.

Jacob slid in next to her, leaving the space on his right for Mr. Fitzhugh. He glanced past Jacob, then murmured "Excuse me" and stepped around him to sit on Cassie's left.

She stared at her lap, waves of heat washing over her. Being in church with Jacob West would be news enough on its own, but to arrive with two escorts? What would people think?

To her eyes, Reverend French seemed to smile in her direction as he moved behind the pulpit. "Our opening hymn this morning is 'And Can It Be?'"

Cassie rose with the rest of the congregation. She shook her head slightly as she reached for a hymnal. Here she stood with Jacob *and* Mr. Fitzhugh. Can it be, indeed.

Jacob moved close when she held the hymnal out to share. She couldn't help but notice how well his resonant bass voice harmonized with her alto. On her left, Mr. Fitzhugh held another hymn book and shot disgruntled glances in her direction while he sang.

After Mrs. French played the closing notes, Cassie sank back onto the pew and listened with half an ear to Reverend French's sermon. He'd chosen as his topic a passage from the book of Deuteronomy, dealing with Old Testament law. She stifled a yawn and prayed Jacob wouldn't be equally bored. To have him accompany her to church, regardless of his motive, filled her with joy. She planned to invite him again next week.

After the final hymn had been sung, Jacob waited until most of the congregation left so that his crutches wouldn't be jostled by worshipers headed for the door. Now he stood with other townsfolk on the lawn outside the square brick church, watching while Cassie and Faith Saxon whispered together.

The service hadn't been as unpleasant as he'd feared. He expected a pulpit-pounding preacher hollering about judgment, like the one who'd conducted his mother's funeral. Instead, Reverend French talked about laws God had instituted for his people, and how each one was for their benefit.

The hymns had soothed him. He'd forgotten how much he enjoyed singing, and Cassie's voice blended perfectly with his. Maybe he'd attend next Sunday, whether or not she invited him to join her.

His fingers tightened on the handgrips of his crutches when Mr. Fitzhugh stopped next to the two women and bowed in Cassie's direction. Their voices carried over the buzz of conversations surrounding them.

"I'll see you tomorrow morning before my train leaves."

"Please, give me the news from my mother now. Surely it won't take that long."

"I'd rather wait until we can be alone." He sent a pointed look at Jacob before lifting Cassie's gloved hand to his lips.

He tipped his hat in Jacob's direction. "Good day, Mr. West."

"The same to you." Jacob wished he could move fast enough to grab the man by the shoulder and force him to allay Cassie's fears. Making her wait for news was cruel.

20

assie watched Mr. Fitzhugh stride south, she presumed toward the hotel. His strong resemblance to Garrett had given her the initial impression that they shared the same nature. But where Garrett had been relaxed and easygoing, she sensed in his brother a desire for control. If only he'd make time to give her news of her mother, she wouldn't have to see him again tomorrow.

She pushed the thoughts away. An afternoon with Jacob lay before her. She wouldn't ruin their time together by worrying.

Faith's voice brought her back to the moment. "Who was *that*? He was rather rude to interrupt us without apologizing."

"His name's Patrick Fitzhugh. He's the brother of my late fiancé." She explained how he'd come to the station in Calusa as she was leaving and then showed up unannounced at the grocery yesterday. "He came to bring me news about Mother, but so far all he's said is that she's well. If that's true, then why is he here? I fear he's hiding something drastic."

"He wants to wait until he can comfort you without Mr. West's presence."

"I don't want his comfort." Cassie shuddered. "I want him to give me whatever news he has, then go home."

"Looks to me like Mr. West would be happy to comfort you." Faith giggled. "Enjoy your buggy ride." She hurried toward her waiting family.

Smiling, Cassie crossed the lawn to Jacob. "I'm sorry to keep you waiting. Sundays are my best time to visit with Faith. She's either busy at home or in the mercantile—and of course, I'm busy too."

"I understand. Perhaps once Becca's familiar with the kitchen, you could take an afternoon off now and then."

"That would be wonderful. The hardest part of my job is the lack of time to spend with friends. Without Mother, my cabin is a lonely place sometimes." She bit her lip. Why would Jacob care about her friendships? As far as she could see, he seemed to get along fine with few friends of his own.

His gaze softened. "This afternoon, we won't think about loneliness." He moved as near as possible, allowing for the barrier his crutches created between them. "I asked Mrs. Fielder to surprise you with a picnic lunch to take with us on our ride. We'll stop by the restaurant on our way."

"A picnic sounds delightful." She slipped her hand beneath his elbow. "Where are we going?"

"Pioneer Lake, although I can't walk far on uneven ground. We'd have to stay in the buggy and watch everyone else do the walking for us, if you don't mind."

"I don't mind a bit."

❧

Sunbeams skated over the ripples on Pioneer Lake. From their vantage point under a weeping willow, Cassie and Jacob watched children running and splashing along the shore. Couples strolled around the water's edge.

Jacob's coat lay folded over the seat back. When he turned up the cuffs of his shirt, Cassie fought the urge to run her fingers over the dark hair on his muscular forearms. Her improper thoughts caused her face to warm more than the heat of the afternoon warranted. What on earth was the matter with her? Her mother would be scandalized.

To occupy her hands, she tucked a cloth over the near-empty picnic basket. "Jenny outdid herself. Chicken, strawberries, biscuits—it was a lovely meal."

"The first of many, I hope." He rested his index finger alongside her chin and turned her face toward him. "Do you think you can work with me as your employer and still allow me to spend time with you away from the restaurant?"

"Oh, yes! With no trouble at all."

She liked the way he appeared gentle and resolute at the same time. She liked the way his voice rumbled when he spoke. She liked his wavy black hair. At the moment, she couldn't think of anything about him she didn't like. She knew her mother didn't share her opinion, but given enough time she'd change her mind. Jacob's fine qualities outshone Garrett's, and Mother had been fond of Garrett.

"Then it's settled." He lowered his voice. "I've never let myself get this close to anyone before."

"But you and my friend Rosemary—"

"We were both lonely. Doc Stewart was the better man for her. Turned out she thought so too."

Cassie leaned against the seat back, knowing the time had come to explain about Garrett, but reluctant to break the spell of the afternoon. After a moment, she straightened. Omission was as wrong as commission.

"As Mr. Fitzhugh mentioned, two years ago I was engaged

to his brother. My fiancé, Garrett, died in an accident shortly before our wedding date."

He stilled. She studied his face, but the leafy curtain over them shadowed his expression. After a few seconds he slipped his arm around her shoulder.

"Two years is a long time. Are you ready to care for someone else?" His rumbling voice drowned out the children's laughter.

"Indeed I am," she whispered.

"Good. We'll agree to let the past stay in the past."

Thoughts of Garrett vanished when Jacob pressed his lips to hers.

After the breakfast rush ended on Monday, Cassie paced from the kitchen to the dining room, her thoughts bouncing between her afternoon with Jacob and Mr. Fitzhugh's promised arrival. The westbound train would depart at nine. So far, he hadn't appeared. Surely he wouldn't leave without seeing her.

"Are you going to make those pies or wear a track in the floor?" Jenny folded her arms around her middle. The aroma of apple cider hung over the room like a sugary cloud. "Becca's got the filling about ready, and I need to use the range. It's time to get stew cooking for dinner."

"I'm sorry." She took pie pans from the shelf. Besides the six that she prepared for the restaurant daily, she had three orders to fill. "I know I'm wasting time, but Mr. Fitzhugh said he'd be here this morning. I don't want to be up to my elbows in flour when he arrives."

Jenny pretended a long-suffering sigh. "I reckon I can wait a few more minutes." She took a cup, filled it with leftover coffee, then sank onto a chair near the worktable. "Might as well get off my feet."

Cassie heard Jacob approach before he reached the kitchen. He stopped at the entrance and glanced around, his gaze settling on her. "Your friend is here. He's waiting in the grocery."

"Oh, good. I was afraid he wasn't coming." She smoothed her hair back from her face, then removed her apron.

She caught Jacob's frown before he turned away. Once they left the kitchen, she placed her hand on his arm.

"After he answers my questions about Mother, he'll be on his way."

"Not a minute too soon to suit me."

Mr. Fitzhugh bounded forward when they reached the grocery. "Mr. West, with your permission, I'd like to have a few minutes of Miss Haddon's time away from your establishment."

"By all means. As it is, she's waited far too long to hear why you came."

Cassie frowned at Garrett's brother. He should have asked her permission, not Jacob's. Did he think she was a child?

He gazed down at her. "Miss Haddon. Shall we get some fresh air?"

She ignored his extended elbow and marched out the door ahead of him, turning right on Main Street. "The morning is quite warm. That tree across the street will offer shade while we talk."

He put his hand on her elbow and guided her to the butternut tree that stood as a sentinel in the middle of the block. As soon as they stopped, she tugged her arm free and faced him. "What's wrong with my mother? She must be dreadfully ill if you needed privacy to inform me of her condition."

"Your mother's in fine health."

"But isn't that why you came? You said my mother sent you."

"No, I said your mother told me where to find you. Actually, Reverend Greeley sent me."

Cassie stepped backward until the flat ridges of the tree's bark pressed against her shoulders. "Reverend Greeley sent you?" Her voice squeaked. "I've spent this whole weekend worrying about my mother. Why didn't you say so to begin with?"

His jaw tightened. "It's rather a delicate matter. Fortunately, your pastor opened the door with his sermon yesterday."

She stared at him, wishing she'd stayed in the grocery with Jacob. Mr. Fitzhugh was obviously deranged. Inching away from the tree, she tried to leave enough space between them so he couldn't touch her.

He held up his hand. "Please listen. If you recall, part of yesterday's passage in Deuteronomy dealt with the duty of the brother of a deceased man to marry the man's widow."

She shook her head slowly as comprehension dawned. "That's Old Testament."

"Reverend Greeley says God's law stands as written. I'm responsible for you now."

"So this is all Reverend Greeley's idea? Tell him I said no."

He gentled his tone. "Give yourself time, Miss Haddon. Cassie. I'm not a bad fellow. Having you as my wife would fulfill my scriptural duty, and it would certainly ease your poor mother's heart for us to live in Calusa. I'm sure in time we'd learn to care for one another."

"No!"

"I realize I've botched this." He took a step forward.

The train's whistle rolled through the humid morning. He

stopped and turned in the direction of the sound. "The next time I come, I'll court you properly."

"Don't come back, Mr. Fitzhugh. The answer will still be no."

She picked up her skirts and bolted toward West & Riley's.

*C*assie burst through the kitchen entrance, her hand at her throat. The screen door banged behind her.

"Good gracious! Was the news as bad as all that?" Jenny bustled over from the stove, concern clouding her hazel eyes. "Did something happen to your ma?"

"No. Far from it." Cassie slumped against the wall to catch her breath.

"Then what's got you all aflutter?"

Surrounded by the familiar kitchen aromas of apple pie filling and breakfast bacon, she wondered if she'd overreacted. Mr. Fitzhugh lived in Calusa. Reverend Greeley could believe whatever he wanted, but his outdated ideas couldn't touch her here in Noble Springs. She dragged in a steadying breath and told herself to be calm. She was safe in Jacob's restaurant.

She glanced between Jenny and Becca and forced a smile. "The reason for Mr. Fitzhugh's visit took me by surprise. An unwelcome surprise, I might add. Thankfully, he's on his way back to Calusa." She dusted her hands together. "Time to start on those pies. Becca, would you please carry that pot of apples over to my worktable?"

"Yes, missy."

Jenny gave her a searching look. "I can tell when you're upset. There's something you're not saying."

"Nothing important."

"Humph. When you're ready to talk, you can always come to me."

"I know. Thank you." She slipped her arm around the woman's ample waist. "We'd better get busy. Time's flying, and Mr. West doesn't pay us to stand around."

"This is your day to be boss, is it?" Jenny faked a grumble and marched to the range, where steam rose from two skillets.

After Jenny turned away, Cassie tied on an apron and walked on wobbly legs to her worktable. She'd never considered such a thing before, but Mr. Fitzhugh's determination left her shaken. Could there be truth in his words? Did Scripture really say Garrett's brother was required to marry her?

While Becca watched, Cassie measured flour and salt into a large bowl, then cut lard into the mixture. "This is the important part," she said, striving to keep her voice level. "Just the right amount of water to moisten." She lifted a pitcher, but the base struck the side of the bowl and most of the water splashed over the floury mix.

Her hands shook when she replaced the pitcher on the table. Using a fork, she tried to fluff the flour and water together. The result stuck to the bowl like wallpaper paste. She fought a desire to panic. Much as she'd like to throw the whole thing out and start again, she couldn't waste that much wheat flour.

She opened the flour bin and dumped several scoops into a smaller bowl, then dropped in additional lard. While she cut through the mixture with two knives, she sent Becca a weak smile. "I'm sorry. This is not the way I usually make piecrust." The knives clattered against the side of the bowl.

Becca's soft brown gaze rested on her. "Maybe I'll go see if Miz Fielder needs me. It don't help none to have someone starin' at you when you're in a fix."

"You're so right. Thank you."

The young woman's kindness threatened to undo the fragile control she'd maintained since her meeting with Mr. Fitzhugh. Somehow she had to get nine pies ready for the ovens in the next few minutes. She scraped the contents of the smaller bowl into the large one and stirred the ingredients together, her wrist aching from the weight of the additional dough. As soon as the crust felt workable, she removed a portion and flattened the sticky substance on a floured cloth.

Cracks appeared in the dough with the first pass of the rolling pin. Her stomach tightened. No matter what, this crust was going in the pans. Their dinner customers expected dessert. She picked up pieces of dough and pressed them together inside the first pie pan, then repeated the technique with five of the remaining pans. After a struggle, she managed to fill and cover each pie, although the results looked more like a patchwork quilt than anything edible.

While Becca carried the completed efforts to the ovens, Cassie stared at the three empty pans, representing customers' orders. Her shoulders sagged. Jacob charged fifty cents for a whole pie—she'd have to do what she could to produce pies worth that much money.

She poked at the dough remaining in the bowl, sprinkled more flour in to balance the stickiness, and flattened another disk on the pastry cloth. Jacob trusted her to fill these orders. She couldn't disappoint him.

Jacob sat at the table in his corner office, fighting to keep his mind from wandering to Cassie and Patrick Fitzhugh. He'd heard the train arrive, so assumed Fitzhugh was on his way back to Calusa. What could the man have had to say that was important enough to keep Cassie waiting for two days? He hoped she'd tell him as soon as she had the opportunity.

It would be just like that mother of hers to come up with a scheme to send Cassie running to her side. He wished he could stand and pace the room, but being on crutches ruined the effect. Instead, he kicked the table with his left leg and stared at a blank sheet of paper in front of him.

He needed to tell Keegan Byrne about operating a bakery from the restaurant kitchen. Writing to him now would help pass the time until he had a legitimate reason to go to the kitchen. He tapped the end of a pen holder against the tabletop.

How to best present the situation to a man who was a stranger to him? Colin Riley had encouraged him to think of ways to help the business grow as the war years faded behind them. He had no idea how Mr. Byrne might react to the news.

Huffing out a breath, he dipped the pen nib into an inkpot.

Noble Springs 22nd June 1868

Dear Mr. Byrne,
This is to inform you that as of last week, I've added a new income-producing department to West & Riley's kitchen. Miss Haddon has proved herself to be a proficient baker, to the extent that her pies are in demand by grocery customers as well as patrons at mealtimes. Thus encouraged, I instituted a bake shop solely for her management. She reports to me, of course.

He strove to keep his words noncommittal. His personal feelings for Cassie were of no concern to Keegan Byrne or anyone else in Boston.

Since the bake shop puts an extra strain on normal kitchen operations, I've hired another employee to assist with preparations, although Mrs. Fielder and Miss Haddon will continue to do the cooking in their respective roles.

The operation is in its infancy this month. In the future, I have every expectation that my decision will result in greater income, which will increase your agreed-upon share accordingly.

At any rate, he hoped so. The venture represented the largest gamble he'd taken since opening West & Riley's. So far, the expenses of the bakery exceeded income. That wouldn't always be the case, but for now every pie sale was important. If profits failed to materialize, he feared he'd have Mr. Byrne on his doorstep.

He rubbed his moist palms on his trouser legs before signing with a bold flourish.

After addressing an envelope, he grabbed his crutches and walk-hobbled to the grocery, smiling at the sight of a cleared space atop one counter. Three of Miss Haddon's perfect pies would be cooling there soon.

Jenny carried a stack of empty serving bowls from the dining room to the washbasin. "Might as well cut those pies. They're not going to improve just sitting there."

"I know." Cassie rolled her shoulders to release tension.

Filling had boiled through the cracked crusts, leaving sticky residue down the outside of the pans. Worse than the first six pies, the crusts she'd assembled to fulfill customers' orders had shrunk away from their crimped edges. Exposed apples were burned brown.

She tried to imagine Jacob's reaction while she cut the crumbling desserts. She could pretend she'd intended to make apple pandowdy for the diners, but nothing could explain away the withered-looking offerings at the end of the work-table. She put her hand over her mouth, trying not to cry.

Within minutes of dessert being served, Jacob entered the kitchen. His gaze locked on hers. "The slices fell apart when the men tried to take them out of the pans. We had to use our spoons. I hope the others are . . ." His voice trailed off when he noticed the three remaining pies. "What will I tell my customers when they come in? Those are pig food."

"Pig food?" Her words boiled with pent-up frustration. "You can tell your customers their orders aren't ready. Something went wrong. Period. They can come back tomorrow." She seized one of the pans and dumped the contents into a slop bucket.

Becca hurried from the washbasin to the table. "Wait!" She faced Jacob. "Mr. West, those are still pretty good. Can I take 'em with me tonight? I'll share with Wash."

"Yes, of course."

Becca's need and Jacob's kindly response cooled Cassie's temper. Maybe those pies didn't look perfect, but obviously they weren't swine fodder. She shouldn't have thrown away something that could be shared.

She shot Jacob a contrite look. "I'm sorry. I haven't been thinking clearly since talking with Mr. Fitzhugh this morning." She wished she could respond to Jacob's questioning gaze, but the matter felt too private to air. "I'll come in earlier tomorrow and have the orders ready before noon. Would that be suitable?"

"It'll have to be, won't it?" The hint of a smile lifted the corners of his eyes. "In the meantime, maybe a few hours away from the kitchen this afternoon would help clear your mind."

She peeked over her shoulder and saw Jenny's mouth drop open. The woman's reaction mirrored her own.

"Th . . . thank you, Mr. West. I'll be happy to go, on one condition."

"You're giving me conditions?"

"Just one. Jenny and Becca should get free afternoons too. You did mention the possibility recently."

"So I did." He looked at the three of them. "Fine. One afternoon a week. Take turns."

After one more glance at the ruined pies, Jacob pivoted toward the dining room. His crutches thumped a cadence across the floor.

"Whoo-ee, missy. You're brave to speak up like that." Becca shook her head in wonderment.

"I'm learning that sometimes I have to be." Her mind flew to Mr. Fitzhugh's stated purpose for coming to Noble Springs. If he ever dared to return, she prayed she'd find the words to send him away permanently.

When Cassie left the kitchen, she halted in the alley and stared across the street at the tall butternut tree where she and Mr. Fitzhugh stood that morning. She wished she'd paid more attention during Reverend French's sermon yesterday. Try as she might, she couldn't remember that he'd said anything about Old Testament laws applying to present-day life.

She bent her head over her clasped hands. Maybe Rosemary

could set her mind at ease. Given all the soldiers she'd tended during the war, perhaps she'd heard discussions on the subject of widows' remarriage.

Stepping from the shade into bright sunlight, she headed down Third Street toward the Stewarts' home, planning a stop at the post office on the way. Regardless of Mr. Fitzhugh's assurances, or perhaps because of them, she felt more worried than ever about her mother's well-being.

As soon as she entered the small clapboard building across from the parsonage, the postmaster, Mr. Lyons, smiled up at her.

"Howdy, Miss Haddon. Looks like you finally got a letter from your mama." He ran his fingers over the tray of mail before him and removed a square envelope. "Mrs. Elmer Bingham, Calusa, Missouri. Right?"

"Yes. Thank you." She plucked the envelope from his fingers, wishing the letter had arrived before Mr. Fitzhugh's visit.

Mr. Lyons leaned across the table. "Wonder how she's getting along?"

"So do I. I'll tell you after I read this."

Rumor had it he sometimes read the mail before recipients did. People claimed that's how he knew so much about Noble Springs' residents. She tucked the envelope in her handbag and hurried out, ignoring his deflated expression. He probably wouldn't be so eager for information if he'd already read this one.

Instead of continuing to Rosemary's house, she doubled back, hastening toward the privacy of her cabin. Once inside, she broke the seal on the envelope and removed two closely written pages.

Cassie scanned her mother's opening sentences containing polite inquiries about her health and a report on the weather. When she read the first lines of the second paragraph, her breath caught in her throat.

Rand is away more than he is at home. He did warn us that would be the case, but I didn't realize how empty this little house could feel. Mr. Fitzhugh and Reverend Greeley have done much to make the lonely days here bearable. The good reverend seems to have made me a special mission project. He calls almost daily. Quite often we discuss passages of Scripture that he feels are particularly relevant to my situation.

Poor Mr. Fitzhugh is at loose ends with school dismissed for the summer. He, too, is lonely, since he has no wife. I must confess I've mentioned your name to him several times in that regard. If only you would join me here, I believe the two of you would find much in common. He'd be a far more suitable match than anyone you'll find in Noble Springs. I'm sure you haven't forgotten the fine home the Fitzhugh family possesses in St. Louis.

Cassie stared at her mother's words. Humiliation rocked her at the image of the three of them plotting her future as though she were a pawn in a chess game. No matter what her mother said, she would not return to Calusa.

Her gaze dropped to the next paragraph.

As much as I value their companionship, I sorely miss having another woman to pass the time with. In hindsight, the days we had together at your Uncle Rudy's were blessed. In some ways I wish we'd never left.

I'm doing my best to be brave here in this desolate town. At church this week, Reverend Greeley introduced me to a woman who operates a boardinghouse. I'm trying to decide whether to call on her. If only you were here, dearest Cassie, I could abide the wind and the incessant dust.

I remain,
Your loving Mother

The letter slipped through her fingers and drifted to the floor. She wouldn't give up everything she'd accomplished here to run to her mother's side. She owed her mother honor, yet in what manner?

Guilt gnawed at her conscience. Mother had to be miserable to look back on life at Uncle Rudy's as a pleasant experience. She'd wanted to find her brother, and now that she'd done so, she was still miserable. Cassie considered the thought that perhaps her mother would be miserable no matter what her circumstances, then pushed the idea aside as disloyal.

The gravel path outside her door beckoned. She had questions, and she prayed Rosemary could supply the answers. She shoved the letter into her handbag and covered the distance between her cabin and her friend's home with brisk strides.

Cassie stood on the doorstep listening to footsteps hurrying in response to her knock. Belatedly, she hoped she hadn't disturbed the baby's nap.

A wide smile lit Rosemary's face when she opened the door. "What a joy to see you! Come in." Her hair was pulled back in an untidy bun, and lavender shadows smudged the skin beneath her eyes. "You picked a perfect time to call. We're having a little rest." She led the way into the sitting room, where her two-week-old baby slept in a cradle in front of the sofa.

Cassie knelt beside the cradle and ran a finger over the infant's soft black curls.

"Josephine Amanda is such a sweet name. Will you call her Josie?"

"Elijah already does. Josephine was his late mother's name, but it's a mouthful for such a wee one." She sank onto the sofa.

Cassie kissed Josie's forehead before standing. Now that she was here, she wasn't sure how to ask her questions.

Her friend patted a spot beside her, at the same time setting the cradle to rocking with the toe of one shoe. "Come, sit." A grin teased at the corners of her mouth. "So, Jacob must have given you the afternoon off. And Faith told me he came to church with you yesterday, along with a handsome blond stranger. You're cutting a swath through Noble Springs."

"Not quite." She hugged her arms across her chest. "But

that's what I wanted to talk to you about. Did Faith tell you who the blond man was?"

"Garrett Fitzhugh's brother, Patrick. How remarkable that your paths crossed. I don't recall that you ever mentioned him."

"I didn't even remember meeting him. He said he saw me at Garrett's funeral, but everything was such a blur at that time."

Rosemary laid her hand over Cassie's. "Of course it was. Faith also said he brought news of your mother. I pray she's well."

"Apparently her health is fine." She dug Mother's letter from her handbag and thrust the pages at Rosemary. "After you read what she has to say, I'll tell you about Mr. Fitzhugh's visit."

Rosemary read the letter, then sent Cassie a look brimming with compassion. "She doesn't make things easy for you, does she?"

"It gets worse." She rose and paced across the room, then swung around to face her friend. "Apparently Reverend Greeley has convinced Mr. Fitzhugh that as Garrett's brother, it's his biblical duty to marry me in order to carry on the family line."

"Impossible!"

"I agree, but that's exactly what Mr. Fitzhugh told me. He referred to a passage in Deuteronomy. His preacher friend claims Old Testament law is still valid. I wondered if any war widows you knew had done such a thing."

Rosemary shook her head. "No, none that I ever heard of. Of course the Old Testament is still valid, but those laws were written to specific people at a specific time. Those days have passed."

"That's what I said. But he seemed so sure."

"The reverend who's advising him sounds like a fanatic.

We'll pray the two of them stay in Calusa—far away from you. And you stay right here," she said in a stern voice, then patted the space next to her again. "Now tell me about you and Jacob. How did you get him to go to church with you?"

Cassie explained her Sunday morning, then relayed the story of the picnic at Pioneer Lake. Tears gathered beneath her lashes. "We had such a perfect afternoon, then Mr. Fitzhugh's words this morning spoiled everything. I ruined nine pies, lost my temper with Jacob, and selfishly threw away good food without thinking of anyone but myself. That's why he gave me the afternoon off. He's probably regretting ever letting me come to work for him."

"I doubt that. Will you tell him what Mr. Fitzhugh said?"

"No. We agreed to let the past stay buried."

"Secrets between couples have a way of exploding at inopportune times."

"My former engagement is no secret. As for the rest, Mr. Fitzhugh's notions will only upset Jacob. Right now, he's upset enough with me as it is."

<hr />

A week and a half following Cassie's pie disaster, Jacob entered the kitchen soon after breakfast had been served. Six pies were lined on the worktable ready to go in the oven. The tangy-sweet aroma of hot blueberries rose from four more cooling beneath a window.

Cassie beamed at him and blotted perspiration from her forehead with a corner of her apron. "Six orders today, plus pies for dinner. Independence Day is keeping us busy."

"That's what I came to see you about." He moved closer, lowering his voice. "There's a fireworks display tonight at Pioneer Lake. Would you like to attend?"

"Oh, yes! I'd love to." Her eyes sparkled with excitement. "I'll hurry home after work and change my dress, then we can leave whenever you say."

He squeezed her hand, ignoring the presence of the other two women in the kitchen. "If we leave by seven, we'll have plenty of time to find a good vantage point."

"I'll be ready."

The look she gave him swirled through his insides like hot butter. Tonight couldn't come soon enough to suit him.

With reluctance, he left the kitchen to return to the grocery. When he'd crutched halfway through the dining room, the street door to the restaurant opened. Two well-dressed men paused on the threshold.

He pointed to a sign on the wall stating mealtimes. "Dinner seating won't be for another two hours, gentlemen. Please come back then."

The taller of the two, a beefy redhead, took a step inside. "We're not here to eat. I'm looking for Jacob West. Are you him?"

"I am. What can I do for you?"

"You can show me around this fine establishment." His boots thudded as he wove his way around the empty tables. When he reached Jacob, he extended his hand. "Keegan Byrne." He pointed at his companion, a skinny man with greased-down hair. "My assistant, Lenny Ruggero."

Jacob's heart threatened to stop beating. He couldn't be sure, but something about Ruggero's appearance seemed familiar. He shrugged off the notion. The fact that Keegan Byrne had come all the way from Boston was concern enough.

He clasped Byrne's hand with what he hoped passed for sincerity. "Welcome. Never expected to see you here. Colin was content with written reports."

"It's bad business to step into something sight unseen.

Colin told me you had a small operation. Then you send me a letter about opening a bake shop and got my curiosity going." His ice-blue eyes bored into Jacob's. "In the two months since I bought his share from Riley, you've added three new workers. Kind of cuts into profits, doesn't it?"

"A necessary expense if we're to increase business." Jacob pivoted toward the grocery entrance. "Please come with me. My office is this way. I'll show you how income has grown."

"I don't want to see your numbers. Show me why you need so much help."

He tightened his grip on his crutches. In spite of Byrne's attempt to dress like a gentleman, he resembled a street brawler. Why Colin had agreed to sell his business to such a man was a mystery.

"Very well. In here's the grocery." He led the way into the spacious room, lined on three sides with floor-to-ceiling shelving. His clerk, Timothy, glanced at them before grabbing a duster and attacking a display of tinned milk.

Jacob waved his hand at the array of tins, bottles, and boxes on the shelves. "I sell everything ladies need to keep their families well fed. Since my wealthier customers learned of the bake shop, trade has increased. They come in to order a pie, and end up buying an additional item or two." He felt a flash of pride in Cassie's efforts. In the beginning, he'd hired her out of a charitable impulse and had been rewarded with a helper of uncommon skill. The greatest reward had been opening his heart to her, something he'd never anticipated.

Byrne gave the well-stocked shelves a brief survey. "So, let's see this bakery."

"Straight through the dining room." He retraced his steps, with Byrne and Ruggero close behind.

Cassie had her back to them when they entered. Her fingers moved rapidly around the rim of a pie plate as she crimped the edges of a crust together. When she saw Jacob, she turned her head and smiled. At the sight of his two visitors, her expression changed to one of curiosity.

Across the room, Jenny paused, chopping knife in hand. Becca rested her hands on the edge of the dishpan.

Jacob broke the waiting silence. "Gentlemen. This is Miss Haddon, the baker; Mrs. Fielder, the cook; and Becca Rowan, their helper." He pointed at each in turn. "As you can see, they're fully occupied with tasks. I couldn't offer three full meals a day and sell pies in the grocery without them."

Byrne leered at Cassie. "I can see why you hired this one. And she can bake too?"

Fire raged in Jacob's gut. One more word and he'd whack the man with a crutch. He took a deep breath. "Now that you've seen everything, I hope you'll have a comfortable trip back to Boston." He stomped through the entrance as fast as his leg would allow.

"Not so fast, Mr. West. I based part of my decision to buy Colin Riley's share on the reports you sent him. Since I've come all this way, I'd like to see some of the businesses you mentioned in your letters. A cooperage, and you said something about a brickyard?"

Jacob slowed. "Yes, but the brickyard is several miles north of town. I'll have Timothy, the clerk in the grocery, show you around."

"I'd rather you accompanied us. I have a rented carriage out front." Byrne and Ruggero moved to stand on either side of him. "Shall we go?"

Jacob sat wedged on the carriage seat between Mr. Byrne and his assistant. The streets bustled with Independence Day celebrants. Young boys ran along the boardwalk waving small flags. Firecrackers popped. Buggies carrying families all seemed to be headed in the direction of the town park across from the railroad tracks.

"Some of the men who come in for meals work in the cooperage. It's on Commerce Street, down past the hotel, if you want to see it. After that I'll direct you to Wylie's wagon shop."

Byrne grunted and guided the horse south. "So, Colin tells me he set you up here before the war." His tone probed.

"He did."

"And before that, you worked for him in Boston?"

"You already know the answer. Why are you asking me now?"

"Just making sure I've got the whole picture."

He turned the carriage onto Commerce Street, then immediately jerked up on the reins. Buggies crowded the road in front of them. On their right, picnickers dotted the park lawn. Customers lined up at concession booths along the boardwalk. Inside the bunting-draped bandstand, musicians tuned their instruments.

Byrne glared at Jacob. "Is this your idea of a joke? If I want to see crowds, I'll stay in Boston."

He returned the man's glare. "Independence Day. The store's open, so I forgot about the celebration down here." Inwardly he, too, chafed at the delay. The sooner the men saw the town, the sooner they'd leave.

Ruggero stirred on the seat and pointed. "Look there. The sign on that booth says 'Beer and Libations.' Want to stop?"

"We're not here to spend the day with a bunch of yokels." Byrne flicked the reins and guided the horse through the commotion, then turned right.

His scrawny assistant shot him a hard look. After shoving his bowler hat over his eyes, he slouched down in the seat.

"Relax, Lenny. We'll have time later." Byrne shifted his focus to Jacob. "Where's this wagon shop?"

"A mile or two south. Follow Third Street out." Jacob strove to maintain a polite tone. By the time they reached Wylie's shop, the hour would be well past noon. He hoped Byrne would forget about seeing the brickyard.

When they reached Wylie's, Byrne stopped the carriage in front of the sun-bleached building. No horses were tied to the hitching rail. The door was padlocked. "Another one of your little jokes, West?"

Jacob fought down an urge to plant his fist in the man's smirking face. "You're the one who wanted to tour Noble Springs today. Looks to me like most folks went to the celebration." He tightened his jaw. "Might as well take me back to the grocery."

Ignoring his suggestion, Byrne turned the carriage around. "How far's the brickyard?"

"From here? About eight miles." Jacob clamped his hands

on his thighs. Eight miles out and back over a rough country road would take too much time. He'd promised Cassie they'd leave by seven. "Going to be the same thing, though. The workers will probably be in town."

"How do I know there's a brickyard out there? You could've invented it to make your decisions to hire extra help look better than they are."

"Sit back." Rugerro sneered at Jacob. "When the boss says he's going to do something, he does it."

As Jacob expected, when they reached the northern end of town the road changed from graded to rocky. Byrne slowed the carriage to avoid the worst of the jolts, but each bump sent a shot of pain up Jacob's right leg. He gritted his teeth and endured. He wouldn't give Byrne the satisfaction of hearing him groan.

They rode in silence until they saw two beehive-shaped kilns when they rounded a curve. After drawing abreast of the yard, Byrne stopped the carriage. "No one's around."

"I didn't think anyone would—"

"We'll get out and have a look." Byrne hopped down and tied the horse to a rail. "Come on, West."

Jacob surveyed the uneven ground. The desire to remain in the carriage and favor his leg warred with his determination not to be intimidated. He huffed out a breath, grabbed his crutches, and joined Byrne and Ruggero inside the brickyard fence.

Afternoon sun slanted across a mud pit. A stack of empty six-brick forms waited nearby. Byrne walked to a storage shed, his head cocked as he studied the contents. Jacob imagined him counting the bricks and estimating how many men the business employed.

In a moment, the man faced him. "Got to hand it to you. Looks like your ideas are sound. Glad you thought of a bakery—looks like a money-maker."

Jacob blinked. The last thing he'd expected was a compliment. He opened his mouth to respond, but Byrne continued.

"Since the business was smaller when you started, I think it's time to renegotiate Colin's agreement. I deserve a larger share."

"The ideas are mine. So are the profits."

"That might have satisfied Colin. I don't work that way."

Jacob thrust his chin in the air. If this Boston bully thought he could intimidate him, he'd better think again. "You'll have to. You *deserve* nothing more than what he originally intended."

"How about I give you a little time to think about it?" Byrne turned to Ruggero and nodded in the direction of the carriage. "Get in. We've got a train to catch."

They strode across the brickyard. Jacob struggled to follow at their pace, but the muddy ground dragged at his crutches.

As the carriage pulled away, Ruggero hollered over his shoulder, "Enjoy your walk, Jake Westermann."

Cassie walked through the deserted dining room, her record book tucked under her arm, while Jenny and Becca finished their chores in the kitchen. Because of the holiday, they'd had few supper patrons. She'd have plenty of time to change her dress and rearrange her hair before Jacob called for her at seven.

When she entered the grocery, Timothy grinned at her. "Time to lock up, Miss Haddon. You going to see the fireworks show?"

"Yes, indeed. I want to give today's receipts to Mr. West first, though. Is he in his office?"

The boy looked surprised at the question. "No. Haven't seen him all afternoon."

"Then what—" She glanced at the shelf where Jacob kept his cash box. "I'd better hide that away. He must be planning to come in tomorrow."

"I expect so, miss. You know how he is about the receipts."

She knew all too well. After Timothy left, she hid the box in Jacob's office, but didn't go near his ledger.

On her way home, she heard snatches of band music coming from the park. Excitement tickled in her throat at the thought of spending the evening watching fireworks. Her uncle had deemed such a pastime worldly, so she hadn't been allowed to go when she and Mother lived in St. Louis.

For a moment she felt disloyal. What if Calusa didn't hold an Independence Day celebration? Maybe her mother was sitting at home alone. Her steps slowed as she recalled Mother's most recent letter. She'd mentioned a growing friendship with a woman who owned a rooming house.

Praying the two of them had plans for the evening, Cassie darted across the street and hurried into her cabin. Tonight she'd wear her rose-colored chintz dress. Jacob hadn't seen that one.

The sun had settled toward the horizon by the time she felt satisfied with her appearance. After draping her embroidered muslin mantelet over her shoulders, she took one final glance at herself in the mirror. Spots of color brightened her cheeks at the thought of sitting close to Jacob as the sky darkened and brilliant rockets blazed across the heavens.

She crossed to the next room and opened the door to catch stray breezes, then perched on the edge of a chair to wait. The setting sun cast on orange glow over the path to her cabin. After a few minutes, the light faded. A breeze scuffed through a patch of coneflowers planted beside the alley.

Cassie stepped outside. The fireworks would start soon. If Jacob didn't hurry, they'd miss the show. She peered down the alley, seeing nothing but a yellow tabby cat licking a front paw. It wasn't like Jacob to be late for anything.

She returned to the cabin and lit the lamp. The last thing she wanted was to be caught staring out the door like a child waiting for Papa to come home. She grabbed a book from her meager collection, plopped down on a chair, and opened a page at random. Her mind wouldn't focus on the words. Instead, she tried to imagine what Jacob might have found so important that he'd forget their plans.

After reading the same paragraph several times, she snapped the cover shut and paced to the open door. The first stars of the evening twinkled overhead. She listened for hoofbeats, but heard none.

She slammed the door and blew out the lamp.

The next morning, Cassie marched to church with her head high. Jacob had attended with her the past two weeks, but if he couldn't be bothered to take her to the fireworks, he probably wouldn't show up at church, either. If he decided to join her, fine. If not, that was fine too.

She slid into a pew next to Rosemary and Elijah.

Rosemary shifted little Josephine in her arms and arched an eyebrow. "Where's Jacob this morning?" She spoke in a whisper.

"I don't have the slightest idea, and I don't care."

Rosemary blinked. "What—" She stopped when Reverend French stepped to the pulpit and opened a hymnal.

He sent the congregation a beatific smile. "Please stand and join me in singing 'O Day of Rest and Gladness.'" Pews creaked and dresses rustled as worshipers rose. Cassie felt anything but glad, but she sang anyway. As her anger at Jacob faded, tears threatened. Had he changed his mind? Was ignoring her his way of avoiding commitment?

She pondered her questions as she listened to Reverend French preach from the first chapter of the General Epistle of James. When he read, "Wherefore, my beloved brethren, let every man be swift to hear, slow to speak, slow to wrath. For the wrath of man worketh not the righteousness of God," she squirmed in her seat. She definitely felt wrathy toward Jacob. She bowed her head. *Please, Lord, help me to know what to do.*

When she stepped outside after the closing hymn, the first thing she noticed was Wash standing at the foot of the steps. Worry creased his forehead.

She ran to him, her heart slamming against her ribs. "Wash! Why are you here? Where's Jacob?"

"His leg took a bad turn on him." He twisted his worn hat between his fingers. "He said to ask if you'd kindly come to the store."

"Come to the store? The grocery's closed on Sundays."

"Yes, missy. But that's where he is. Would you come?"

She stared down at her clasped hands. When she asked the Lord to show her what to do, she hadn't expected such a quick answer. Lifting her head, she met Wash's anxious gaze. "All right. I'll go with you."

24

Cassie walked the block up Third Street to West &
Riley's, Wash following a few paces behind. Her stomach churned. Jacob left her waiting all last evening without
sending word. Now he expected her to meet him in the store,
rather than calling for her with his buggy. And why did Wash
appear so anxious? She exhaled a long breath. In a moment
she'd have her answers.

Upon reaching the grocery, she stepped to one side while
Wash unlocked the door. Mingled aromas of vinegar, coffee,
and tobacco greeted her when she entered the quiet room.
She glanced around, expecting to see Jacob.

"He's in back, missy. In his office." Wash paused at the
entrance to the deserted dining room. "I'll wait in the kitchen
'til he's fixing to leave."

"Thank you." She crossed to the storeroom and peeked
around the doorway.

Jacob sat at his workable, his injured leg resting on a packing crate. In the lamplight, his skin looked gray. Deep grooves
channeled either side of his mouth. The lines disappeared
into a broad smile when he saw her.

"I was afraid you wouldn't come today. You must be thinking the worst of me."

"I don't know what to think." *Be swift to hear, slow to speak.* "I waited for you until well past dark."

He winced as though she'd delivered a blow. "Will you forgive me? You were on my mind every moment, but I had no way to reach you."

"You could've sent Wash, like you did this morning." She perched on a chair facing him.

"Wash wasn't with me, or I would have."

"Then what happened to you? Wash said something about your leg."

"I'm afraid I might have set back the healing. The pain is . . . rough." He swallowed, his face grim. "But I had to see you this morning. I have to know you'll forgive me."

"Oh, Jacob. Of course I forgive you." She reached for his hand. "You can't be blamed for an accident. What happened? Did you fall?"

An uneasy expression crossed his face. "Yes. I was walking on rough ground and stumbled."

"Walking on rough ground? With crutches? Why would you do such a thing?" She clapped her hand over her mouth. "I'm sorry. I have no right to speak to you like that."

"You have more right than anyone. I'm grateful you care."

"You know I do."

"Cassie, I—" He clamped his lips shut and sucked in a long breath. "I'm going to stay at home and rest my leg for the next week. Would you take care of the receipts . . . and the ledger?" He patted the green leather book.

She felt a swell of triumph. He trusted her. "I'd be glad to." She grinned at him. "See, you're not too old to change after all."

After Cassie left, Jacob unscrewed the posts that held his ledger together. He lifted the front cover and removed the page where he'd listed names. After folding the sheet into a rectangle, he tucked it into his pocket and then replaced the cover.

Cassie's caring attitude tempted him to tell her the whole story behind his miles-long walk back to Noble Springs. He'd come close, but lost his courage at the last moment. The risk was too great. If she'd known him during his early days in Boston, she'd have crossed the street when she saw him coming. In fact, she wouldn't have walked on the same streets he frequented.

Ruggero's taunt was as much a setback as the pain in his leg. He doubted that sending Byrne a larger share of West & Riley's profits would protect him from eventual exposure.

When he heard footsteps, he turned his head toward the entrance.

"Wash?"

"Right here. You ready to leave?" He'd filled out in the weeks since he'd been hired. Now his bulk complemented his height of over six feet.

Jacob nodded. "Please help me to the buggy." Gritting his teeth, he tried to suppress a groan when Wash hoisted him from the chair.

"Did you tell her how bad you're hurtin'?"

"I said I was staying home to rest my leg."

"She cares about you. Maybe she'll bake you another pie." Wash chuckled as he handed him the crutches. "I brought the buggy around front so's you don't have far to walk."

"Thank you." With the other man's help, he crossed to the boardwalk and stopped at the passenger side of the buggy. Wash held him steady while he negotiated the step.

Jacob fell back against the seat. "Again, thank you."

"That was a sorry trick those two pulled. If I hadn't been late leaving last night, I'd never have seen you."

He managed a mirthless laugh. "You'd have seen me sooner or later. I'd have slept on the floor of the grocery rather than walk another step. The bottoms of my feet are bruised from the rocks, not to mention the pounding my leg suffered."

Wash untied the reins, then guided the buggy west on High Street. Noontime sun glared down on their heads. After a moment or two of silence he said, "You're not goin' to let this go, are you?"

"No, I'm not." He turned his head away, staring at the roadway as the buggy rolled out of town. His mind buzzed with the implications of Lenny Ruggero calling him by his former name. He and Byrne had not merely disrupted his time with Cassie, they threatened him with exposure.

The day would come—soon—when he'd have to take action.

After West & Riley's closed the following Saturday evening, Cassie sat in Jacob's office entering the day's receipts into the ledger. Another good week. Jacob would be pleased when he returned on Monday.

"Missy?"

She swung around and smiled at Wash. "Thank you for waiting with me. I'll be finished soon."

"No hurry. Someone's at the back door asking for you. I didn't let him in."

"Who is it?"

"Never saw him before."

Her mind raced as she tried to think of who might seek

her out. As far as she knew, Wash had never met Curt Saxon, Faith's husband. If something happened to Faith, he'd be the only person she knew who'd expect to find her at the business after closing time.

She snapped the ledger shut and rose. "Only one way to find out."

"The boss said to watch out for you." Wash stepped closer. "I'll stay right nearby."

"That's a comfort. Thank you."

When they entered the kitchen, she hesitated a moment and then strode to the screen door.

Light from the room shone on the visitor's blond hair. Cassie stepped backward, her hand at her throat. "Mr. Fitzhugh."

He gave her an easy smile. "I went to your cabin first, then figured you might still be here. I told you I'd be back to court you properly."

"And I told you I wasn't interested."

"Your mother sent you a gift." He held out a small parcel. "May I at least deliver it to your hands?"

From behind her, Wash made a noise like a growl. Judging by the expression on Mr. Fitzhugh's face, she could imagine how imposing he looked. She pushed the door open partway and took the package.

"Please give Mother my thanks."

He stepped into the opening, but remained in the alley, keeping part of his attention on Wash.

"She enclosed a message. I realize it's late. Since no doubt you'll be at church tomorrow, I'll wait until then for your reply."

Cassie huffed out a breath. The man was as persistent as a swarm of ticks. "Fine. You can take my response back with you when you leave."

He flashed the same easy smile. "Until tomorrow, then."

She closed the screen with more force than necessary, then slammed the inner door shut and sank onto a chair.

"Should I have said you wasn't here?" Wash leaned against the closed door.

"No. I wouldn't want you to lie." She clutched her mother's gift, wondering what had possessed her to use Mr. Fitzhugh as a courier. Upon further thought, she was sure she knew the answer.

❧

Cassie sat at the table in her cabin and untied the ribbon binding the paper-wrapped parcel, exposing two folded pillowslips. She smoothed her finger over the soft linen and then unfolded them. Each one displayed the initial C surrounded by flowers, done in her mother's exquisite embroidery.

Her heart warmed at the memory of sitting in their parlor at home watching her mother work colored floss into beautiful designs. Most of her handiwork had been lost during and after the war years. Cassie pressed a pillowslip against her chest, grateful that Mother was making an effort to return to former pastimes.

An envelope remained in the package. Since her mother sent Mr. Fitzhugh to deliver the message, and he was expected to carry a reply back to Calusa, things apparently weren't going as well as she hoped. She tensed as she removed the letter.

9th July, 1868

My dearest daughter,
I hope this gift pleases you. I thought of your long-lost trousseau with every stitch, and pray you'll set these pillowslips aside for a new beginning. Mr. Fitzhugh was

most anxious to deliver them when I told him what I was working on. He is such a dear young man.

She blinked. Trousseau? And Mother told Mr. Fitzhugh to deliver the package? She felt the jaws of a trap closing around her. Gripping the paper so hard it wrinkled, she read the remainder of the letter.

What with the way that Mr. West keeps you busy with your job, you may have forgotten that my birthday is coming up on the 15th of this month. My friends here (few they may be) are planning a small celebration for me. Of all the gifts I could receive, a visit from you would be the finest. Thus the reason for asking Mr. Fitzhugh to deliver this message, rather than trusting to the post. I pray you'll make every effort to be with me on my special day.

I anxiously await his return with your reply.

Your loving Mother

Cassie dropped the letter on the table and paced the room. She *had* forgotten her mother's birthday. Today was the eleventh. For her to travel to Calusa, she'd have to depart in four more days. Even if she only spent one night with Mother, that would leave Jacob with no one to bake pies while she was gone.

She ran her fingers along the sides of her head, dislodging her braids. She hadn't seen Jacob since he'd asked her to take care of the accounts. Mr. Fitzhugh expected a response tomorrow, and Jacob wouldn't return to work until Monday.

Stumbling past the wrapping paper and pillowslips strewn on the tabletop, she fell to her knees beside her bed. *Lord,*

Ann Shorey

*help me. I want to please you. I want to please Jacob. I want
to please Mother. I ask you to show me what you want.*

✦

On Sunday morning, Cassie walked to church along the
alley rather than the boardwalk, hoping to avoid Mr. Fitzhugh
until she was safely seated next to her friends. She'd talk to
him afterward. She skirted around the cemetery at the rear
of the churchyard and slipped inside just as the bells ceased
pealing.

When Rosemary saw her, she scooted closer to Elijah to
make room on the pew. Cassie settled into the space with a
grateful smile.

"You're late today," Rosemary whispered.

"I had trouble sleeping last night, so naturally I overslept
this morning."

She darted a glance around the sanctuary and spotted Mr.
Fitzhugh sitting near the front. He turned and nodded in her
direction as if he sensed her gaze. She quickly tipped her head
so her bonnet would hide the flush that warmed her face.

After going through the motions of standing and singing, she listened to more about Deuteronomy from Reverend
French. She didn't know whether to feel relieved or sorry
when he didn't return to the passage about a brother marrying a widow. She hadn't paid attention the first time and
wished she knew the reverend's opinion of Mr. Fitzhugh's
interpretation.

More than that, she wished she possessed the courage to
talk to the reverend about her concerns. But as a newcomer
to his congregation, she didn't believe he'd want to spend
time explaining something to her that she felt sure everyone
else already knew. She sighed and scooted down in the pew.

179

As the sermon continued, part of her mind circled the dilemma of her mother's birthday. She'd had no lightning bolt of insight during the night. By the time the service dismissed, she still had no idea what message she'd send back to her mother.

When she moved down the aisle, Mr. Fitzhugh elbowed in next to her. "You read your mother's letter?"

She nodded.

"And your response?"

Taking a deep breath, she blurted, "Tell her I'll be there on her birthday." Her heart hammered. Now she'd have to tell Jacob what she'd done.

Mr. Fitzhugh gave her a benevolent smile. "I'm glad. Your presence will make her happy. The poor woman misses you." He tucked his hand under her arm as they descended the steps. "I'm just sorry you'll have to make the trip unescorted."

"I did it before and no harm came to me." She twitched her arm free of his touch.

He put out his hand and stopped her before she could reach the boardwalk. "I know we got off to a poor start last month, and I apologize. Can you overlook my rash comments and allow me to be your friend?"

Put that way, how could she refuse? His expression reminded her of Garrett at his most appealing. Besides, his presence in Calusa helped her mother adjust to life without her. She extended her gloved hand. "Very well, Mr. Fitzhugh. We will be friends."

❧

That afternoon, with Mr. Fitzhugh on his way to Calusa carrying the message to her mother, Cassie's conscience pricked her. She'd spoken too soon. She should have asked Jacob before committing two days out of the middle of the workweek. If they were to be together in the business, as well as in their personal lives, she couldn't go dashing off on a whim.

She'd have to call on him at his home.

Today.

After church, she'd slipped on a comfortable old cotton skirt and bodice, and hung her green taffeta dress up for next Sunday. Now, with a resigned sigh, she went to the bedroom and removed the dress from a hook. Then she paused. Because he missed their Independence Day engagement, Jacob hadn't seen her in the rose chintz. He wouldn't be pleased when he heard her request, so she ought to look her best when she called on him.

Smiling to herself, she fastened matching rose-colored buttons on the fitted bodice, then smoothed the skirt over her cage crinoline. Her cheeks glowed pink when she checked her reflection in the mirror. Although the visit today was a necessary one, she had to admit she had more than the bakery on her mind. She missed Jacob.

Since suppertime was near, she prayed Wash would be at the restaurant collecting Jacob's evening meal. She'd ask him to take her. If he'd already left . . .

She'd cross that bridge when she came to it.

Once outside her door, afternoon humidity smothered the air in her lungs. Leaves on the oak tree next to her cabin drooped in the heat. Thankful she didn't have far to walk, she unfurled her parasol and reached the entrance to the alley in fewer than five minutes.

Jacob's buggy wasn't there. Hoping Wash hadn't already come and gone, she hurried to the screen door. Jenny would know.

When the door squeaked open, Cassie and the kitchen's occupants stared at each other in mutual surprise.

"Wash? Becca? Where's Jenny?"

Wash jumped to his feet with such haste his chair tipped over. "In the next room. Is there somethin' you need? Want me to fetch her?"

"No, thank you. You're the person I came to see."

Becca grabbed a rag and headed for the basin, where dishes waited on the slanted drain board. "I was just resting my feet a minute, missy."

Clearly, she'd interrupted the two of them in a private moment. She hid a pleased smile at the realization that Wash and Becca had feelings for one another. After all they'd endured in their lives, they deserved happiness.

"Please don't apologize. No reason you shouldn't rest if you're tired."

Becca plunged her hands into the soapy water, but not before Cassie caught the relieved glance she sent in Wash's direction.

He bent and stood the fallen chair back on its legs. "What can I do for you, missy?"

"I hoped you could take me to Mr. West, but I don't see the buggy."

"Be happy to take you out there. The buggy's down at the livery. Needed a wheel repaired." He rested his hand on the screen door. "Should be done by now. I'll go fetch it."

"Thank you." When he left, she gazed across the room for a moment, an idea forming in her mind. Then she walked over to where Becca stood at the basin.

"How about resting your feet again? I'd like to ask you something."

25

Cassie's heart rapped a couple of extra beats when she spotted Jacob sitting in the shade of his veranda. He looked even more handsome than she remembered. By the time Wash assisted her from the buggy and she reached the porch, Jacob had risen from his wicker chair.

His crutches made a hollow sound on the floorboards as he met her at the top of the steps. "Cassie." His smile lifted his lips, his moustache, and rose to the corners of his eyes. "How good of you to visit. This has been a lonely week." He rested his fingers on her cheek. "You look pretty in that pink dress."

"I hoped you'd like it." Oh dear. She should have said something less flirtatious, like "This old thing?" Too late now.

"I mean, thank you." Her face flushed. "I'm happy to see you too."

"Come, let's sit in the shade while you tell me the reason for your visit." He stepped back and allowed her to precede him to one of the two chairs on either side of a square table. A pitcher rested on a tray in the center, with a half-filled glass of lemonade at one side. Jacob moved forward to peer through the lattice. "Wash, would you please bring a glass for Miss Haddon?" He leaned his crutches against the wall and eased himself into his chair.

"Right away." Wash looped the horse's reins through a hitching post and sprinted into the house.

Cassie wished she didn't have to spoil their time together by discussing her mother's request. To postpone the moment, she glanced between Jacob and his crutches. "Has your leg recovered?"

"I think resting has undone most of the damage. I'll be back at work in the morning. Did you have any trouble with the receipts?"

"None." She related the amount of the past week's business and how well Timothy had handled the grocery on his own.

"Sounds to me like you're the one who responded well to a challenge." He reached across the table and patted her forearm. "We make a good team."

Butterflies danced in her stomach at the meaning behind his words. She placed her hand over his. "I think so too."

"'Scuse me." Wash broke the spell by moving between them, lifting the pitcher, and filling a glass for her.

She leaned back in her chair. There would never be a good time to broach the real reason for her visit, so she plunged ahead as soon as Wash left.

"I had a visitor last evening while I was finishing the accounts."

He jerked upright. "Who was it? Were you there alone? I told Wash to stay with you."

"He was there. You'll be happy to know he didn't let the man into the building." When Jacob relaxed, she knotted her fingers together in her lap and continued. "Mr. Fitzhugh brought me a message from my mother."

"The postal service in Calusa broke down?" He arched an eyebrow at her.

"Believe me, I was not glad to see him. However, Mother's message concerns both of us. She reminded me her birthday is this Wednesday and asked that I come to see her. She sent Mr. Fitzhugh rather than trust the post due to the shortness of the time."

"So you'd like to go, I suppose."

She dropped her gaze. "I already told him I'd be there," she whispered. When Jacob didn't respond to her confession, Cassie peeked at him.

His lips were stretched into a thin line. "I don't know what to say to you. Your mother calls, off you run. Are you planning to be gone all week?"

"Just Wednesday and Thursday. I'm so sorry! I know I should have asked you first. I responded to Mother's request without thinking."

"In your haste, you apparently forgot about the bakery. How will we fill orders with you gone? Now that you've seen the ledger pages, you know what a large part those profits play in our success."

She took a quick breath. He had said *our* success. Swallowing, she forced herself to return to the subject at hand.

"I did not forget about the bakery. Before coming out here, I asked Becca if she would make the pies while I was gone."

"Becca? She's a kitchen maid."

"She's been helping me on busy days. I've watched her handle the crust—I think she'd do well."

"The pies won't be the same. No one makes piecrust as flaky as yours."

She wondered if he knew how much his praise meant to her. "You're very kind, but I'll only be gone two days. That's not terribly long."

He leaned his elbow on the arm of his chair and rested his

chin in his hand. A half smile tipped the corner of his mouth. "All right. For two days."

"Thank you." Her mind jumped back to his previous statement. "A few moments ago, you said *our* success. Did you mean that the way it sounded?" She slapped her fingers to her lips. She had to learn to stop saying the first thing that popped into her mind. Her question was beyond forward.

He nodded. "I did. I've thought about you all week." He shifted to look directly into her eyes. "Would you allow me to court you—officially?"

"Oh, Jacob, yes!"

"You're sure?"

"Absolutely." She reached across the table and took his hand. "I was afraid you'd be angry about my visit to Calusa."

"I am. But that doesn't change how I feel about you." He squeezed her fingers, then released them. "You have a responsibility to the bakery now. You can't continue leaving on a whim. A birthday's not that important."

Her mind reeled at the swift change from business to courtship, then back to business again. She frowned at him. "Birthdays are important to Mother. Wouldn't you leave if your mother needed you?"

"She died when I was thirteen. I don't think she ever needed me—I was nothing but a burden."

"What . . . what about your father?"

His face hardened. "I never knew him."

Kindly Jacob West, growing up on his own. She'd assumed his parents taught him his caring ways toward others. Questions perched at the tip of her tongue, but from the set of his jaw she knew they'd have to wait. She lifted her glass and took a sip to moisten her dry lips.

"I had no idea." Her voice shook. "I apologize for bringing up a painful subject."

"You need to know if I'm to court you. I'm not a fine gentleman like Mr. Fitzhugh."

"I like you just as you are."

He grabbed his crutches and raised himself out of the chair, moving so he could stand beside her. He laid his hand on her shoulder. "I feel the same way about you."

Her heart soared. As soon as Mother's birthday celebration ended, she'd come straight back. She didn't want to be away from Jacob one minute longer than necessary.

On Wednesday, Cassie stared out the window of the nearly empty passenger car as the train approached the Calusa station. The platform appeared deserted. Surely Mr. Fitzhugh had given Mother her message. At the very least, she'd expected her to be waiting.

Cassie blew out an exasperated breath. Now she'd have to traipse across the street to the café to learn which of the houses belonged to Uncle Rand. Gus, the heavyset man who operated the restaurant, had said something about her uncle living in the fourth house from the west end. Or was it the second house?

After gathering her carpetbag, she accepted the conductor's assistance and descended the steps into the muggy afternoon. As soon as she stood on the platform, the train rolled forward and began its turnaround in the wye junction. Steam shot from beneath the wheels. The bell clanged.

Cassie waited a moment, hoping the sounds would bring someone to meet her. Men on horseback passed by on the wide street. A black-and-white spotted dog lay panting in the shade under the boardwalk. A puff of wind stirred the dust, then subsided.

She lifted her skirt above the toes of her boots and marched across to the restaurant. When she pushed open the door, Gus lumbered out of the kitchen, a cigar stub protruding from one corner of his mouth.

"Supper's not ready. Come back in an hour." The cigar bobbed between his lips when he spoke.

She dropped her carpetbag at her feet. "I'm not here for a meal. I'm hoping you can tell me where Rand Carter lives. I'm Mrs. Bingham's daughter—Rand Carter's niece. I was here with my mother last month."

"Thought you looked familiar." He scratched his belly. "Likely you can find your ma at Miz Gilforth's. Pretty sure she ain't at Rand's."

Cassie swallowed impatience. She suspected he was one of those people who slowed down in proportion to how hard she pushed. Keeping her voice sweet, she asked, "Then will you please direct me to Mrs. Gilforth's home?"

"Reckon I can. Across the next street over you'll come to the schoolhouse. Then go some more. When you see a two-story place that could use a good coat of paint, you found it. Sign out front says Gilforth's Board and Room."

"Why would my mother be in a boardinghouse?"

Using his lips, he maneuvered the cigar from one side of his mouth to the other. "Best ask your ma."

"I intend to. Thank you for your time." She grasped the handle of the carpetbag and stepped back into the merciless sunshine. Across to the schoolhouse and go some more. What kind of directions were those? "Some more" could be twenty feet, or twenty miles.

Wishing she'd remembered to bring her parasol, she walked until she saw the school, then paused and looked up and down the street. Perspiration trickled from under her bonnet. Several houses to the west, she noticed a two-story building, the only one within view.

Her boot heels tapped on the boardwalk as she covered the distance from the school to the house. Gray showed through faded white paint on the clapboard siding, and a sign by the front door stated GILFORTH'S BOARD AND ROOM.

Still wondering what reason her mother had to be in a rooming house, Cassie climbed the four steps to the covered porch and rapped on the knocker. After a few seconds, she heard footsteps, then the door opened.

A woman with hair redder than Mother's stood in the entrance. Her cheeks were bright with rouge, and her ears glittered with ruby-colored earbobs. "If you're looking for a room, honey, I'm filled up right now."

Cassie tried not to stare. "The man at the restaurant told me I'd find my mother here. Her name's Eliza Bingham."

"Well, sure enough she's here. You must be Cassie. I'm Claramae Gilforth." She pulled a man's gold watch from her pocket and clicked open the lid. "My land, we forgot the time. Your ma and I planned to meet you, but we got busy with laundry in the kitchen." She stepped aside. "Come on in."

As soon as Cassie entered, Mrs. Gilforth hurried toward the rear of the house. "I'll fetch your ma," she called over her shoulder.

Faded wallpaper did little to brighten the dim entryway. Cassie set her carpetbag next to a coat rack, then perched on a bench to await her mother. In her most far-fetched imaginings, she wouldn't have pictured Mother in such a setting. Why she wasn't in Uncle Rand's house was one mystery—why she was here helping with laundry was another.

26

assie blinked and took a second look as her mother dashed toward her across the entryway. With her sleeves rolled to the elbows and a voluminous apron wrapped around her middle, Mother resembled Jenny Fielder—except for the hennaed hair.

"My sweet girl! I'm so sorry I didn't meet your train." She held out her arms.

Cassie stepped into her embrace, nestling close. She hadn't realized how much she'd missed her mother's presence until this moment. "Mrs. Gilforth said you were busy in the kitchen. Whatever were you doing there?"

Mother's face flushed. She tugged at her sleeves, then buttoned them at the wrist. "Just lending a hand. Claramae's been kind enough to cook a small supper for my birthday tonight."

"But why are you here? Why aren't you at home with Uncle Rand?"

"I wrote you that Reverend Greeley suggested I befriend Claramae. You might say this has become my second home. You'll share my room tonight." She fumbled with the ties on her apron, avoiding Cassie's eyes. "Rand's gone most of the time. He's in Price City right now."

Cassie struggled to absorb the information. Mother didn't have the funds to stay in a boardinghouse. That's why she'd gone to such lengths to live with Uncle Rand.

Then an unwelcome thought pressed into Cassie's mind—was she expected to settle a bill with Mrs. Gilforth? She had last week's salary in her handbag, but with her own rent coming due, she couldn't risk spending her money on Mother's boardinghouse fees.

"I . . . I hate to ask, but is Uncle Rand paying for your stay here?"

Mother patted Cassie's cheek. "We'll talk about this after the party." She headed toward a steep flight of stairs. "Come, let's get you freshened up before supper. You'll be glad to know Mr. Fitzhugh will be attending."

Cassie swallowed a groan. An entire evening spent in his company would make her anything but glad. She prayed there'd be enough guests to form a barrier between the two of them.

"My dear Miss Haddon. You've scarcely touched this wonderful meal. If my mother were the cook, she'd forbid you any dessert." Mr. Fitzhugh faced her across the table, where he sat beside Reverend Greeley. He regarded her with a smug expression. "I'm sure Mrs. Gilforth has something delectable waiting."

Ignoring Mr. Fitzhugh's comments, she turned to the landlady, who sat at the foot of the table. "I do apologize for my lack of appetite. This has been a tiring day."

Much to her disappointment, her prayers for a large gathering hadn't been answered. Mr. Fitzhugh and Reverend Greeley were the sole guests. Mr. Fitzhugh talked throughout the meal, while the reverend maintained a watchful silence. She squirmed under his constant scrutiny.

Mrs. Gilforth's earbobs sparkled in the light from the overhead lamp. "Don't you worry, honey. You're not going to miss dessert on your mama's birthday. I baked a special rose geranium cake."

"I recall you were especially fond of rose geranium." Mother reached for Cassie's hand. "You used to ask for this cake on every birthday."

"I remember. Thank you."

Cassie sensed unease beneath her mother's cheerful façade. She prayed Uncle Rand would return soon. Surely he hadn't left her here to fend for herself.

Once Mrs. Gilforth served the dessert, Cassie avoided the watchful stares from across the table by keeping her gaze fixed on her plate while she savored each fluffy bite of pink icing and delicate white cake. As Mother remembered, it *was* her favorite. But the minute she lifted her head, Mr. Fitzhugh leaned toward her.

"There's still enough daylight left for a stroll. I'd like to show you the schoolhouse."

"I really should help Mrs. Gilforth with the washing up."

"Nonsense, honey. You young folks go on and enjoy yourselves." The landlady beamed at them as though they were well-loved children.

"You two need to get better acquainted." Reverend Greeley leaned back in his chair, arms folded over his chest. "There are too many miles between you."

Her heart thrummed. She'd hoped Mr. Fitzhugh's offer of friendship meant he'd dismissed the idea that, as Garrett's brother, he was obligated to marry her. Apparently Reverend Greeley had other thoughts. She glanced at her mother and caught her exchanging a pleased smile with him. No help there.

She squared her shoulders. A few minutes this evening wouldn't hurt anything. After all, tomorrow afternoon she'd return to Noble Springs. If Mr. Fitzhugh raised the subject of marriage while they were alone tonight, she'd have the perfect opportunity to remind him she had no intention of becoming his wife.

"All right. For a short while."

He hurried to her side. "Thank you. I hoped you'd agree."

After they excused themselves, he hustled her out the door and onto the boardwalk. Fireflies circled under a scrubby oak tree next to the rooming house. Crickets chirped. If the temperature were a bit cooler, an evening walk would be tolerable. Cassie fanned herself with her hand.

He turned his back on the fiery sunset and grasped her elbow. "The school's this way. I thought you might be interested to see where I spend my days when classes are in session."

The man was harder to discourage than a muddy dog. She tightened her jaw. "Really, Mr. Fitzhugh, I have no interest in knowing where you spend your days."

His head jerked up. "Miss Haddon, are you quite yourself?"

"Please forgive me for being blunt. I came here to be with my mother on her birthday, and that's the only reason. From what she's written, you and the reverend have been faithful visitors since she arrived. I do appreciate that, but come fall I expect you'll be too busy."

He squeezed her elbow. "I'll never be too busy for your mother. The poor woman is lonely here without you. Especially now, since her brother has left."

"Left? You mean permanently?" She swung around to face him. "I had the impression he was only away for a day or so."

"Perhaps I've spoken out of turn." His face flushed. "I'm sure your mother will explain."

"She hasn't said a word. Why didn't you tell me this when you were in Noble Springs last week?" She pivoted forward and strode toward the schoolhouse, her heels rapping on the boardwalk. Crickets ceased their song when she marched by.

He hurried to catch up with her. "I thought you knew."

"Apparently I'm the only one who's ignorant of my mother's circumstances." She bit off the words. To spend the day traveling, then to learn from Mr. Fitzhugh, of all people, that her mother was alone in Calusa . . .

She leaned against the schoolhouse gate. "I feel quite weary all of a sudden. Would you please escort me back to Mrs. Gilforth's?"

⁂

Cassie planted herself in front of the window in her mother's small bedroom, hands on her hips. "Why didn't you tell me Uncle Rand left? I'd have come to get you."

Mother sank onto the single chair next to the door. "To live in that little cabin while you slave away for Mr. West? It pains me to see you living such a dismal life."

"I manage my own bake shop in the kitchen. Customers request my pies."

"You were raised to be a lady, not a cook."

Cassie took several deep breaths to push the hurt away. "I hoped you'd be proud of me." Her voice wavered.

"I'll be proud the day you make a good match. Reverend Greeley believes Patrick Fitzhugh—"

"No more about Mr. Fitzhugh, please. Just tell me what *you* plan for yourself. If you don't want to return to Noble Springs, what will you do?"

A calculating expression crossed her mother's face. "Rand said he'd make room for me in Price City if I could find a way to get there. He's opening a travelers' hotel. When the rail line is complete, he'll be ready."

Shoulders sagging, Cassie realized she'd been manipulated. "Why didn't he take you along when he left?"

"He traveled in a wagon with a work crew. Hardly the situation for a lady."

"So you want me to arrange for the stage to take you to Price City."

"And travel with me. You know I don't feel safe traveling alone."

The lamp on the bureau burned low, sending a coil of oily smoke into the stuffy room. Cassie stared out at the few lights that burned in windows across the street. She'd promised Jacob she'd return on tomorrow's train. If she traveled with Mother to Price City, she'd likely be gone for several more days.

Becca hadn't been hired as a baker. If her pies didn't meet customer's standards, then there'd be no customers by the time Cassie returned. She leaned her forehead against the window. Disappoint Jacob? Disappoint their customers? Or disappoint her mother? She turned away from the glass.

"All right. I'll take you to Price City."

27

The next morning, Cassie entered a shack next to the railroad platform and waited for the telegrapher to acknowledge her presence. After several seconds of rapid clicking on the key, he leaned back in his chair. "You want something?"

"I'd like to send a telegraph to Noble Springs, please."

"Well, you come to the right place." Chuckling at his own humor, he raked his fingers through his sand-colored hair. "First of all, who're you sending it to?"

"Jacob West, at West & Riley's Grocery." She winced at the thought of Jacob's reaction to her telegram. If Uncle Rand had stayed put, in a few hours she'd have been headed home on the train, not on her way farther west in a stagecoach.

He scribbled Jacob's name on a piece of paper. "Message?"

"Taking Mother to Price City. Home as soon as possible. Sign it 'Cassie.'"

"Why not say, 'home soonest'? Save you three words."

"Fine. Whatever you think best."

After copying her message onto the paper, he held out his creased palm. "That'll be eighty cents. I'll send this right away."

Eighty cents. And she had yet to buy tickets for tomorrow's trip on the thrice-weekly coach. She took a deep breath and dug in her handbag for the coins.

❧

On Friday, Cassie and her mother stood near the entrance to the restaurant while the stage driver hefted Mother's trunk to the top of the coach.

"You ladies traveling alone?" he asked, with a leer in Cassie's direction.

She lifted her chin. "Yes, we—" She wheeled around at the thudding of footsteps on the boardwalk.

Mr. Fitzhugh pounded up to the driver. "D'you have room for another passenger?"

"Could be." The man directed a stream of tobacco juice at the ground. "Where you headed?"

"Price City. I'll be escorting these ladies."

Cassie jammed her hands on her hips. "Mr. Fitzhugh. We didn't ask for your company."

"Please, call me Patrick. Reverend Greeley suggested I come along." He removed his hat with a flourish and bowed. The sun glistened on his oiled blond hair. "That way you won't be alone when you return."

Mother fluttered to his side. "You're the most thoughtful young man. We'll appreciate an escort. Don't you agree, Cassie?"

"Since Mr. Fitzhugh is willing to make the trip, why don't you have him accompany you so I can return to Noble Springs?"

"And miss an opportunity to spend time together? If we have an escort, we can enjoy the scenery and not worry about our safety." Mother directed her gaze toward the driver to underscore her meaning.

Cassie glanced at him. His grubby black hat cast shadows over his unshaven face. Perhaps an escort would be a good idea, but why didn't Reverend Greeley accompany them himself?

She knew the answer.

The prospect of spending seven or more hours in Mr. Fitzhugh's company—she would *not* call him Patrick—stretched ahead like a bad dream. She felt herself slipping back into the old Cassie—the girl who agreed with everyone and had no opinions of her own.

Then she thought about her job in the restaurant. With the Lord's help, she'd accomplished much since arriving in Noble Springs. He'd see her through this next challenge as well.

She turned to Mr. Fitzhugh. "If you insist, we will accept an escort for propriety's sake. Mother and I will wait inside the coach while you pay your fare." Turning her back, she held out her hand to the driver. "Would you please assist us?"

<hr />

Cassie sat next to her mother as the stagecoach rattled over uneven ground. Patrick Fitzhugh rode on the seat facing them. At first, he'd attempted conversation, but after a half hour or so of bouncing and swaying in the stifling coach, he subsided.

To avoid his gaze, she stared out the window opening at the flat land rolling past with monotonous sameness. When she thought she couldn't stand another mile of jostling, the stage jangled and creaked to a stop in the midst of a forlorn group of houses.

Beyond the main road, laborers pounded spikes through rails into crossties. The clang of their sledges played a rhythmic chorus across the settlement. Other workers hunched over shovels as they dug holes to erect telegraph poles. Soon, trains would travel this far west and eliminate the need for uncomfortable stagecoaches.

The driver swung open the door. "This here's Delion Junction. Got to change horses." He pointed to a frame house with a corral at one side. "You go on in. They'll feed you before we go on to Price City."

Cassie peered at the humble building, wondering whether she felt hungry enough to risk whatever the owner might serve.

The driver worked a wad of tobacco from his cheek to the front of his mouth and spat on the ground beside the coach. He held out his hand to her. "Step lively. This ain't supposed to take all day."

She grasped his rough palm and fitted her foot to the tiny rung below the door. After her feet touched the ground, he repeated the action with her mother, then stepped back and waited for Mr. Fitzhugh to descend.

"You take the ladies inside and get 'em settled at the table. We'll stop for about twenty minutes." He climbed up on the driver's bench and guided the horses toward the corral.

Cassie brushed at the grit on her soiled taffeta skirt. If she'd known this journey was in the offing, she'd have brought a more practical garment. Her faded work dress would have been perfect.

Mother huffed while she arranged her fringed shawl over her brown poplin dress. "I can see why trains are taking over this country. I'd forgotten how dreadful coach travel is."

"It's miserable indeed." Mr. Fitzhugh held out his arm to her mother, and she grasped his elbow. He looked down at Cassie as the three of them moved toward the doorway.

"I'll have a word with the cook to be sure you get the best of whatever they're serving." He beamed as though he were escorting them into Auguste Reynard's French restaurant in St. Louis.

She glanced around as she stepped into the dingy room. A bare wooden table, set with tin plates and utensils, waited a few feet from a black iron range. Flies bumped against the glass of a single window at the left of the door. When the sour smell of boiled cabbage and bacon fat assailed her nostrils, her stomach rebelled.

"A slice or two of bread will be plenty, thank you."

Her mother stood beside the table and waited while Mr. Fitzhugh seated her. Once settled, she smiled up at him. "I'm quite hungry. If you will, I'll take a large portion."

Cassie flushed. A lady never admitted she was hungry. Mother seemed to have forgotten her manners—normally she went out of her way to remind people of her well-to-do background.

Stamping hooves and jingling harnesses warned them of the coach's return. A shadow blocked the light when the driver stopped the stage in front of the building. While Mother and Mr. Fitzhugh gulped down their cabbage soup, Cassie finished one slice of the coarse brown bread she'd been served and wrapped the second piece in her handkerchief to save for later. No telling how long they'd be traveling before they reached Price City.

Late afternoon sun brushed long shadows over a collection of tents scattered in a low spot next to a thin trickle of a river. Wagonloads of what appeared to be railroad crossties sat parked some distance away. Beside the wagons, men swung pickaxes into the ground while teams of horses followed, pulling scrapers to smooth a roadbed.

The stagecoach rumbled to a stop in front of an unpainted two-story building, one of the few wooden structures that met Cassie's eye.

She stared out at her bleak surroundings. "Where are we?"

Mr. Fitzhugh straightened the lapels of his dust-covered jacket. "I have no idea, but I'll certainly find out for you." He flung open the door of the coach and called up to the driver, "Why are we stopping here?"

The stage bounced, and in a moment the driver faced them, thumbs tucked in his belt. "You bought tickets to Price City. This here's it."

Cassie leaned forward. "Impossible. This isn't a city. It's not even a village."

"Once the railroad's done, the place will grow. They always do." The driver waved toward the building beside him. "Soon as you ladies get down, I'll take your trunk into the hotel there."

Mr. Fitzhugh jumped out of the coach. "Let me assist you, Miss Haddon."

Suddenly grateful for his presence, she offered her hand and allowed him to help her to the ground. Mr. Fitzhugh would look after them until they learned where they could spend the night. That rickety-looking frame structure couldn't possibly be her uncle's hotel.

First thing in the morning she and Mother would take the stage back to Calusa. Then she remembered—no weekend travel on this route. The stage ran Monday, Wednesday, and Friday to the west. But only Tuesday and Thursday to the east. She felt like collapsing in the dusty road and crying.

There wasn't a telegraph pole to be seen in the scalped landscape. She was stranded here until next week with no way to get word to Jacob.

Cassie surveyed what passed for a lobby when Mr. Fitzhugh led them inside the two-story building. Three straight-backed wooden chairs sat around a square table in one corner of the small space. Keys dangled from a rack on a wall behind a narrow counter. Without rugs to deaden the sound, their footsteps echoed on the rough pine floorboards.

She darted an angry glance at her mother. "Are you sure this is a hotel? There's no one here. Doesn't Uncle Rand know you're coming?"

Mother lifted her hands in a defenseless gesture. "How was I to tell him? I didn't know myself until you agreed."

Cassie tilted her head back and closed her eyes. Would she never learn?

In seconds, she sensed Mr. Fitzhugh at her side.

"This day has been a trial for all of us. If you ladies will wait over there, I'll find the proprietor and secure a room for you." He strode off down a dim hallway.

Cassie perched on the edge of a chair and rubbed at a headache throbbing in her right temple.

Mother slumped beside her. "I had no idea Price City looked like this. Rand described everything as though he'd invested in a prosperous community and this hotel was a booming business." She laid her hand against Cassie's cheek. "I'm sorry, dear."

Cassie took her mother's hand and kissed her fingers. "I know you didn't do this deliberately. We'll just make the best of things for the next few days until the stage comes back through."

Mother straightened. "If Rand is here—"

"Do I hear my name taken in vain?" Uncle Rand burst into the room, his untucked shirt billowing behind him.

His bushy red beard made him look like a hennaed bear. He strode over to them.

"By gar, Lizzie, you got here. You're one persistent gal." His stained teeth showed when he grinned at Cassie. "Been hoping your ma would come and help me run this place. Glad to have the two of you. Heard they're finishing the track twenty miles east—trains will be here in another month. And where the train goes, telegraph follows." He rubbed his hands together. "Things are bound to pick up soon."

Cassie put her hand to her throat. "I'm not planning to stay."

"Sure you are. Families help one another. You want to be useful, don't you?"

She stared up at her gruff uncle, the name she'd been called in St. Louis ringing in her ears.

Useless.

Mentally, she groped for a response, but the words wouldn't come.

Cassie startled awake. The door to the room she and her mother shared rattled in response to pounding on the flimsy boards.

"You gals going to sleep all day? Thought you was going to help with breakfast."

Mother sat up in bed. "We'll be down in a shake, Rand."

He grunted and stomped away.

Cassie gazed out the window at the gray pre-dawn. "What are you saying? Doesn't he already have a cook?" she whispered.

"He does, but the man is unreliable."

Cassie pushed herself up on her elbow. "I didn't promise I'd help with breakfast or anything else."

"I might have said something after you went to bed."

"You didn't! What happened to your claim that you reared me to be a lady, not a cook?"

Mother ignored her question and swung her feet to the floor. "Hurry. Foremen for the work crews will be here soon."

"You know even less about feeding workmen than I do. Besides, I have nothing suitable to wear. I intended to leave for Noble Springs two days ago, so all I brought with me was a change of undergarments."

"You can wear this." Mother rummaged in her trunk and drew out a faded yellow calico skirt and bodice. "With an apron on no one will be able to see that it's a little large for you."

Groaning, Cassie threw off the bedcovers and stood. "How can you offer to work in a kitchen? Do you even know one end of a skillet from another?"

"You can teach me."

"I bake pies—I don't cook breakfasts."

Mother tightened her jaw. "I'm going to overlook your sass. My brother is expecting help, and we need to do what we can."

Cassie wondered what had become of the weepy woman who drooped and complained at every mishap. More and more, her mother reminded her of Jenny Fielder.

Floorboards creaked as she stalked across the room. She slipped on the yellow calico garments, rolled the waist over to tighten the fit, then braided her hair and pinned the braids at the back of her head. If her uncle expected her to be useful, she'd show him what useful looked like.

"I'm ready. Where's the kitchen?"

Cassie followed her mother into a kitchen half the size of the one in Jacob's restaurant. The sweetish-sour smell of spoiled food greeted them when they entered. With its small range, one worktable, and narrow shelves near an interior door, the room would have been better suited to a private home rather than a hotel. A pang of loneliness for West & Riley's clean and orderly restaurant caught her by surprise.

She'd never dreamed a kitchen could feel like home, but Jacob's did.

A grizzled man stepped through an open door leading to the rear of the hotel. He kept one hand on the small of his back as he hobbled toward them.

"Rand said you two was going to take my job away."

"Not at all," Cassie said. "I'm only here for—"

"My brother informed me you needed help." Mother bit off the words in a no-nonsense tone of voice.

Cassie blinked at the steel of authority beneath her mother's words. She sounded like her old self, ordering their servants around in the days before the war.

"Don't need no help. Been cooking here since I got down in the back. Had to quit the railroad. You git me fired, I got no place to go."

"We're not here to get you fired, are we?" Cassie sent her mother a pointed glance. Then she looked at the floor, littered with crumbs and food scraps. "I'll sweep while you get the fire started. Tell us what you're cooking this morning so we can work together."

He clumped to the stove and threw kindling into the firebox. "Gonna make biscuits and ham gravy. You want to sweep, fine. Then go on with you."

"That's it? What about eggs?"

His face reddened beneath his patchy whiskers. "See? That's why you got no bidness in here. You don't know nothing about railroad camps. Won't have no eggs 'til the next supply wagon comes through."

Cassie grabbed a broom from a corner. "Then as soon as I've finished the floor, I'll start on the biscuits. How many men usually come for breakfast?"

"Eight or ten. The crew bosses. Rest of 'em eat in the camp. But I already told you—"

"We'll work together, Mr. . . ?"

She remembered how uncertain she'd felt about keeping her job when Jacob first hired her. Uncle Rand's cook had more to lose than she'd had. At least she was young and healthy.

"Just call me Fred." He shook his head, glancing between Cassie and her mother. "The flour's in a bin under the table. Make plenty."

She hid a triumphant smile and worked the broom across to where her mother stood in the doorway. "I've helped make biscuits for Jenny, the cook at West & Riley's. I'll show you what she taught me. By the time I leave on Tuesday, you'll be an expert."

Mother lowered her voice to a sibilant whisper. "You expect me to work with this old man? Rand wants both of us here."

"He doesn't need both of us." She patted her mother's arm. "Don't worry. Uncle Rand's hotel is a long way from being crowded. By the time the rail line is finished, you'll know all there is to know about this kitchen."

"You've changed. Mr. West has been a bad influence on you."

Cassie let the comment bounce off without responding. If Jacob's influence helped her to stand up for herself, so much the better. She crossed to the shelves and selected the largest bowl she saw, then took down several baking pans.

"Let's get started on the biscuits. By the time the stove heats we should have them ready for the oven."

"Humph." Mother stuck her nose in the air and stalked to the worktable. With her head tipped to one side, she watched while Cassie used two knives to cut lard into the flour mixture. After a minute, she cleared her throat. "Aren't you forgetting something?"

"What?"

"Milk." Mother took a step toward Fred and tapped him on the shoulder. "Where do you keep the milk?"

He snorted. "See them tins on the shelf? That there's our cow."

"In that case, we'll need some water too. Where can I find that?"

"Pitcher's right there." He waved his hand in the general direction of a washstand outside the open back door. "Refill it from the pump after you're done."

Cassie hid a grin when her mother gave him a withering glance before seizing the pitcher in one hand and a tin of milk in the other. She slammed the two containers on the worktable next to the bowl. "Odious man! I don't see how you can be so pleasant to him."

Grumbling to herself, Mother took a spoon and formed a well in the center of the flour mixture. After opening the tin, she poured condensed milk and water together into the bowl.

Dumbfounded, Cassie watched while her mother stirred the mixture to perfect consistency, scattered flour on the tabletop, and scraped the biscuit dough out of the bowl into the mound of flour.

"Where did you learn to do that?"

Mother's face reddened. She backed away from the table. "Just makes sense is all. Now, show me how you knead the dough and cut biscuits."

As Cassie kneaded, she stole glances across the table. Her mother appeared to be paying close attention, but questions rose in Cassie's mind. Mother had avoided anything resembling kitchen work for as long as she could remember. Perhaps instead of taking all their meals at Calusa's restaurant, she'd been forced to cook for Uncle Rand from time to time. Cassie hid a smile at the rumpus that must have caused.

When the time came to serve the breakfast, Cassie and her mother filled bowls with biscuits. After Fred poured the ham gravy into tureens, he grabbed a bowl of biscuits and headed for the door to the dining room.

Mother lifted her hand to stop him. "Rand wants my daughter to serve the tables. The men are more likely to return if someone young and pretty brings them their breakfast."

"Fine by me." He plunked the bowl back on the worktable. "I'm ready to set a spell, anyways."

Cassie recalled her first day at Jacob's restaurant. He'd sent her to the kitchen and asked Jenny to serve the tables. At the time, she believed his actions were the result of her inexperience, but later she recognized he was being protective. She closed her eyes and wished she were back in Noble Springs at this very minute instead of trapped under her uncle's roof.

She gaped at her mother. "I said I'd work in the kitchen, not act as a lure for Uncle Rand's customers. How could you agree to such a thing?"

"It's important that we help my brother succeed." Mother pushed a tureen into Cassie's hands. "Put the food on the tables and stay out of reach. You'll be fine."

When she entered the dining room, her cheeks burned at the appreciative murmur rising from the men seated at the tables. Before she could take a second step, someone tapped her on the shoulder. She jumped and spun around, almost dropping the gravy-filled tureen.

"Mr. Fitzhugh! You startled me."

He leaned forward and spoke close to her ear. "I didn't mean to eavesdrop, but I heard your mother. If she insists that you do the serving, I'll stay at your side. This is no task for a lady."

Cassie felt she'd melt with gratitude. "Thank you. I accept your offer."

"You bringing the food or ain't you?" one of the men called.

"Right away." She walked to the first table, Mr. Fitzhugh at her side.

The man glanced between them, then looked down at his plate. "Thanks," he mumbled when she placed the tureen in front of him.

"You're welcome." Mr. Fitzhugh spoke before she could respond. "We'll have the biscuits out in a minute."

Mr. Fitzhugh's voice wasn't as resonant as Jacob's, but at this moment his words sounded like music.

When they returned to the kitchen, her mother stalked over to them. "What are you doing?" She glared at Mr. Fitzhugh. "She doesn't need help serving just two tables."

"With respect, Mrs. Bingham, she does. There are no lawmen in a railroad camp, and some of these men may have unsavory backgrounds. It's best if they know your daughter's protected." The look he gave her cut off any room for argument.

Cassie lifted two bowls of biscuits from the worktable and handed one to him. "Customers are waiting, Patrick."

On Monday evening, Cassie sat on the back porch of the hotel with her mother and Uncle Rand. Smoke from railroad workers' campfires scented the air. Tents dotted the land to the north, some glowing with lantern light while others faded into the dusk.

Uncle Rand's chair creaked when he leaned over to look at Cassie. "They'll be bringing rails up any day now. Once they're in, trains will be right behind. You're making a big mistake by leaving."

"Noble Springs is my home. I'm happy there." *Especially since that's where Jacob lives.*

"You could be happy here. Food's improved with you in the kitchen, and once that dandy's gone, you'll really bring in the customers."

Cassie thought he winked at her, but in the dim light she couldn't be sure. She hated to think an unkind thought, but she'd never understand how this oaf could be her mother's brother. She pushed to her feet.

"Please excuse me. It's time I packed my things. What time do you expect the stage in the morning?"

He stared out at the horizon, as though the answer were

211

written on the looming thunderclouds. "Usually around nine. Sure you won't stay at least a few more days?"

"You don't need me. Soon Mother will be as much a help as I am. She's catching on in the kitchen very quickly."

"Lizzie? Catching on? Why, she—"

The crash of breaking glass interrupted him.

"Oh my heavens! I dropped my tea. I'll get the broom." Mother jumped out of her chair and dashed for the kitchen.

Cassie hurried after her. "Let me help."

"Nonsense. You go ahead with your packing. I'll have this cleaned up in a jiffy."

Shaking her head, Cassie wondered again at the change in her mother. Three days in the hotel kitchen seemed to have transformed her into a new person—one she didn't recognize.

Patrick joined her as she passed through the sparsely furnished lobby on the way to her room. His bright smile gleamed in the lamplight. "Would you like to join me on a farewell stroll along the street?"

She hugged her arms to her waist. Much as she'd appreciated his protection, he mustn't get the wrong impression about their circumstances.

"No, thank you. I'm rather tired this evening."

"Quite understandable, after the long days in your uncle's kitchen." He touched his finger to his forehead in a mock salute. "I'll see you when the stage arrives."

"Yes." Seven hours to Calusa, then the train to Noble Springs and Jacob. She sped down the hall to her room. One more day.

<hr/>

Pounding on the bedroom door roused Cassie the next morning. Mother had already left for the kitchen. Why was Uncle Rand knocking? He knew she was leaving today.

"Cassie! Hurry! You'll miss the stage." Patrick's voice cut through her drowsiness.

She swung her feet to the floor and grabbed her wrapper. After opening the door a cautious crack, she peered into the hall. Patrick faced her, a valise at his feet.

Clutching the wrapper close at her throat, she asked, "What do you mean, 'miss the stage'? It's way too early."

"It's after seven. He's right on time."

Cassie jolted wide awake. "Uncle Rand lied to me! He said the coach came through at nine." Her pounding heart threatened to choke her. "Please . . ." She drew a ragged breath. "Please ask the driver to wait five minutes. I'll be there."

"I'll do my best. He's already been waiting. I told him you'd be along any minute. Your mother and uncle are out front with him."

She frowned at the mention of her lying uncle. If Patrick hadn't knocked, she'd have been stranded for another two days.

"Tell the driver I'm hurrying." She banged the door shut and threw off her night things, jamming them into the carpetbag. Thankful that she'd sponged her taffeta dress clean the night before, she laced her stays, stepped into her crinolines, and dropped the dress over her head. With no time to comb out her hair, she gathered her nighttime braid and looped it in a circle at the base of her neck. Quick pins held the hasty coiffure in place. Her bonnet completed the preparations.

Clutching her bag, she threw open the door and dashed the length of the hall, praying the stagecoach still waited out front.

When she pushed through the entrance, she bumped into a young man who looked as though he'd ridden into Price City behind a herd of cows.

"Whoa there!" He tipped his hat and sent her a flirtatious

grin. "I'm not used to waiting while ladies primp, but I'd say you're worth it."

She glanced between him and the stage. "You're the driver? What happened to the man who brought us here from Calusa?"

"He up and quit. Said he's going to St. Louis to find something better to do than eat dust all day." He held out his hand for her bag. "Soon as you're inside, we'll go."

"One more minute, please." She stalked over to her uncle. "You said the stage didn't leave until nine. If you think stranding me here is going to make me want to work for you, you're quite mistaken." Her voice shook.

Uncle Rand glowered down at her. "Fine thing, when a man's own family can't be bothered to lift a finger to help him."

Her mother stepped between them. "Now, Cassie. Don't be upset with Rand. You know how much he wants you to stay—and so do I." She tugged a handkerchief from her sleeve and dabbed at her eyes. "You're going to be so far away. My only comfort is knowing you'll have Patrick to look after you."

Cassie stiffened. "We'll be together until we reach Calusa. That's all."

"Of course." Mother kissed her cheek, then turned to smile at Patrick, who stood next to the coach step. "Give Reverend Greeley my best."

"Indeed I will." He beckoned to Cassie. "Come. It's time to get inside."

She tightened her lips at his peremptory tone. One reminder of Reverend Greeley and helpful Patrick became haughty Mr. Fitzhugh.

Last evening's clouds hung like gray laundry over the landscape. As she walked toward the stagecoach, she prayed rain wouldn't delay their journey. If she figured correctly, they'd reach Calusa in time for her to board the train to Noble Springs.

Tomorrow morning she'd see Jacob.

When Patrick helped her through the door of the coach, her heart sank at the sight of an overweight couple occupying the forward-facing bench. She'd hoped she and Patrick would be the only passengers, so she could have one of the seats to herself.

The plump man's bulbous nose shone red, as though polished. The woman, whom Cassie assumed was his wife, held a large basket on her lap. The contents were covered with a blue-striped cloth, but from the aroma that filled the small coach, Cassie believed they carried enough food to last the journey and beyond.

She settled on the empty bench, scooting as far as she could to one side when Patrick took the space next to her. She folded her arms across her middle and sighed. This was going to be a long trip.

The coach bounced as the driver climbed up to his perch. With a snap of a whip and a holler at the team, they lurched into motion. Once underway, Cassie offered a polite smile to the woman sitting across from her. "Are you traveling far?"

"Far enough. Too far, some might say." She rested a hard look on her husband.

"Now, Emma—" A cough interrupted his statement. He coughed again, then pulled a dingy handkerchief from his coat pocket and honked a mighty blow into its soiled depths.

Cassie recoiled, praying the man wasn't consumptive. She placed her gloved hand over her mouth and nose.

"You don't want to make Otis talk," Emma said. "He coughs." She leaned her head against the back of the seat and closed her eyes.

"I'll remember that." Cassie glanced to her left and caught Patrick's sympathetic gaze.

He reached inside his jacket and removed a pristine white handkerchief. "Perhaps you'd like to borrow this." He pitched his voice low.

"Thank you." She took the offering, noting the initials *PF* embroidered in scrolling letters on one corner. "This looks like my mother's handiwork."

"Indeed it is. The dear lady has been gracious enough to monogram several of these for me."

Cassie almost groaned. Her mother was drawing Patrick into their lives with every stitch. She turned her head and stared out the window. Somehow there had to be a way to mend the gap between Mother and Jacob. But with Mother now living in Price City, the gap had grown wider.

The coach swayed and rattled along the road, the journey punctuated by bouts of Otis's coughing. Halfway to Calusa, Cassie's fears about the weather were realized when the sky split open and the temperature plummeted. Canvas coverings over the windows did little to protect them from blowing rain.

She scooted toward the center of the bench seat in an effort to stay dry, wishing she'd brought more than a shawl as a wrap.

Patrick slipped out of his frock coat and held out the garment. "You're cold. Cover yourself with this."

"No, thank you. Then you'll be cold."

"I insist." He moved until their thighs touched. Leaning forward, close enough for her to smell the spicy pomade on his hair, he draped his coat over her shoulders.

In spite of the warmth of the garment, she froze under his contact, conscious of his nearness within the close confines of the coach.

A wounded look crossed his face. He moved back, resting his hands on his knees. "You needn't fear me. I want to protect you, not harm you."

"I don't fear you, but I don't like you hovering over me."

"You didn't object when I helped you in your uncle's dining room."

"Patrick, I—"

She noticed Otis watching them with ill-concealed interest and swallowed the remainder of her sentence.

"Perhaps we can finish our discussion later." She shifted her position to peer out at the downpour through a gap in the canvas.

Patrick blew out an exasperated breath. "As you wish," he muttered.

Otis bent forward, wracked by a spasm of coughing. His wife roused and handed him a flask from the basket on her lap. "Here, this will help."

He took a swig, then coughed again.

Cassie clutched Patrick's handkerchief to her nose to smother the odor of spirits that blew in her direction. The promise of Jacob waiting in Noble Springs glimmered like a beacon on a distant horizon. Would this journey never end?

❧

Cassie rose as soon as the stage driver opened the door in front of Calusa's only restaurant. They'd left the rain squall behind at some point, and the boardwalk and streets appeared as dry and dusty as they'd been when she left.

She nodded a courteous farewell to their traveling companions, grateful to be free of Otis's hacking cough, then turned to Patrick.

"Please, help me down. I need to learn whether the train has left yet."

Patrick held out his hand to assist her. "Allow me to inquire for you. I'll only be a moment. You wait here."

"No thank you. I can manage a simple question by myself. I believe the driver is waiting for you to collect your valise." Clutching her carpetbag, she strode across the street and entered the telegrapher's shack.

"Excuse me, sir."

The telegrapher raised his eyebrows when he recognized her. "You was here last Thursday. You needing to send another message?"

For a moment, she debated. Assuming she hadn't missed the train, she could send a telegram informing Jacob she was on her way home, or she could simply surprise him by arriving at work in the morning. She smiled to herself. She'd surprise him.

She met the man's inquiring gaze. "No, I don't believe so—that is, if the train east hasn't already left."

"Nope, it hasn't." He snapped open a pocket watch. "You got another few minutes or so—she's running slow today. Lots of freight to unload."

"Thank you so much. That's what I was hoping to hear."

"You care about freight?"

"No, I care about going home." She whisked out of the building and stood near the edge of the platform, watching a plume of smoke on the horizon grow larger as the train approached.

Patrick jogged across the dusty boards and faced her when the engine roared into the station. Panting, he dropped his bag at his feet. "I'll accompany you to Noble Springs to be sure you're safe."

"No, thank you. I don't require an escort."

His face reddened. "Hang it, Cassie! This is no life for you—or your mother. It's not fitting for ladies to travel from pillar to post alone. And what are you going back to? A job as common kitchen help." He placed his hand on her shoulder. "I can make you quite comfortable. I trust your experience in Price City and the journey you just endured have helped you see the folly of ignoring Scripture."

"Please desist, Mr. Fitzhugh. I'm not ignoring Scripture when I look after my mother. What we do is not for you to decide."

"Ah, you must be tired." He gentled his voice. "I'll give you time to go home and rest. We can make plans during our next visit."

She stamped her foot. "There will be no more visits. How can I make you understand? I don't wish to see you again."

Lips pinched in a firm line, she marched to the train and entered the passenger car. She'd done it! The old Cassie would never have had the courage to send Patrick away permanently, but then the old Cassie would never have made other decisions on her own, either.

She liked the new Cassie better.

30

Jacob lifted the telegram from the table beside his armchair and read it again.

```
TAKING MOTHER TO PRICE CITY STOP  HOME
SOONEST STOP  CASSIE
```

How soon was "soonest"? She'd left last Wednesday, the telegram arrived Thursday, and now another Wednesday morning blossomed on the horizon. The sky shone silvery with the first light of dawn.

After blowing out the lamp, he wrapped his fingers around the crook of his cane and paced to the stable. Might as well go to work. At least there he'd have some company.

Attending church Sunday morning had helped for a short time, but seeing Cassie's friends chatting on the lawn after services sent a sharp pang through his chest. Had she attended church with her mother in Price City? What if she decided not to come back?

As he rode Jackson toward the sunrise, he tried to focus his thoughts on the coming week's business. He didn't know how much longer customers would accept Becca's pies. Good as they were, they weren't Cassie's. A dip in income would reduce the amount he sent to Keegan Byrne, a thought which filled him with dread.

In Reverend French's sermon on Sunday, he'd quoted a passage about casting all care on the Lord, but Jacob knew such a solution couldn't apply to a man like him. He'd brought his troubles on himself. He'd have to find his own way out.

He rode past the livery stable, the town square, and the butcher shop, then turned in to the alley behind West & Riley's. Golden fingers of dawn traced a path toward the water trough where he tied Jackson. Wash would tend to the saddle and blanket later.

After removing his cane from a scabbard behind the saddle, Jacob limped toward the kitchen door.

"Jacob? Jacob!"

He spun toward the sound of the voice. Cassie ran to him, her skirts flying, and threw her arms around his middle.

"I hoped to get here before you did, so I could surprise you."

"This is even better." He bent his head and kissed her waiting lips, then rested his cheek on top of her soft hair. She fit in his arms as though they'd been sculpted together. "I was afraid you weren't coming back." His voice sounded gruff to his ears. He cleared his throat. "I missed you, more than I thought possible."

She took a step away and held his gaze with her emerald eyes. "Knowing you'd be waiting was the one bright spot in my days. Price City was . . . well, to begin with, it wasn't a city. It's a railroad construction camp in the middle of nowhere. My mother's brother is there managing a stage stop—he calls it a hotel—for the Union Pacific."

He studied her animated face while she went on to explain her delay. To his ears, the circumstances pointed to her mother manipulating her once again. Cassie's innocence was one of the qualities he loved about her, but how she could continue to respond every time her mother beckoned was a mystery. When she described her uncle's plan to use her as an attraction in his hotel's dining room, he'd heard enough.

He bent down and kissed her lips to stop the flow of words. "You can tell me the rest later, when we're truly alone. Mrs. Fielder and Becca are probably inside, praying for your return."

She grinned at him. "They can't be praying any harder than I did. This has been one of the longest weeks I can remember." She threw her arms around him and hugged him again before opening the door.

As he expected, the two women in the kitchen greeted Cassie with broad smiles.

Becca rested her hands on the floury worktable. "Praise God. No more pie baking. Sure am glad to see you."

Mrs. Fielder dashed to her side. "You're back! We thought you'd be gone only a couple of days."

"I'll tell you both everything that happened while we work. We don't want the boss angry with us for wasting time." She turned her head and sent Jacob a barely perceptible wink.

The warmth that filled him raced all the way to his toes. His Cassie was home.

❦

Jacob stood behind the counter in the grocery, listening to the clink of utensils on plates and the low murmur of men's voices coming from the dining room. Three of Cassie's pies sat atop a display case waiting to be claimed. He took a deep breath and inhaled the sweet fragrance of warm blackberries rising through the perfectly browned crust. From the sounds reaching his ears, his patrons were enjoying their dessert, as well.

He gave a contented sigh and was about to return to his office when a paunchy man with an unshaven face approached from the dining area.

"I don't have one of them meal tickets, so guess I need to pay you for my supper."

"You can buy a ticket if you'll be here for a few days. Save you some money."

"Nope. Leaving on the morning train for St. Louis." He dug in his pocket. "How much?"

"Thirty cents." He picked up a pencil and noted the amount on a sheet of paper.

After the man laid the coins on the counter, he tipped his head toward the open kitchen door. "That little red-headed gal in there—saw her last week when I drove the stage to Price City. She was with a blond fella. Now she's in your kitchen." He smirked. "She gets around, don't she?"

Jacob lowered his voice to a growl. "You must be mistaken. Miss Haddon was traveling with her mother."

"There was two ladies all right, but the blond fella couldn't keep his eyes off the young one." Shrugging, he turned away. "Guess what she does on her own time is her business, ain't it?"

The pencil snapped in Jacob's grip. The "blond fella" could only be Patrick Fitzhugh. Why hadn't Cassie told him the truth?

He wished he'd brought the buggy today, so he could drive her somewhere for a private word. Since he'd arrived on horseback, the office space in the storeroom would have to do. Glancing around, he spotted his helper.

"Timothy, mind the store. I'll count the receipts later."

The boy hurried toward him. "Yes sir. Want me to lock up if you're delayed?"

"I'm not leaving. I'll be at my desk." He grabbed his cane and marched to the kitchen, ignoring the patrons still seated at the tables.

When he entered, Cassie held up a plump blackberry between her thumb and forefinger. "I don't know who supplied these, but they're beautiful, aren't they?" She gestured toward several baskets brimming with fruit. "We'll have plenty for pies tomorrow, and maybe the next day, as well."

He grunted acknowledgment. "Soon as you're finished with those, would you please come to my office?"

Her pleased expression changed to one of surprise. She dropped the berry into a basket and untied her apron. "This can wait. What's wrong?"

"We'll talk in my office."

Mrs. Fielder and Becca stared at him as Cassie walked to the doorway. From their expressions he realized his tone had been uncharacteristically harsh. Well, if they'd heard what he just heard, they'd feel harsh too. He stepped to one side to allow Cassie to precede him.

She passed him with her head held high and her cheeks redder than an unripe blackberry. He tried to tamp down his anger as they crossed the dining room and entered his office space. He knew the events of the past month had left him on edge. Maybe she'd have a good explanation. But what if she didn't? What if she confessed an interest in Mr. Fitzhugh?

He waited until she was seated, then hooked his cane on the edge of the table and faced her. With an effort of will he kept his gaze from her soft lips.

Before he could say anything, she placed her hand on his arm. "Jacob, please tell me why you're upset. Did I do something wrong with the customers' pies? Leave out the sugar?" Her voice sounded hoarse.

"The pies were perfect, as usual."

"Then, what?"

He pinned her with his sharpest gaze. "Why didn't you tell me you went to Price City with Mr. Fitzhugh? Why did I have to hear the news from a stranger who passed through here at suppertime?"

"I didn't go *with* Mr. Fitzhugh. I went with Mother, and he invited himself along to—" She paused and coughed, then cleared her throat. "To protect us on the journey. He felt the long stagecoach ride wasn't safe for unescorted ladies."

Hot jealousy burned through him. If the coach ride wasn't safe, he should have been the one to protect Cassie. "Admirable." He spun the word with sarcasm. "But why did you conceal the information?"

She sprang to her feet, hands planted on her hips. "If you recall, you stopped me right in the middle of my story this morning. You said we'd talk more later." Her lower lip trembled. "I've been counting the days until I'd see you again. But I didn't expect this! You've accused me of deception. I'd never deceive you—you should know that by now."

Tears glittered in her eyes. "If you're finished, I'd like to go home. Suddenly I feel very tired." She darted from the room without waiting for a response. In a moment, he heard the door to the grocery slam.

Jacob slumped forward in his chair and rested his head in his hands. Why had he been so hasty? He'd dug himself into a pit and now he had no idea how to climb out.

❧

Blinking back tears, Cassie left the store behind and strode to the corner of Third Street, then turned toward home. She would not cry. Not in public. She passed Mr. Slocum's white clapboard house and dashed down the gravel path to her cabin. Once inside, she leaned against the closed door and buried her face in her hands. If only Jacob had listened to the rest of her account before accusing her.

Sobs shook her body. She didn't know him as well as she thought she did. Weren't couples supposed to discuss their differences? Perhaps their courtship was a mistake. In the morning, she'd offer to release him. No, she'd write Jacob a letter explaining the entire journey and leave it on his desk. The next move would be up to him.

She sniffled. Grabbing a handkerchief from her pocket, she wiped her eyes, then dropped the linen square on the table.

Sunset's vermillion rays tinted the shelf where she kept her writing paper and ink. If she started the letter now, she wouldn't need to waste oil by lighting the lamp. With heavy steps, she carried the materials to the table and sat on one of the chairs Jacob had provided when she first rented the cabin. Closing her eyes, she leaned back, the memory of his help with furnishings a heavy weight in her chest. "Things change," her father had often said. Indeed they did.

She dipped her pen in the ink and wrote "Dear Jacob" at the top of the page. Then she crossed out "Dear" and began.

> *Here's what happened when I arrived in Calusa last week: Mother's brother was gone and she was staying in a boardinghouse. She asked me to accompany her to Price City, where Uncle Rand supposedly was managing a hotel. The stage runs to Price City three times a week, so we couldn't leave until Friday. When the coach arrived, Mr. Fitzhugh . . .*

Her throat ached from her bout of tears. She laid the pen aside and stepped outside to fill a pitcher with water from the pump in the lean-to.

Long shadows traced the yard with fingers of gloom. What a difference from today's bright morning, when she'd been eager to see Jacob. Sighing, she carried the dripping pitcher into the cabin and gulped down a cupful of cold water, then took her seat at the table and stared at the unfinished letter. Fatigue crept over her bones. She'd finish tomorrow—tonight all she wanted to do was crawl into bed and pull the blanket over her head.

31

*J*acob paced between the grocery and the kitchen. Mrs. Fielder and Becca had prepared and served the breakfast, and now Becca stood at the basin washing dishes. Cassie had not come to work.

He raked his fingers through his hair, cursing himself for his harsh words the night before. He'd planned to apologize the moment she arrived this morning, but as the hours ticked by worry overrode his remorse. The nine o'clock train going west left a half hour ago. What if his unfounded jealousy had driven her straight to Mr. Fitzhugh's arms?

When he paused in the doorway, Becca turned to him.

"Since Missy ain't here this morning, I reckon you want me to make pies today."

"Yes, please. We have two orders to fill."

He turned to leave, then stopped. Cassie lived alone. Someone could have noticed her on the street and followed her home. Strangers were always coming and going through Noble Springs. Although Jesse Slocum lived next door, he might not hear her if she cried out.

Jacob stared at the floor while possible scenes played out in his imagination. If anything happened to her, it would be his fault for sending her out in a distressed state. That being the case, he needed to be the one to make sure she was safe. Then he would apologize—immediately and profusely.

"Becca?"

"Yes, sir?"

"Leave the pies for now. I'd like you to accompany me to Miss Haddon's house."

"I don't know where she lives."

He clenched his jaw to prevent himself from snapping his response. "I do. I want to be sure nothing bad has happened to her and don't want to compromise her reputation by going there alone."

She stared at him for a moment, then untied her apron and followed him out the door.

❧

Jacob's steps crunched on the gravel walkway leading to Cassie's door. Becca stayed several paces behind until he reached the stoop and knocked. Then she caught up with him and waited to one side.

After a long moment, he knocked again. Nothing moved inside the cabin. He clenched his fists. No doubt she'd left on the train, or had seen him coming and refused to open the door. He'd stepped back onto the walkway when the door opened a crack.

Cassie peered at him with purple-shadowed eyes, clutching her wrapper at her throat.

"G-go away," she said in a raspy voice. A tremor shook her body.

His breath hitched at her ravaged appearance. "Are you injured?" He reached a hand toward her, but she backed away.

"I'm ill." Her teeth chattered. "I said . . . go away."

Becca moved in front of him. "Let me help you, missy. You needs to be in your bed."

Without waiting for permission, she stepped through the entrance and tucked her hand under Cassie's arm. Jacob followed into the combined kitchen and sitting room and waited while the two women crossed into the bedroom. A half-filled sheet of paper rested on the table beside a crumpled white handkerchief.

In the next room, Becca rolled back the covers. "You lay down and let me rub your feet. Might help you warm up some. I seen people with ague before."

"Th . . . thank you. I'm . . . so cold. Would you . . . could you get me another blanket? Mr. Slocum . . . my neighbor . . . would probably have—" Her body arched as a spasm of tremors overtook her speech.

"Just tell me where he's at."

Jacob dropped his gaze to Becca, who knelt beside the bed, chafing Cassie's bare feet. "Mr. Slocum lives in the house in front of this cabin. I'll go for a blanket."

Cassie stared at him for a moment, then turned her head away.

His harsh words last night had wounded her more deeply than he'd thought. An apology would have to wait—she needed a doctor, now. Fear rattled him. Ague was a merciless illness that struck again and again.

"As soon as I fetch the blanket, I'm going for Doc Stewart." She didn't turn her head.

Something hard inside crumbled when he spoke the doctor's name. He'd resented the man since the day he married Rosemary. Now he realized how unforgiveness had distorted his thinking.

On his way out the door, he hoped Cassie would forgive his hasty accusations faster than he'd forgiven the doctor.

When she recovered—if she recovered—he had an important question to ask her.

❧

Jacob doubled back to the alley behind the restaurant for his horse. Doc's office was too far to walk on his aching leg. He steered his thoughts away from the question of what he'd do if the doctor wasn't in his office.

After dropping his cane in the scabbard, he flung himself into the saddle and urged Jackson to a gallop over the three blocks to Commerce Street. As he passed the church, he remembered Reverend French's admonition to cast his cares on the Lord. The reverend had claimed the Lord cared for all his people.

Jacob swallowed. *Lord, I don't know how you could care for me, but I know you care for Cassie. Please help her get well.*

When he rounded the corner, his anxiety eased at the sight of the doctor's horse and buggy tied to a rail outside his office. He dismounted and fastened Jackson's reins next to the chestnut mare's. Cane in hand, he limped into the reception area, relieved to see there were no patients waiting.

Dr. Stewart met him at the entrance to the examining room. Surprise crossed his face, followed by a welcoming smile.

"Jacob. Is your leg troubling you again?"

"No. Seems to be healing fine." He sucked in a breath to steady his voice. "It's Cassie Haddon. She needs you. She didn't come to work today and when I went to see what was wrong I found her weak and shaking. Says she can't get warm." He took a step closer and gripped the doctor's arm. "You don't suppose it's ague, do you?"

"Won't know until I take a look." He raised an eyebrow. "She's not alone, is she?"

"Our kitchen maid, Becca, is with her."

"Good. Let me get my bag and I'll follow you."

Jacob settled into a chair to wait while the doctor conducted his examination. The door between the two rooms was closed. He heard Doc's deep voice and Cassie's abbreviated responses, but couldn't distinguish their words.

He dipped his head, staring unseeing at the paper before him. After a moment, his eyes focused on Cassie's handwriting.

~~Dear~~ *Jacob.*

His heart lurched at the bold line drawn through "Dear." No doubt he deserved the slash, but the heavy stroke cut like a sword. He scanned to the end where she'd stopped in the middle of a sentence. The temperature in the small room seemed to have risen several degrees as the shame of his behavior filled him.

He grabbed the crumpled cloth next to the page and mopped his forehead. *Lord, it's me again. Please help her to forgive me.* He smoothed the handkerchief. When he folded the linen into a neat square, his thumb traveled over the letters *PF* embroidered in cream-colored floss on one corner.

Alarm bells rang in his head. Patrick Fitzhugh. Whatever else her letter would have said, she had his handkerchief.

Jacob stared at the ceiling. If he couldn't mend the rift between them, he'd be responsible for sending Cassie straight to Fitzhugh's arms. He couldn't allow that to happen. The sight of her lying sick and helpless roused feelings he hadn't known he possessed.

Cassie was meant to be his wife. But before he dared ask, he had to eliminate the problem that had arisen in Boston. Then his position in Noble Springs, and with Cassie, would be safe.

The bedroom door opened and Dr. Stewart joined him.

Heartened at the smile on the doctor's face, he stood, one hand braced on the back of the chair. "Will she be all right?"

"Give her a few days and she'll be fine. She's got a case of the grippe." He plopped his medical bag on top of the folded handkerchief. "I'll bring Rosemary by this evening with some of her special chicken soup with peppers, along with an infusion of boneset. Guaranteed to help."

Jacob grinned to himself at Dr. Stewart's reference to an herbal remedy, recalling Rosemary's accounts of the many disagreements she and the doctor had over such treatments when they first met.

Apparently Jacob didn't hide his grin with much success, for the burly physician winked at him. "She's made me a believer." He lifted his bag and strode toward the entrance. "See you this evening."

He responded with a noncommittal nod. Cassie had made her feelings clear. She didn't want him there.

⌁

As daylight dimmed outside her window, Cassie pushed back a layer of blankets. "Becca, please help me get up. I want to be presentable when Rosemary arrives."

"Doctor said you was to rest. Miz Stewart knows you're sick. No need for you to be out from under them covers."

Gooseflesh prickled over her when she uncovered her shoulders and arms. "Just for a minute? The chills are better. If you'll please bring me my brush and comb from the bureau, I'll tidy my hair. Then I promise I'll cover up again."

Becca raised a skeptical eyebrow, but handed her the items

she'd asked for. While Cassie brushed out her tangles, Becca crossed to the next room and gazed out the window.

"Here comes Miz Stewart. My land, she's carrying a big basket. Must have a lot of chicken soup in there."

Cassie gathered her hair into three sections and plaited the strands in haste. After dropping the comb and brush onto the table next to her bed, she propped pillows behind her and pulled the blankets up to her chin. She'd have no trouble obeying Elijah's orders to rest if a little thing like brushing her hair left her struggling to breathe.

Becca swung open the front door. "Come in, ma'am. Missy's been waiting for you." She took the basket from Rosemary's hands and deposited it on the table while Rosemary hastened to Cassie's bedside.

The sight of her friend brought tears to Cassie's eyes. She'd tried all day to wall off thoughts of Jacob, but Rosemary's sympathetic gaze sent a crack through her defenses.

"I'm so glad you're here. This has been a horrible day."

"Of course it has. The grippe can be miserable."

"More than that. Jacob—" She remembered Becca's presence, and bit off the rest of her sentence. To change the subject, she leaned forward and peeked at the basket on the table. "Do I smell chicken soup?"

"I'll bring you a bowlful right now." Rosemary bustled into the next room and lifted a towel-wrapped crock from the basket.

While she spooned a portion into a bowl, Becca came to the doorway. "Mr. West said I should stay with you today, but now that Miz Stewart's here, do you think I could go? If I get back to the kitchen before Wash leaves, he'll fetch me home."

"Of course you may leave." She groped for her handkerchief and blew her nose. "Thank you for looking after me."

"You sure now?"

The expression on Becca's face spoke more clearly than words. She was smitten with Wash.

"I'm sure." Cassie tried to draw a deep breath, but coughed instead.

"Thank you, missy." Becca whisked out the door.

Rosemary dragged a chair next to the bed and then carried in a bowl of soup and a spoon, which she placed next to a candleholder on the small table.

Cassie pushed her feet toward the edge of the bed.

With gentle pressure, Rosemary pressed them back under the blankets. "Tomorrow you may feel well enough to get up and eat. Tonight stay right where you are."

Too tired to argue, she flopped back against the pillows and accepted the bowl and spoon.

Between swallows of the spicy mixture, she told Rosemary about her trip to Price City and Jacob's reaction to his customer's insinuations.

"He accused me of deliberately deceiving him. That's the same thing as calling me a liar, isn't it?" She handed the empty bowl to Rosemary. "Before I left he asked to court me, but now I'm not sure he's someone I should consider marrying."

Rosemary set the bowl on the table. "Jacob's a lonely man. He desperately needs the softening influence of a lady in his life. From what I've seen of the two of you at church, you're that lady."

"But he seemed so angry. He's the one who stopped me yesterday morning when I started to tell him about the trip—then he got upset because he didn't hear the whole story." Her throat tickled and she turned her head away to cough.

"He came here today to look for you when you didn't come to work, didn't he? Then he went for Elijah when he saw how sick you are."

"He probably missed his precious pies."

Rosemary laid her hand over Cassie's. "You don't believe that."

"No. I don't." Tears pooled in her eyes. "I'm sure I love him, but when he acts the way he did, I don't believe he loves me. With Garrett, everything unfolded as though it was meant to be. Mother was happy. Garrett was happy. I was . . . content." She paused to draw a shallow breath. "But with Jacob, Mother doesn't like him and I don't understand him. How can he be happy to see me in the morning and accuse me of deception that same afternoon?"

"Maybe he has reasons to fear being deceived. When you're well, perhaps you can ask him."

"Do you think he'd tell me?"

"If he loves you, he will."

After Rosemary left, Cassie burrowed under the blankets as though she could hide from thoughts of Jacob. Her entire body ached—her heart most of all.

She wished she hadn't told him to go away.

❧

The following Thursday, Cassie took extra pains with her hair and dress before leaving for work. A week at home, coupled with Rosemary's soups and tinctures, had vanquished the grippe's worst symptoms. Despite an occasional cough, she felt eager to return to the restaurant—and Jacob.

She tucked the letter she'd written into her handbag. Somehow she'd find a way to leave it on his office table when he was busy elsewhere. By this time, surely he'd gotten over his anger and would be willing to listen to reason.

Excitement fluttered in her stomach when she pictured his response. His rumbly voice would express his regret at hurting her feelings and he'd take her in his arms and . . .

She gave herself a little shake. First things first. Put the letter on his desk.

The July morning promised a hot, humid day. By the time she reached the kitchen, perspiration dotted her forehead. Pausing outside the screen door, she took a deep breath, savoring the fragrance of coffee boiling on the stove. Then she stepped into the kitchen and took several quick steps with her arms outstretched toward Jenny and Becca.

"I've missed you both." She glanced at the worktable where the pie plates were stacked in their usual place. "I've even missed baking pies in this heat."

"Sure glad you're back, missy." A smile wreathed Becca's face. "I'd rather chop potatoes any day than fuss with them pies."

Jenny drew Cassie close with a one-armed hug. "I'd rather have Becca chop potatoes too. Cooking three meals a day is getting to be too much for me. 'Course, I agree it's mighty good to have you back. We all missed you."

"Mr. West, too?" She hated herself for asking, but he hadn't come to see her one time since the day she took sick. Her imagination had traveled down many lonely roads wondering why he hadn't visited.

"Him, too, I'm sure."

"Is he here yet?" If he wasn't, she'd go lay the letter in the middle of his table where he'd be sure to see it first thing.

Jenny and Becca exchanged surprised glances. Jenny spoke first.

"He's been gone since last Friday. Didn't say where he was off to, just that he'd be away for a couple of weeks. Thought maybe he told you."

"No, he didn't." Cassie frowned as she tried to comprehend his absence. Did he leave because of her? She leaned against her worktable. "But . . . what about orders for pies? And who's taking care of his ledger?"

"Timothy takes the orders and brings them to us each morning. Reckon he'll be here in a few minutes."

"The ledger? Surely he wouldn't expect Timothy to handle that too."

Jenny grinned at her. "Nope. That's your job. Mr. West said you'd know where to find everything."

Cassie blew out a relieved breath. So Jacob still trusted her with the accounting. She hoped that meant he still thought of them as partners—in the business at least. She'd have to wait to learn whether he wanted her as his partner in life.

32

*J*acob stepped off the train into the humidity of a Boston summer. His gray suit was rumpled from long days riding one train after another to reach his destination. The first thing he'd do after collecting his valise would be to locate a tailor's shop and hope for ready-made trousers and a jacket that fit. He wanted to look his best before making any calls on former associates.

Since leaving Boston eight years ago, he hadn't returned and had no desire to do so. Until Byrne and Ruggero paid him a visit. Then everything changed. He had to protect his future in Noble Springs by neutralizing the threat the two thugs represented, regardless of the cost.

He gazed around the tile-floored station until he spotted a baggage claim sign toward the street exit. Joining a line of fellow passengers, he shifted from one foot to the other, the pistol in his boot bumping against his ankle. Once he retrieved his valise, he straightened his shoulders and strode through the double glass-paned doors out to the city of his birth.

Horses and buggies moved both ways along the cobbled street. Pedestrians crowded along the walks, everyone going someplace as fast as they could travel. The noise of hoofbeats and shouted conversations sounded much louder than he'd remembered. Too much time spent in the quiet of West & Riley's, he thought with a wry grin.

Once he'd been part of the bustle, welcomed the noise as a distraction that prevented his activities from being overheard. No more. Not for seventeen years. Long enough that he'd grown complacent.

A cab driver hollered at him from the curb. "I can take you wherever you're going, mister."

Jacob lifted his chin. He'd stay in the fine hotel that had been constructed while he worked for Colin Riley in the North End. "The Parker House, please. It's on School Str—"

"You don't have to tell me where the Parker House is. Everyone in Boston knows that hotel. You must be from out of town."

He smiled inwardly while he handed the driver his bag. Apparently his time in Missouri had been sufficient to soften his accent. "Yep, I'm visiting for a week or so."

The carriage jolted over the uneven pavement as the driver guided his team away from the train station and into the flow of traffic. Jacob rested against the seat back and surveyed his surroundings. Boston looked just as he remembered, a teeming city filled with bitter memories.

He wondered what Cassie would make of his hometown. She'd lived in St. Louis, but Boston's energy far exceeded that of Missouri's largest city.

Cassie. Loneliness stabbed at him. If not for her, perhaps he wouldn't have decided to take the steps he had planned. He thought he could stand up under Byrne's threats, but he couldn't risk dragging a lady like Cassie into his troubles. One whiff of scandal and that mother of hers would snatch her away like a mama bear protecting a cub.

"Here you be. Parker House." The driver jumped down and handed Jacob his valise.

After he paid the man, Jacob took a moment to admire the multi-storied hotel that dominated the area. "Jake Westermann, staying at the Parker House," he whispered to himself, then shook his head in disbelief and entered the plush lobby.

When he reached the registration desk, the clerk gazed down his nose at Jacob's wrinkled suit. "What can I do for you?" His voice held disdain.

Aware that his mother's Italian heritage showed in his skin's dark tone and his wavy black hair, Jacob met the man's eyes without flinching. "A room for the week, please." He reached in his pocket and splashed a handful of gold coins on the marble counter. "I'll be paying in advance."

The clerk snapped to attention. "Yes, sir." He pushed a register toward Jacob. "Please sign here. I'll have the bellboy show you to your room."

"Thank you." After pocketing his change, he leaned on the counter. "Can you tell me where I can find a tailoring establishment nearby?"

"Yes, sir. Indeed I can. Markham's is but a block away. He's quite popular with our local politicians."

Jacob thanked him again, then leaned on his cane as he followed the bellboy up two flights of stairs to his room. His thrifty nature chided him for the amount of money he was spending. Maybe the hotel laundress could brush and press the clothes he wore. And yet . . . if he wanted to be seen as successful, he needed to look the part.

When they reached the third floor, the lad flung open a door and placed the valise on a bench at the foot of the brocade-covered bed. A carved mahogany bureau and matching chair occupied the facing wall. The window was draped in the same moss-green brocade as the spread on the bed.

"There's fresh water in the pitcher," the boy said, pointing to a washstand stacked with thick white towels. "You need anything else, just ask for Rob."

"I'll do that." Jacob handed him a tip, then turned the key in the lock after Rob left.

He settled in the chair and admired his surroundings. A far cry from his boyhood home in the tenements of the North End. His errands would take him there soon enough, but for now he'd enjoy the quiet serenity of this room.

Two days later, Jacob hailed a cab and asked to be driven to the Charles Street Jail. The driver studied Jacob's fawn-colored trousers and black frock coat with raised eyebrows.

"Going to visit a prisoner? Better watch yourself, dressed like that."

"Thanks for the warning. I'll be careful."

The carriage wound around Beacon Hill and rolled toward the Charles River. Within minutes a walled-off granite building came into view. As memories swamped him, Jacob fought a desire to flee. Coming here had been a poor idea. He could do what had to be done without calling on Warden Dwight.

"Driver, I changed my mind. Please take me back to the hotel."

The carriage stopped in front of a high iron gate topped by a stone arch. "You're here now. I'll wait if you want." He rested a sympathetic gaze on Jacob. "Got a brother in there myself. Know how hard it is to go in. Them prisoners are a sorry lot."

"All right. If you'll wait."

A voice in his head screamed "hypocrite." In his new clothes, he looked like the respectable citizen he'd become.

He wondered how the driver would treat him if he knew why Jacob wanted to visit the jail. The man probably would have refused the fare.

Gripping his cane, he paced to the entrance. A uniformed guard stepped out of a shelter when he approached. "You a lawyer here to see a prisoner?"

"N . . . no." He cleared his throat. "Is Warden Dwight here today? He's the person I'm looking for."

"He retired a couple years back. Want to talk to the new man?"

"No thanks." Relieved, Jacob turned toward the waiting carriage.

"Don't be in such a hurry. Warden Dwight comes in on Tuesdays for a checker game with one of the guards. You're in luck." The guard drew a ring of keys from a peg inside the shelter and opened the gate.

The creaking hinges sounded like the opening of a cell door. Jacob shuddered.

Inside the compound, a stone path led to another guard shack outside the main prison doors. As he walked, he tried to remember what he planned to ask the warden. His thoughts were clearer at the hotel. Now he couldn't think over the pounding in his ears.

The second guard left him standing in the octagonal rotunda while he sent a clerk to find Warden Dwight. Light from the high atrium flooded the area but couldn't conquer a prevailing smell of damp stone and iron bars.

As he waited, a jailer led a group of men from one wing toward a flight of stairs leading to the basement. The men wore black-striped prison uniforms and walked with their heads down, each person with his hand on the shoulder of the man in front. Jacob backed away until he stood pressed against a wall. His heart thudded.

"Westermann?"

Jacob startled and fought the impulse to duck his head to avoid notice.

Warden Dwight approached with his hand extended. The buttons on his vest strained over his belly. "Most of you fellows don't come back—at least not voluntarily." He chuckled and pumped Jacob's hand. "Last time we shook, you were leaving."

"Never figured to return, but you and this place have been on my mind lately."

"That so? Well, what can I do for you?" He put his hand on Jacob's shoulder and guided him toward a bench.

"I have a question." One question, but the answer would affect his decisions from this moment on.

"What do you want to know?"

"Do you—that is, does the jail—let anyone see your records?"

"Records of what?" The warden frowned. "Our expenses? Prisoner totals?"

"Prisoner names and offenses." Jacob blurted the words, then braced himself for the response.

"Ah. Those records." He shook his head. "You can rest easy. Our goal is rehabilitation. You stay out of trouble, no one will ever know you were here."

Jacob realized he'd been holding his breath and released a long sigh before standing. "Good to know. Thank you."

⁂

Jacob left his room the next morning, rested and ready for the next phase of his plan. Vehicles jammed the street in front of the hotel. Delivery wagons, carriages, and horse-drawn carts jostled their way back and forth on the wide road. The sound of hoofbeats echoed between the buildings.

Jacob scanned the line of cabs and drivers waiting at the curb, hoping to see the man who'd taken him on yesterday's mission. After a moment, he spotted him at the far end of the conveyances.

The driver noticed him at the same time and hopped down from his perch. "I remember you. Where to this morning?"

"The North End. Riley's Grocery."

"You sure you got the right address? Not the best part of the city for a gent like yourself."

"I've been there before. I'm not worried." He dropped his cane on the seat and climbed into the cab.

Once they pulled away from the curb, Jacob bent forward and patted his left boot to reassure himself of the presence of his pistol.

As he rode, the streets grew narrower and the buildings more run-down. After traveling for fewer than ten minutes, the driver stopped.

"The store you want is a block or two that way." He pointed down a street crowded with peddlers' carts, shoppers, and loiterers. "You'll have to walk from here."

Jacob paid him and made his way into the maelstrom of humanity. The once-familiar smell of rotten garbage and human waste wrinkled his nose. Thankful the walk would be a short one, he pushed past shawl-draped women picking over contents on the carts. Children chased each other up and down narrow stairs leading into the shoulder-to-shoulder brick tenements.

As he neared Riley's Grocery, he picked up his pace. Colin's business occupied the first floor of a building that was in better repair than its neighbors. Jacob bypassed the entrance and instead stepped through a narrow doorway and climbed a steep flight of stairs to the second floor. His right leg throbbed from the extra walking he'd done since arriving in Boston.

Three closed doors lined the hallway, but Jacob would never forget which one belonged to his former partner. He knocked on the first door on his right.

Soon he heard footsteps. A voice called, "Who's there?"

"Jacob West. Jake."

A key turned in the lock. A skinny man with thistledown white hair and piercing blue eyes beamed at him.

"Saints alive. I thought I'd never see you again." He gripped Jacob's shoulder, then threw his arms around him and thumped his back. "Come in. Tell me what brings you to Boston."

Jacob took in the familiar furnishings in Colin's sitting room. Round tables draped with lace coverings, armchairs upholstered in faded red plush, ornate lamps flickering against the dimness. The apartment smelled of tea and pipe tobacco.

In a blink he felt himself to be twenty-one again and being taken to Colin's lodgings above the grocery for the first time. He gazed at his old friend through a film of tears.

"I should have come back long ago. Thanks to you I have a good life now. I can't think what would have happened if you hadn't seen something in me that no one else did."

Colin waved a dismissive hand. "Helping you blessed me. You know what the Lord said about helping 'the least of these.'"

Jacob remembered hearing those verses when he attended Reverend French's church. If Colin could forgive him, maybe the Lord had too.

His friend's next words drew him back to the present.

"I miss getting your monthly letters since Byrne bought my share in your business." Colin lifted his bushy white eyebrows. "Tell me, did he change the name to West & Byrne?"

"Hah. Not likely. You're the man who gave me a chance. Your name will be on my store as long as I own the place."

He settled onto one of the chairs. "In fact, that's the main reason I came to Boston."

"To tell me my name will remain on your sign? I doubt that." His gaze sharpened. "Knowing you, there's more to the story."

Jacob drew a deep breath. He didn't know what he'd do if Colin refused his carefully rehearsed proposal. Leaning forward, he rested his moist palms on his knees. "First, I have to ask an unmannerly question."

"Go ahead."

"Did Byrne buy your share in West & Riley's outright, or does he still owe a portion?"

"I wouldn't answer such a question from anyone but you. Byrne is paying me monthly."

"How much is his debt?"

Colin pushed his hands against the arms of his chair and stood. "I'm ready for some tea. Want to join me?" Without waiting for an answer he entered the adjoining kitchen. Metal scraped against metal as he dragged a kettle to the front of the stove. He reached into a cupboard and placed two mugs on a tray beside a teapot, then added an open biscuit tin along with a sugar bowl.

The abrupt change of subject left Jacob wondering whether his former partner had lost some of his acuity over the years. A case clock ticked in the corner while Colin waited for the water to boil. Neither man spoke.

Once steam issued from the kettle, Colin measured leaves into the pot and poured the boiling water over them. "Important discussions can't take place without a cup of tea," he said as he carried the tray into the sitting room.

Jacob doubted the knots in his throat would allow him to swallow, but he accepted one of the mugs. With his hands cupped around the warm surface, he repeated his question. "How much is his debt?"

His former partner named a figure.

Taken aback, he did a quick calculation of the sum he'd brought with him to Boston. Most of his savings. His hands tightened around his mug. "So you're holding a promissory note?"

"Aye."

"How about if I pay you the same amount, and half again. Would you sell the share to me?"

Colin laced his fingers together over his paunch. "Why now? You could have offered to buy me out at any time."

"Two reasons. Keegan Byrne has made indirect threats to reveal my past if I don't make larger payments than the ones you and I agreed upon. I believe since the ideas are mine, the profits belong to me."

"And the second reason?"

"I hope to marry soon, if she'll have me." Heat crept up his neck that had nothing to do with the stuffy apartment. "When you and I were partners, I had no concerns about my history following me to Noble Springs, but with Byrne . . . He could destroy my future with a few well-placed words."

"You've lived in Noble Springs for eight years. People know you and respect you. I'd be willing to wager that folks won't care what you did as a youth."

"Cassie would care." Jacob hung his head as he mumbled the words. "She was raised to be a lady. She'd be scandalized if she knew my past."

Colin scooted forward and rested his hand on Jacob's shoulder. "Let Byrne do his worst. If your young lady loves you, she'll understand that you're a new man."

He swallowed disappointment. "Does that mean you won't sell me the share?"

33

Cassie crimped the crust on the last of Wednesday's orders. Five customers had requested her plum pies. Now all she needed was access to the ovens. She paced back and forth while she waited for Jenny's pans of cornbread to finish baking.

What the kitchen lacked was a second range, one that would be dedicated to the bakery. Becca could cook pie fillings without having to fit her work around the needs of the dining room. Pies could go into the oven as soon as they were ready, rather than sitting on the worktable with the crusts sagging in the summer heat.

She stopped pacing and cupped her chin with one hand, studying the room's arrangement. If they moved the shelves from her side of the room to Jenny's, a small range would fit in the space across from her worktable. Cutting a flue hole in the ceiling ought to be a simple matter. She clasped her hands. What a perfect solution. She'd visit the mercantile on her free afternoon tomorrow to see if Faith would help her select the right model. That way when Jacob returned all he'd have to do was find a carpenter to cut through the roof—assuming he agreed with her plan, and she felt sure he would.

After all, he'd told her that if she needed anything for the bakery, she had only to ask. Well, she needed a second range. Since he left her with his ledger in his absence, he obviously trusted her judgment.

Her thoughts drifted from the kitchen to his prolonged absence. One week had become eleven days, and no word. She'd give anything to hear his deep voice rumble in her ear, to see his dark eyes glow when he looked at her.

Hugging her arms to her waist, she blinked back tears. The last words she'd said to him were "Go away." What if something happened, and those words were all he had to remember her by?

"Oven's ready," Jenny called from across the room. "Want me to stick the pies in?"

"Please." She wiped her eyes, then turned around. Time to set out plates for the noon dinner. She took a stack from the shelf and carried them into the dining room. Busyness was the best cure for melancholy.

Cassie sat at the small table in Jacob's office that evening, entering the day's receipts into the ledger. The business had fared well in his absence. She hoped the totals would make him smile.

Next to the ledger, Timothy had left the current stock list she'd requested. She scanned the items, noticing with a ripple of dismay that sugar, flour, and lard were among the goods in short supply. Maybe Timothy knew where Jacob obtained his merchandise—she certainly didn't.

"Oh, Jacob. Come back," she whispered. "I need you. We all need you."

She lifted her head when she heard soft footfalls behind her.

"Missy?" Becca stood outside the lamp's bright circle. Her shoulders drooped. "Can I talk to you?"

"Of course you can. Come sit over here."

"I'll stand."

Cassie closed the ledger and swiveled in her chair so she faced Becca. "What's troubling you? I know we've been extra busy this week. Have I asked too much of you?"

Becca shook her head. "It's nothing you done. It's Mr. West." She rubbed her hands against her red calico skirt, then squeezed them together. "I'm hoping there might be something you can do."

"You're having trouble with Mr. West?" Cassie's voice rose to a squeak. Jacob was the last person she would have suspected of trifling with colored girls. She shoved her chair away from the table and stood. "I'm glad you told me now, before I—"

"No, no. Nothing like that. I know you set quite a store by him. He ain't done nothing wrong."

Cassie tipped her head back until a wave of dizziness receded. "What, then?"

"He let Wash move into a little room behind the kitchen in his house to be a watchman, like. Wash told me how nice everything is." She took a step closer. "But now that he's up there at night, I only get to see him for a few minutes after he's done with his work. He walks me to where I'm living, then goes to Mr. West's."

"He can't spend some time with you before he goes . . . home?"

"No, missy. He's supposed to keep an eye on things, so he's got to hurry on. He don't want to leave me, but the boss has been so good to him. Wash is afraid to let him down." She covered her mouth, but a sob escaped.

"Oh, Becca, please sit." Cassie slipped an arm around the young woman's shoulders and led her to a chair.

"I'm sorry for cryin' like this. But things have been so hard all my life, and then I met Wash. He treats me like the boss treats you. You know—like he loves me."

Cassie's heart warmed at Becca's words. Jacob did treat her like he loved her. Her quick tongue had been her downfall yet again. She'd been wrong, so wrong, to be angry with him.

She resumed her seat facing Becca. "What can I do to help?"

"If me and Wash was married, I could live in the little room with him."

Cassie sat bolt upright. "You could! That's a perfect solution. Has he asked you?"

"We talked about it some. But we don't know what Mr. West would say about me living there too. Could you . . . would you talk to him?"

"I'll be happy to talk to Mr. West for you." She patted Becca's arm. "I'm sure he wouldn't object."

"There's something else." Becca picked at a spot on her skirt, then met Cassie's gaze. "We got no colored preacher around here, neither. Who'd marry us? Sundays some of us do church on our own, but a colored man reading a Bible over Wash and me wouldn't make us married—not legal-like. Now that we're free, we want to act free."

Becca's plight tore at her. Jacob's approval was one thing—finding a preacher willing to perform the ceremony for them was quite another. Reverend French's name sprang to Cassie's mind, but she hesitated before speaking. She barely knew him. Still, if Wash and Becca wanted to marry, he was Noble Spring's only preacher. *Lord, please give me the courage to speak up for Becca.*

Cassie left the restaurant kitchen the following afternoon and headed for Lindberg's Mercantile. Her head buzzed with ideas for a new range. She could bake four pies at a time in one wide oven, and a smaller size than the double-oven model Jenny used would fit nicely in the space now occupied by storage shelves. Her steps slowed as she approached the parsonage. She'd all but forgotten Becca's dilemma in her excitement over her upcoming selection.

She should stop and talk to Reverend French, but why would he listen to her? Her weekly tithe reflected her small salary, probably not enough to earn her any favors. She didn't help with the Ladies' Missionary Society or teach a Sunday school. He probably didn't even know who she was.

Another day. After she had time to gather her courage. Head high, she increased her pace, turning right on King's Highway and covering the distance to the mercantile with brisk steps. The bell over the door jingled when she entered. To her dismay, Sheriff Cooper, rather than Faith, stood beside one of the counters. He tipped his head to acknowledge her presence.

"Miss Haddon. Something you need?"

"Good afternoon, Sheriff. Actually, I hoped to see Faith here today."

"She's in the storeroom unpacking bolts of calico. Got a new shipment in, and you know how she is about that fabric display. Things got to be just so."

Cassie smiled. Even though Sheriff Cooper managed the store, Faith had kept the items for ladies under her control. The sheriff could sell shotguns and plows, but he didn't know much about lace and buttons.

"I'll just go on back. Thank you." She crossed the length of the building, remembering the first time she'd visited the mercantile. Then, a row of cookstoves lined the center of the room. Over time, they'd been sold and now had to be ordered individually. A bubble of excitement tickled her throat at the prospect of paging through a catalog to find the right one.

Faith turned from her task when Cassie walked into the storeroom.

"What a nice surprise!" She kissed Cassie's cheek. "It's been a long time since we had a chat."

"Too long." She glanced around the room. "Where's Alexander?"

"Curt's watching him for a couple of hours. He had a free afternoon, so I took advantage of his willingness."

"Well, I'm happy to find you here. I need your help in selecting a new range."

"For your cabin? How perfect. You should have a proper place to prepare meals."

"My little stove is fine for the small amount of cooking I do at home. The range will go into the kitchen at West & Riley's. I decided yesterday that the bake shop needs its own oven."

Faith clapped her hands together. "How splendid! Let me get Mr. Tyler's catalog and show you what's available." She dashed out of the storeroom and returned a minute later with a thick book in her hand. She placed the volume on one of the shelves. "Now, tell me what kind of a range you need."

As Cassie explained her desire for a wide oven and warming shelves for pie fillings, Faith flipped pages until she came to an illustrated model that had everything Cassie wanted. She pointed to the drawing.

"Like this?"

"Yes. Exactly." She bent over the page, admiring the design. She closed her eyes for a second and pictured the range in the restaurant's kitchen. "If Jacob approves, how long before delivery?"

"Tyler's Stove Works is in Massachusetts. Your purchase

would come by rail, so I expect you'd have to wait no longer than a week."

"And how much does this model cost?"

Faith tipped her head and met Cassie's gaze. "Twenty-five dollars."

Cassie pressed her hands to her lips. Jacob sold her pies for fifty cents each. At that price, her baking had already earned more than the cost of the range. "Jacob's away right now, but we expect him to return any day. I'll ask him as soon as he gets back."

After all, he did say she had only to ask if she needed anything.

34

assie dropped the flour scoop to the floor, where it landed with a clang. "What did you say?"

"The boss wants to see you in his office." Timothy spoke with an air of importance. "As quickly as you can, he said."

"He's back?"

The boy grinned at her. "He was here when I came to work this morning."

"I didn't see his horse in the alley."

Timothy shrugged as if to say "So?"

"Did he say what he wanted?"

"No, miss, he didn't."

Cassie's heartbeat pounded in her throat. If she'd known Jacob planned to return today, she would have come in early to review the ledger and be sure her work was faultless.

He'd left without saying good-bye, and returned unannounced two weeks later. Uncertainty tempered her excitement at the prospect of seeing him again. He may believe she'd deliberately deceived him and used his time away to decide how best to end their courtship. Why else would there be such a long silence? And why send Timothy to fetch her, when he could have stopped by the kitchen?

Timothy waited by the door. "Shall I tell him you're on the way?"

"Yes. Thank you."

She patted the sides of her head to be sure her hair looked tidy. From the burning in her face, she knew there was no need to pinch her cheeks to bring out their color. Shoulders straight, she sailed across the dining area and into the storeroom.

A broad smile lit Jacob's face when she entered. "I'm glad you could spare a couple of minutes. There are a few matters I'd like to discuss."

His business-like tone crushed her hopes that he'd forgiven her. "Did you find errors in my bookkeeping?"

"Not at all." He lifted Timothy's list from the tabletop. "I see you're running low on the supplies you need for the bakery. How long do you think the inventory will last?"

"A week, maybe more."

He made a note on a scrap of paper. "Have you seen any increase in customers for the dining room?"

She wondered why he asked the questions. The ledger had totals for every day. Still, if he persisted in treating her like a clerk, she'd respond in the same manner. "We have. Railroad workers are stopping in Noble Springs for the night before continuing west."

"Good." He made another note, then leaned against the back of his chair with a relieved expression. "I wanted to share this news with you first. I made a large expenditure while I was away, and need to watch every penny for a month or so."

Cassie's knees wobbled and she sank into a chair. "Watch . . . every penny?" Her dreams of a new range took wing and flew away. Light-headed, she bent forward and took a deep breath. Her mouth opened but no words emerged.

"Cassie, what's wrong?" His voice spiked with urgency. "Are you ill?"

She stared at her lap until he gripped her hands.

"Talk to me."

"Oh, Jacob. I've done something presumptuous. I should have waited until you got back."

He tipped her chin up with his thumb. "Why don't you tell me, then we'll see if it's presumptuous or not." The warmth in his gaze flowed over her like a balm.

What a homecoming. She'd expected him to be happy with the store's success in his absence and hoped that happiness would spill over into forgiveness of the way she'd spoken to him when they parted. She cast about for a way to gloss over what she'd done, but in her heart she knew truth was best served unadorned.

"Between serving meals and filling orders for pies, we're often tripping over one another in the kitchen when we juggle use of the range." She swallowed, then blurted, "I went to Faith yesterday and picked out another range. Smaller, just what we need for the bakery. But she didn't order it," she added hastily.

He gaped at her. After a few seconds, a corner of his mouth twitched. "You are full of surprises." He pushed himself to his feet and held out his arms. "Come here," he said in a husky whisper.

Without a second thought, Cassie fell into his embrace. He pulled her close and kissed her forehead, then bent his lips to meet hers. His arms tightened around her. After a long, tingling moment, she drew away.

"You're not upset?"

He dropped a kiss on top of her head. "We are partners, after all."

"I was afraid you left because you were still angry with me."

258

He stroked her cheek with his forefinger. "I left for you, not because of you."

"What does that mean?"

"Would you be willing to go on a buggy ride with me this evening to find out?"

She snuggled back into his arms. "You know I would."

⸙

Cassie glanced out when Wash drove Jacob's buggy past the screen door. She untied her apron and dropped the soiled garment into a basket for Timothy's mother to launder. Within a minute or two, Jacob entered the kitchen, Wash a few steps behind him.

Jacob's mesmerizing gaze settled on her. "If you're ready, Miss Haddon, I'll see you home now."

"Thank you, Mr. West. I'm quite ready."

When she turned to say good night to Becca, she noticed that Wash had moved close and rested his hand on her shoulder. The pleading in the young woman's eyes stopped the words in Cassie's throat. She'd been so absorbed in her own happiness that she'd forgotten her promise.

"I'll ask him," she mouthed in Becca's direction before turning to join Jacob at the door.

Twilight shadowed the alley. As soon as they were out of sight of the kitchen, Jacob drew her close to his side. "I thought today would never end."

"I felt the same way." Warmth from his body radiated along her arm. She wished she'd had time to go home and change into her rose chintz dress. The blue calico she wore had been washed so many times the garment had faded to the color of smoke.

The sorrel whinnied when he saw them coming. Jacob

helped her into the buggy, then lit the lantern and untied the reins. Keeping the horse to a slow walk, he turned south when they reached the street. Fireflies danced beneath trees as they traveled through the quiet neighborhood. With each sway of the buggy, Jacob's shoulder brushed hers, sending tingles over her.

She wiggled a bit closer. "Where are we going?"

"You'll find out soon." He guided the horse around the block and up to High Street, where he turned left. They passed homes with lighted windows, the closed livery stable, then traveled on west.

Puzzled, Cassie glanced at him. "We're not going to your home, are we?"

"No. Just be patient another minute or two."

She saw the road to Pioneer Lake through the dusk, but he didn't turn there. A short distance farther, he pulled onto a grassy verge and stopped the buggy. He tied the reins to the brake.

"Look." He pointed below, where a full moon reflected its light across the satin surface of the lake. A fish jumped and ribbons of moonlight spread a circle in the water.

She drew in a sharp breath. "How beautiful."

"I hoped you'd think so." He shifted on the seat and clasped her hands. "I brought you here because I have something important to tell you."

Her heart threatened to stop beating. A warm evening, moonlight. The setting couldn't be more perfect. She tipped her face to his.

"What do you want to tell me?" she whispered.

"I've been in Boston this past week and a half."

She blew out a long sigh. Her expectations had run off with her once again. "You didn't need to bring me here to give me a report on your travels."

"I know I'm awkward, but please let me have my say." His jaw tightened. "I was born in Boston, but haven't been back since before the war. I went there now to settle several matters, business and personal, from my past. I needed to know I was free . . . to ask you to marry me."

Cassie pulled her hands away and pressed them to her chest. Leave it to Jacob to over-explain. She didn't care why he went to Boston. All she cared about was that he'd come back and was asking her to marry him. She couldn't be sure. She cocked an eyebrow at him.

"And are you?"

"Am I what?"

"Jacob! Are you asking me to marry you?"

"Yes. Yes I am. Will you?"

"Only if you love me."

"Are you giving me conditions again?" He swept her into his arms. Nuzzling his face in her hair, he spoke in her ear. "I've loved you since the day you came in to ask for a job. It just took me some time to realize it." He kissed her earlobe. "The expression on your face . . . you were so determined to try. You're a wonder, Cassie Haddon."

She ran her index finger over his moustache, then lifted her lips to his.

If it weren't for his arms holding her, she knew she'd float away.

When Cassie awakened the next morning, she burrowed down in the bed and let her mind drift to the previous evening. Jacob asked her to marry him. Warmth flooded her. The memory felt like a dream, but her heart told her otherwise.

She wanted to remember every detail, so when her children

asked when she and their papa had decided to marry, she could tell them precisely. Her mother had always refused to talk about how she and Cassie's father had met. Even questions about their wedding elicited vague answers.

An icicle stabbed through her daydreams. Her mother had made her feelings about Jacob quite clear.

Cassie swung her feet to the floor and hunched on the edge of the bed with her head bowed. She'd have to let Mother know of her engagement.

Perhaps she and Jacob could elope. At twenty-five years of age, she could do what she wanted. After all, judging from her last letter, Mother was happy enough in Price City. She hadn't mentioned Patrick Fitzhugh at all.

Then Cassie shook her head. Regardless of what her mother's reaction might be, Cassie was obligated to honor her. She had to tell her of Jacob's proposal.

She threw her wrapper over her shoulders. She'd write a letter now, before leaving for the restaurant. Then when she had a free moment this afternoon, she'd dash to the post office and send the news to Price City.

While she performed her morning ablutions, she tried to think of how best to phrase her letter. As she donned her faded blue dress, she mentally composed and discarded several different approaches. At last, she threw her hairbrush on the bed and stomped to the next room. *Just tell her straight out.* No matter what she said, or how she said it, Mother would be unhappy at the news.

She carried writing paper and ink to the table. The first paragraph flowed with good wishes for her mother's health, comments on the hot weather, and a brief account of last Sunday's church service. Then she paused and chewed the end of the pen holder. If the telegraph extended to Price City, she could say everything in ten words or less.

The ink dried on the nib while she pondered her next words. Finally, she bent over the page and dashed off her news.

Last evening, Jacob West asked to marry me. Of course I said yes! I love him so very much, and have for the longest time. He's kind, gentle, and protective—all the qualities I could hope for in a husband. Since Father is dead and you are far away, we had to dispense with the formalities of asking permission. I pray you will forgive the lapse of etiquette.

You'll be happy to hear he possesses a fine home, although I'd marry him if he lived in a cabin.

We haven't set a wedding date yet. Perhaps before winter sets in?

I will, of course, keep you fully informed and hope you and Uncle Rand can take time away from your duties at the hotel to attend our union.

Praying for your blessing, I am your affectionate,

Cassie

Feeling like a soldier who'd fired a shot into enemy camp, she tucked the letter into her handbag and hurried out the door.

Given the difficulty of transportation to Price City, she hoped for at least a two-week silence before receiving a return volley.

35

The minute Cassie entered the kitchen, Becca sped to her side.

"What did he say?"

Cassie frowned, wondering why Becca would ask her about Jacob's proposal. Then comprehension dawned.

"I'm so sorry." She laid her hand on the young woman's arm. "Something totally unexpected happened last evening, and I forgot my promise."

Becca dropped her gaze to the floor. "White folks is always forgetting their promises. I thought you was different."

She spoke so softly Cassie had to strain to hear. The words stung. Becca was right—she'd been so wrapped up in her time with Jacob that she'd thought of nothing else. "A promise is a promise. I'll go talk to him right now."

"Don't be gone too long," Jenny said from her listening post next to a worktable. "If you hurry, you can get a couple of pies ready to bake when the biscuits are done."

"I won't be but a minute." She zipped out the door, smiling inside at an excuse to see Jacob first thing.

As though he'd read her thoughts, he met her in the dining room. "Good morning, sweet Cassie."

"Good morning to you too, Jacob." She maintained a proper distance in case Timothy happened to be watching them. "I forgot to ask you a question last evening."

"I have one for you as well. Tell me yours first."

"Did you know that Wash and Becca would like to be married?"

His eyes crinkled at the corners. "No, I didn't, but I wish them all the best." Then his brows shot up. "They're not leaving, are they? I'd hate to lose Wash. He's a good man."

"That's not the issue. They're both content working for you. But since Wash now lives at your house, they're worried that you wouldn't want both of them there." For a brief second, she marveled at herself advocating for two people she'd only known for a couple of months. Useless Cassie had become bold Cassie, no doubt about it.

Jacob moved closer to a table and rested his free hand on the back of a chair. A hint of a smile appeared. "The question now is, would *you* want both of them there? My house will be your house soon."

She slapped her hand against her cheek. "Oh my word. I didn't think about that." She and Jacob, living in the same house. Sharing everything. The thought left her breathless. "Of course they could both live in . . . our home."

He took her hand and kissed her fingertips. "Now it's my turn with a question."

She heard shuffling footsteps behind her and turned toward the sound. Jenny stood in the kitchen entrance, arms folded across her stomach. When she saw Cassie looking at her, she cleared her throat and pointed toward the range, then mouthed "pies."

Cassie nodded, then looked up at Jacob. "She's urging me to get started on today's baking."

"She's right. We can talk later, perhaps after everyone goes home." He pivoted toward the grocery.

Cassie longed to follow him, take his arm, and slip away for a picnic somewhere. Instead, she joined Jenny in the kitchen.

Becca stood at the basin watching her. Her hands gripped the edge of the counter as though if she released her hold she'd collapse.

"What did he say, missy?"

"He left the decision to me." She gulped. She should have asked Jacob if he wanted to share their news with his employees before saying anything. Too late now.

"Why you?" Jenny jammed her hands on her hips. "It's his house."

"Last night he asked me to marry him." She beamed at the two women. "I said yes."

Jenny wrapped her in a plump hug and kissed her cheek. "I wonder what took him so long. He's been mooning over you like a lovesick schoolboy for months."

Becca took several steps away from the basin. "I'm happy for you, missy. But what did you decide about me living in Mr. West's house?"

"We'd both be glad to have you there with Wash."

A brief flicker of joy flashed across her face, then she bent her head. "Now alls we need is a preacher. That's not going to be so easy."

Cassie brushed away a flutter of apprehension. Talking to Reverend French would not be easy, but she'd have to call on him, and soon.

Late in the day, a lull between the noon meal and supper gave each of them an opportunity for a short rest. Cassie saw her chance to dash down the street to the post office and send her mother's letter on its way.

Jenny sat at one of the worktables with her feet stretched out in front of her. A mug of coffee rested near her elbow. Becca leaned against the door frame, staring out at the alley. Cassie suspected she watched for Wash to arrive with Jacob's buggy.

She folded her apron over a chair, donned her bonnet, and stepped out into the stifling afternoon. Thank goodness the post office was but a few yards down Third Street.

Mr. Lyons smiled at her when she stepped through the door. "Nothing for you today, I'm afraid. Your mama doesn't write as regular as she used to."

"Mail is slow from Price City. When I was there, train service hadn't arrived, and the stage only comes east two days a week."

"How's she liking being so far from everything? I recollect she's a pretty citified lady."

"I believe she's content."

Anything she shared with the postmaster would be common knowledge in town within a day, so she kept her response brief. She dug in her bag and handed him the letter.

He read the address, then dropped the envelope into a canvas bag. "This'll be on its way first thing tomorrow. Your mama will be happy to hear from you, I reckon."

"I hope so." However, she doubted Mother would be happy. Whatever happened next was in the Lord's hands.

After thanking Mr. Lyons, she paused outside the doorway and gazed at the parsonage across the street. She could go now and speak to Reverend French about Becca and Wash. The conversation wouldn't take long. He'd either say yes or no—or maybe he wouldn't be home and she could procrastinate a bit longer.

Gathering her courage, she crossed the boardwalk and stepped onto the dusty street, then hopped backward when a horse and buggy rolled toward her.

"Cassie." Jacob pulled up on the reins. "Mrs. Fielder said you'd gone this way. Did you get a letter from your mother?"

"No, I sent one telling her of our plans."

"Guess that was the right thing to do." A muscle twitched in his jaw before his smile returned. "I'm going to the mercantile. Will you come with me?"

After casting one last glance at the parsonage, she climbed into the buggy. She'd talk to Reverend French tomorrow after church services.

Jacob squeezed her hand. "I want you to show me a picture of the range you'd like to have. I agree with your plans, but I hope to do a little bartering and get Cooper to shave the price."

She flushed. "I pray you're successful. I'd never have talked to Faith if only I'd known . . ."

"I'm sure Cooper will be willing to dicker." He shook the reins over the horse's back and turned onto King's Highway. "This is what I started to ask you this morning—would you come with me." He grinned. "Now that I've kidnapped you, you can't say no."

"I wouldn't say no to a buggy ride with you, no matter where we're headed."

When they reached the mercantile, he lifted his cane from the buggy floor and descended to the boardwalk. After tying the horse's reins to a hitching rail, he offered Cassie his hand, holding hers for an extra moment when she stood next to him. She sent up a prayer of thanks that he'd accepted her decision so calmly. If he could barter successfully, she'd feel even better.

⤙⤚

Jacob spotted Thaddeus Cooper as soon as they entered the store. "I'm here to see the picture of that range Miss Haddon looked at a couple of days ago."

"Tyler's Stove Works catalog. Right here." Thaddeus reached beneath a counter and dropped the book into Jacob's waiting hand. He pointed to a scrap of paper protruding near the center. "There's the page you want, but Miss Faith will have to place the order. You need to talk to her."

Jacob laid the book on the counter and flipped to the marked page. He turned to Cassie. "Is this the one?"

She stepped closer, her lavender fragrance teasing his senses.

The thought that she'd soon be his wife filled him with wonder. With his past behind him once and for all, the future glowed with promise. Cassie didn't know it, but she could have asked for an expensive new carriage and he wouldn't have minded. Having her beside him made him happier than he'd ever been.

"Yes, this would be the best range for the kitchen." She looked up, her eyes shining. "See the wide oven, yet the total space is little more than half of the range Jenny uses to prepare the meals." Then her face clouded. "I should have talked to you first," she whispered.

He patted her hand. "I'd have chosen the same one. It's just what we need." His heart warmed to see a smile return to her lips.

"So, d'you want to talk to Miss Faith?" Thaddeus moved from behind the counter.

"Yes, thanks."

"I'll fetch her. She's in the back room, counting buttons, of all things." He shook his head. "Ladies and their fripperies."

While he waited, Jacob struggled with doubt. Would Cassie think less of him for confessing he currently lacked funds to purchase the range outright? What if Faith saw him as a poor marriage risk for her friend?

As Faith hurried toward them, he forced himself to return

her smile. No sense borrowing trouble—he'd soon have her reaction.

After offering her hand to him and hugging Cassie, Faith pointed to the open catalog page. "Are you pleased with Cassie's choice?"

"This one is exactly what we need." He fingered his bow tie, then gripped Cassie's hand. "Unfortunately, while I was away I invested a large sum in the business, which Cassie had no way of knowing when she chose the range. If you would accept, say a month's worth of kitchen necessities—flour, coffee, and the like—could you reduce the price?"

Faith's gaze bounced between Jacob's eyes and his hand clasped over Cassie's. A knowing smile crept over her face. "Please don't be concerned. I'm sure we can work out the details so we're both happy."

"Good. If you write up a list of your needs, I'll have Wash deliver everything to your home."

"I know you will, Mr. West. You're an honorable man." Her smile grew broader when she looked at Cassie. "Do you two have an announcement to make? You're positively glowing."

He nodded at Cassie. "Tell her."

"Jacob has asked me to marry him. Of course I said yes right away before he could change his mind."

"How splendid for both of you!" Faith drew Cassie into a tight hug. "You deserve happiness after all you've been through. I'll gather my fashion books and on your next free afternoon we'll select a perfect wedding dress." She hesitated. "Have you written your mother?"

Jacob gritted his teeth. From Faith's troubled expression, he gathered that she shared his opinion of Cassie's mother.

36

*C*assie stood on the lawn near Jacob the next morning after church, accepting the good wishes of her friends. Rosemary kissed her cheek and whispered, "You're perfect for each other. I know you'll be happy."

"Thank you. I think so too, or I wouldn't have said yes." Cassie smiled and stepped back, glancing over Rosemary's shoulder to look for Reverend French. Her joy at the prospect of marrying Jacob contrasted sharply with Wash and Becca's uncertainty. She'd made up her mind to talk to the reverend today, and talk to him she would.

Spotting him across the churchyard, she excused herself and headed in his direction. Tension fluttered in her chest. How did one talk to a preacher? The parson in the church she'd attended with her family was old and crotchety. As a child, she'd done all she could to avoid him.

Reverend French apparently noticed her approaching, because he paused and smiled at her. His graying hair ruffled in the slight breeze that fluttered the ribbons on her bonnet.

"Miss Haddon, isn't it?"

"Yes, sir. I wonder if you have a minute? I have a matter I'd like to discuss."

"I'm sorry. I promised my wife we'd leave right after services to visit our son and his wife." Regret tinged his voice.

She bit her lower lip. "I understand. Forgive me for bothering you."

"You're no bother at all. I'd be pleased to meet with you tomorrow afternoon. Can you come to the parsonage at one o'clock?"

The hour he named was her busiest time. As soon as Jenny finished with the noon meal, Cassie had to get pies in the oven for the customers in the grocery. She knew she could manage the bakery with Becca's help, but wondered how she'd explain her absence without raising the young woman's hopes.

She considered his request for less than a moment. "Yes, I'll be there. Thank you."

Now she had to tell Jacob of her planned absence from the kitchen. She blew out a long sigh. Lately all of her actions turned into knotted balls of yarn.

Lifting her rose chintz skirt above the narrow toes of her Sunday shoes, she crossed the lawn to Jacob's side and blurted out her news. "I'm meeting with Reverend French tomorrow at one. Becca can take care of the baking for an hour or so."

"Shouldn't we go together to discuss our wedding?" He stared at her with one eyebrow raised.

"Oh, yes, absolutely. But this isn't about us."

He took her arm and turned toward the brick pathway that led behind the church, stopping when they reached the shade of a willow tree next to the burial ground. "You're going to talk to a preacher and it's not about us? I don't understand."

"Wash and Becca have no one to marry them. She told me there's no Negro preacher in Noble Springs. So I plan to ask Reverend French if he'd perform the ceremony."

"You're going to be disappointed." He gathered her hands in both of his. "Why would he listen to such a request?"

"I have to try. How would you like it if we couldn't get married because we didn't have a preacher?"

"That's different. We could always go to another town."

"They can't travel easily the way we can. If Reverend French refuses . . . well, I'll cross that bridge when I come to it."

He shook his head. "My Cassie. When you're determined, I'd better not stand in your way."

Mindful that they stood in a churchyard, she squelched her desire to wrap her arms around him and rest her head against his chest. He was the kindest, most honest man she'd ever known.

<hr />

Cassie dumped flour and salt into a mixing bowl, then added chunks of lard. As she sliced two knives through the mixture, Becca leaned over the table to watch.

"You got a lot of git-up-and-go for a Monday. What's the hurry? This don't have to be done before noon."

"Maybe not, but I want to leave for a while after the dinner hour. If I get the pies ready early, you won't be left with extra work to do." She smiled to herself, thinking she'd dodged any further questions.

Jenny sauntered over to them. "You leaving again today? You were gone almost all afternoon on Saturday." She winked. "Marrying the boss has its advantages."

Cassie's face burned. She enjoyed being in the kitchen with Jenny and Becca and hadn't considered how they'd view her new status.

"That's not the case. I can't change today's commitment, but from now on please treat me like you always have. I'll be here the same hours you are."

"I was teasing you." Jenny gave her a brief hug before returning to the bacon sputtering on the range.

Sometimes teasing contained nuggets of truth. Cassie took a steadying breath while she sprinkled water over the flour mixture. Jenny had become almost like a beloved aunt, although a peppery one, over the months in Jacob's kitchen. She couldn't allow misunderstanding to come between them.

She glanced up and caught Becca watching her. "When you have time, could you please peel those peaches and cut them up for pie?" She pointed to a flat wooden box filled with a single layer of ripe fruit. The tantalizing fragrance made her mouth water.

Grinning at Becca, she added, "You could slice a few to go with our breakfast, if you want."

"Yes, missy, I'll do that for sure." She sent her a rare smile.

Satisfied she'd warded off a problem, Cassie fluffed the flour and water together until the texture looked right, then patted balls of dough into disks. She worked without ceasing while Jenny and Becca served breakfast to the morning customers. Before noon six pies cooled on a shelf and she began work on three orders.

Her shoulders ached from tension, but she didn't stop. Kitchen aromas changed from bacon and eggs to fried steak and onions. By the time Becca carried the final serving plates to the noon diners, Cassie had all her orders ready for the oven.

She flopped on a chair and undid the two top buttons on her bodice. Her body sagged. Fanning herself with an old newspaper, she glanced at the wall clock over the doorway to the dining room.

Twelve thirty-five.

She jumped to her feet.

After removing her apron, she smoothed her hair and refastened her buttons. "I'll be back as soon as possible. Please mind the pies, Becca. They should be ready in forty minutes or so."

"Yes, missy."

She sensed the two women gazing after her as she left the kitchen. *Please, Lord, let me bring back good news.*

✎

Reverend French's wife answered Cassie's knock. "The reverend is expecting you. I'm Clarissa French. Please, come in."

She stepped into the spacious entry. The wood floor shone in the sunlight flowing through the open doorway. A mirrored hall tree reflected a comfortable sitting room on her right. The house smelled of coffee and fresh-baked cookies.

Mrs. French closed the door. "If you'll follow me, I'll show you to his study." With brisk steps, she proceeded to a room at the rear of the house.

Reverend French stood when she entered. "Please have a seat, Miss Haddon."

She chose an armchair upholstered in a floral fabric. To her surprise, Mrs. French took the chair next to hers.

Apparently noticing her expression, he gave her a reassuring smile. "Sometimes it's easier for young ladies to talk to another lady, so my wife keeps me company."

A flush warmed her face. "I . . . I'm not here because I'm in any trouble." She hesitated. How best to explain her errand? Now that she faced Reverend French her resolve wavered.

He rested his hands on the surface of his spotless desk. "There's nothing you can tell us that the Lord doesn't already know. Please don't be nervous."

In spite of his compassionate expression, her heart thrummed. She straightened her shoulders to remind herself she was now bold Cassie. "A friend of mine wants to get married, so she needs a preacher."

"Why doesn't she come to see me instead of sending you?"

"She didn't send me. In fact she doesn't know I've come."

He steepled his fingers under his chin. "Can you tell me a bit more about this . . . friend? Why are you here in her place? Is she ill?"

"No, sir. She's a Negro."

She heard Mrs. French gasp.

"And her intended? He is Negro also?" His face remained serene, as though he heard requests like hers every day.

Cassie relaxed a bit. "Yes, sir. They both work for Jacob West."

When she said Jacob's name, a gentle smile lifted the reverend's lips. "I've seen the two of you at church. You make a fine couple."

"You've noticed? I thought with so many people there you couldn't keep up with everyone."

"I'd be a poor pastor if I didn't pay attention to my congregation. The Lord sent me to minister, not give Sunday speeches and ignore you the rest of the week." He chuckled before turning serious. "So you'd like me to marry them?"

"There's no Negro preacher here. You're their only hope."

Mrs. French leaned forward to face her husband. "You can't do it, Ethan. A colored couple in our church! What would the ladies in the Missionary Society say? They'd drop over in shock."

"You're right, I know." His bristly gray eyebrows furrowed when he looked at Cassie. "We have a mixed congregation here, Miss Haddon. Not everyone supported the abolitionist cause, although many did, myself included. But some of our members were and are firmly on the side of the Confederacy. I have to tread a fine line."

"Does that mean you're saying no?"

"It means I'll pray about what to do and let you know what answer comes to me."

She rose. "I see. Thank you for listening."

A sodden lump of disappointment weighted her insides. There were some things all the determination in the world couldn't fix. Wash and Becca's dreams were one of them.

*L*indberg Mercantile's yellow delivery wagon rattled to a stop in the alley behind the kitchen midmorning on Friday. Cassie dashed to open the screen door.

"Our new range is here," she called over her shoulder to Jenny and Becca.

"Couldn't have picked a worse time." Jenny grumbled her way across the room. "Smack in the middle of a busy day. And you've got pies waiting."

Sheriff Cooper stepped inside and tipped his hat at Jenny. "The range came in on the morning train. Sorry for the disturbance, ma'am, but no sense hauling something this heavy to the store. We'd just have to turn around and bring it over here. Thing must weigh as much as an elephant."

He turned his gaze on Cassie. "Would you fetch Jacob? I brought three helpers with me. He needs to tell us where he wants his range."

She bristled. "I'd think that empty place on the wall over there would answer your question."

"Rather talk to Jacob, miss. No offense."

"Fine. I'll be right back." She stomped toward the office, fuming. Of all the high-handed, condescending . . .

Jacob met her at the entrance to the grocery. "I heard the wagon arrive. Is that our range?"

"*Your* range, to hear Sheriff Cooper. He sent me to fetch you. He has to have you tell him where you want it placed."

"Doesn't do any good to be upset. That's the way he is, and we can't change him." He squeezed her hand. "This is a big day for us. I'm proud of you."

Her heart swelled. His praise was the antidote she needed to overcome her irritation with the former sheriff. "I'm eager to put the range to use. We can handle more orders if I don't have to wait for Jenny's ovens to be available."

When they reached the kitchen, she stood beside Jenny and Becca to watch while Sheriff Cooper and his helpers hefted the crated shipment from the wagon and maneuvered through the doorway. Grunting with the weight, the four men staggered to where Jacob leaned on his cane next to the empty wall space.

"Right here," he said, sending Cassie a subtle wink.

Jenny sniffed. "How are we supposed to cook dinner with a roomful of people?" she muttered.

The range hit the floor with a thud as they released their burden. The sheriff straightened, rubbing the small of his back while the other three men escaped to the alley.

"I brought a crowbar. You want me to open the crate?" He addressed his question to Jacob.

"Yes, please. You can pile the scraps over in the woodbox."

With creaks and flying splinters, the strips of wood encasing the new range fell away.

Cassie gasped. "It's beautiful. The drawing in the catalog didn't do it justice." She inched past Sheriff Cooper and traced her index finger over the sunburst design embossed over the shiny black exterior. Whirling around, she shared a smile with Jenny and Becca. "Imagine how much we'll enjoy having an extra oven for baking."

"It's mighty pretty, missy." Becca's smile didn't reach her eyes.

Cassie bit her lip, feeling guilty for her pleasure. If only finding a preacher to marry Becca and Wash were as easy as ordering new equipment for the kitchen. She wondered how much time ministers needed to receive answers to their prayers.

"There's a couple things I got to show you before you use this range, Miss Haddon. You too, Miz Fielder."

Jenny folded her arms under her bosom. "I've been cooking since I was ten. I think I can figure out how to work a range."

Jacob cleared his throat. "I'll see you out, Thaddeus. We're grateful for your help."

After they left, Jenny moved to Cassie's side. "Anytime you have a question, just ask me. I'm thinking you won't have a bit of trouble. Soon as the flue is up, we'll start us a fire. Maybe bake a test pie, just for the three of us."

Becca walked to the range and ran her hand over the smooth iron top. "Wash is going to cut the hole in the roof for the flue." This time her smile lit her face. "He's a good carpenter."

"I'm sure he is." Cassie's heart ached for Becca. Why didn't Reverend French just tell her "no" straight out, instead of pretending he might agree? His promise to pray sounded a lot like her parents saying "We'll see" when she was a child. A delayed no was still a no.

❧

Jacob sat in his office staring at the totals in his open ledger long after everyone but Wash had left.

Now that he no longer needed to send a portion of his earnings to Keegan Byrne, he should be able to rebuild his savings within a month or two. He'd kept July's portion when he left for Boston, hoping his visit with Colin would go as it had. When he reached the end of August, he'd be able to put another payment in his own bank account, instead of giving his profits to Byrne.

But for the moment, his funds were stretched thin. He needed to order more stock for the grocery, and soon. He twirled the pen between his fingers. If he ordered just enough to finish out the month, he'd be in a better position in September to restock his supplies. He noted the amounts he'd need, based on Timothy's list, then tallied the total. Barely sufficient.

No matter. He'd done the right thing in purchasing his share. No one could threaten him again.

From the kitchen, he heard metal clank as Wash mounted a collar to the opening in the top of the range. Further metallic rattles told him the flue had been shoved through the ceiling.

After a few minutes, Wash rapped on the entrance to the storeroom. A dusting of sawdust clung to his hair. He wiped beads of sweat from his forehead with the back of his arm, then brushed debris from his trousers.

"All done. Want to take a look?"

"Absolutely." Jacob blew out the flame on the lamp and followed him.

He whistled when he reached the kitchen. The range, with its shining nickel trim, fit perfectly into the spot Cassie had envisioned. The flue rose to the ceiling and disappeared through a precise opening. Wash had swept the sawdust away, leaving the room immaculate.

"Good work. The ladies will be pleased when they come in tomorrow."

Wash ducked his head. "Hope so. I been trying to think of ways to make Becca smile."

"Miss Haddon told me about your plans to marry."

"That's about all we got is plans." Wash balled his fists. "No colored preacher around here."

Jacob opened his mouth to make a comment about Cassie's visit to Reverend French, then decided to say nothing. The minister said he'd pray for a solution, but that was four days ago. He'd give the matter some thought. Perhaps he could move things along.

After taking a final glance around at Wash's work, he reached in his pocket and handed the man a dollar gold piece. "I appreciate you staying late. You did a fine job on that range flue."

Wash's eyes brightened. "Thank you, sir." He took a step toward the back door. "If you're ready to go home, I'll fetch the buggy."

"I'm ready." Wash had worked hard and looked exhausted. The stock order could wait.

<hr />

Jacob strolled into the kitchen after the noon meal the next day. Heat radiated from the new oven, spreading the aroma of peaches through the room. Cassie stirred a pot of what appeared to be clear syrup on the range top.

"Are you happy with your choice?"

She sent him a smile that weakened his knees. No one had ever looked at him like that before.

"Happy as I can be! The morning seemed far less rushed with two baking areas. Didn't you think so, Becca?"

"Yes, missy." She lifted a platter from the washbasin and set it upside-down on the drain board. "We got our work done a lot faster, for certain."

Jacob moved closer to Cassie. "If you're caught up, would

you come with me for a few minutes? I have an errand and would like your help."

A plate clinked against the platter. Becca stood rigid, hands unmoving in the soapy water.

Cassie glanced at her, then up at him. "I'm afraid I can't today. This is Becca's free afternoon, and I've already been gone twice this week."

"But that's why—" He swallowed the rest of his sentence at the sight of the gratitude on Becca's face. "This evening then."

Cassie gave him another muscle-melting smile. "That will be fine."

He walked toward his office marveling at the way she'd taken his gruff nature and turned it into something resembling soft pie dough. He'd try to change the arrangements he'd made. This evening ought to be soon enough to accomplish his purpose, assuming they left right after the restaurant closed.

Jacob shook the reins and guided the horse and buggy out of the alley and south on Third Street.

"Where are we going?" Cassie smiled at him through the soft light. She placed her hand over his. "Not that it matters."

"I made arrangements for us to see the reverend this evening."

She jerked her hand away. "The reverend? Why?"

"Wash and Becca have waited long enough for their answer. I'd like to hear a yes or a no. If Reverend French won't marry them, maybe tomorrow after church you and I will go to Hartfield to find a preacher. I know there are a number of free Negroes in that area."

He turned the buggy toward the curb and stopped in front of the Frenches' house. Lights glimmered in the windows.

She stared at him, fanning herself with her hand. "I thought you wanted to discourage me from asking, now here you are stepping forward."

"I talked a bit with Wash last night. Telling him Becca could share his lodging in my—our—house was almost cruel. They have our permission to be together, and no legal way to marry."

A minute later she stood next to him on the doorstep, waiting for someone to answer his knock.

Lamplight spilled over them when Reverend French opened the door. "Mr. West. Miss Haddon. You're very prompt. Please, follow me."

He led them through the doorway at the end of the hall. "We're less likely to be interrupted in here. Please sit anywhere you like."

Jacob surveyed the study as he held one of the armchairs for Cassie. Bookshelves lined two of the walls, with a draped window behind the reverend's chair. A lamp hanging from a brass chain glowed above their heads. He nodded silent approval. One day he'd enlarge West & Riley's to include a real office that resembled this one.

Reverend French rested his folded hands on the surface of his desk. He glanced between them, a sparkle in his eyes. "Are you here to discuss your wedding? Mrs. French reports that you're planning to be married, and I must say I'm pleased at the news. Have you set a date?"

"We have. The twenty-fifth of September."

"Any particular reason you chose that specific day?" He raised a questioning eyebrow.

"It's Jacob's birthday," Cassie said. "And my favorite time of year—the fall colors are coming on. The leaves are gorgeous."

Jacob cleared his throat. "But tonight we've come to discuss a different wedding—that of my employees Wash Bennett and Becca Rowan."

The minister rubbed his fingers over his flushed cheeks. "Miss Haddon must have told you of our visit. I said I'd pray about the matter, and I have. My answer is yes—and no."

38

$\mathcal{J}$acob half rose from his chair. "What do you mean, 'yes and no'? Will you perform the ceremony or not?" He heard the harshness in his voice and subsided. "Forgive me. I need to learn patience."

"I understand your frustration. Let me explain." Reverend French laid one hand flat on the desktop, fingers spread. "I'm happy to marry the couple you're concerned about. But not in the church building. Unfortunately, too many members in my congregation have strong feelings about this subject."

Cassie stirred. "Then your yes isn't really a yes at all, is it?"

"If you can suggest another location—"

"My house." Jacob thumped his fist on the arm of the chair. "What better place? Would you be willing to marry them there?"

Reverend French tipped his head to one side, smiling. "You're a noble soul, Mr. West. Just tell me the day and I'll promise you a fine wedding."

"When I see Wash tonight, I'll give him the good news. You'll have the date as soon as they decide." He rose and extended his hand. "Thank you."

The minister gripped his palm. "You're the answer to my prayers. Thank *you*."

After they left the parsonage, Cassie squeezed his arm. "How kind of you to offer your home. Becca will be overjoyed. You truly are the answer to many prayers, I'm sure."

He didn't know about being the answer to anyone's prayers, but after his rough Boston past, he knew plenty about being on the outside of proper society. If he could help Wash and Becca get a start in a new life, he'd be on the road to repaying those who had helped him.

When Cassie and Jacob took seats next to Faith in church on Sunday, Faith leaned close and whispered in Cassie's ear.

"Can you come by the mercantile after services? I have a surprise for you."

Shocked, she stared at her friend. "You're open on Sundays now?"

Faith gave her head a decisive shake. "No. Never. But I have something to show you. I'll unlock the front door and we can slip inside." She reached to her right and clasped her husband's hand. "Curt can drop us off and then take Alexander and Grandpa on home."

Mrs. French played the first notes of the opening hymn, cutting off further conversation. As Cassie followed the order of service, her mind wandered to the image of Reverend French standing in Jacob's parlor performing Wash and Becca's marriage ceremony. She scooted a bit nearer to Jacob. In five weeks it would be their turn.

Once the final hymn had been sung, she followed him out into the brilliant sunlight. "Faith has something she wants to show me. Curt's going to take us to the mercantile now."

"Is that what you two were whispering about?" His moustache lifted in a smile.

"Yes. I know we have a picnic planned this afternoon. Would you be disappointed if we delayed our departure for a half hour or so?"

"Not at all. You go find out what Faith's secret is all about. I'll call for you at the store after a bit." He raised her gloved hand and kissed her fingertips.

She wished she could throw her arms around him but contented herself with clasping his hand before joining Faith and her family in the Saxons' buggy.

"Just wait until you see," Faith said while they traveled the short distance to the mercantile. As soon as Curt deposited them at the door, she opened her handbag and removed the key.

The interior felt stuffy from being closed up on such a warm afternoon. Cassie slipped her mantelet from her shoulders, draping the embroidered garment over her arm.

"Where's my surprise?"

"Right here." Faith led her to the fabric display. Tissue paper rustled as she unwrapped a protective covering. She held a bolt of shimmering ivory silk toward Cassie and said, "For your wedding dress."

The mantelet fell to the floor as Cassie reached out to stroke the smooth fabric. "This is beautiful." She kept her voice low, as though the silk were magical and her words might cause the illusion to disappear. "I never dreamed you'd order something so fine for my dress." She gulped. "I . . . I don't know if I can afford silk."

Faith placed the bolt on the cutting table and hugged her. "This is my gift to you. Sheriff Cooper's wife, Amy, will sew your gown." She pushed a *Godey's* magazine toward her, opened to a page near the center. "Here's the style you chose. Ruffles around the bottom and appliquéd lace at the neck. Silk is the perfect choice."

Fighting tears, Cassie pressed her fingers to her mouth. "How can I thank you?"

"Your friendship is thanks enough. It's been a blessing to see how you've blossomed on your own. And now you have Jacob in your life. I want to celebrate with you."

Cassie bowed her head and sent up a silent prayer of thanks.

Cassie's mind continued to buzz with thoughts of weddings when she entered the kitchen Monday morning.

Becca left Jenny's side and hurried to her. "Wash told me what you and Mr. West did. I can't think how to thank you." Her face shone with happiness. "Mr. West said we could get married anytime we want."

"That's so. Have you chosen a day?"

"Maybe this Friday after we close?"

"If Reverend French has no other commitments, that sounds perfect." Cassie looked up and caught Jenny's smiling nod. "Jenny and I will bake a cake for you, and I have a friend who grows flowers. I'll ask her for a bouquet."

Becca hugged her arms to her middle. "I can't hardly believe this is happening. A real wedding with a real preacher." She twirled around. "Just like white folks."

Cassie blinked back tears. She'd taken too much for granted in her life. Even after the devastation of the war, her privileges were so great, and Becca's were so few.

Thank you, Lord, for answering this prayer with a yes.

She turned when she heard a spoon tapping on the side of a bowl. Jenny sent her a mock frown. "We'd best get breakfast cooked. We'll do our dancing on Friday night."

"Indeed we will." Cassie patted Becca's shoulder, then slipped on an apron and arranged kindling in the new range's firebox. Once the flames burned steadily, she added larger pieces of wood and slid the damper partway closed.

"While the oven heats I'll go tell Mr. West that you've chosen Friday for the wedding." Without waiting for a response, she whipped out of the kitchen and sped toward the grocery.

Jacob's eyes softened when he saw her. "Good morning, Miss Haddon. You look like a lady on a mission."

Her heart tingled when he said her name in his growly voice.

"Good morning to you too, Mr. West. I have news. Becca said they'd like to be married this Friday evening. Will that be suitable?"

"Definitely. They've waited long enough."

She clasped her hands beneath her chin, certain she was engaged to the kindest man in the world. "Would you have time today to ask Reverend French whether he's free on Friday?"

"I'll call on him this afternoon."

"Thank you. Oh, I have so many plans! Jenny and I will bake a special cake for them, I'll see Rosemary about flowers . . ."

He glanced around. Seeing they were alone, he kissed the tip of her nose. "This will be good practice for us. Our wedding day will be here before we know it."

"I'm counting the hours! But in the meantime, I want Becca's wedding to be perfect. May I have Wash drive me to your house Friday afternoon so I can decorate the parlor just a bit?"

"Decorate to your heart's content. Like I said, this is good practice for us."

She couldn't keep the smile from her lips as she returned to the kitchen. If not for Jacob volunteering his home, this wedding wouldn't be happening. She'd do all she could to make the event memorable.

❧

Cassie stood in Jacob's parlor on Friday afternoon, a basket of flowers at her feet. Rosemary had supplied her with rose verbena, purple blazing stars, and black-eyed Susans, along with two glass containers for arrangements.

She surveyed the room. Assuming Reverend French would stand in front of the fireplace to perform the ceremony, she'd place the flower-filled vases at either end of the mantel. Timothy and Jenny were the only invited guests, aside from her and Jacob.

Wash hovered in the entrance to the parlor. "The boss said to help you. Is there anything you need done, missy?"

"Yes, please. While I fill these vases with water, would you bring four chairs from the dining room? Set them so they face the fireplace. That's where the minister will stand when he marries you and Becca."

He shook his head, an expression of wonder on his face. "Lord be praised. Never thought I'd see the day when I'd be free to take a bride and not worry about her being sold off." He stepped forward and lifted the basket from the floor. "Let me take this to the kitchen for you. There's water in a pitcher next to the stove."

While she arranged the flowers, she heard him crossing back and forth between the parlor and the dining room. When the vases were arranged to her satisfaction, she carried them into the parlor and placed them on either side of two glass candlestands. Then she stepped back and admired her handiwork. With the chairs in place, the parlor resembled a small chapel. Giving a sigh of satisfaction, she returned to the kitchen.

Wash sprang to his feet when she entered. "Got something else for me to do?"

"No, thank you. Everything's in place for this evening. Please take me home now."

The buggy lurched over rocks as Wash guided the horse down the dusty track. Cassie leaned back to admire the soft blue of the sky that stretched, cloudless, from horizon to horizon. Soon after they turned onto the road toward town, they passed the grassy overlook where Jacob had asked her to marry him.

She felt a pang of longing, wishing he'd come with her today. She hoped he wouldn't mind that she'd rearranged his parlor. Then she closed her eyes. Before long they'd share not only the parlor but the upstairs portion of the house. A flush crept up her neck and she forced her thoughts to Wash and Becca. Everything was in place for a perfect wedding.

Wash stopped the buggy in the alley behind her cabin, then jumped off the seat and helped her down.

"Thank you. I appreciate you taking time from your work to drive me to Mr. West's and back." She tucked the empty basket under her arm.

"You done so much for us, missy. Anytime you want my help, you holler."

"Indeed I will." She smiled up at the big man. "I'll see you this evening."

She stood watching for a moment as he drove away. The

remainder of the afternoon stretched before her. Perhaps she'd heat water for—

"There you are, Cassie!"

She whipped around at the familiar voice. Mother charged down the gravel path toward her, Patrick Fitzhugh trailing in her wake.

39

Cassie gaped at her mother. Her eyes must be playing tricks.

The peacock feathers on Mother's hat bobbed as she grabbed Cassie's hands. "I came as soon as I received your letter. I just pray I'm not too late."

"Wh . . . what are you talking about?"

"Mr. West. I couldn't believe your words. You haven't married him, have you?"

Cassie firmed her spine. "No, but I plan to. In September."

"Why would you defy Scripture and marry a shopkeeper when you know Patrick is the person the Lord intends for you?"

"I know no such thing." She glanced at Mr. Slocum's house, which stood barely twenty feet away. If he happened to be home, he'd hear every word of their conversation. The next thing she knew, Faith's woodstove regulars would have the report all over town.

She opened the door of her cabin. "Please come in. You're evidently exhausted from your journey."

Mother flounced inside, her royal blue skirt swaying as she passed and settled on one of the chairs around the small table.

Cassie glared at Patrick. He must have the thick hide of a range cow. She'd told him in no uncertain terms that she didn't wish to see him again and yet here he stood.

"You may come in too, if you wish."

Patrick cast a sorrowful look in her direction when he entered. "Miss Haddon. Cassie. Your poor mother was sorely distressed at the contents of your letter. I can't say I blame her."

She stood in the center of the room with her hands on her hips. "Forgive me for being blunt, but why are you involved? This is a matter between my mother and myself."

"I'm the one called to be responsible for you, not Mr. West. Reverend Greeley suggested I accompany her the moment she showed him your message."

She spun around to face her mother. "You showed Reverend Greeley my letter? Why would you do such a thing?"

"Because I care about your future."

A wave of dizziness staggered her. She groped for a chair as her thoughts swung to the two men who held her mother in their spell. She could spend all evening sorting out the motives behind this visit, but she didn't have all evening. Jacob would be here soon to escort her to Wash and Becca's wedding.

Mother reached across the table and patted her hand. "May I please have a cup of tea? I'm rather weary."

"I'm sure you must be." Cassie tried to keep sarcasm from her voice. She rose and opened the firebox on her stove, stirred the coals, and dropped kindling over the embers. After filling a kettle, she placed it on top of the stove. "While we wait for the water to boil, perhaps Mr. Fitzhugh would be good enough to leave us so you can rest."

"That won't be necessary. He kindly engaged two rooms for us at the hotel." Mother glanced through the open doorway into Cassie's bedroom. "Seeing you living in such circumstances makes me feel like a failure. I devoted my life to molding you into a lady, so you could marry well. Instead here you are, living in a cabin, working as a cook . . ." She dabbed at her eyes with a handkerchief.

A plume of steam rose from the kettle. Cassie jerked her teapot from the shelf and dumped in a scoop of tea. Her hands shook as she poured water over the leaves. "I am going to marry well. In five weeks I'll be Mrs. Jacob West."

Patrick lifted his hand, palm out. "As Garrett's brother, I'm obligated to take his place. I cannot disobey God's Word."

She ignored him and splashed tea into a cup, placing the brew in front of her mother. "As soon as you've finished, I must excuse myself to change my dress. Jacob is coming in a few minutes. He's hosting a wedding for two of his employees."

"Oh mercy sakes." Mother fanned herself with her handkerchief. "His employees? Do you see why I'm concerned? I'm sure they have no social standing whatsoever." She lifted the cup and took a small sip. "You wouldn't have any sugar, would you?"

Honor your mother. Honor your mother. Cassie repeated the words to herself while she crossed the room for the bowl and a spoon. As she placed the sugar on the table, she heard someone rap on the door frame.

How like Jacob to be so eager to see her that he'd arrive early. And how unfortunate that the two people he'd least want to see were sitting in her home. Her shoulders sagged when she turned to answer his knock.

Jacob rested his hand on the jamb when the door opened. "I know I'm early, but—"

Cassie's strained expression stopped him. He noticed she still wore her work dress, and loose tendrils escaped her pinned-up braids.

"Forgive me. I thought you'd be ready. Did something go wrong this afternoon?"

Tears shone in her eyes. "You might say that." She moved away from the entrance.

Her mother sat at the table, nailing him with a glare that could have burned leather. He took an involuntary step backward, then noticed Patrick Fitzhugh standing in the shadows.

"Mrs. Bingham. Mr. Fitzhugh. What a—" He couldn't say "pleasant." "A surprise."

"I'm sure it is," Fitzhugh said, his tone silky. "Mrs. Bingham was most anxious to see her daughter. As a family friend, I offered to help her make the journey."

Jacob shot a glance at Cassie, eyebrows raised.

She folded her arms across her chest. Her lips thinned. "Mother and Mr. Fitzhugh arrived after Wash brought me home this afternoon. They'll be staying at the hotel. I've already informed them of our plans for this evening."

"Miss Haddon was most apologetic. I do understand that we arrived unannounced." Fitzhugh sketched a bow in Cassie's direction. "We will visit more tomorrow." With a pointed look at Jacob, he continued. "After working hours, of course."

He clenched his fist over the head of his cane. One more word and he wouldn't be responsible for what happened next.

Mrs. Bingham pushed her teacup to the center of the table and moved to Cassie's side. "Have a pleasant evening, dear." She dropped a kiss on her cheek. "I trust you'll keep tomorrow evening free. Patrick has an important matter to discuss with you."

Nodding as she passed Jacob, she said, "Good-bye, Mr. West."

When the door closed behind them, Cassie leaned against the frame and rubbed her temples. "Of all the days, why did she pick today?"

His temper heated. "I'm not as concerned about the timing as I am with Fitzhugh's 'important matter.' Is there something between you that you haven't mentioned?"

"There's nothing between Mr. Fitzhugh and myself." She bustled to the table and carried her mother's teacup to the washbasin, refusing to meet his eyes. "Mother seems to like him, but I don't."

When he opened his mouth to respond, she stopped him by placing her finger over his lips. "I must excuse myself to change my dress. After all we've done to arrange this wedding, we can't be late."

The door to the bedroom closed.

He straddled one of the chairs and fought to rein in his imagination. Regardless of Cassie's claim, Fitzhugh wouldn't travel all the way to Noble Springs without an ulterior motive. Men like him never did.

Now that he had a moment to think, he tried to remember what she'd said in the letter she'd written explaining the circumstances of her stay in Price City. Seemed to him that she'd glossed over Fitzhugh's presence. Perhaps the man had made improper advances and she was too embarrassed to confess.

He rubbed his moustache. Now wasn't the time for a confrontation. He'd find a way to ask her after the wedding.

Cassie smoothed the skirt on her rose chintz dress as she settled into the chair Jacob held for her. He'd said little on the trip to his house. She knew the arrival of her mother and Patrick had put a damper on his anticipation of Wash's wedding. When he took the chair beside her, she laced her fingers through his. "This event wouldn't be happening if not for you."

His eyes brightened for a moment. "You had as much to do with the arrangements as I did. The flowers look pretty on the mantel."

Jenny leaned over from her seat between Timothy and Cassie. "Don't forget about the cake in the dining room. I worked a long time getting that icing just right. Had to slap Timothy's fingers a time or two on the way out here to keep him from tasting a sample."

Timothy's face reddened.

"I haven't forgotten," Jacob said. "We'll all enjoy a slice after the ceremony."

Cassie peeked over her shoulder in time to see Reverend French enter. He took his position in front of the screened fireplace and nodded toward the doorway.

Becca and Wash entered hand in hand. She wore a yellow calico dress Cassie hadn't seen before, with a crocheted white collar pinned at her throat by a shell brooch. Green glass earbobs sparkled against her skin. Next to her, Wash walked tall and proud. His white shirt gleamed almost as brightly as his smile.

They stopped in front of Reverend French and for a few moments the room fell silent. Then he opened the book he carried. After glancing at the page, he lifted his eyes to Wash and Becca.

"Dearly beloved, we are gathered here today to join Washington Bennett and Rebecca Rowan in holy matrimony, which is honorable among all men and is an estate which is not to be taken lightly."

Cassie sighed and clutched Jacob's hand. Before long they'd be hearing these same vows spoken over them. She stole a glance at him and met his warm molasses gaze. Tingles coursed over her skin.

By the time Reverend French pronounced Wash and Becca husband and wife, Cassie had to wipe tears from her eyes. She heard Jenny sniffling next to her.

Wash turned and strode to Jacob. "God bless you, sir, for all you done. You're a mighty good man."

As she led the way into the dining room, Cassie's heart swelled at his words. She couldn't agree more.

Jenny had centered the cake on the oval pillar-style dining table. Light from an overhead lamp shone on delicate china plates and silver dessert forks. Once the bride and groom entered, Jenny cut the first slice of cake, handing the plate to Becca.

Tears slipped down the young woman's cheeks. "I feel like I'm dreaming. When I got to Noble Springs I never thought I'd end up married, and find white folks who cared what happened to me."

"The Lord has a plan for each of us," Reverend French said. "He was guiding you all along."

Cassie took a breath for courage. Here was her opportunity to settle the question of Patrick Fitzhugh once and for all. She tucked her hand under the minister's arm and skirted them around the table to stand in a quiet corner.

"I believe that's true for all of us, Reverend. But when things happen, how do we know whether they're the Lord's guidance, or man's plan?"

He raised an eyebrow. "That's a serious question for such a happy occasion."

"I'm asking because I need your advice."

"Well then, I can tell you two of the best ways." He held up his index finger. "First of all, seek your answers in Scripture." He raised a second finger. "Then seek godly counsel. You should find the guidance you need."

She stared at the floral-patterned rug while she considered his response. Patrick claimed Scripture supported his position, but his counselor was a person she neither knew well nor trusted. Reverend French had proved himself to be a godly man, sincere in his desire to do the Lord's bidding.

Lifting her chin, she met the minister's gray eyes. "Would you be able to meet with me tomorrow evening after I finish at the restaurant? Please? There is a man who seems to think I'm endangering my soul if I don't marry him." She felt she'd choke on the knot in her throat.

He cast a startled glance at Jacob. "I had no idea—"

"No, not Jacob. Someone else."

Jacob's head shot around at the mention of his name. He took a step toward them.

Reverend French patted her wrist. "Tomorrow evening will be fine. I'll be most happy to discuss this matter with you."

"Thank you." Her legs trembled as she walked to Jacob's side. She prayed with her whole heart that Mr. Fitzhugh would be proved wrong. The alternative was too heartbreaking to contemplate.

⁂

Cassie sat next to Jacob on the buggy seat as they bounced their way down the track to the main road into Noble Springs. In spite of the lateness of the hour, she didn't feel a bit sleepy. Tomorrow evening's meeting with Reverend French boiled through her thoughts. She'd blurted out her request before remembering her mother and Patrick were expected at the same time. Somehow she'd have to juggle the two visits.

She blew out a long sigh and cuddled closer to Jacob's side. The image of the happiness on Wash and Becca's faces swept her concerns away for the moment. "What a happy night."

"Yes." He guided the horse onto the road and within a short distance pulled off onto the verge where he'd asked her to marry him.

The waning moon hung low over the water of Pioneer Lake, casting shadows over Jacob's face. Her heart fluttered. The romance of the evening had affected him too. She lifted her lips for his kiss, but he clasped his hands over hers instead.

"We're alone here. No one will bother us."

Her heartbeat increased from a flutter to a pounding. What on earth was he suggesting?

He tightened his grip. "All through the ceremony my mind kept returning to Fitzhugh and his important matter. Is he the 'someone else' you mentioned when you were off in the corner with the reverend?"

Cassie wished she could disappear. Why hadn't she told Jacob the whole story about Patrick from the beginning? Instead of going away as she'd hoped, Patrick had persisted with his claim. Tugging her hands free, she rubbed her sweating palms on her skirt, then forced herself to meet his gaze.

"Yes, he is."

He lowered his voice. "Are you carrying on with both of us?" His face was emotionless, waiting.

"Good heavens, no!"

"How can I believe you? Fitzhugh turns up like a bad penny every few weeks."

"I've told him more than once I'm not interested." She bit her lip to keep from weeping. "I have no control over his comings and goings."

"So, if you told him you're not interested, he must have had reason to believe you were taken with him in the first place."

She slid across the seat and scrambled down from the buggy. She couldn't think with Jacob so near. The brake grated into place, and the next thing she knew he stood beside her.

"Please give me a minute to myself."

His feet crunched on the dry grass as his footsteps receded. "Take all the time you need. I'm not leaving."

Pressing her fist against her lips, she stared out at the moon-lit lake. If she evaded the truth, he'd find out sooner or later. Her mother would probably tell him, bless her. But sharing Patrick's claim might end their engagement tonight.

Her father's words came back to her. *There are many ways to do the wrong thing, but only one way to do what's right. Let your conscience be your guide.*

"Yes, Papa," she whispered, then stepped to Jacob's side.

He tucked his thumbs in his front pockets when she approached. He didn't smile.

She lifted her chin. "I first met Patrick Fitzhugh when I escorted Mother to Calusa. You already know that. What I didn't tell you is that he believes that as my former fiancé's brother it's his scriptural duty to marry me. If I marry anyone else I'm going against God's Word."

"What?!"

She held up her hand. "Please let me finish. I didn't want to tell you at first because I hoped if I ignored him he'd go away. Obviously that hasn't happened, so this evening I asked Reverend French if I could call on him tomorrow after work. He should be able to tell me whether there's any truth to Patrick's assertion."

Jacob clutched her shoulders and drew her closer. "What will you do if Fitzhugh is correct?"

"I don't know."

assie sat up in bed and slid her feet to the floor. Perhaps a glass of water would help her fall asleep. After lighting the candle on her bedside table, she padded through the cabin to the shelf where she kept a filled pitcher, then sighed and turned back to her bedroom without the glass. Water wouldn't slow her tumbling thoughts.

She flopped back on the bed and tried to find a comfortable spot within the tangled sheets. She'd been so sure Patrick was wrong that she'd never given serious consideration to the alternative. If she couldn't have Jacob, she didn't want anybody. Being a spinster forever would be better than marrying a man she didn't love.

When she awakened at daylight, she longed to stay locked away in her cabin until time to meet with Reverend French. Such a choice wasn't possible. Becca had been given the day off.

She groaned. Jenny would be full of chatter about the wedding. Jacob would . . . She didn't know what Jacob would do. Their parting last night had been strained.

As she left her cabin, she prayed for strength to last the day. Without Becca she'd have to bake all the pies herself as well as help Jenny with the meals. Then after work Mother and Patrick would be waiting.

One step at a time. If she didn't heap all her worries in a pile, they might seem less overwhelming.

Jenny paused in her breakfast preparations when Cassie arrived. Her round cheeks shone like apples from the heat radiating off the oversized range.

"Didn't Becca look nice in that yellow dress my daughter gave her? What a fine thing Mr. West did to let them get married in his house." Jenny swiped perspiration from her forehead. "Not too many folks around here would've been so open-minded."

"No, I suppose not. He's a kindly man." She lowered her head to hide the tears stinging her eyes. What if the reverend agreed with Patrick?

"Here, now. What's the matter?" Jenny slid her arm around Cassie's shoulders. "Did you two have a tiff?"

She leaned against the other woman's side. "Not . . . not exactly. My mother arrived unexpectedly yesterday afternoon and—"

"Say no more. She may be your mother, but I must say that woman's a trial."

"She can be. But she was a different person before the war. Content, busy with her needlework and overseeing our home. That's the mother I see when I look at her."

Jenny sniffed. "We were all different before the war, but we don't take our griefs out on other folks."

"I know." To change the subject, Cassie took an apron off the shelf and tied the starched waistband around her middle. "What would you like me to do to help with breakfast before I start the pies?"

"Get the tables ready, please, then chop up a mess of potatoes while I fry the ham steaks."

Grateful for tasks to keep her hands occupied, Cassie paused in front of her new range and stuffed kindling into the firebox, then headed for the shelves where they kept the crockery.

Jacob stood in the entrance to the grocery watching her with a somber expression as she arranged place settings on the tables. A sheet of paper dangled from his fingers. She suspected he held the letter she'd left for him after her return from Price City.

Her hands trembled. His steady gaze reminded her of her first days in the kitchen, when she could do nothing right. When he had the power to dismiss her from her job. Now the threat was greater. If Patrick was correct, Jacob might be forced to dismiss her from his heart.

Cassie trudged home at the end of the workday, dreading the visit from her mother and Patrick. There had to be a way to make both of them understand she had her own plans for her life. As soon as she made herself clear, she'd hurry to her meeting with Reverend French.

Her heart raced. She couldn't remember a time when she'd been so fearful. Then a verse she'd memorized slipped between her ragged thoughts.

For God hath not given us the spirit of fear; but of power, and of love, and of a sound mind.

What would she do if she weren't afraid? She'd face her mother. She'd talk to the reverend. She'd trust in the Lord for the outcome.

When she stepped onto her gravel walkway, she saw her mother and Patrick waiting in the shade of the oak tree next to her front door. She squared her shoulders.

Mother held out her hand. "My dear, I hope you're not totally exhausted."

"No, I'm not," she said, surprised at the truth of her response. "Let's go inside. I'll brew some tea if you like."

"No thank you." Patrick moved between them. "We wouldn't want to put you to any trouble. You've spent a tiring day working in that kitchen."

She frowned at him as she opened the door. "Then please sit and tell me the important matter that brought you here." She knew why he'd come, but she wanted the opportunity to tell him no with Mother as a witness.

Patrick sat across the table, with her mother between them. "I came to formally ask for your hand. I can provide you and your mother the type of life you deserve."

Mother folded her hands in her lap and beamed at him.

"Do you love me?" Cassie held her breath, waiting for his answer. What would she do if he said yes?

"I know love will grow after our marriage."

She heaved a relieved sigh. "Without love, and given the fact that we hardly know one another, I cannot accept such a proposal." She clenched her hands in her lap so tightly the nails bit into her palms. If this didn't send him on his way, nothing would.

"I was afraid you'd feel that way. Unfortunately, Scripture is clear." He sent her a pleading glance. "It's my duty to take you as my wife."

God had opened the door and she'd step through it. She pushed her chair away from the table. "Since you're so sure, I'd like you to come with me."

"Where?"

"We're going to the parsonage in the next block. I want you to explain your reasoning to Reverend French."

"Cassie . . ." Mother scrambled to rise.

Patrick touched her arm and she settled back on the chair. "This will only take a moment, Mrs. Bingham. You stay here and rest. We'll be back quite soon, I assure you."

❧

Reverend French opened the door at her knock. "I'm pleased to see you again, Miss Haddon." He cocked an eyebrow at Patrick. "And you've brought a guest?"

"Yes. This is Mr. Fitzhugh. He's raised an issue that I pray you can settle."

After the men shook hands, he led the two of them to his study. By now Cassie felt comfortable enough in his presence to relax somewhat when she seated herself on one of the upholstered chairs.

He moved several papers and an open Bible to one side before placing his hands flat on the desktop. "Well, Miss Haddon, what's the issue you're concerned with?"

She shot a glance at Patrick. He sat with his hat on his lap and an expectant expression on his face. Lamplight gleamed on the Macassar oil in his hair.

Her fingers tightened on the arms of the chair. "Mr. Fitzhugh is the brother of my late fiancé, Garrett Fitzhugh. I met Patrick quite by accident when I first escorted my mother to Calusa. Then yesterday afternoon, the two of them arrived unexpectedly as I was preparing for Wash and Becca's wedding . . ." Her voice faltered.

Reverend French nodded. "Please go on."

"Yes, Miss Haddon. Please do. I'd like to hear your version." Patrick's mouth tightened.

She glared at him. "To put it bluntly, Mr. Fitzhugh believes it is his scriptural duty as Garrett's brother to marry me. I've refused on more than one occasion, but he persists." She slumped against the chair back and drew a shaky breath.

The minister stared at Patrick. "Your scriptural duty? Where did you get that idea?"

Patrick's fair skin turned a mottled red. "My good friend, the Reverend Alfred Greeley, supplied me with the verse. As a matter of fact, I heard you quote the same verse right here in your church."

"What verse might that be?"

Cassie leaned forward. She should have asked that question long ago, instead of trusting Patrick's word.

"Deuteronomy 25:5." He gave a haughty lift to his chin. "Scripture is quite clear on the matter."

"Let's see about that." Reverend French lifted his Bible and riffled pages toward the front, stopping when he found the verse in question. As he ran his finger along the lines of print, a wrinkle formed between his eyes. "Have you read this for yourself, or did you rely on your friend's interpretation?"

"Of course I've read it." Patrick's Adam's apple bobbed. "Why?"

"Here's what the verse says: 'If brethren dwell together, and one of them die, and have no child, the wife of the dead shall not marry without unto a stranger—'"

"Exactly what I've told Miss Haddon."

"Let me finish. '—her husband's brother shall go in unto her, and take her to him to wife, and perform the duty of an husband's brother unto her.'"

"Precisely."

She sank lower in the chair. Her doom was sealed.

Reverend French tapped his index finger on the page. "In your haste to interpret Scripture to suit your desires, you've overlooked one important fact."

"And what would that be?"

Cassie sat taller, head cocked to hear the reverend's reply.

"The verse pertains to the *wife* of the dead brother, not his fiancée. There's no reason Miss Haddon should be required to marry you."

"But Reverend Greeley said—" Patrick stood, clenching his hat brim. "I see." Without another word, he pivoted and left the room. His footsteps thudded along the hallway. The front door slammed.

She leaped to her feet. "Oh, thank you!" She felt like twirling around the room for joy. Free of Patrick, free to marry Jacob.

"You're more than welcome, Miss Haddon. Please come to see me whenever you have questions. Misapplied Scripture has been the cause of far too much unhappiness in our world."

"Thank you again, for everything." She held out her hand and he took it in both of his.

"I'll look forward to discussing wedding plans with you and Mr. West when you two are ready."

Cassie wished she could run to Jacob's side right now, but her mother waited at the cabin.

She wouldn't take the news well.

41

Cassie marched to her cabin, prepared to face an angry Patrick and a weeping mother. Twilight softened her surroundings. Beneath the butternut tree, fireflies spun and danced to a tune played by crickets. Her heart danced with them. Reverend French had given her the best news possible. Her mother would be unhappy, but Cassie hoped Uncle Rand would keep her too busy to attempt any further matchmaking.

She opened her door, surprised to see Mother sitting alone. Instead of tears she wore the expression Cassie remembered seeing after they received the news of her father's death in a prison camp during the war.

She gazed at Cassie with dull eyes. "Patrick's gone."

"Back to the hotel?"

"I suppose so. He's planning to leave on the late train. He said he'd bring my bag over before he goes." She held up a blue pasteboard square. "He paid my fare back to Price City."

Her heart softened at her mother's bleak tone. "Why don't you stay with me for a while? You can get to know Jacob."

"I already know Jacob. He's a grocer."

"He's so much more than what he does for a living. If you'd only—"

"I'm just staying for tonight. I know tomorrow's Sunday, but I'd like to be on the morning train."

Guilt pricked at her. She shouldn't be happy that Mother wanted to leave, but her disapproval of Jacob was a continual thorn.

As if thinking his name brought him to her doorstep, someone knocked. She pushed down a bubble of excitement. Praying it was Jacob, she flung open the door, eager to tell him Reverend French's opinion.

Her smile flattened when she saw Patrick. He thrust Mother's carpetbag at her, his gaze fixed somewhere in the vicinity of her shoes. "Good-bye, Miss Haddon," he muttered.

"Good-bye to you, Mr. Fitzhugh." She closed the door with a sharp click.

Her mother watched as she carried the bag into the bedroom. "Thank you," she said in the same bleak tone she'd used earlier.

Cassie opened the firebox on the stove and stirred the ashes, then stacked a few sticks of kindling over the coals. "You'll feel better if you have some tea."

"No I won't." Mother rose. "I'm very tired. If you'll excuse me, I'd like to go to bed."

After she left, Cassie sat at the table and waited for the water to boil. Her poor mother. She'd endured such a comedown since the war, and now she didn't even have Patrick. His attentions had apparently been motivated by Reverend Greeley's interpretation of Scripture.

She poured water over the tea leaves and watched the color inside the pot change to honey-brown. If only it were that simple to change her mother's opinion of Jacob.

Creaking floorboards roused Cassie in the middle of the night. She snapped awake, fear clutching at her throat. She groped for the candlestick on her night table.

Shuffling footsteps. A chair scraped against the floor.

She grabbed for the matches and lighted the candle, then at the same moment remembered her mother's presence. Tiptoeing into the kitchen, she spotted her standing by the window staring into blackness.

"Why are you walking around in the dark?"

"I'm trying to decide what to tell Rand when I return to Price City."

"Tell him the truth. Patrick was misled by Reverend Greeley." Misled sounded kinder than accusing Patrick's advisor of ignorance. Perhaps he wasn't a preacher at all, but a charlatan, preying on weak women.

"You don't understand. Patrick was my best hope."

"There's no need to worry about my future. You may not like Jacob, but I love him and plan to marry him."

"I'm not thinking about your future, Cassiopeia. I'm facing mine. If you married Patrick, I could return to living a gracious life instead of spending my days slaving in a kitchen. Heaven knows I've had enough of that."

"You've only been helping Uncle Rand for a month."

The candlelight flickered against her mother's face, leaving dark furrows in the lines around her mouth. Gray strands showed in the loose hair cascading over her dressing gown. She sank onto one of the chairs and rested her head on her hand.

"My life is a failure. Everything I fought to achieve is gone. Now I'm back where I started, working in a kitchen."

Cassie took the chair next to her. "You must be tired. We

had a lovely home and servants. You didn't set foot in the kitchen unless you were planning menus."

Mother cupped her hand around the back of her neck and rotated her shoulders. "The truth is I was a kitchen maid in your father's parents' home. That's how we met. You've asked why we never talked about our wedding, or our families. I wouldn't allow it."

"You weren't a maid! That can't be true. You've always been a perfect lady."

"Kitchen maids have eyes. I copied the mistress—your grandmother. By the time your father married me, no one would have guessed my background. We moved far away. Your father lived the life of a gentleman farmer, and I raised you to be a lady."

Cassie drew several deep breaths. Her mind reeled. Every childhood memory she possessed was based on a lie. Needlework, piano lessons, literature appreciation—all pretense. Her mother played a part and she was expected to do the same.

"What about Uncle Rand? Is he really my uncle?"

Mother nodded. "He apprenticed to a blacksmith before I married your father, then wandered from place to place until the war began. I didn't tell a soul back home that he fought for the Union—we'd have been ostracized."

She stared blankly at her mother, then whispered, "And now everything's gone anyway, isn't it? We start over."

Jacob paced the length of his parlor on Sunday morning, a letter from Keegan Byrne crumpled in his fist. He'd planned to show it to Cassie on Friday, but her mother's arrival with Fitzhugh squelched his intentions. Then after the wedding, when she told him about Fitzhugh's claims, all thoughts of his own troubles fled.

He watched her all day Saturday going through her duties without her usual smile. His prayers went with her when she left for home that evening. He wished he knew the Bible better, so he'd understand why Fitzhugh believed she belonged to him.

When he called to take her to church she'd tell him the minister's response. His gut clenched. Regardless of Reverend French's opinion, starting today he'd fight for Cassie.

He tossed the crumpled paper onto the floor and strode to the stable for his buggy.

Cassie waited next to her mother at the train depot. Within minutes, Mother would board and Cassie would be left to sort out her childhood memories, images that resembled a kaleidoscope filled with scattered fragments.

The rails sang with the rhythm of the approaching train. When the engine drew near, Mother broke the prolonged silence between them. "You had to know sooner or later. I'm sorry. What more can I say?"

"Nothing. I just need time to think."

"I wish you'd come with me."

"My life is here, with Jacob."

The train roared to a stop, wheels screeching against the rails. Passengers disembarked. After a few minutes, the conductor hollered the boarding call.

Mother leaned close to kiss Cassie's cheek. "Whatever you may think of me, I love you."

Tears blurred her vision. "I love you too." She spoke from her heart. Despite their frequent clashes, love for her mother didn't change.

Her shoulders sagging, Mother walked toward the passenger car. Her steps dragged. She turned and lifted her hand in a half wave before disappearing down the aisle.

Steeple bells pealed as Cassie left the station. Instead of walking toward the church, she turned north a block away. Spending the morning in church without breaking down would be impossible. She had all she could do to keep from sobbing aloud as she ran toward home.

After services ended, Faith joined Jacob as he left the sanctuary. "I wanted to tell Cassie the muslin pattern for her dress is ready for fitting. Is she sick today?"

"I wish I knew. She wasn't at home when I called for her."

"Not home? On a Sunday?"

"She didn't answer the door." He spread his hands. "I thought she might have left for church early, and would meet me here. I'm going to her house again now."

"Good gracious. If she's desperately ill, please come for me. I'll be glad to sit with her."

"Thank you. I will."

He didn't confide his galloping fears. When Cassie wasn't waiting at the church, he assumed Reverend French told her she had to marry Fitzhugh. She'd taken the morning train with him and her mother. The thought twisted a dagger in his heart.

He knew he shouldn't, but if her door was unlocked he planned to go inside. Maybe she'd left a letter for him on her table. Cassie would never go away without telling him good-bye.

His leg pained him more than usual as he limped toward his buggy. He swung onto the seat and shook the reins over Jackson's back. A couple of minutes and he'd know. Sweat popped out on his forehead. The last time he'd been this apprehensive was in Warden Dwight's office, waiting for his release papers.

Jacob tied his horse in the alley, then marched to Cassie's cabin and knocked. His fingers trembled on the head of his cane. When she didn't answer, he reached for the knob. She opened the door at the same time.

"Oh, Jacob, praise God it's you. I've never been so glad to see anyone." Her eyes were red and swollen. He glanced over her shoulder for her mother and Fitzhugh, pleased to see they were still at the hotel.

"Come in." She sniffled, then wiped her eyes. "I'll leave the door open in case Mr. Slocum is watching." As soon as he stepped out of her neighbor's view, she threw her arms around him. "I've had the most dreadful shock."

He tightened his hold on her waist. As he feared, Reverend French had confirmed Fitzhugh's claim. "Don't worry," he whispered in her ear. "We'll think of a way to stay together, no matter what the reverend says."

She gave a half laugh, half sob, then leaned back in his arms. "I forgot. You don't know. Reverend French informed Mr. Fitzhugh that he was sadly mistaken. The Scripture he based his claim on was meant for the *wife* of a deceased man, not a person's fiancée."

Jacob's knees sagged. He released her and collapsed on a chair. "I've been dreading what you might have to tell me. This . . . this is the best news I've ever heard."

"You should have seen Mr. Fitzhugh's face. He looked like someone had punched him in the stomach. He left on last night's train."

"Then where's your mother? Is she at the hotel?"

Cassie's eyes brimmed. She grabbed her handkerchief and patted the corners of her eyes again.

"N-no. I took her to the depot this morning. She's on her way back to Uncle Rand."

She drew a chair away from the table and sat close enough for her knees to touch his. Her tears spilled over.

He patted her arm. "You miss her."

"No I don't!" She jerked her arm away. "I'm shocked, angry, and bereft. Last night she confessed that her entire life has been a lie. She's not the great lady she pretended to be. Mother was a kitchen maid when she met my father."

Cassie jumped to her feet and stalked across the room, then whirled to face him. "All this time she's scorned my job at the restaurant. She looked down on you as though you weren't good enough for me. Not good enough for the daughter of a kitchen maid! How could she?"

In his mind, he saw the crumpled letter from Byrne lying on the floor in his parlor. The contents seared his memory.

So you paid Colin off. Makes no difference to me. If you want to keep your masquerade I'll expect July and August payments. The choice is yours.

He had less than two weeks until the end of August. If the man carried out his threat, Cassie would agree with her mother.

Jake Westermann wasn't good enough for her.

Jake Westermann. The name haunted him as he drove his buggy away from Cassie's house. Warden Dwight had assured him no one had access to jail records. Colin Riley gave him a new start and a new name seventeen years ago. If he surrendered to Byrne's demands now, Jake Westermann would live on, a chain anchoring him to his past.

He snapped the reins over Jackson's back. The horse picked up speed, trotting past the town square and on beyond Judge Lindberg's home. Noble Springs knew him as Jacob West. All ties to Westermann had long since disappeared.

The buggy bumped through a rut, jarring the pistol in his left boot against his ankle. An icy chill prickled the hair on the back of his neck. As long as he carried that pistol, Jake Westermann traveled with him wherever he went.

When he changed his name, he vowed to be a new man. Jacob West should have disposed of the weapon years ago. Why had he clung to a piece of the life he'd renounced? Habit? Protection? Whatever happened, he knew he'd never point a gun at another person again.

Giving the reins an abrupt tug, he guided the horse down the track to Pioneer Lake, passing buggies tied under trees. Families sat on blankets enjoying a Sunday evening picnic. He slowed Jackson's gait, following wheel ruts around to the deserted eastern side of the water until swamp willows and thick brambles blocked the trail.

Before leaving the buggy, he glanced in all directions to be sure he was alone. Then he climbed down and tied the reins to a stout willow. Sweat soaked his shirt as he fought to push his way through the brush to reach the water's edge. His cane sank into the sandy soil. Mosquitoes buzzed around his ears.

Maybe he should return in the cool of the morning. He paused to catch his breath and turned to look behind him, tracing the path he'd taken to the shoreline. He'd come too far to go back now.

A few more yards through the undergrowth and he stood inches from the lake. Water bugs skated on the glassy surface while dragonflies swooped and darted above. He leaned over, pulled up the hem on his trouser leg, and slid his pistol from the holster. Clutching the grip in his right hand, he pitched the gun as far as he could. It splashed into the water thirty feet from shore.

Jake Westermann was gone forever.

42

assie spun in front of the framed mirror in Faith's spare room. The double row of flounces on the skirt of her silk gown shimmered in the light. She held her hands out to admire the lace ruffles at her wrists. "This will be the most beautiful dress any bride ever wore. Amy is so gifted."

"She'll be happy to know you're pleased." Faith spoke from a slipper chair next to the mirror. Little Alexander played on the rug next to her, waving his legs in the air and grabbing for his toes.

"When do you think she'll remove the final basting and finish the seams?"

"She should have the dress ready by the end of next week. Plenty of time."

Cassie moved carefully across the room and turned so Faith could help her out of the dress. "Not so much time. Today's the third. The twenty-fifth isn't that far away."

Faith paused in removing pins from the back of the gown to pat Cassie's shoulder. "September was upon us before we knew it this year, wasn't it?"

"So many things happened in August. I'm glad the month is over."

"Have you heard from your mother?" Faith's voice carried sympathy.

"No, but it's only been a couple of weeks." A familiar ache settled around her heart. "Maybe she doesn't know what to say now that she's not playing a role."

"Give yourselves time. Healing will come." She removed the last of the pins and held the shoulder seams while Cassie stepped out of the gown.

"I do hope so. Jacob needs to forgive her as well. She's treated him shamefully. He hasn't said as much, but I know he's glad she's in Price City and not here with me."

$\approx$

Jacob tapped the end of a pen holder on the ledger page. The totals looked promising, but not what he'd hoped. Certainly not enough to comply with Byrne's demands—if he planned to comply, which he didn't. The purchase of the new range pushed August's expenses over what he'd anticipated when he paid Colin for his share.

He smiled to himself. Cassie's pleasure at having her own oven for pies made the additional expense worth every penny. Stock orders for September would need to be trimmed, but he'd find a way. Perhaps Mrs. Fielder could offer suggestions for lowering meal costs.

Since the dinner hour had passed, he knew she'd be relaxing with a mug of coffee before commencing supper preparations. He tucked the ledger into a drawer and crossed the empty dining room.

As he'd assumed, Mrs. Fielder sat beside a worktable with a mug in one hand. Becca and Cassie were bent over another table, assembling pies. When she noticed him, Cassie flashed a brilliant smile.

"Jac—Mr. West. Did you come for an afternoon snack? There are a few biscuits left from dinner."

"Not today." He stepped close enough to give her hand a squeeze. "I came for advice from Mrs. Fielder about cutting food costs for the next month or so."

The mug thunked on the tabletop. "I never knew you were short of cash." Mrs. Fielder stared at him with wide eyes. "We've been plenty busy."

He held up his hand. "It's temporary. I made an investment in the business last month, then bought the new range, so I'm stretched right now."

Fresh admiration for Cassie swept over him. He'd confided his money situation to her almost a month ago, yet she hadn't shared the news with Mrs. Fielder. A good quality in a businessman's wife.

Mrs. Fielder rested her chin on her fist. "Well, I can make more stews. Beans and bacon can be dressed up with ketchup and molasses so no one knows they're eating cheap. Did it for years with my young'uns. More potatoes and gravy, not so many steaks and chops."

"I knew I could count on you. Is there some way to cut down on the amount of flour and lard you use?"

"I can make more cornbread, but most of the flour and lard goes into the pies." She leveled her gaze on Cassie.

Cassie's face flushed. "I don't know how to make a pie without flour and lard."

He shook his head. "Don't change a thing on the pies. With Mrs. Fielder's help, we'll shave costs elsewhere."

"How about we render our own lard now that we got two ranges? You can get pork fat cheap."

No doubt about it. Mrs. Fielder was a gem. He'd increase her salary as soon as he could.

"If you teach me, I can make the lard," Cassie said. "Seems only right, since I'm the one who uses the most."

"Be happy to show you how. You're a good learner."

His heart filled with love as he looked at Cassie's eager face. Three weeks and she'd be his wife. Everything he'd ever hoped for had come his way.

He turned when he heard footsteps. "Sorry to interrupt, Mr. West," Timothy said. "There's a man here to see you. He's waiting in the grocery."

"Did he say what he wanted?"

Keegan Byrne's bulk filled the entrance. "I'm here to collect a debt." His gaze skimmed over the room. "Or else."

Jacob's breathing slowed. His surroundings appeared in sharp focus. Cassie and the other two women watching him with wide eyes, Timothy fidgeting from foot to foot, tidy worktables, cookstoves—his life. He clenched his teeth.

Byrne lunged into the room, stopping a few feet in front of him. "I'm sure you don't want your workers involved in our dealings. Shall we go to your office?"

"We can talk right here, Byrne." Jacob let his cane fall to the floor and straightened to his full height.

"I don't think you want to do that."

"Do your worst, Byrne. I'm through hiding from my past." He glanced at Cassie, wondering if she'd walk out the door when she learned what he'd done.

"You're even dumber than I thought you were." His icy blue eyes narrowed. He held up his index finger. "I'll give you one minute to think this over."

"I've had two weeks. I don't need another minute. You're not getting a cent out of me."

Byrne shook his head in mock sorrow. "You can't bluff your way out of this, Westermann." At Cassie's gasp, he gave her a cold smile. "Bet he never told you that, did he, girlie? Did he tell you he's spent time in jail for armed theft? More than once, isn't that right, Jake?"

He held Cassie's gaze and replied directly to her. "Yes. Three times." He refused to justify himself. A confession was worthless if it came wrapped in excuses.

He shrugged. "Awhile. What difference does it make? He's a jailbird."

Cassie stared into Jacob's eyes. His mother died when he was thirteen. No telling what he did to survive. She sidled next to him, took his arm, and faced Mr. Byrne. "How long ago did this happen?"

He shrugged. "Awhile. What difference does it make? He's a jailbird."

"No, he isn't. He's a well-respected man in this town. Your once-upon-a-time tales can't change who he is now." Her knees trembled, but she glared at Mr. Byrne without flinching.

Jenny moved to Cassie's side. "What a boy does don't count when he's a man. I've worked for Mr. West since he came here eight years ago. He's a good man through and through."

"He gave me and my ma work when no one else would help." Timothy's young voice squeaked. "We'd be starvin' if it weren't for Mr. West."

"His name's not Mr. West. He's Jake Westermann, from the Boston slums."

Cassie raised her eyes to Jacob's and he nodded confirmation.

"It was. I stood before a judge and changed it to Jacob West seventeen years ago. Jake Westermann doesn't exist."

"I know it's not my place to interrupt white folks, but you're houndin' the wrong man." Becca's voice shook. "Don't matter what his name is. No one here cares what he done back in Boston."

"Maybe no one in here cares. After all, he pays you good, doesn't he? I'll go see what the men at the wagon factory or the brickyard think of your boss." He swung toward the door, then stopped short.

Wash stood in the entrance, arms folded across his broad chest. He glowered down at Byrne. "Best you go back where you come from. Now." Menace laced his deep voice. He stepped to one side and waited, his gaze never leaving the man's face.

Byrne ducked around him. After a moment, a door slammed.

Cassie slumped against Jacob's chest, not caring that they weren't alone. "What a horrible man."

His arms tightened around her. "He won't be back, thanks to you—thanks to all of you." She heard tears in his voice.

After Jacob returned to the grocery, she collapsed onto a chair. "I never dreamed I'd be able to stand up to someone like that. I was terrified."

"You could've fooled me." Jenny patted her shoulder. "You're going to make Mr. West a fine wife. A man likes a woman who'll take up for him."

Poor Jacob. What a miserable life he'd led as a young man. She planned to spend the rest of her life making every day a joy.

43

A delivery wagon stopped outside the kitchen door the following Monday afternoon. Wash propped open the screen before carrying a vat filled with slimy-looking, pinkish-white chunks into the room.

Cassie felt her dinner rise in her throat. Swallowing hard, she stared at him. "What on earth is that?"

"You never seen pork fat?"

She shook her head. "On bacon maybe, not like this." She backed away and bumped into Jenny.

"We told Mr. West we could save money by rendering our own lard, remember? You said you wanted to learn how. This is the main ingredient—in fact, about the only ingredient."

"You mean I'm putting *this* in my piecrust?"

Wash chuckled. "I'll leave you to your work." He rubbed Becca's shoulder on his way out the door.

"I'll learn how if you want, missy."

"No, thank you, Becca. I said I'd make the lard, since I use most of it." She prayed her dinner would stay down while she learned.

Jenny opened the firebox on the smaller range and pushed a few pieces of wood inside. "We don't want too hot a fire."

She took a fork and transferred several slabs of fat onto a cutting board. "Chop this into little squares, not much bigger than your thumb." Using a cleaver, she demonstrated with quick whacks, then handed the heavy knife to Cassie.

"Soon as you're done chopping, dump the pieces into this kettle." Grabbing the wire handle, she swung a cast iron pot onto the table. "When you got it half full, put in a teacupful of water and set it on the range. You're going to simmer this, not fry it."

Cassie curled her lip, but followed Jenny's instructions. White lumps piled up in the kettle.

Becca hung over her shoulder, watching. "I could do this part if you don't want to."

"No, I need to learn."

After adding the water, Cassie set the pot on the range, thankful to be finished handling the slimy pieces of fat. "Now what?"

"Leave it simmer. Stir every so often. When the cracklings float, your lard's done."

Cassie hurried to the washbasin and scrubbed her greasy fingers. She hoped when she and Jacob married they could afford to buy lard already rendered for their home use. She'd ask him tonight before they met with Reverend French.

<hr />

"You want me to promise what?" Jacob almost laughed until he noticed the serious expression on Cassie's face.

"Promise you'll purchase lard for our home. Jenny showed me how to render fat today. What a disgusting job."

He leaned close on the buggy seat and inhaled. "Is that why you smell like old beef?"

"Jacob!" She gave his arm a playful swat. "It does stink

when it's cooking. That's another reason I want you to buy rendered lard for us when we're married."

"You don't know stink until you've visited my old neighborhood in Boston." He enjoyed the freedom to speak of his past. He hadn't realized how evasive he'd had to be until the threat of exposure evaporated with Byrne, when the man's campaign to harm him came to naught.

Cassie looked down at her hands. "I'm sorry. I didn't mean to bring up bad memories."

He kissed her cheek when he stopped the buggy in front of the Frenches' house. "The past is past. You can talk to me about anything you want."

Joy lifted his steps as they walked to the door. Tonight they'd discuss their plans for the wedding. His wedding. To Cassie. *Thank you, Lord. She's more than I deserve.*

She slipped her hand into his as they followed the reverend to his study. Once they were seated, he rested a smile on both of them.

"Less than three weeks now. Are you both sure of your intentions?"

"We are." They spoke at the same time, then grinned at each other.

"The church is reserved for Friday evening, the twenty-fifth." Reverend French placed a sheet of paper in front of him and dipped a pen in an inkwell. "How many guests do you expect?"

"Rosemary and Elijah, Faith and Curt, Mr. Slocum . . ." Cassie counted off names on her fingers as she spoke, then stopped and looked at Jacob.

"Do you know the exact number?"

"Probably twenty-five. More if folks want to come." He had all he could do to keep a silly grin off his face. "We'll close the restaurant after the noon meal, so everyone can be there."

The reverend made a note on the paper, then directed his attention to Cassie. "And will your mother attend?"

"I . . . I don't know. I haven't heard from her in some time."

Jacob didn't express his thoughts. He hoped his prospective mother-in-law would stay in Price City. Permanently.

Cassie helped Jenny with the washing-up after Saturday's noon meal since Becca had the afternoon off. Once they were finished, Jenny untied her apron and draped it over a chair.

"I won't be gone too long. Mr. West said I could give my daughter a hand for a couple of hours. She wants to wash quilts."

"There's a nice breeze blowing. They'll probably be dry by nightfall."

Jenny chuckled. "I'll be back long before then." She pointed to a tub of pork fat on the worktable. "You'll be busy, looks like."

"I'll never get to where I like rendering." She wrinkled her nose. "The fat is slimy and smells bad when it melts."

"Once you get it on the stove, you can do something you like better." Jenny gave her a quick hug and bustled out the door.

Cassie stabbed a piece of fat with a long-handled fork and dropped the slab on a cutting board. While she chopped, she allowed her mind to drift to her wedding next Friday. Her gown hung in her bedroom. With Faith's help, she'd assembled a small trousseau, including a white cambric nightdress with roses embroidered around the neck and hemline. Her cheeks heated as her imagination strayed to their wedding night. Only six more days. With an effort of will, she herded her thoughts back into the kitchen as she heaped pieces of fat into the iron kettle.

After dropping more wood in the firebox, she moved the kettle to the top of the range. Holding her greasy hands in the air, she crossed to the sink and plunged them into the dishwater.

"I'm looking for a Miss Haddon." A boy with a bag slung over his shoulder peered through the screen. "D'you know if she's here?"

"I'm Miss Haddon." She dried her hands on her apron and opened the door.

"I have a telegram for you, miss."

Cassie bit her lip as she reached for the message. She'd never received a telegram, but knew without looking that the news wouldn't be good. No one ever sent good news by telegram.

"Thank you." Her voice quivered.

The boy touched his cap and ran down the alley.

She opened the envelope, noting the sender's location. Price City.

With shaking fingers, she unfolded the yellow paper inside.

```
RAND KILLED STOP  AT HOTEL STOP  PLEASE
COME STOP  MOTHER
```

Tears burned Cassie's eyelids. Her poor mother, alone again. After all the months she'd spent searching for Uncle Rand, now he was dead.

"Oh, Mother, I'm so sorry," she whispered. She'd leave tomorrow and bring her mother back to Noble Springs. If she didn't want to share Jacob's house, she could live in Mr. Slocum's cabin.

Cassie sprinted from the kitchen to the grocery to share the sad news with Jacob.

When she entered, he smiled his wonderful smile. Then a frown creased his forehead. "You're upset. What's happened?"

Before she could reply, he glanced at Timothy, who stood with a customer near a display of tinned soup. Jacob took her hand and led her to his office. "Sit down and tell me what's wrong."

She thrust the telegram at him.

Color rose in his cheeks as he read the message. "Her brother's dead and she's at the hotel? How did she send a telegram? You said there's no telegraph there."

"The telegraph follows the railroad. The line through Price City must be complete." Cassie choked back a sob. "If I leave tomorrow, I can bring Mother back with me on Monday or Tuesday."

"You can't!" He jumped to his feet. "Our wedding's Friday. If you're delayed like you were last time . . ." His voice trailed off.

"I have to go. Don't you understand? She's all alone. I'm all the family she has now."

"Wait a week, please. She won't be any more alone than she is already."

"How heartless of you. I'm going. What would you do if—" She stopped. Jacob truly didn't understand. She could talk all day and nothing would change.

"Is this going to be our life? Your mother calls, you run?"

"She's my mother and I owe her—"

"Choose, Cassie. Your mother or me. I won't accept second place."

The sound of her heart thudding echoed in her ears. "Fine. I'm choosing—"

"Wait." He pivoted abruptly, turning his back to her. "I smell something burning."

"Oh my heavens. The lard!"

She hoisted her skirt and ran toward the kitchen, jolting to a stop when she reached the entrance.

The open damper glowed. Flames raced over the top of the range.

44

assie screamed and ran into the kitchen. She grabbed
a pitcher and threw water over the burning fat. The
fire traveled with the rivulets, down the sides of the range and
across the floor until flames contacted the wall. They roared
upward, jumping from board to board while she watched,
horrified.

Jacob grabbed her shoulder. "Get out! Now! I've sent
Timothy to ring the fire bell." He pushed her toward the
door. "Go. Help will be here soon."

"Come with me."

"I need to save the ledgers and cash box." He ducked away
from the burning wall and limped toward his office, his cane
pounding the floor.

"Jacob! No!"

The fire bell next to the courthouse pealed a steady *clang,
clang, clang.* Within minutes the steeple bell joined in, sending a request for help across the community.

The flames reached the ceiling and found the opening Wash
had cut for the flue. In another moment they burned around
the flue and spread overhead. Dazed, she stared at the growing conflagration.

A hand clasped her upper arm and yanked her out the door. A fresh breeze whipped around the building, tugging at her skirt as Timothy pulled her out to the street. "Get back, Miss Haddon. You're in danger."

Men in the fire brigade ran toward them, water sloshing from the buckets they carried. Someone yelled, "It's on the roof. We'll never stop it now. This wind ain't helping, neither."

Tears poured down Cassie's cheeks. Jacob's beloved business, burning, and she'd caused the fire.

Jacob. She clutched Timothy's shirt. "Jacob's in there. He went to get his papers."

He glanced down the alley toward the grocery. Black smoke curled from the roof of the storeroom. A window shattered somewhere behind them.

Timothy shook his head. "He probably went out the front door," he said, without conviction. His face mirrored her fears.

She whirled away and ran around to the front of the building. Fragments of ash swirled overhead like malignant snowflakes. Cinders fell on her dress. Through smoke-blurred windows she saw fire raging in the dining room. Pounding past, she stopped at the grocery entrance and reached for the door handle.

Someone pushed her out of the way and then threw a bucket of water against the clapboard siding. Sweat ran down the stranger's face. "Git out of here, miss. You could be hurt."

"Jacob—Mr. West is inside. Please, help."

He stared at her, then back at flames eating their way around a window frame. "No one's going in there."

She lunged for the door, but he shoved her aside. "Git along. We got a fire to fight."

Sobbing uncontrollably, she crossed the street, skirting around men running back and forth with buckets. Every time water hit the fire, the snakelike flames hissed and ducked, then rose somewhere else. She scanned every sooty face, looking in vain for Jacob.

A cry went up. "The roof's going. Back off." Firefighters scattered as the center of the building collapsed in a shower of embers. Flames shot toward the sky.

Cassie bowed her head and stumbled toward her cabin.

45

assie sat in numb silence for what felt like hours. The commotion from the street gradually quieted. Somehow the silence was worse than the shouts. West & Riley's was gone, and Jacob with it.

The last words she'd hurled at him were angry ones. Dropping to her knees, she pressed her blistered hands against her ears to muffle the echoes of their argument, then huddled into a ball and yielded to shattering sobs.

Metal grated on metal as someone turned her door latch. She opened tear-blurred eyes and saw a soot-covered apparition leaning on a stick. His clothes were torn and pocked with holes. Dark brown eyes shone from his blackened face.

She rocked back on her heels, certain she'd lost her senses.

In another moment, strong hands lifted her from the floor. "I thought I'd lost you for good. Timothy said you'd gone in the front of the store."

"Jacob." She touched his dirt-streaked face. "I thought you were dead." Her knees buckled.

He wrapped his arms around her and rocked her back and forth. "I'm here." His deep voice rumbled in her ear.

She twisted away. "The store's gone. It's my fault. How can you stand to look at me?"

"When I thought you'd died, I realized you matter more than anything else. We can rebuild the store."

"You said . . . we?"

"Everything that was in that building can be replaced—but you're irreplaceable." A smile lifted his singed moustache. "I love you, Cassie. While I searched for you, I made a bargain with God. I promised him as soon as we're married I'd take you to your mother."

She flung her arms around his waist and breathed in his smoke-tinged Jacob smell. "I love you, Jacob West."

His grip tightened around her as their lips met. For a long, breathtaking moment she sampled the bliss that their marriage promised.

When he released her, she smiled up at him.

"Just think," she said, "we'll be the first honeymoon couple to stay in the Price City Hotel."

Epilogue

Cassie stared out the window of the passenger car as the train rolled into Price City. Her stomach tumbled at the prospect of bringing her mother and Jacob together.

He squeezed her hand. "I promise I'll be polite."

"I'm not worried about how you'll act." She leaned close and kissed his cheek. "Mother's bound to be distraught. I just pray she doesn't take her loss out on us."

Jacob stood and brought his valise down from the overhead rack, then reached up for Cassie's. "We'll find out soon enough. Our telegram told her we'd arrive today, so at least she's had time to prepare herself."

The setting sun blazed over their surroundings as they stepped from the train onto the platform. Since her July visit, Price City had fulfilled Uncle Rand's prediction and showed signs of growth. Streets had been graded between the railroad tracks and the hotel, a few small cabins dotted the landscape, and several larger buildings were in various stages of construction. A telegrapher's shack sat at the far end of the platform.

Cassie scanned the people milling about while Jacob collected their trunk from the baggage car. No sign of her mother. Perhaps she'd taken to her bed, the way she'd done when they got word of Cassie's father's death.

"Baggage master said there's a driver—" Jacob stopped and pointed. "Isn't that your mother?"

A woman dressed in black tied a team and buckboard to a hitching rail behind the telegraph shed. When she spotted Cassie and Jacob, she turned and moved toward them with hesitant steps, then at the last moment opened her arms and ran to Cassie.

"I'm so thankful you're here! Until I received your telegram, I was afraid you wouldn't come." She hugged her daughter and stepped back, extending a trembling hand to Jacob. "Mr. West. It was good of you to escort Cassie. Thank you."

Jacob took her hand in both of his. "She's my wife now, Mrs. Bingham. That makes us family. Please call me Jacob."

Cassie's spirits soared at his gracious tone.

"Jacob." Mother's voice emerged in a croak. "How is it you can leave your store to travel?"

"The building burned week before last. Right now I have no store."

Cringing at the memory, Cassie sucked in a breath, wishing they could talk about something else.

Mother's eyes widened. "Burned! But . . . how will you support my daughter if you don't have an income?"

As though sensing Cassie's discomfort, Jacob slid his arm around her waist and pulled her close. "The business was insured. As soon as we return, we'll begin construction on a new West & Riley's—with a bigger bakery for Cassie."

She smiled up at him and relaxed against his side, certain the Lord had blessed her with the best husband in the world.

"Well." Mother blew out a breath and shifted her gaze to the buckboard. "I brought the hotel wagon for your baggage. As soon as you're ready, we must get back. I need to help Fred with supper."

Surprised at her mother's casual reference to the cook she'd once called an odious man, Cassie followed her to the buckboard.

A wide veranda stretched across the front of the hotel. Several rocking chairs waited in the shade of the roof. A tidy sign next to the door read

CARTER HOUSE
ROOMS BY DAY OR WEEK

"'Carter House'?" Cassie turned to her mother as the three of them climbed the steps to the entrance. "When did you name the hotel?"

Mother's eyes moistened. "Rand made me half-owner shortly before he died. We chose the name together." Her voice quivered. "He told me to be proud of my past and stop trying to be someone I wasn't. Together we were turning this into the hotel he dreamed of. Then . . . ten days ago he slipped while repairing the roof and fell to his death." She pulled a handkerchief from her sleeve and wiped away a tear.

Jacob held the door open for them. "What do you intend to do now, Mrs. Bingham?"

"Eliza."

He smiled, then took Cassie's hand. "Eliza. You're welcome to live with us in Noble Springs, if you wish."

"Thank you, but I plan to continue managing the hotel."
She drew a deep breath. "That's what Rand would want."

Cassie glanced around the lobby, which now had rag rugs
on the floor and colorful cushions on the chairs. Her mother's
touch, no doubt. She and Jacob had been worried about
Mother's ability to manage alone, without considering that
the Lord had his own plans—for each of them.

Mother untied the bow under her chin and laid her bonnet
on the reception counter at the rear of the lobby. She handed
Cassie a key from a rack on the wall. "This is for our . . . my
best room, number four, at the end of the hallway. Supper
should be ready in about thirty minutes."

She took a few steps away and paused. When she turned,
she rested a shrewd gaze on Jacob. "Would you mind coming
with me? I have a few questions about how best to run
this kitchen."

"I'd be happy to help. Lead the way." He tossed Cassie a
wink before following her mother.

She blew him a kiss and watched them go, her heart full
of love. Ever since the rainy day she'd left St. Louis, the Lord
had been guiding her to Jacob—and this bright and perfect
moment.

Acknowledgments

I'm beyond grateful to have had the support of my husband, Richard, during the process of writing this novel. Without complaining, he's endured late meals and a wife who suffers from ongoing "book brain syndrome." Thank you, my love.

The team at Revell who produce my books are also at the top of my gratitude list. Vicki Crumpton is a fabulous editor whose sense of humor makes the process a pleasure. It's also my continued joy to work with Barb Barnes and her editing staff. Again, the process is a pleasure.

This beautiful book cover is the result of Revell's talented art department, led by Cheryl Van Andel. Thank you for working so closely with me to perfectly reflect Cassie's personality. Special gratitude goes to the marketing department's bubbly Michele Misiak, who's never too busy to respond to my requests.

I've loved working with all of you!

Tamela Hancock Murray, my agent, is everything an agent

should be. Helpful, supportive, and a fabulous cheerleader for my work. I appreciate you, Tamela.

I'm blessed with gifted critique partners whose suggestions never fail to improve my chapters. Hugs to Sarah Sundin, Bonnie Leon, and Linda Clare. A special shout-out to Judy Gann for taking on extra chapters—and most of all, for praying me through to the ending of the novel.

And speaking of prayer, the Lord should be listed as coauthor of this book. As the greatest creator of all, he is my guide. All glory goes to him.

Every author needs readers, and to you I offer my heartfelt thanks for contacting me to share what you've enjoyed about my books. I hope you'll take Cassie's story to your hearts and love her as much as I do. As always, I look forward to hearing from you.

For more information about my books, as well as my contact information, please visit my website (www.annshorey.com). If you're a Facebook user, you'll find me by typing Ann Shorey Author into the search line.

Ann Shorey has been a full-time writer for over twenty years. She made her fiction debut with the At Home in Beldon Grove series in January 2009.

When she's not writing, she teaches classes on historical research, story arc, and other fiction fundamentals at regional conferences. Ann and her husband live in southern Oregon.

Ann loves to hear from her readers, and may be contacted through her website, www.annshorey.com, or find her on Facebook at http://www.facebook.com/AnnShorey.

Meet
Ann Shorey

Visit AnnShorey.com
to Learn More about Her Books,
Life as a Writer,
and Upcoming Events

f

SPANNING A CENTURY IN AMERICA,
THIS COLLECTION LEADS READERS ON A JOURNEY
THROUGH THE LANDSCAPE OF LOVE.

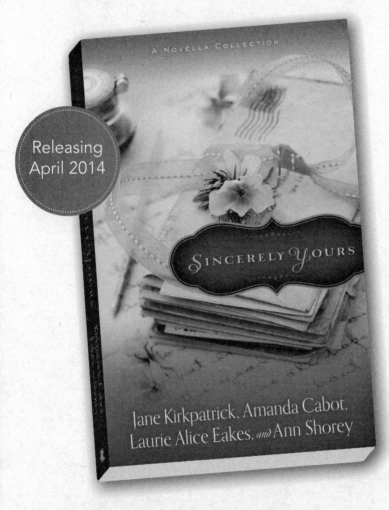

Releasing
April 2014

A NOVELLA COLLECTION

SINCERELY Yours

Jane Kirkpatrick, Amanda Cabot,
Laurie Alice Eakes, *and* Ann Shorey

In this inspiring collection of historical romances, four young women
each receive a letter that will change the course of their lives.

How far will she go to follow her dreams?

Faith Lindberg longs to go west on the Oregon Trail until she realizes the love of her life may not be the man of her dreams.

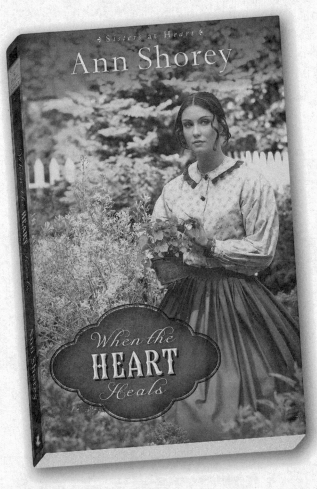

Be the First to Hear about Other New Books from REVELL!

Sign up for announcements about new and upcoming titles at

RevellBooks.com/SignUp

Don't miss out on our great reads!

Revell

a division of Baker Publishing Group
www.RevellBooks.com